Rock & Roll Homicide

R.J. McDonnell

Copyright © 2008 by R.J. McDonnell
All rights reserved.

No part of this book may be reproduced in any form or by any electronic or mechanical means, to include information storage and retrieval systems, without the expressed written permission of the publisher, with one exception: Reviewers may quote brief passages.

Killeena Publishing
PO Box 3611
Scranton, PA 18505

(Killeena Publishing utilizes the SAN System)

In cooperation with RJ Communications LLC
New York

First Edition

This book is a work of fiction. Any similarity to real people, alive or dead, is purely coincidental and not intended by the author.

Printed in the United States

ISBN: 978-0-9814914-1-7

www.rjmcdonnell.com
rjmcdonnell@yahoo.com

Cover Photography: Maryann Nebraski – Morrison's Memories

Prologue

JACK said, "That sounded like a keeper to me, Terry," as the band finished the 12th take of *Full Moon Following*. Terry glanced at the recording engineer who nodded his approval.

"If I waited until everybody got it exactly right, this CD wouldn't come out till our fans were all dead or in nursing homes," Terry replied. Ten songs down, four to go.

"Take fifteen while I check my notes for the next song," Terry said authoritatively. "And, don't get lost."

As the band members exited the studio, Terry turned again to the recording engineer behind a wall of soundproof glass and asked, "Do you need a break?"

"No, I'm gonna review that last take, just to be sure," he replied.

"Good man," Terry commented. He then set his guitar on its stand and carried a red nylon bag to a small table a few feet away. He removed an iPod, a set of headphones and a custom-made audio recorder. He plugged in the recorder and inserted the iPod into its dock. Then he put on the headphones, which were a heavy-duty model, guaranteed to eliminate almost all external noise. Terry hated when his concentration was interrupted by roadies making equipment changes or other musicians tuning up for the next song.

He took a deep cleansing breath and assured himself that the last take was fine. It was time to move on. The next song would probably be the #1 track on the CD. Cerise Records had already signed an accomplished director for the video. When the band returned from their break he would give them one of his infrequent compliments to set the tone for the making of their next blockbuster. But first he needed to review his audio notes.

After one more deep breath Terry pushed the "Power" button on the recorder and both of the cups of his headphones exploded. Terry died instantly. Blood and brain matter spattered his white guitar.

Chapter 1

CHELSEA Tucker entered my office exuding the kind of attitude I had come to expect from my financially privileged clientele. I took the lead. "Before we get started let me express my condolences. Although I never met your husband, I found him to be a truly gifted musician."

"Thank you," Chelsea replied. "I understand you were a rock & roll musician yourself before you became an investigator. I've got to tell you, that's a major concern for me. For every responsible adult I know in the music business there are a thousand flakes."

"I played the San Diego club scene for ten years. But I wasn't in it for the party lifestyle. I financed two degrees playing cover tunes until 2:00 AM most nights," I replied.

"I went to college too, Mr. Duffy. I met as many flakes there as I did in the music business. Put my mind at ease. What can you do for me that other investigators can't?" she asked.

Since this would be my first homicide investigation I couldn't dazzle her with a track record of success and, since I've only been an investigator for two years I couldn't impress her with my vast network of contacts. "The music business is very unique. Most PI's work either in a world of corporate executives or unfaithful spouses. I understand what motivates musicians, promoters, club owners, agents, roadies and groupies. Also, I liked Terry's music and truly want to see his killer brought to justice."

Sitting forward in her chair, locking her intense green eyes with mine, Chelsea asked, "Can you give me some references of clients you've worked with in the past?"

"A very important part of the service I provide is complete confidentiality. I'm sure you'd like me to show you the same consideration when we conclude our business," I said.

"Right answer," said Chelsea.

"Why don't you tell me how I can help you," I said, assuming I passed the audition.

"The San Diego Police Department has been investigating Terry's death for the past two weeks. I don't like the direction they're taking. I have a pretty good idea of who did it. But, apparently they prefer to spend their time trying to link it to me because we took out an insurance policy within the last year. I understand that the police have to investigate me, but it doesn't seem like they're doing much of anything to track down Terry's real murderer. That's why I'm here," she said and pushed her long black hair away from her face.

"The police managed to keep many of the details out of the press about what actually happened in the recording studio. I know it was a bomb that killed Terry. What else can you tell me?" I asked.

Chelsea replied, "Terry was a perfectionist. When the band was recording he'd work night and day to get just the right sound. He had a high-quality portable recorder that he worked with at home to note ideas, changes and things that needed improvement. During recording sessions he kept the recorder on a little table next to him in the studio. Between songs he listened to his notes, then told the band what to do."

"Was the bomb in the recorder?" I asked.

"No, it was in the headphones. Terry complained that his old headphones weren't able to screen outside noise. His band mates and sound techs were distracting him. So, he asked me to buy a heavier set, designed for noisy environments. On the day he died, the band finished one of their songs and took a break. Terry put on the headphones, pushed *play* and they exploded, killing him instantly," she said as her voice shook noticeably for the first time.

"Who do you think is responsible, Chelsea?" I asked.

"Most of the guys were established musicians when they formed about three years ago. Terry and the lead guitarist, Nigel Choate, were both prolific songwriters. So, it didn't take long until they had enough material for their first CD. They thought with their experience and hot demo they'd be in a position to, if not dictate terms to a recording company, at least manage to not get screwed. But the timing was really bad. All of the record companies were freaking about shared files on the Internet gutting their CD and download sales. The established record companies were in a wait and see mode, and it looked like the market was going to stay that way indefinitely until some legislation passed to eliminate piracy, or at least limit it. There was no way the band was going to sign one of the usual rip-off contracts the record companies use to swindle unsuspecting new bands. Just when things were looking their worst, this salesman-type Texan approached our manager with an offer that was about half-way between what Terry was looking for and what everybody else was offering."

"How was the contract set up?" I asked.

"In the first part, the band agreed to record three CD's. The money for the first two was marginal. But, the contract stipulated that if the first two CD's hit their sales goals that the money for the third CD would be increased relative to how the first two sold." It was obvious that Chelsea knew what was going on and did not emerge from the groupie bimbette gene pool.

"The first two CD's more than doubled their performance goals. But, when it came time for the record company to sweeten the pot for the third CD, the company president was supposedly out of the country on other business. The band proceeded with the recording sessions, but it became apparent they were getting the royal run-around."

"You mentioned it was a two part contract. What was the other part?" I asked.

"It called for locking the band up for another three CD's, but it had an escape clause if they couldn't reach an equitable agreement on the third CD. That's why Terry started recording without definitive answers on the contract re-negotiation. The band figured there was no way they would risk losing their biggest asset. I'm convinced

Cerise Records was behind Terry's murder. I want you to find out why and point SDPD in the right direction," she said.

After explaining the details on my fee, Chelsea reverted to the businesswoman persona she displayed at the beginning of our meeting. "I'm sure you're a great detective, but I'm not committing to a long-term relationship until I see some results. I'll pay you for one week, then decide if I want to continue. Is that satisfactory?" she asked.

"Only if you don't expect me to solve the case in that time," I replied.

"I expect significant progress, not a miracle," she said as she stood up. "I'll also expect regular progress reports." She then walked out of my office without the customary handshake or goodbye.

As a musician I put up with drunks, hecklers and club owners who refused to pay up. In my three years as a mental health counselor I butted heads with several bureaucrats who routinely put their career self-interest far ahead of the needs of their clients. But these confrontations paled in comparison to what I knew I needed to do next. I had to ask my dad for a favor.

James Duffy spent thirty years with the San Diego Police Department, ten in a squad car and twenty as a detective. He retired the year I became a private investigator. I wish I could report a warm, supportive relationship, but no such luck. From the day Mom bought my first guitar when I was in 7th grade, Dad was sure he would find me dead in an East San Diego crack house. As a cop he saw too many rockers end up on a slab in the morgue to let it slide when he saw his only son going down the same path. I don't remember Mom and Dad having any serious fights until I started rocking out. Mom argued successfully that I had the benefit of good parenting and a strong sense of right and wrong. She wanted me to follow my dreams and Dad started spending a lot more time at the local cop bar. Whenever I started practicing, Dad considered it an open invitation to hang with his cop buddies. The bottom line is that their relationship suffered quite a hit, particularly while I was still in high school.

Dad hasn't said much about my career as a PI. I get the feeling he's keeping his opinions to himself to prevent more problems with Mom. He's happy that I'm no longer a working musician. But, I think he's counting the days till I do something that will embarrass him in front of his cronies.

Mom has a fantasy that he'll become my mentor, help me become a success and feel needed in the process. More importantly, she's hoping we'll patch things up and be more of a family now that we have some common ground. For these reasons, Mom was a willing co-conspirator when I called to ask her to keep him around the house so that I could get his advice on the case.

I found him in the backyard watering the lawn. "Hi Dad. Been doing any fishing with Kerrigan?"

"Cut the chit-chat. Your mother tells me you want something. Let's just get to it," he said with his usual amount of tact.

At that point I did the only thing Dad would go for - I gave him exactly what I had. When I finished he asked, "So, what do you want from me?"

He knew exactly what I needed but he wanted to hear me ask. "I need to talk with the primary investigator on the case."

"Son, I know we've had our differences, but I've always been on your side. I'll do what I can to get you a sit-down. But, I'm going to ask you to take a tip from your old man," he said.

"I did ask for your advice," I replied, hoping the lecture would be mercifully short.

Dad shut off the hose to give me his full attention and read my reaction. "Most cops think of PI's as pains in the ass. They think you guys are there to tap them for information with nothing of value to trade."

"These days, everybody who thinks he's been wronged, files a civil suit. They usually hire lawyers and PI's who cite chapter and verse of the damned Freedom of Information Act and expect the cops to help them make their cases. Most cops act tough, like they're not afraid of these jackals. But, the truth is that their chances for promotion go right in the shitter if one of these assholes files a lawsuit against the Department. The sad part is that the cops end up jumping through hoops and hate every minute of it. If you tell the primary you're there to do the legwork for a civil suit against the record company, he'll probably cooperate and thank God you're not wearing a Brooks Brothers suit."

"I like it," I said.

"Don't forget to fill in your client and, for God's sake, don't mention that it was my idea," he said.

"Dad, I had no idea you could be so deceptive," I said.

"You're welcome. Now go say hello to your mother and let me finish the lawn," he said concluding the conversation on his terms.

As I walked into the kitchen Mom was waiting for me with an anxious look on her face. "How did it go?" she asked.

"Call 911 and tell them to bring the defibrillator. We actually had a productive conversation with no yelling and no sermons. I'm in shock," I said, knowing Mom would be elated with my report.

"I'll be sure to tell Father Lavelle that my prayers are finally being answered," she said with a genuine smile. "I think he's mellowed out a bit since he retired."

"Or was it since my band hung it up?" I asked.

"Hard to say. It all happened around the same time. What do you think?" she asked.

"I think we shouldn't overanalyze it. Count it as a good day and hope it's the start of a trend," I said.

"Amen," she replied as Dad walked in the back door.

"One more thing, son," he said. "I know the vic was a rock star, but I think it would be in your best interest not to mention your musical career to the primary."

Chapter 2

JEANNINE Joshlin has been my administrative assistant since I opened the agency. She was also one of my first clients when I went to work as a mental health counselor for the San Diego County Department of Social Services. She is a tall, blond, intelligent, beautiful, obsessive-compulsive 25 year-old. At first glance she adds a huge measure of class to an otherwise modest office space in La Jolla. Fortunately, most of my clients don't stick around the office long enough to pick up on her numerous idiosyncrasies. She's also honest, sincere and willing to work hard at the business and on her problems. I buzzed her on the intercom.

"Yes Jason," she said as she walked into my office.

"I've got a very busy day planned for you," I said as I handed her a *To Do* list. "First I need you to call Chelsea and ask for a copy of the recording company contract. I also need a list of names and phone numbers for each of the band members, support staff and manager; a copy of Terry's address book would be even better. Let her know that if a cop calls asking about a civil suit, tell him she can only discuss it with her attorney at this point. Ask her for the name, title and phone number of the president of Cerise Records. Try to set up a meet for this afternoon. Mention that we're working for Chelsea and they should bend over backwards to try to avoid a lawsuit."

Jeannine is a whiz when it comes to computers, especially the Internet. I have no doubt she'll come up with twice the info I would have found and in half of the time. Right after I got back to my own *To Do* list, she buzzed me, "Your dad is on Line 1."

"Hi, Dad. Any luck?" I asked.

"Am I going to have to go through that every time I call here?" he asked with a large measure of irritation in his voice.

" What?" I asked.

"That nut-job receptionist of yours just called me Dad. I never met the woman in my life and she acts like she's my long-lost daughter. I don't need to ask where you found her," he carped.

I replied, "Yeah, but she does Windows."

"What?" asked Dad.

"I thought you liked getting to the point. Do you know the primary?" I inquired, hoping I had successfully changed subjects.

"It's Walter Shamansky and I do know him. We're not exactly the best of friends, but he agreed to a meet. Call him at Metro; my old number," he said.

"Thanks Dad. Any advice on how to approach him?" I asked.

"Go with what we talked about. Form your own opinion. I gotta go," he said and hung up.

Three minutes later I was patched through. "Shamansky," said the burly voice.

"This is Jason Duffy. I'm a Private Investigator working for Chelsea Tucker," I said.

"Duff's boy. Yeah, the wheel's been greased, as if you didn't already know. I don't have a lot of time for this sort of thing. The case is very high-profile and that means I have the brass up my ass looking for results," he said.

I replied, "You've got to take a break occasionally. You name the time and place; I'll be there."

"I do have to eat lunch," he offered.

"Great! When and where?" I asked.

"Larabee's at noon," he said.

"Where's that?" I inquired.

"It's in that yellow research manual they give to everybody who owns a phone. If you cross-reference it with a Thomas Brothers

Map Book, you'll have an hour and a half to figure it out. Think you can you handle it?" he asked with much sarcasm.

"I can't wait," I said and he hung up. Who says there's no such thing as a free lunch? Ten to one lunch sets me back at least $50. I hope Chelsea isn't a grinder when it comes to expense reports.

My next call was to Bernie Liebowitz. Of all of the club owners I worked for, Bernie was the best. He's a former rock & roll agent who got out of the business because he couldn't stand seeing his clients constantly getting ripped off by the recording companies. He agreed to meet me at the start of happy hour.

As expected, Larabee's turned out to be an upscale restaurant just off of La Jolla Boulevard. It's a white Spanish building with a red tile roof, built into the side of a hill overlooking the Pacific. The restaurant had several terraces filled with alfresco diners. Inside the beveled glass entranceway was a hostess who looked very familiar. I'm sure she played the part of a mom on one of those sitcom's that has been in reruns for years.

"Do you have a reservation?" she asked with the warmth and charm you might expect from Beaver Cleaver's mom.

"I'm afraid not," I said. "Do you think you could squeeze in a party of two?"

"We're booked solid until at least 2:30," she said.

"Actually I'm meeting someone. It's quite possible he made a reservation. His name is Walter Shamansky," I stated with raised eyebrows and a hopeful inflection in my voice.

Beav's mom made a big production of perusing the reservation list carefully. When she finished she gave me a sad, sympathetic expression and a little shake of the head. "Mind if I wait until Mr. Shamansky arrives?" I asked.

"Not at all," she replied and extended her arm toward a church pew adjacent to the door. Just as I was thinking Shamansky stood me up, in walked a muscular, 50-something guy with a shaved head. Beaver's mom lit up like Disneyland's Main Street Electrical Parade.

"Howdy stranger!" she enthused. "I thought you lost our address."

"Not a chance. Where else in La Jolla am I going to find four-star food and a five-star hostess," he said, laying it on thick.

"Where's the benevolent benefactor today?" she asked.

He replied, "I'm supposed to be meeting a PI." Beaver's mom gave a head nod in my direction. Walter Shamansky turned to face me and asked, "Son of Duff?"

I raised my hand and stood. "That's me." He flapped his palm indicating he wanted me to fall in line behind him as he turned his attention back to the hostess. As I approached I said, "I thought you didn't have a reservation for a Walter Shamansky."

Beav's mom looked at Shamansky and asked, "Is that your name, Kojak?"

"You can call me anything you want, beautiful," he replied with a wink. She feigned embarrassment and showed us to a window table with a view of the ocean.

I started to launch into the spiel I had prepared, but got halted by a raised palm as Shamansky focused on his menu. I wanted to ask if he'd recently been promoted from Traffic Division, but held my tongue. After a couple of minutes the poster girl for anorexia nervosa stopped by our table and asked for our orders. Shamansky flirted as shamelessly as he had with the hostess. Surprisingly, this twenty-one-year-old also knew Shamansky and treated him like a friend.

Once our orders were taken Shamansky said, "OK, let's hear it." I proceeded with the scenario I worked out with Dad. When I finished Shamansky said, "I gotta give your old man credit. For a guy who's three years retired, he set you up with a very believable story. Almost any other cop in the department would have bought it."

"What are you talking about?" I asked.

He replied, "Your dad and me never saw eye to eye. He was with the In Crowd, the Irish Mafia, and I wasn't."

"Are you saying my dad was dirty?" I asked with a pugnacious tone.

"No. Nothing like that. The Irish Mafia in SDPD is a clique. A large group of Irish cops who hang out together and watch each other's backs in the field and at promotion time," he said with a bit of acrimony.

"I have a flash for you, Shamansky, he never made it past detective," I noted as the tension mounted.

"Don't get me wrong. I like your dad. When we were both at Western Division we had two of the highest clear rates in the department. He was a damn good cop. I just didn't care for the company he kept," he said with a notable drop in hostility. Just as the smoke was clearing, Olive Oyl arrived with lunch.

We ate in silence for a couple of minutes, then Shamansky said, "Here's what I've got to offer. If you read the papers you probably know the assholes on city counsel cut our budget to shit. No overtime; hiring freeze; and something they're calling 'total accountability,' which is short for more paperwork/less field time." He shoved an artichoke heart into his mouth and, once again, held up his palm, telling me it was not yet my turn to speak. "Your little scam about a civil suit tells me you're willing to do some legwork in exchange for some information. Here are the rules: If I give you an assignment, you give me exactly what you find - no holding out on me and no partial truth. If you can do that I'll keep you in the loop on the investigation. Deal?"

"I can live with that, on one condition. No bullshit assignments to satisfy the brass. You ask me to do something we need to know to move forward, I'll give it to you straight," I said while returning his stare with equal intensity.

"You are definitely the son of Duff. That's a good thing. OK, no bullshit assignments. What do you need to know?" he asked.

Before I could launch into my questions our server rolled a dessert cart to our table and looked like she was auditioning for the role of game show hostess as she hand-gestured from one confection to the next. When it was mercifully over we ordered coffee. "What did forensics have to say about the bomb?" I asked.

Shamansky replied, "It was a combination of BBs and a blasting cap in each ear pad of the headphones."

"Wouldn't that make the earphones noticeably heavy" I asked.

"Here's something you'll find very interesting. The headphones were a recent gift from your client. According to her, he had been asking for a heavier, tighter seal to block out extraneous noise. A studio sound tech confirms that he asked for a recommendation on a pair that had those features," he said.

I asked, "Is that the only reason you like my client?"

"Not at all. She inherits five million bucks from an insurance policy. Her husband, like all rock stars, may have had infidelity issues. And, everyone I've talked with tells me Terry Tucker was a sonofabitch," he said with confidence.

"Don't tell me you're relying on clues from the National Inquirer," I said, defending my client.

"Talk to the band," he retorted as he stood up from the table.

"Anything else?" I asked.

"Yeah," he replied, "Leave a big tip."

I waited until I got down to the street before calling Jeannine. "Were you able to get me an appointment at Cerise Records?" I asked.

"Everything else on the list is going very well. But, Cerise Records was really weird," she said.

"Weird, how?" I asked.

She replied, "I told the receptionist who I was and everything, then she put me on hold. She must have put her hand over the phone, but I could still hear her explaining it to her boss. He said, 'Tell them I am out of the country and won't be back for at least a couple of weeks.' When she came back on the line she told me what her boss said."

"What's the boss's name?" I inquired.

"John Koflanovich. I couldn't hear him very distinctly, but he definitely had a foreign accent," she added.

I got the address and decided to try a drop in. It's infinitely easier to blow someone off on the phone than it is in person. Twenty minutes later, I entered a large business office complex that was decidedly more upscale than my modest quarters, but definitely not in the same league as the major record labels. Fortunately, they had an on-site management company listed on the marquee.

As I walked out of the elevator I was disappointed to see an interior hallway with no windows. There were only two office suites on

Cerise's side of the hallway. The other was Cleason Enterprises. As I walked into the Cerise reception room I was again disturbed by the absence of interior windows. No way of telling the size of the suite or how may people were in their offices. The receptionist was an attractive blond in her mid-twenties.

"Hi. I'm with Cubic Property Management. We're having an electrical problem on this floor and I need to take a look at your panel," I said.

She replied, "Let me speak to the boss." She then left her desk and opened a heavy, walnut door just to the side of her reception desk. When she returned she said, "I'm sorry. There's a confidential meeting going on right now and no one is allowed in the interior suites. If you would like to leave your name and number I can call when it's OK. Or, I can just call Cubic."

"I'm afraid you don't understand," I pleaded. "I just came from Cleason and their computers are completely down. They're losing money by the second."

"We work with some very big name acts in the music business. When they're in negotiations it's imperative that we maintain the highest standards of confidentiality. Entertainment Tonight, the Hollywood Tattler, California Confidential and the tabloids are constantly snooping around here. I'm sure you are who you say you are, but if a new talent or his agent sees you wandering around back there it could easily cost us a big contract."

I responded, "I understand. But Cleason is very important to us, so I'll just wait until the meeting is over if you don't mind."

"That'll be fine," she said.

After about ten minutes of watching the receptionist primp and preen, a plan came together. Without her noticing, I took my Swiss Army knife out of my pants pocket and the vitamins I forgot to take after lunch, out of my shirt pocket. I poked a small hole in one of the pointy ends of a Vitamin E gel cap. "Excuse me," I said to the receptionist. "Did you go out for lunch today?" I asked.

"Yes. Why do you ask?" she inquired.

"When you turned I saw something in the back of your hair," I said. She immediately started reaching for the back of her head. "Don't touch it!" I exclaimed as I stood up and walked toward her. "It looks like bird dookie. Turn around." When she did I squeezed the Vitamin E into the back of her hair as I touched it lightly. "Eeeeewwww!" I exclaimed as I quickly withdrew my hand, revealing a strand of clear, sticky liquid spanning two of my fingers. "Tell me this isn't what I think it is!"

The receptionist took one look at my fingers, made a high-pitched sound and bolted out the front door toward the hallway Women's room. After wiping my fingers, I let myself into the interior office suite and noted three offices on either side of the hall. There was no identification on any of these doors. However, at the far end of the hall was an ornate door with a brass plate displaying the name John Koflanovich. As I cautiously made my way down the hall I heard a noise behind me and, before I could turn around, felt the cold steel of a large-caliber handgun poking into the flesh below my chin as the shaft of the gun rested on the side of my neck. "Don't move or you're dead," said the owner of the handgun with a heavy Russian accent.

"That's it! You Ruskies are getting an eviction notice today!" I barked with all the righteous indignation I could muster. "Cubic Property Management does not allow firearms in this building. It's in the lease you will soon be responsible for losing."

"Bullshit!" was his reply.

"The computers are down at Cleason Enterprises, your next-door neighbor's suite. We're not going to lose them as a tenant because you think you can deny us access to the electrical panel when it says very clearly in your lease that we have access whenever it's necessary," I said with conviction.

"Turn around and show me some identification," he said as he withdrew the gun from my neck. When I turned around I saw a man in his late thirties of medium build, holding a pistol aimed at my chest.

As I reached for my wallet he gestured excitedly with the pistol and said something in Russian. I retrieved my movie rental card from my wallet. As I reached out to hand it to him I said, "You keep waving that gun at me and you'll not only get evicted, you'll get deported." When I said this he pointed the gun away from me for the first time. I made my move.

You already know that I'm a man of many talents: detective, musician, and dispenser of psychological advice. So, it's completely understandable if you mistakenly assume I'm an expert at karate. Unfortunately, the only black belt I own is currently holding up my pants. I developed my best move in my childhood as a result of defending myself against my sister. She is two years older, but I passed her in height and weight when I turned seven. In spite of her lack of stature, Lisa packed exceptional punching power. If I teased her, took stuff out of her room or any number of minor transgressions, I could count on her to come in with a hard right to the breadbasket. When she first started doing this Mom was appalled, but Dad recognized it as a way for her to fend off unwanted advances as she transitioned into her teenage years. The bottom line was that Lisa could pummel me to tears, but I could only learn how to block, evade or trap her punches. Being a survivalist at heart, I became quite proficient at sidesteps and trapping her right hand under my left arm, like a boxer tying up an opponent with a clinch. I also learned the effectiveness of a good body punch and have first-hand knowledge of exactly where such a punch will do the most damage.

So, when the Russian pointed the gun to his side, I trapped his gun hand under my arm and, in one motion, brought a power punch up into his solar plexus. His knees buckled and I shouldered him backward two steps into the doorjamb behind him. He banged his head hard on the corner of the doorway and his lights went out. I then saw Koflanovich's door open part way and heard the unmistakable sound of large dogs growling. I was on the other side of that walnut door faster than a heavy metal drummer on double-espresso.

As I exited Cerise Records I ran into the receptionist in the hallway. "Did you put that stuff in my hair?" she asked angrily.

"Are you kidding? Most of the time I don't even kiss goodnight on the first date," I replied without breaking stride toward the exit.

By the time I got back to my Acura NXS, reality had set in. My heart could have kept time for a drum and bugle corps. My hands were shaking and I was too light-headed to drive. I sat in my car with the windows up and the air-conditioning on full-blast. I kept visualizing myself lying in the hallway of Cerise Records being fitted for a toe tag by an Assistant Coroner. After about ten minutes I calmed down enough to navigate over to the Dali Lama Yo Mama, Bernie's nightclub. It was only 5:30 PM and the night clubbers wouldn't be out for several hours, but Bernie opened up at 5:00 to catch the Happy Hour crowd from the nearby office buildings. I sat on a barstool near the server station, hoping to connect with a familiar face.

I ordered a double vodka gimlet from a bartender I vaguely remembered as a rookie back when I was leaving the music scene. I'm normally not a big drinker. I had to deal with too many drunks as an entertainer to ever want to join their ranks. But, I needed to steady my hands before my chat with Bernie.

"Hey stranger, I thought you got married and moved to the valley," said a voice I recognized, from directly behind me.

"Gag me with a spoon," I responded with a Valley Girl inflection. "And it wasn't me who was engaged last time we talked. What happened to that Matthew McConaughey wannabe you were hooked up with, Jasmine?" I asked.

"I married him," she said.

"Oops," I said, "I always thought Matthew McConaughey was pretty cool."

She replied, "Matthew is very cool. But that dick-head I married is history."

"I'm sorry. Is that why you're waiting on the suits now instead of the rockers?" I asked sympathetically.

"I thought you got out of the head-shrinking business?" Jasmine retorted in a way that brought back memories of her feisty nature.

"I did and for the same reason you got out of your marriage. I couldn't live with the dick-heads either. Most of the bosses I met needed more help than the clients. At least you don't have that problem working here," I said.

"You got that right. Bernie is the real deal. I've been working here for six years now and for at least the first two I kept waiting for Bernie to show a little bit of a dark side," she said then shook her head. "Never happened."

"Is he around yet?" I asked.

"Yeah, he's in his office. I'll tell him you're here after I help the white collars get happy," she said with a smile.

I finished my drink and ordered another double. As I was reaching for my wallet, I felt a hand clamp down on my shoulder while Bernie told the bartender, "This one's on the house." Then to me he said, "Since when did you start slamming doubles."

"Since about an hour ago when a thug stuck a gun in my neck," I said, knowing it would be counterproductive to hide anything from my mentor.

He replied, "I thought your practice was limited to the foibles of the rich and famous."

"I'm working on the Terry Tucker murder. I'm sure you've been following it in the papers," I said.

"Terry played my club a few times in the early days when he was with Caliber 9," he said. "I was saddened, but not entirely shocked."

"How come?" I asked.

"Terry was a perfectionist. The first time he played here he very politely asked if his band could rehearse some new songs at the club the afternoon before their performance. I agreed and showed up at noon to let them in. Terry worked them non-stop until 4:30 PM. He was pretty confrontational in the way he addressed his band mates when they didn't measure up to his expectations," he said.

"Are we talking obvious mistakes or nit-picky stuff?" I asked.

"I have a pretty good ear and half the time I couldn't hear anything that sounded remotely off. It was clear that the guys in the band weren't hearing it either. They were pissed," he said.

At this point I launched into what I knew of the contract with Cerise Records. "I was hoping you could take a look at it and see if you could spot anything that might give the record company a motive to kill him."

"Do you have it with you?" he asked.

"No," I said. "Jeannine was supposed to get a copy from Chelsea Tucker today, but after my near death experience, I forgot to call to see if it came in."

Bernie said, "Why don't you call her from my office. If it's there she can fax it over."

It was almost 6:30 PM and Jeannine had surely left for the day, but who knows how many times her OCD compels her to check the lights now that she lives within walking distance of the office.

I tried calling her at the office and didn't get lucky. I called her house and connected. "Hi, Jeannine. Have you settled in for the evening?"

"Uh-huh," she replied in a quivering voice.

"Are you OK" I asked in a panicked voice, fearing the Russians had come looking for me.

"No. I'm not OK," she replied with a sob.

"What's wrong?" I asked.

"Lassie's dead!" she cried. "One minute she was standing next to the river and the next minute she's going down the rapids. Now she's dead." Jeannine began to wail. She was letting it all out, like I'd never heard her cut loose before. It could have been the basis for a very therapeutic session. But, since I'm no longer her therapist I did what any other self-respecting detective would have done. I ruined the movie by telling her how it ends and got her to walk over to the office and fax the contracts. About twenty minutes later thirty-one pages of legal bullshit came steaming out of Bernie's fax machine.

While we waited, Bernie reminded me of a night at the club shortly after I started carrying a gun. At the time, a stick-up man was ripping off local bands. We were usually paid in cash after our gigs and would frequently find ourselves in a dark alley behind a club at 2:30 AM. Since my dad was a cop and I handled the money, I got elected for security detail.

One night, after collecting our pay and hanging with Bernie until the band had time to load the equipment into our truck, I walked into the alley behind the club. I immediately heard a voice screaming about money. As my eyes adjusted to the darkness, I saw a crazed junkie holding a hypodermic needle less than an inch from our bass player's neck. "I've got AIDS!" he screamed. "Give me the money or this guy's as good as dead!"

The rest of the band was frozen in front of the junkie, saying the money guy hasn't come out yet. I had the gun on a belt holster in the small of my back. I quietly pulled it out, took careful aim and yelled,

"Put the needle down or I'll blow your fuckin' head off!" As the junkie turned to look at me I screamed, "RIGHT NOW!"

It was very clear to me, the band and especially the junkie, that I wasn't bluffing. He carefully laid his spike on the ground, raised his hands and said, "I crashing man. I wouldn't have stuck him." Then he sprinted down the alley. My first instinct was to chase him, but Kyle, the bass player, started hyperventilating and I thought he was having a heart attack. I stopped to help and the junkie was long gone.

"That was a life or death situation and you handled yourself very well, as I recall," Bernie said.

"I thought of that scene many times when I was weighing my decision to become a detective. Until today, I thought I'd be a lot cooler under fire," I said.

"Actually, you are," Bernie said. "I'm sure you've replayed that scene in your head a thousand times, but you probably forgot that we sat here in this office and talked until 10:00 the next morning. You were on an adrenaline high that the junkie would have died for. Tonight you're not even a quarter as amped as you were that night."

"Really?" I asked. "I forgot all about what happened afterwards."

"The last thing San Diego needs is a detective who thinks shooting people is part of the job description." As he was finishing his point, the fax machine stopped printing.

He got me set up with pen and a notebook and began analyzing the content. When he read a section he thought could have a bearing on the case he gave his expert opinion and answered all of my questions.

"Bernie, what do you think? What stands out the most?" I asked.

He replied, "As you know, I worked as an agent for 17 years. Since I became a club owner a lot of bands, managers and agents have asked my opinion on record contracts. The thing that screams at me is that the owner or ownership group has business experience, but not recording industry experience."

"How so?" I asked.

"The contract has a couple of giant loopholes that could easily be exploited by somebody who knows the established legal precedents in recording industry contract law," he said.

I asked, "What would be the record company's motive?"

"There was no way of telling if the Internet piracy issue would be resolved quickly when the contract was written. You had a talented new band with some name recognition and some terrific new material, jumping into a bad contract market. Along comes a new record company, anxious to attract talent. I know from personal experience that Terry got involved in contract negotiations and knew how to mix charm with a knack for getting his way. I'd guess it didn't take long for him to figure out he was dealing with amateurs and he managed to plant a hidden time bomb in the contract that would enable him to call the shots if the first two CD's performed well," he said.

"Was Terry the kind of guy who'd screw the recording company and piss them off enough to get himself killed" I inquired.

Bernie replied, "Most of the recording industry executives I know have ego's that wouldn't fit in this room. If their meal ticket had 'em by the balls the way Terry had Cerise Records, I wouldn't put anything past them."

"Wouldn't that be like killing the goose that laid the golden eggs?" I asked.

"It would if the whole band died in the explosion. There's a lot of talent in that group and, if memory serves me, Terry wrote only half of the songs," he said.

"Can the band survive without Terry?" I asked.

"I'd give them a listen," Bernie said.

Chapter 3

I RARELY work on Saturday mornings. So far, most of my clients have been either spouses who suspect infidelity or rich parents looking to bail their kids out of scrapes with the law. Business booms on Friday night. Saturday morning is for sleeping.

My first task was to call each of the band members to schedule a time to meet on Monday. I reached the bass player, Jack Pascal, who was quite cooperative. I left messages for drummer, Ian Davis, and lead guitarist, Nigel Choate.

Over the next two hours I reviewed the Internet research that Jeannine dug up yesterday. I immediately went to the material on Cerise Records and John Koflanovich. She tracked the business through two dummy corporations to a business called Yuliya, Inc. This is an electronic parts manufacturing operation based out of Tecate, California, which is a border town southeast of San Diego. Most of Yuliya's officers share the sir name, Chofsky. Yuliya is a small, publicly held corporation on an over-the-counter exchange. Jeannine found it listed in the local stocks section of the *San Diego Union-Tribune* newspaper. In the paper's archives she found a two-page feature on the company from 1990. It appears Yuliya has been essentially the same size since the early 1900's. It was a privately held company based out of San Francisco until 1979, when it went public to finance the move to Tecate in 1980. Before doing so, Yuliya was known as Rasputin Enterprises. In the early days, Rasputin traded in machine parts and slowly transitioned to electronics as technology developed.

The phone rang. "Duffy Investigations," I said.

"Is this Jason Duffy?" asked the caller with a heavy British accent.

"It is." I said.

"Nigel Choate. Your message said you were hired by Chelsea Tucker," he stated.

"I appreciate your time and I'm sorry for the loss of your friend," I said.

"Friend? Terry wasn't a friend. I don't think Terry had any friends. I don't usually speak ill of the dead, but if you're conducting an investigation you're going to find this out sooner or later," he said and paused. "What do you want from me Mr. Duffy?"

"I'd like to get together and talk about what the recording sessions had been like; if you noticed anything unusual. Those types of things," I said.

"I went through all of that with the police. Does Chelsea think one of us did it?" he asked with stress becoming apparent.

I replied, "Nothing like that. Actually she thinks Cerise Records may have been involved because of what was happening with the contract. I'd really like to get your take on it, as well as your thoughts on the record company rep who was at all of the sessions."

Nigel started to relax, "I think she may be onto something. The cops didn't really ask many questions about that Neanderthal from Cerise. I don't like him; I don't think any of the lads do." Nigel agreed to meet me on Monday to go into details.

As soon as I hung up, the phone rang again. After answering with my usual salutation, I heard my girlfriend, Kelly Kennedy, say, "When did you start going to the office on Saturday?"

"Since I started working a high-profile murder case earlier this week," I replied with some enthusiasm.

"Are we still on for the Padres game tonight or will you be holding a press conference?" she asked.

"Let me call my people and I'll get back to you," I replied.

"Your people are probably all in group therapy at this hour. You're just going to have to decide all by yourself," she said, enjoying the exchange.

I replied, "Well, we can't disappoint all of those fans. I'm sure they're expecting us."

"What about dinner?" she asked.

"I thought we'd go with the cylindrically shaped, all beef, non-kosher specialty of the house," I retorted.

"If I have to eat another hotdog I'm not going to want to come within ten feet of anything that even remotely resembles a wiener for a long time," she said.

"As a former therapist I feel duty-bound to help prevent wiener aversion. How does the buffet at the park restaurant grab you?" I asked.

"I'll be ready by 6:00. See you then," she said and hung up.

After a lunch break at the local deli, I was back at my desk by 2:00 PM. I decided to try Ian one more time. After six rings and a brief silence, a smoker's grunt told me a semi-conscious human was attempting to communicate. "Is this Ian Davis?" I asked.

"Who's this?" was the phlegmy reply.

I started by telling him I work for Chelsea and briefly explained what I wanted. He agreed to a meet on Monday, though I got the impression he wouldn't remember the conversation, since it was apparent he was still drunk from the night before. I managed to find out where he would be on Monday afternoon to help avoid getting stood up.

As 3:30 PM approached I was getting ready to call it a day. I had just finished outlining another *To Do* list for Jeannine when I heard the front door open. I was sure it was Jeannine, since I definitely locked the door behind me when I returned from lunch. Fortunately, I had a convex mirror installed in the upper corner of my office when I first moved in, primarily to avoid old mental health clients who couldn't let go of me as their therapist. But that was no familiar face walking through the door. I quietly rolled the middle drawer of my desk open and withdrew my snub-nosed .38 revolver. I then inched my way to a spot behind the door and wondered if he could hear the pounding in my chest. He rustled a few papers on Jeannine's desk, then made his way for my office.

As he walked through the door I stepped behind him and put

the .38 against the nape of his neck. "Freeze," I said, knowing I sounded exactly like one of my Dad's favorite cop shows.

The intruder was in his mid-thirties and built like a professional wrestler. I ordered him up against the wall and frisked him while maintaining the gun's contact with his spinal column. He was carrying a large pistol and two extra clips. After lightening his load, I walked him back out to the reception area, where I could move him out of lunging distance before turning him around. "What are you doing here?" I asked loudly. He didn't reply. "You can either talk to me right now or you can talk to the cops in ten minutes."

He replied with a thick Russian accent, "You call cops anyway if you don't kill me."

"That depends on what you have to say," I offered, hoping to get some answers before arranging his accommodations at our county lock-up. "Did Koflanovich send you over here?"

"Like you visit Koflanovich yesterday?" he responded.

"I went over there to ask him a few questions. I didn't break in," I said.

"You trick girl and knock Nicky unconscious. Not quite friendly visit," he said.

"Tell me about Koflanovich. Why all the strong-arm security?" I asked.

"Your boss no tell? American Mafia keep many secrets," he stated.

"Koflanovich is in the Mafia?" I asked.

"Not him, you!" was his reply.

"I'm not in the Mafia and I'm not the one who needs to start answering some questions." I walked over to the phone on Jeannine's desk, picked up the receiver and said in a forceful way, "Tell me about Koflanovich or you're off to the gulag right now!"

"Ivan is legitimate businessman. He move to US after daughter, Ivana, kidnapped in Ukraine. After your pig comrades cut off finger," he said with disgust.

"I have no pig comrades," I said. As I was about to ask my next question Jeannine walked through the front door. When I turned to look at her, the Russian sprinted toward the balcony, smashed through the screen door and dove over the rail. I ran to the edge of the balcony in time to see the Russian dislodge himself from a couple of oleander branches, two stories below, and run down the street.

When I walked back into the office Jeannine looked to be in shock. "Are you OK?" I asked.

"I told the salesgirl I couldn't wear this perfume. She said it would drive men wild. Is he dead?" she asked.

"He just ran down the street, and it wasn't your perfume. He broke in and just escaped to avoid going to jail," I said.

"I'm going to wash it off anyway. I'll be in the girl's room," she said and walked out.

Chapter 4

KELLY loves going to baseball games, though she doesn't seem particularly attuned to what's happening on the field. She grew up in a dysfunctional family with two alcoholic parents and two older brothers who followed their parents lead down the same road. Kelly got out at 18 to attend school on the East Coast, primarily to get away from the family. I think she likes engaging in what she perceives to be normal family activities. While I'm watching the game she does a lot of people watching, which is OK until she feels compelled to share. A little sharing is fine. Getting nudged in the bottom of the ninth with the game on the line is not.

We're both constantly amazed that we are dating someone of Irish heritage. Kelly associates the Irish with alcoholism and her bad childhood. On the other hand, I think of how Mom had to spend so many lonely nights while Dad was hanging out with his Irish buddies. As a teenager I would feel guilty leaving her alone while I went out with friends or played gigs with the band. I grew up not far from San Diego's Little Italy section and dated girls of Italian heritage almost exclusively, until I met Kelly just over a year ago.

As is our routine, I slept over at Kelly's house Saturday night, and we planned to have brunch after reading the Sunday papers, then go our separate ways. However, about once every month or two the Kennedy clan goes on the warpath and calls Kelly to be the arbitrator of who's right and who's wrong. They used to call at all hours, sometimes from jail. About the time we started dating, Kelly laid down the law and told them if they called before 9:00 AM she would change her phone number and make sure none of them ever got it again. At 9:01 AM Sunday her phone rang and she talked with them for over an hour. When she finished she asked if we could spend the afternoon at the mall and take in a movie. I managed to negotiate a no chick flick codicil to the agreement, and we had a fun day.

On the drive home I cruised the neighborhood surrounding Cerise Records and got lucky on two counts. First, the building offers underground parking for employees, requiring a keycard for entrance. There are two, labeled visitor parking spots per tenant around the perimeter of the building. Second, there is a park directly across the alley from Cerise's parking spots. Cory, my stakeout photographer, could easily sit at one of the picnic tables with a book and his trusty Nikon to keep tabs on the comings and goings of Cerise's visitors. I called Cory and set up a meeting at the office for first thing tomorrow.

At 8:00 AM on Monday morning I met with Cory Pafford, who suffers from Tourette's Syndrome. This is a very unusual psychological disorder that results in many victims uncontrollably uttering the foulest language you can imagine. Cory is forty years old and has been unable to hold a job for any length of time. He's a truly gifted photographer who had a few of his photos printed in major magazines. Unfortunately, most of the steady jobs in photography involve working with journalists, babies, mommies and numerous others who are immediately incensed by the symptoms of Cory's affliction. When I worked with him at the mental health center, I helped him get a job with a National Geographic journalist I had dated briefly. To make a long story short, apparently there is a lot more English fluency in Ecuador than you might imagine. When they got unofficially deported Cory got officially sacked.

Since most of the obscenities Cory spews are not germane to the conversation, I'll spare you as much of it as I can. I laid out his assignment and sent him on his way.

At 10:30 AM I rang the doorbell of Doberman's Stub bassist, Jack Pascal. He lives in a large old house in a lower-middle class neighborhood. On the outside, it looked like most of the other houses on the block, in need of a paint job and some minor repairs. Inside was a very different story. A small entranceway was kept to match the outside; undoubtedly to lead pop-in neighbors, girl scouts and delivery people to believe he was just like them. However, once we walked into the living room it was obvious that Jack had an artist's eye for detail, and excellent taste. The furnishings were modern, but not trendy. The art was phenomenal and his use of electronics to conceal computer, sound system and TV was inspired.

"I'll bet the neighbors think you're a regular Joe Lunchbucket," I said.

"That's the idea," he said.

"Don't they get curious when the bass riffs rattle their windows?" I asked.

"Check this out," he said and led me out of the living room and into a room where all of the walls and ceiling were completely covered by one-foot square cubes, designed to absorb and dissipate sound. The soundboard, amplifier, speakers and cased guitars were all laid out and arranged as if he had prepped for an MTV Cribs photo shoot.

"If I had a set-up like this, my Dad could have actually spent time at home during my teenage years," I said.

"You play?" he asked. I explained a bit of my background and he selected a gray suede case that housed a 1959 Gibson Les Paul. The neck was as straight as any new top-of-the-line guitar you could buy at a quality shop. Jack got us plugged in and we jammed for about 20 minutes.

"You sound familiar. Did you play the club scene?" Jack asked.

"Yeah. I played rhythm guitar and sang for a band called Tsunami Rush until three years ago," I said.

"I heard you a few times. Good stuff. So, what do you want to know about Terry?" he asked.

"Could you take me through what happened the day he died?" I asked.

"OK. We all met at the Denny's on Broadway, near the studio. I got there first and read the paper while I waited for the others. We ordered before Ian arrived, since he's not very punctual. But, he was only about 15 minutes late, which is as close to on time as he gets," Jack said.

"What did you talk about?" I asked.

"We covered the two songs we were going to be working on that day. We planned on finishing one up by early afternoon and starting on the other. Terry was excited about the second song. We had played it several times over the past month and Terry felt it had potential to be big. But, he also couldn't get comfortable with Ian's drum line. To me, it seemed like Terry was blaming Ian's lifestyle for why it wasn't coming out like he wanted it. But Ian was playing it like Terry was telling him. Terry was just having a time making it measure up to his standards. Ian had about two bites of his breakfast before he and Terry got into it. The argument accelerated quickly and Ian left with most of his breakfast still on his plate."

"Did Nigel take sides?" I asked.

"No. We usually tried not to do anything that would get Terry pissed at us. Terry was a lot mellower when it came to playing Nigel's compositions. If it wasn't his baby he didn't feel the need to be the parent," Jack said.

"Were the headphones in Terry's car while you were at Denny's?" I asked.

"I guess so. He usually brought his recorder and headphones into the studio when he got there," Jack said.

"Did you go straight from Denny's to the studio?" I asked.

"I did. But I think Terry stopped at 7/Eleven for a gigantic iced tea. He'd work on it all day," Jack said.

"Did he carry everything in one trip from the car?" I asked.

Jack replied, "I don't think so. It was too much stuff. He also had a briefcase for his sheet music and notes."

I asked, "Did he keep the headphones in the briefcase."

"No," he replied. "It was one of those thin, Italian leather cases. The headphones were big and bulky. He carried them and the portable recorder in a nylon carry bag. He'd bring his guitar home, too. So I'm sure he made more than one trip to his car, or had one of the studio guys help him."

"Did he usually lock his car?" I asked.

"If he was going in the studio for the day he did. But he wouldn't lock up in between trips to the car, I'm sure," he said.

"What about a quick stop at 7/Eleven?" I asked.

"Probably not," he replied.

"How about at Denny's?" I asked.

"Probably yes, but I'm not sure. There's a view of the parking lot at that Denny's. But, his guitar was in there, so, I'm guessing he locked," Jack said with an uncertain look on his face.

"Was the rep from Cerise Records at the studio when you arrived?" I asked.

"If we were there, he was there," he responded.

"What's your take on that guy?" I inquired.

"He creeps me out. He acts like he suspects everybody of everything and it's his job to control through intimidation," he said. "Most record companies ply their talent with hookers, booze and dope as an incentive to put out a hit. Cerise has Vlad the Impaler acting like we better make a hit or else!"

"Did you see him touch the recording equipment at any time?" I asked.

"No," he said.

"Is it possible he helped Terry carry in his stuff?" I asked.

"I don't know. He certainly wouldn't offer, but Terry liked to butt heads with him and would tell him to do manual labor tasks just to piss him off," Jack said.

"Would he do what Terry told him?" I asked.

"Sometimes," he said. "Terry would tell him to make himself useful and not be the only one in the studio not earning his keep. Terry was very good at getting his way."

"Did you see anybody else around the headphones?" I asked.

"Just our roadie, GI Jo-Jo. Terry would put his stuff on a bench by the door and Jo-Jo would put it where it belonged," Jack said.

"Could Jo-Jo have carried the headphones into the studio that morning?" I asked.

"I wasn't really paying that close attention. But, I heard one of the cops ask Ian that question and Ian said Jo-Jo was helping him realign the glass partitions in front of his drum set when Terry walked in. I guess Ian was trying something different to get Terry off his ass."

I said, "Jack, you're a bright guy. Who do you think killed Terry?"

"I've given it a lot of thought and here's all I've got. Our name is Doberman's Stub. Terry was definitely the Doberman. That's not necessarily a bad thing. When dealing with record companies and promoters, every band could use a Doberman Pincher. If somebody pushed Terry, he would push back twice as hard. I'm a Golden Retriever myself. I'm convinced Terry was killed by a Pit Bull or another Doberman."

As I drove away from Jack's house I was starved and not very focused. I couldn't get the dog analogy out of my mind. If Dad's a Police Dog and Mom's an Irish Setter, what am I? Should I drive to the pre-scene of the crime and check out Denny's "Moons Over My Hammy" or drive straight to PetCo. for some kibbles and bits? My cell phone interrupted my ramblings. "Hello," I said.

"Time to pay the piper," said Walter Shamansky.

"Kojak! I thought you forgot all about me. Then again it is almost lunchtime," I said with much enthusiasm.

"Not today. I've already got a date," he said.

"Then what can I do for you?" I asked.

"Your boss is still number one in the charts for the homicide. But, in the interest of being thorough, I thought I'd give you a chance to see if there's anything to her theory about the record company," Shamansky said.

"Have you actually talked with John Koflanovich at any time?" I asked.

"He's out of the country a lot. But, I see where you're going. The Cold War is still very much alive at Cerise Records. Do I think they killed their top moneymaker? Not a chance. Business is business. It would be moronic. But, getting stonewalled by the Ruskies is enough to make me want to punish them by putting <u>you</u> on their tail," he said.

"How about this? There's a park on the other side of their building. Cerise has two visitor parking spaces facing the park and it also faces the entrance to the underground employee parking lot. I can put one of my staff members in the park with a camera to track the comings and goings of the employees and visitors. How does that sound?" I asked without telling him the plan was already in action.

"Staff members?" he queried with much skepticism.

"What's so…?" I started to say when Shamansky cut me off.

"No wait. Don't tell me. I got it. It's an out of work keyboard player or some nutcase from the Mental Health Clinic," he said ebulliently.

"Does SDPD have a policy against hiring the handicapped?" I asked.

"Aha! Nutcase it is! Do you expect me to rely on the work of a mental defect if I have to go to court?" he asked.

"He does stakeouts for me all the time. He's a top quality photographer whose photos were published in National Geographic and other major publications," I said with some pride.

"Tell me those other publications weren't Hustler and other porno rags," he stated.

"Nothing like that," I said authoritatively.

"Can this guy testify if I need him on the stand?" he asked.

"I don't think that would be a good idea," I said.

"OK. What's his major maladjustment?" Shamansky asked.

"He has Tourette's Syndrome," I replied.

"Oh that's just great. I can see it now. The prosecutor says, 'Mr. Pottymouth, tell us in your own words what you saw outside Cerise Records,' and he says what?" Shamansky asked sarcastically.

I replied, "You don't need to use him on the stand. His photos have time and date stamps. Didn't you ever hear the expression, one picture is worth a thousand words?"

"Why don't you personally sit on the place?" he asked.

"My pictures are awful. When they aren't blurry it looks like I'm stalking Marie Antoinette," I said. "Cory can get recognizable faces through rolled up windows of moving cars going in and out of that garage. I've seen them. They're great."

"In other words, Cory's already there. This is no skin off your nose. So, I didn't actually use up that favor. You still owe me," he said.

"Great minds think alike," I said.

"Then tell me when and where I'm thinking about viewing those Rembrandts," he said.

"My intuitive powers are revealing an expensive, hillside eating establishment, sometime around lunch hour tomorrow," I said with mystical inflection.

"Bingo! Make it 12:45," he said and hung up.

While Jack Pascal chooses to blend into a working class neighborhood, Nigel tries to stand out in an upper class section of Rancho Santa Fe. The entrance to his driveway features a wrought iron gate adorned by two, rhinestone encrusted ceramic guitars. I cruised up a fifty-yard driveway with perfectly maintained flowerbeds on either side.

The entranceway had a huge awning extending out from the second floor of the house, supported by polished marble columns. A beautiful outdoor chandelier hung from the awning. Although it had an aesthetically attractive look, it was totally impractical for San Diego, where it rains about as often as you hear the phrase, "who needs fire insurance?"

When I rang the doorbell, instead of the usual chimes I heard a 30-second guitar solo from one of Nigel's compositions. The door opened promptly at the end of the solo. I was expecting a white-gloved butler to greet me with a large measure of British stoicism, but instead, was pleasantly surprised to see a bikini-clad brunette in her early 20's. Maybe you <u>can</u> get good help these days. I was shown into a music room where Nigel sat on an armless swivel chair between a guitar in its floor-stand and an ultramodern blue glass desk.

"Come in Mr. Duffy. I've been expecting you," he said in the accent I was expecting from the butler. "I'm afraid I don't have a lot of time. We're going back into the studio for the first time since Terry's death tomorrow and I'm expected to take up the slack."

"How far are you from finishing?" I asked.

He replied, "The CD was supposed to be 14 cuts. We just finished number ten when Terry died. Our record company has agreed to reduce it to 12 cuts, but three of the last four were Terry's."

"I thought you usually split up the number of cuts pretty evenly," I said.

"We did. It's just that Terry liked to fuss with his songs and put off laying down the tracks until he was completely satisfied. I'm just the opposite. Once a song is written I can't wait until it's recorded," he said.

"Nigel, what can you tell me about the day Terry died," I asked.

"Well, for starters, Vlad the Impaler was at the studio, as usual," he said.

"Is this the Cerise goon?" I asked.

"Exactly."

"What's his real name?" I asked.

"His first name is Vladimir. I don't know his last name. He's definitely not a real executive producer. This guy is muscle and nothing more. He wears a suit, but he's definitely a Teddy Boy," Nigel said.

"Teddy Boy?" I asked.

"A hood; an enforcer," he said and I nodded. "Vlad and Terry had an adversarial relationship. Terry felt Vlad was there to get the tracks down as quickly as possible and spare expenses for the record company."

"Did Vlad ever tell Terry or any of you to speed it up?" I asked.

"Not in so many words. But, he always acted tough and liked to think he was in charge. Terry belittled Vlad as a way of keeping him in line. You could tell Vlad hated being treated like the imbecile he is. When you said on the phone that Chelsea suspects him, I couldn't agree more."

"I haven't been able to get near him at Cerise. Any suggestions?" I asked, trying to wrangle an invitation to the studio tomorrow. Nigel accommodated as expected. "I just had a studio guitarist cancel for tomorrow. I'll tell Vlad you're filling in for him. I was planning on laying down the rhythm tracks myself anyway."

"I actually do play rhythm," I said.

"Even better. Can we pick this up after the session?" he asked. "I'm not even close to where I need to be on this song." I agreed and showed myself out. As I reached the entranceway I looked across the living room and through the glass wall into the backyard. Seated at the pool, facing me was the butler minus the bikini top. She smiled and gave me a finger wave as she sipped a drink through a straw. I returned her wave and exited the mansion.

It was only 3:00 PM and I wasn't scheduled to meet Ian until 4:30 PM. So I called Jeannine to see if there were any new developments. She said that Cory called about an hour ago and said to tell me a truck from Formal Affairs Catering had just visited Cerise Records. I had Jeannine look them up on her computer. As I drove over, I stayed on the phone with Jeannine as she checked out the catering company online. There was no indication that they had any affiliation with the Russian community.

When I reached their reception desk I told the receptionist that John Koflanovich from Cerise Records had just sent me over and I needed to speak with the Catering Event Manager handling their affair. I did this using my best impression of a Russian immigrant. The Event Manager was a well-groomed woman in her late 40's. "What can I do for you, sir?" she asked.

"Mr. Koflanovich insist I serve on wait staff to help non-English speaking guests," I said.

"This is very last minute. The party is tonight. We didn't discuss this. We only use our own people," she said.

"It a, how you say – afterthought," I said with a smile.

"I'm afraid that would be impossible," she said.

"More than half of guests speak only Russian. How many staff members you have speak Russian?" I asked.

"We have no Russian waiters, but I'm afraid our insurance and workers compensation would not allow us to let you work the party tonight. There's just no time to get you approved," she insisted.

"Mr. Koflanovich say to tell you if you no let me work, to cancel alcohol part of order. He bring in Russian bartenders," I said.

She smiled, blinked about eighteen times and said, "Tell Mr. Koflanovich that Formal Affairs Catering still believes the customer is always right. I'll have a little form for you to sign that says you are working for Mr. Koflanovich and not our company and, as such, are not covered by our worker's compensation. If you get hurt you are not our responsibility."

"Understand," I said.

"You don't need to be there for the set up. Guests should start arriving at 7:00 PM. That time will be fine. See Suzy at reception to get fitted for your uniform," she said. Besides the uniform I got directions to the Ukrainian Citizen's Club in North Park.

The Tillerman's is a British rock & roll bar in Mission Beach. Rock was king and a large Doberman's Stub framed poster hung on the wall behind the bar. I swung onto a barstool in front of the poster and ordered a Beck's. As the bartender was pouring my beer into a glass I nodded at the poster and asked, "Are you a fan?"

"Yeah. They're pretty cool," he said. "In fact, if you stick around long enough you just might run into the drummer."

"I heard he's the wild one in the band," I said.

"You heard right. He definitely likes to party and has incredible stamina," he said.

"Does he ever bring any of the other band members in here with him?" I asked.

"Hardly. He doesn't get along with them and makes no secret of it," he said.

"Not even his fellow Brit, Nigel?" I asked.

"I think he feels like he owes Nigel for getting him into the band, since Ian is the youngest and wasn't nearly as established when the band formed," he said.

"Couldn't they be friends, just not drinking buddies?" I asked.

"One night at 2:00 AM I was closing up and Ian was potted. He found out that day that an uncle in Leeds had died and he couldn't go home because of the band's schedule. He was nowhere near passing out and needed a friend. I asked him if he wanted me to call Nigel and he said Nigel would tell me to throw his ass in jail. I thought he might just be feeling sorry for himself, but he wasn't. He honestly believes Nigel would like him out of the band," he said.

"That sucks!" I said with a sincere expression.

"Speak of the devil," he said. "Look who's here." Ian made his entrance through the back door. He looked like a young Billy Idol with his wild blond hair, muscles and sleeveless shirt. Ian ambled the length of the bar toward us, surveying the tables as he walked.

When he reached us I said, "Ian, I'm Jason Duffy. Can I buy you a drink?"

"I like the way you think," he said to me. Then he turned to the bartender and said, "Bushmills." As the bartender prepared his drink Ian said to him, "So, Bert, I see you've been talking to the private dick. I hope you haven't been telling tales out of school."

"Just extolling your virtues, Ian me-boy," he replied.

"How about if we grab a table and talk a bit," I suggested.

After a long gulp of Bushmills Ian replied, "You think I don't want to be seen at the bar with a dick."

"We haven't been called dicks since the thirties. You really should have taken an *English as a Second Language* course before immigrating," I said with a smile.

Ian looked at Bert, nodded at me and said, "A comedian. Maybe we will have some fun tonight after all." Then to me he said, "If you want to do the cloak & dagger we can take the table by the loo. If Bert's been in there recently no one will come near us. But first give me a little topper, Bert." Once Bert refilled his empty glass we settled into a booth under a Rolling Stones poster. "OK, grill away. I'm as lucid as you're gonna find me tonight."

"Don't you have a recording session first thing in the morning?" I asked.

"You're on top of things. I didn't find out about that until I listened to my answering machine a half hour ago," he said.

"I just came from Nigel's. He's working overtime to get a song together for tomorrow," I said.

"And I'm fucking off in a bar as usual. Did he send you over here to keep me sober for tomorrow?" he asked.

"I don't work for Nigel, I work for Chelsea," I said, trying to get him on a positive track. "She thinks the record company had something to do with Terry's murder. What do you think?"

"She thinks the blond Bolshevik blew her husband's mind?" he asked enthusiastically. "I concur wholeheartedly. I knew that fucker was bad news from day one."

"Did you see him touch the headphones that day?" I asked.

"Yeah. I think I did. Terry was always trying to get him to do things. I'll bet he planted the bomb while me and GI Jo-Jo were adjusting the partitions," he said.

"Weren't the partitions and your drum set pretty close to the explosion?" I asked.

"Yeah. Thank God for the partitions or the best drum set I ever owned would have been covered in blood," he said, then quickly added. "That didn't sound right. I probably told Terry to sod off every day I knew him, though not always to his face. But I'd trade me drums and swear off the booze forever if it would bring him back. He made me famous. I'm not too sure Nigel can keep the band together without him."

"Let me ask you about the partitions. I don't get it. You were halfway through a song and you adjusted the partitions. Isn't the idea to maintain the continuity of the sound throughout the song?" I asked.

"My bad. I was a little hung over and I just had a row with Terry at breakfast over my part in his big song that we'd be starting later in the day. I thought about what he said on my way to the studio and figured out a way to finally please him, if that's really possible. I was so excited about my idea that I forgot we weren't finished with his other tune. Terry was about to go totally ballistic when GI Jo-Jo told him he marked the exact placement of where the partitions were, and could put them back in ten minutes. Terry chilled and things went pretty well till the explosion."

"Shouldn't you and Jo-Jo have been re-setting the partitions while Terry was listening to his recording?" I asked.

"Terry's a workaholic. I don't suffer from that affliction. I took a little break out at my car. A little taste of the Bushie," he said holding up his glass. "I needed a little fortification before being browbeaten by the master."

"What about Jo-Jo?" I asked.

"I'm sure he was making time with his groupie girlfriend," he replied.

"I didn't think roadie's had groupies," I said.

"Delitah has been using GI Jo-Jo to try to get to Terry," he said.

"Does GI Jo-Jo know this?" I asked.

"Of course," he replied. "But GI Jo-Jo has always been shy around girls. He's happy to have a good looking babe toastin' his buns, even if it's just a temporary arrangement."

"Ian, can I give you a bit of friendly advice?" I asked.

"Here it comes. Go ahead, get it over with," he replied.

"You only have two more songs to go on the CD. The public's probably going to like it no matter how good those songs are. You guys are in the middle of contract negotiations with your label. Cerise and every other major label will be paying very close attention to those two songs to decide whether or not Doberman's Stub can make it without Terry. You're going to be in the studio for what; maybe a week? Why not tone the partying down for one week, then throw yourself and your mates the biggest bash you've ever had? You seem to like this business. Why not give it your best shot to keep it going as long as possible?" I asked.

"Biggest bash ever. I already told you I like the way you think. Good advice," he said.

At 7:00 PM I walked in the rear entrance to the Ukrainian Citizen's Club in my waiter uniform. The Event Manager briefed me on my duties. I was to circulate with a platter of caviar, focusing on the Russian-speaking guests. About 100 people arrived in the next half-hour. The occasion was Ivana Koflanovich's seventeenth birthday. I got a glance at the guest of honor and she was indeed missing half of her left pinkie finger. Daddy looked like a successful businessman in a gray pinstriped suit. He was in his mid-fifties and had a bodyguard accompanying him at all times. Ivana had to endure both a male bodyguard and a matron shadowing her every step. What a way to live.

Most of the conversation was in Russian and seemed pleasant and cordial. I heard a couple of guys in their mid-thirties discussing business in Tecate, but nothing that stood out as illegal or sinister. About an hour into the party I heard a couple of elderly women chatting when one said, "Ivan thinks the American Mafia has found him."

"Oh my God!" replied the other. "What's he going to do?"

"Double the security, upgrade alarms. What can he do? He can't go back to Russia and he can't keep running," she said.

"I honestly didn't think the name change was going to fool them for very long," said the second woman.

Just as she said this I felt a gun in my ribs and a voice in my ear saying, "Try same move again and I pull trigger."

"Is that a new cologne, Nicky? You definitely weren't wearing it on Friday," I said, hoping to defuse the tension this man was exuding.

"Walk toward front door. No funny business," he said.

As we made our way around the dance floor I saw my opportunity and took it. Koflanovich was dancing with his daughter and I could see our paths were going to come very close. I assumed Nicky wouldn't take the chance of inadvertently shooting his boss or the daughter. When they were within two feet of me, in one motion I spun away from my captor, tapped Koflanovich on the shoulder and said, "Mind if I cut in." When he let go of her to turn and see who was making the request, I grabbed Ivana and danced her toward the middle of the crowd. When I reached a point where I could make a dash for the door I said, "You're a wonderful dancer. Great party. Gotta run." When I reached the door I slowed my pace, knowing there would be more guards at the entranceway. As they checked me out in my waiter uniform I smiled, said good evening, walked around the corner of the building, then broke into a full sprint toward the parking lot. As I reached the lot I heard a silenced bullet whiz past my head. I then ducked down and wove my way through the cars toward my Acura parked at the far end of the lot facing the street. Three bodyguards worked their way up and down the rows of cars in a pattern that kept me away from my vehicle. As I was about to make a dash across an open space to the next row, a shadow crossed my path and I dropped to my stomach and rolled under a Ford Explorer.

I reached to the small of my back for my revolver, then realized I wasn't carrying because the short waiter jacket couldn't adequately conceal it. Suddenly, a pair of black, shiny shoes were directly in front of my face. "Nicky, over here!" called a voice in perfect English.

"Do you see him?" asked Nicky.

"Go down this row and wait at the end. I'll try to flush him out," he replied.

Just as I thought I was safe a cigarette butt bounced under the Explorer and came to rest against the side of my left hand. I managed to squelch my instinct to yell in pain, but I couldn't keep myself from drawing my hand back quickly from the burning tip. The scraping noise my hand made against the pavement seemed incredibly loud.

"Nicky wait!" he exclaimed.

Nicky sprinted back. "What is it?" he asked.

"Make sure you look inside the vehicles, he's probably been looking for one that's unlocked," he replied and they both walked away.

I worked my way back to the Acura and was thankful that the remote door locks didn't make a chirp as I clicked. When the Russians got to a point far enough away to make me feel comfortable I started the engine and peeled out across the sidewalk, over the curb and onto the street. Within five minutes I was on the freeway and out of danger.

Chapter 5

ON Tuesday morning I stopped at the Denny's where Terry had his last meal. I used my powers of persuasion and proclivity for bullshit to get seated in the section staffed by the waitress who served the band. After some minor flirting I said, "I heard you served Doberman's Stub the day of the murder."

"How do you know that?" she asked.

"I overheard a couple of your coworkers talking. What were they like?" I asked.

"At first they were pretty cool. But then they got into a fight and the cute one took off without eating his French Slam," she replied.

"Did the rest of them leave together?" I asked.

"No," she replied. "The guy that got here first, left after the cute one. Then, a few minutes later, the other two got up together, but the English guy went to the bathroom while the guy that died paid the bill and took off."

"Cassie, pick up," said a voice from behind a row of steaming plates.

"Gotta go," she said with a smile. I gave Cassie a $5 tip for a $3.95 breakfast and departed.

Twenty minutes later Cory showed me the fruits of his labor; not bad for one day's work. First, he came up with the tip about the birthday party. Then he gave me a veritable rogue's gallery of thugs pulling in and out of the Cerise visitor parking spots. If I didn't know better I'd think Koflanovich was casting for the Russian version of The Godfather.

Cory photographed every vehicle entering and exiting the building. I was able to pick four guys out of Cory's array who were at the party last night. He was also able to get license plate numbers on three of the four guys. I took all of the pertinent photos and put them in a zipped satchel to show Shamansky over lunch.

Jeannine did a bang up job of getting background on people affiliated with Yuliya, Inc. and its predecessor, Rasputin Enterprises. Six years before the Russian Revolution, Josef Chofsky founded Chofsky Enterprises in San Francisco, which was renamed Rasputin Enterprises ten years later. The business became profitable almost immediately because they had connections in Moscow with the Romanov family. Chofsky exported as much technology to Russia as possible.

Besides advanced sales, the other facet of Chofsky's business prowess involved training cheap labor to perform assembly tasks. In San Francisco, they employed Chinese immigrants for less than a quarter of what they would have to pay a US citizen. When human rights groups began protesting and picketing in the 70's, they switched from Chinese laborers to a Maquilladora operation using cheap Mexican labor. The company needed trained Electronics Technicians for key phases of the assembly process. San Diego was perfect, since it has an endless supply of trained Electronics Technicians being honorably discharged from the US Navy and in need of employment.

Once the USSR broke up, Yuliya shifted the majority of its business interactions to Russia. Obviously family ties remained strong. They even changed the way they did business; relying on Russian Electronics Technicians to do most of the sophisticated finish work rather than using ex-Navy personnel.

Jeannine dug up an interesting report written by a stock market analyst. Yuliya initiated an extensive expansion into the Ukraine, then reversed itself within one year and pulled out of Russia altogether. The analyst believed the pullout was caused by extensive piracy perpetrated by the Russian Mafia. The pullout happened one year prior to the start-up of Cerise Records. That would give Koflanovich about the right amount of time to shut things down in

Russia and get set up in California. Unfortunately, the article didn't name any executives in the Ukraine.

I arrived at Larabee's at 12:40 PM. Mrs. Cleaver gave me a look of vague recognition, so I told her, "Kojak, party of two."

She immediately brightened and said, "Of course. If you'll have a seat I'll see if your table is ready."

"Kojak sure gets the red carpet treatment around here," I said. "Is it his witty Polish charm or does he know the owner?"

"Is he a friend of yours?" she asked.

"We're both detectives working on the same case," I said.

"Detective Kojak saved our little restaurant a couple of years ago. The owner used to have a partner until one day he cleaned out the bank accounts and disappeared with a nineteen year old waitress," she said.

"And Kojak found the partner and the money and everybody lived happily ever after?" I asked.

"Something like that," she replied. "Your table is ready. Would you like to be seated now?" she asked.

Shamansky rolled in at 1:00 PM looking sharp in his suit and tie. "You didn't have to get all dolled up on my account," I said.

"Court sucks!" he exclaimed with considerable frustration. "I work my tail off to bust these sleezoids, then help the prosecutor make his case, only to have some left-wing judge give a dead-to-rights repeat offender a free pass so he can qualify for Liberal of the Year at the ACLU picnic."

As I was scrambling to come up with something to get Shamansky out of his foul mood, a Julia Roberts look-alike server came over and gave him a kiss on the top of his shaved head. She said, "I always feel so safe whenever you're around," in a voice that would instantly melt ice from across the dining room. "I'll be with you guys in a couple of minutes."

Shamansky had an immediate change of mood and said to me, "Let's figure out what we're going to eat, then have a look at those pictures." For a moment his voice lost that cop-tone quality and it was quite obvious he was head-over-heels for our *perfect 10* waitress. The thirty-year difference in their ages did nothing to deter his fantasy that he actually had a chance with this beauty. I think I became immune to love at first sight when I got to know Jeannine.

I had the feeling Shamansky would be riding the pink cloud through the end of dessert and I could probably get a lot more info than I had imagined if I played my cards right. Once his heart-throb disappeared into the kitchen he asked, "Are the pictures in the satchel?"

I started off by showing him the crew from visitor parking. "That's Josef Kozlofsky. He was a minor contender on the heavyweight boxing scene until a couple of years ago. I saw him box at least three times. What he lacks in skill he makes up for in ferocity; and man, can he take a punch," Shamansky said. I made a mental note to scrap Plan A of hand-to-hand combat if I came across Josef in a dark alley. I was pretty sure I could take him with Plan B – the hundred yard dash.

Shamansky recognized three more of the 15 scary-looking visitors. He didn't think any were known felons, but all had several scrapes with the law and all had reputations as very bad dudes. "What do you make of it?" I asked.

"Something is definitely going down at Cerise Records. But these pictures aren't enough to be able to get a requisition for more manpower from the brass," he said.

"Why not?" I asked emphatically.

"Because my boss is going to cite the names of about five gangster rap bands and tell me this is probably just a bunch of white guys trying to Gravy Train the idea," he said. We then looked at the rest of the photos I had selected and Shamansky was able to supply a few names to go with the faces. At this point our food arrived and our sexy server made another huge fuss over Shamansky.

"How could your boss not put two and two together. First you have a murder; then an uncooperative suspect who ducks you; then you have half of San Diego's Russian bent noses popping over shortly after the murder," I said.

"I think that's putting three and three together, but who's

counting," he said. "It's not so much that this doesn't look suspicious; it's more that the case against your boss is looking better every day."

"How so?" I asked.

"Let's just say you better put in for your expense reimbursement soon. If I had to make an educated guess, I'd say your client will be wearing a numbered shirt by this time next week," he said.

"C'mon Shamansky," I said. "I gave you some good stuff here. What have you got that makes her look so bad?"

He replied, "There are a few things, like the fact that she gave him the headphones, had access to them and was seen fighting with Terry a couple of days before the murder. But the one that stands out the most is the fact that Chelsea's dad owns a construction company that uses blasting caps for excavation. And, she took out a five million dollar insurance policy on him less than a year ago."

"Most married couples have insurance policies and, from what I can tell, everybody that knew Terry fought with him on a regular basis. He was not your proverbial sweetheart by any stretch of the imagination," I said.

"What about the blasting caps?" he asked.

"Is there any evidence that she was in possession of blasting caps or came anywhere near where they're stored?" I asked.

"We're working on that right now," he said.

"We both know that you can find almost anything about anybody if you know your way around the Internet. Also, everybody knows that the spouse is always the top suspect. Framing Chelsea would be the easiest thing in the world. Especially if the police decide they don't want to look at more than one suspect," I ranted.

"You're lucky I'm in a good mood, Duffy. Why don't you leave fifty for the meal and take off. I'll take care of the tip," he said.

Not at all pleased, but also not wanting to burn any bridges, I left the cash on the table and said, "I suggest the cherries jubilee for dessert."

I arrived at Perfect Pitch Recording Studios at 2:30 PM. The band had just taken a break and was still gathered in the studio.

I was immediately accosted by a blond behemoth in khaki slacks, blue blazer, white shirt and striped tie. "What are you doing here?" he shouted.

"Nigel Choate invited me to stop by," I said as all three of the band members watched the exchange.

"No visitors! Get out now!" he exclaimed.

Jack Pascal stepped forward and said, "This guy is a rhythm guitar player. He's going to fill in for Terry Tucker's part so that the rest of us can stay in rhythm while we do our thing."

"No one told me this. I was told an African man named Skeezie Johnson would be filling in," he said as he glanced at the clipboard in his left hand.

Jack replied, "Skeezie's a little queasy. He won't be joining us today."

Vladimir Torhan looked perplexed, so I added, "Too much vodka. I just came from his place and he's blowing borscht chunks all over the bathroom floor.'"

"Ah, hangover," he said with a smile. Then, changing his expression he yelled, "I don't believe you. Musicians always walk in with instrument. No guitar; no musician."

"I was told I had to play Terry's guitar to match up the sound," I said.

"Play something right now," he demanded.

A couple of minutes later Jack had me plugged in and I was instinctively playing the riff I used to reserve for dates that I was trying to impress as being third base-worthy. By the time I had finished, Torhan had buttoned his blazer and Nigel said, "Blyme! He's bleedin' decent." He then handed me a photocopy of the sheet music for the next song and said, "I'm not going to ask you to sign a waiver because we're not going to be using your tracks. But, it would definitely help us out if you could fill in for the Skeezer today."

"Sure. Whatever," I replied.

"GI Jo-Jo will set you up in a practice room behind the recording engineer. Here's the sheet music and a disk of what it's supposed to sound like, with me playing both lead and rhythm. Stand behind the engineer and give me the high sign when you're ready to go," Nigel said.

GI Jo-Jo stands about 6'2" and weighs around 225 lbs. He carried a Marshall amp into the 5' by 9' practice room, then went back for the guitar. When he returned I said, "Terrible thing that happened to Terry."

"He was a hellofa good musician," he said.

"Was he a friend?" I asked.

Jo-Jo thought about this for about 15 seconds before responding. "I don't know. There were four roadies on the tour and I'm the one he picked for the studio gig; so, I guess so."

"Why do you think he picked you?" I asked.

"Because I worked with electronics in the Army. I can do cabling, sound board, minor repairs and I'm not a complainer like most roadies," he said.

"Not even when your girlfriend talks about wanting to be with him?" I asked.

"Who told you about that?" he asked.

"One of the guys in the band mentioned it. I didn't think it was a secret," I said.

"You're all set to go here," he said and walked out of the room.

Along with the amp and guitar, Jo-Jo had set up a modular recorder with headphones for me to listen to Nigel's disk. I wondered if it was the same make and model that had killed Terry. I gave the headphones a thorough pat-down before putting them on. After about twenty minutes I emerged from the practice room and stood behind the sound engineer. From that vantage point I could tell that the engineer had the best view of the blast, looking through the glass into the recording studio.

Nigel signaled the recording engineer to stop. While he spoke with Ian I said to the engineer, "It looks like you had a clear view of the explosion that killed Terry."

"That's what the cops thought, too," he said. "But I was looking at the mixing board the whole time."

"I thought you were on break, between songs," I said.

"Maybe the band takes a break between songs, but that's usually my busiest time. I was multitasking, splitting time between critical listening and instrument review. I had to make sure we were set with what we had just recorded and didn't need another take. That day it was especially important because I knew the drummer was planning on resetting the partitions. I was completely focused on what I was listening to and how it related to the sound levels I was looking at on my panel," he said.

"Did you notice anybody near Terry's table during the day?" I asked.

"No, but you sure ask a lot of questions for a rhythm guitarist," he said.

"I guess multitasking is big around here," I said as I noticed Nigel waving me into the studio. It felt good to be playing with a band again. We spent the next 45 minutes wading through a couple of takes that didn't please Nigel at all. On the third take he was giving everybody a smile and nod. Unfortunately, as we were coming out of the bridge, one of the bodybuilders that visited Cerise yesterday wandered into the studio and Nigel went nuts.

Torhan did his best to smooth things over, but Nigel was too distracted to continue. He called for a half-hour break and left the building. I walked over to Torhan, who was complaining about how much money a half-hour break would cost and decided it would be my best shot at pumping him for information. I said to him, "That's it for me, I'm outta here and I'm not coming back in a half-hour."

"What are you talking about? There's no reason to leave," he said tensely.

"I didn't like the idea of taking a gig where a musician got murdered in the first place. Then, I'm out there for less than an hour, standing right next to where Terry was blown away and you guys let this thug come strolling in," I said excitedly. "Your security sucks. I can't work under these conditions."

"Boris Melsin is not a thug," he said looking at his comrade. "In fact, he was just assigned to the security detail here at the studio. It's his first day on the job. He didn't know where he was going. You see, there is no shortage of security."

"How much security was here the day Terry was killed?" I asked.

"Just me that day," he said.

"I thought you're supposed to be an executive," I said.

"I am, but I was also an amateur boxing champion in the Ukraine eight years ago. So, I am quite capable of handling myself in a fight," he said.

"The guy who killed Terry used a lot more firepower than fists," I said.

"I've got it under control," he said as he unbuttoned his jacket and revealed his shoulder holster and what appeared to be a Glock pistol. "If the killer returns, he's dead meat."

Nigel came back considerably more relaxed. I got the impression the band smoked a joint during the break. We then recorded his song in one take. Afterwards, he came up to me holding a single sheet of paper. "I think I'll have you sign a release after all. That wasn't half bad," he said.

I accommodated his request, but signed it "Jason N. Daffy," as in "Jason not daffy enough to sign his rights away." Nigel wanted me to stick around for the last song, but I had an appointment with the band's manager, Kirby Kaufmann, and the band's attorney, at Kirby's insistence. So, I turned my back on potential rock & roll immortality to go do my job. Maybe the rock & roll dream finally is out of my blood. Then again, it could also be that I'm enjoying my role as a detective more than at any time since I hung out my shingle.

Kirby Kaufmann presents himself as your stereotypical music industry sleezebag. He's in his mid 50's, about 60 pounds overweight, wears a toupee that probably makes squirrels horny, and he has the worst looking facelift in history. His picture should be on the wall of every cosmetic surgery clinic in California with the warning, "See what happens when you settle for the cheapest surgeon in town!"

At first it was hard to imagine that an astute businessman like Terry Tucker would place his future in the hands of an obvious hack like Kaufmann. Then again, they say you can't judge a book by its cover. Maybe Kaufmann is some kind of rock & roll savant. On the other hand, it is much more likely that Terry selected someone he could control with absolute authority; a puppet that wouldn't be able to figure out what was going on with the recording contract.

Also present, and at least looking the part, was Attorney Elden Dumanis. At first they were friendly and asked that I express their condolences to the widow. But once I wanted to change the subject to the contract negotiations, it got acrimonious.

Kaufmann said, "I'm afraid we're not at liberty to discuss the contract with you. It's privileged information."

"I work for Mrs. Terry Tucker. She inherits all of Terry's publishing and recording interests," I said.

"We work for Doberman's Stub. As much as we were sorry to see Terry die and all, he's no longer a member of the band. We're now accountable to the surviving three members and not to Terry or his widow," said Kaufmann.

"Do you agree with this?" I asked Dumanis.

"Certainly. We're talking about privileged information. If we share anything with you we are betraying confidentiality," he said, then looked at Kaufmann and smiled.

"Then you won't mind if I call my firm's Entertainment Law Attorney?" I asked.

They both looked a bit flustered at this suggestion, but agreed. Of course my firm doesn't have an Entertainment Law Attorney on retainer, so I did the next best thing and called Bernie Liebowitz. I made the call from the desk phone. When Bernie picked up I said, "Attorney Liebowitz, this is Jason Duffy. I need your expert opinion on a contract matter."

"I take it you're scamming some unsuspecting schmuck as we speak," he replied.

"That's correct. I'm meeting with the manager of Doberman's Stub, Kirby Kaufmann and their attorney, Elden Dumanis. Can I put you on speaker phone?" I asked.

"Give me a minute to shove this stick up my backside. OK, I'm ready," he said.

"Thanks. Here we go," I said and switched to speaker mode. "Let's be informal. Bernie, this is Kirby and Elden. Guys, this is

Bernie." After everyone said hello I said, "Bernie, I'm working for Terry Tucker's widow. I'm sure you read about the murder in the papers."

"Of course," Bernie said.

"Kirby and Elden feel they can't talk with me about the contract they were working on with Terry since, being deceased and all, he's no longer a member of the band. Now I feel Chelsea Tucker still has a right to be kept informed, particularly since her husband wrote about half of the songs and performed on the new album," I said.

"Does Chelsea inherit?" Bernie asked.

I replied, "She gets everything. There are no ex-wives, no children, and not even any parents. Chelsea is the sole heir."

"Then here's the deal. Kirby and Elden are right. They can tell you as her representative or tell her face-to-face to take a hike and not share a thing about the contract," Bernie said and the guys lit up like a Christmas tree. "However, if they choose to do that Chelsea can file an injunction against both the band and the record company, delaying the release of the album indefinitely. All of the proceeds of past albums would be put into a trust fund and held without disbursement until the matter is settled. She could even submit the court documents to ASCAP and hold disbursement of royalties from airplay until the case is decided," Bernie said.

Elden chimed in, "If we fight this thing she could be broke for years."

"Actually, her father owns a very profitable construction business. She doesn't need the money," I said.

Bernie added, "The only one who would profit from a fight is you, Elden. If it went on long enough you could own Kirby's house."

"Nobody's puttin' up their house over this thing. We just didn't want to get sued by the band members for disclosing financial information to a non-band member. If the law says we have to talk, then as law abiding citizens we'll talk till we're blue in the face," Kirby said.

"Thanks Bernie," I said, ready to disconnect.

"I'll just bill you for a half-hour on this one," Bernie replied and hung up.

Over the next hour I confirmed two things. First, Terry was completely in charge of all facets of the negotiation with Cerise Records and second, he hired these two clowns based on their level of incompetence. Elden conceded that Terry retained another law firm to do the detail work on the new contract. Fortunately, Elden was a pack rat and had a copy of each version that had been prepared by the firm to date. I made copies of everything, determined their whereabouts at the time of the murder and asked for their opinions on who killed Terry.

Elden said, "I don't have any idea who did it. But, I can tell you this; the last couple of times we got together he was worried about something."

"That was just the pressure of getting the CD done and having to negotiate with the Russian Mafia," said Kirby.

"What?" I asked loudly. "What makes you think Cerise Records is connected with the Russian Mafia?"

"That's what Terry called them all the time. Have you been in Koflanovich's office? It's like visiting somebody at a maximum security prison," said Kirby.

"Tell me about it," I said.

"On the outside it looks pretty normal," he said. "But once you get past the receptionist you've got armed guards, attack dogs, a laser security system, hidden cameras and Koflanovich's office can be instantly turned into a safe room. Fort Knox should be so secure."

I said, "I know in contract negotiations you usually ask for the sun and settle for the moon. Do either of you know where Terry was hoping to end up."

They looked at each other, Kirby nodded and Elden said, "He had a Plan A and a Plan B. In Plan A, Cerise gives Doberman's Stub a new contract starting with the CD they're finishing now. Like you said before, he knew he had Cerise over a barrel and figured he could get headliner money."

"What about Plan B?" I asked.

Elden replied, "In Plan B, if and only if Cerise didn't negotiate in good faith, Terry said something about getting them busted and going free-agent."

"Do you know what he had on them?" I asked.

"He didn't talk about that," Elden replied.

"Was anybody helping him gather information?" I asked.

"I think so," said Kirby. "He got a call on his cell when I was with him a couple of weeks before the murder. I only heard one side of the conversation, but it sounded like he was getting some dirt on Cerise or Koflanovich and he definitely liked what he was hearing. He told the caller to, 'keep digging,' and said 'good work,' or something like that."

"Did he mention a name?" I asked.

"Not that I recall," he replied. "But there is one other thing you might want to know."

"What's that?" I asked.

"The week before he died, Terry told me he was being followed," Kirby said.

Chapter 6

I SPENT all of Wednesday morning pouring over the legalese in four different preliminary versions of the new recording contract. Terry's initial proposal was, as expected, well beyond where he hoped to end up. The following three proposals gave a strong indication that Terry felt he had a great deal of leverage and was not willing to settle for anything short of a contract befitting a business savvy, headline act. The contracts also revealed a major surprise. In each of the proposals there was a clause allowing the band to fire one of its members.

Jeannine popped into my office with a handful of papers. "I think you're going to want to look at this right away," she said. I reviewed Internet printouts as Jeannine gave me a summary. "When Yuliya shifted a significant portion of its assets into a joint venture with the Ukrainian company, they were required to file a report with the SEC naming the officers of the corporation. For the first time I saw the name Ivan Chofsky. I then got into an English language search engine for Tass, one of the major news services in Russia. When I ran Ivan Chofsky, I found several articles on the kidnapping of his daughter," she said. Jeannine then picked up the stack she had handed me and pulled out one titled, *Gruesome Development on Chofsky Kidnapping*. "This one tells about how the kidnappers cut the daughter's pinky off at the knuckle and mailed it to her father."

"It sure looks like proof positive that Ivan Chofsky is John Koflanovich," I said. "Excellent work, Jeannine."

She smiled and gave me a shy look, then said, "There are several more articles on the kidnapping that I haven't read yet. I clicked through and read headlines and first paragraphs, but none of them looked like they would explain how the case ended."

"Keep digging," I said. "It's important to find out if Chofsky cut a deal with the Russian Mafia to get his daughter back."

Did you ever have one of those ideas where you know you should ignore it, but you do it anyway? This idea would allow me to go on my usual mid-week date with Kelly and also work on the case. But, that little voice inside of me was screaming, "You're an idiot if you do this." I ignored the little voice and called my mother. "Hi, Mom. I have an idea I think you'll like, but I'm worried that it could turn out badly."

"What is it dear?" she asked.

"Would you and Dad like to accompany me and my girlfriend to the Padres game tonight. I could get a little more advice from Dad on my case and both of you could meet Kelly," I said with apprehension.

"That sounds marvelous," she said enthusiastically.

"I think the two of you would get along well. I'm just worried Dad will say something that will make me regret doing this," I said.

"I can certainly understand why you would feel that way. It was very insensitive of him to use the word Wop in front of that lovely Italian girl you brought home before the prom," she said.

"That's just one of many times he's offended a friend of mine," I said.

"He's actually gotten much better since he retired. He hardly ever uses ethnic slurs anymore, and now he only curses at strangers when he's driving," she said with a small measure of pride in her voice.

"If we do this, we should probably meet at the ballpark," I said.

"That would be best," she said reassuringly. After a brief pause she added, "Why don't you sit between your dad and Kelly, and I'll sit on the other side of her. This way you'll be able to chat with your dad and I can pull her attention away if he starts to say anything I think would upset you."

"Great plan, though I still feel like I'm going to regret this," I said.

"Kelly sounds Irish. What's her last name?" she asked.

"Kennedy," I replied.

"Your dad will be thrilled. What could go wrong?" she asked.

"For one, her family is alcoholic," I said. "I can see the first words out of his mouth being, 'I'll bet you've had some wild parties on St. Patrick's Day.'"

"What a shame," she said sympathetically. "Your Uncle Bert in Cleveland is a mess. That's why he's never been invited out to visit. And, your third cousin, Matilda, has liver damage from her bad habits. I'll tell your father about her situation and give him a list of taboo topics. OK?" she asked.

"OK. Let's meet in front of Gate C at 6:45. I'll get the tickets. If Kelly has a problem I'll call back," I said.

Mom replied, "Relax. We're going to have a wonderful time."

I called Kelly and, although two baseball games in one week was definitely not what she had in mind for the evening, she was thrilled that I asked her to finally meet my parents. We'll see how thrilled she is after the game.

On our drive to the park I said, "Kelly, I know you've been very up-front with me about your family and I haven't said much about mine. I think you'll get along well with my mother. In fact, she asked that you sit between us, which I think is a great idea."

"That's fine with me," she said.

"But Dad is another story. As you know, he was a city cop for 30 years," I said. "When you spend that much time interacting with the dregs of society, you can get very insensitive. Dad tends to say things that I find embarrassing. I'm just worried that he'll offend you and I'll spend the next two months wondering if you think I'll turn out just like him."

Kelly replied, "There is nothing your father could say or do that could come close to what I've experienced with my family."

"Maybe not," I said. "But, I'm still going to feel embarrassed and wonder what you're thinking."

"I'll tell you what. If your dad says anything that I think will embarrass you, look at me. I'll give you a wink that means he's still not in the same league with my family. OK?" she asked.

"OK," I replied as we pulled into the parking lot.

She said, "All I ask is that you make an effort to have a good time tonight and don't let your dad get under your skin, or I'll pinch you."

"What!" I exclaimed.

"You heard me. And, if I catch you throwing gasoline on the first little spark, you're going to owe me a month of chick flicks. Do we understand each other?" she asked authoritatively.

"Yes Miss Kennedy," I replied, like one of her students being taken to task.

I secured the best seats available, which turned out to be quite good since the Padres were ten games out of first place in mid-August. After I did the introductions, Mom insisted Kelly call them Molly and Jim. This was a first. Dad seemed to choose his words carefully, and managed to keep his foot out of his mouth, as we made our way through a concession stand line and to our seats. Mom took charge when we arrived and got everyone situated in the desired spots. Dad was on the aisle, followed by me, Kelly and Mom.

Once we got settled in and Mom engaged Kelly's attention, Dad asked, "Any new developments in the case?"

Over the first three innings I gave Dad a summary of all that had transpired, except for the gunshots in the parking lot of the Ukrainian Citizen's Club. I stopped only for the Star Spangled Banner, and when Kelly asked me to hail a soda vendor. After I had finished Dad asked, "What do you think you'll find in Tecate?"

"I'm convinced that the money to finance Koflanovich came out of Yuliya," I said. "Do you think it's possible the that the guy with the money might be calling the shots at Cerise?"

"That's good thinking son," said Dad. "I guess that matchbook-cover detective school is finally paying off. Did you hear anything at the birthday party that might help confirm your suspicion?"

"Most of the older men were speaking Russian. The *Learn Russian at Home in your Spare Time* course must have been on another matchbook," I said. I hadn't realized my voice had gotten louder until I felt Kelly's fingers drumming on my leg. When I looked, her fingers moved into the pinch position and tapped my leg twice while she continued a pleasant conversation with my mother. That engineer at Perfect Pitch has nothing on Kelly when it comes to multitasking.

The women took a rest room break in the sixth inning and came back with refreshments, including beers for the guys. Mom said, "Jim, you haven't had much of a chance to get to know Kelly. She's really a lovely girl."

Dad looked over me at the women and replied, "It's hard to be sociable when your son's chewing your ear off. Do you like baseball, Kelly?"

"Oh yes," she said. "I don't watch it on TV, but I love coming out to the ball yard."

"That's great. I thought this one," he said pointing a thumb in my chest, "was going to grow up to think second base meant an extra four-string guitar. But he's turning out alright." Dad smiled at me, actually thinking he paid me a compliment.

Kelly could sense that I was getting angry. I opened my mouth to say something, but she beat me to the punch by saying, "Jim, have you ever seen the movie *Steel Magnolias*?"

Dad replied, "Isn't that a chick flick? I don't go for them, but I'm sure Molly's seen it."

Kelly said, "I just saw it and really enjoyed it. I'm going to talk with Molly about it while you two go back to your shoptalk. OK?"

Dad said, "Sure, you do that." Then he turned to me, and in a quiet voice said, "Does she drag you off to see those things?"

"Not yet," I replied.

Over the next couple of innings Dad shared stories about cases he worked that had some similarities. When we got into the top of the ninth inning he said, "I've got a confession to make. I made a lot of my cases working closely with Forensics. O'Hara said he'd check with them about your case and meet me at Casey's Bar. When I got there he was sitting with Dennis Fallon, the Forensics Department night supervisor. As he was giving us the grisly details, O'Malley and

McCoy joined us. When he was done, O'Malley, who has a bunch of relatives in Belfast, said the IRA has been using blasting cap bombs for the past 50 years."

"Dad, I appreciate your help, but, unless the IRA and the Russian Mafia worked out a merger that nobody knows about, I don't see how that's gonna help," I said.

He responded, "Since I retired I've been helping your mother with her jigsaw puzzles. It seems like with every puzzle I work on I come across a couple of pieces that look like they don't belong. Do you think I should throw those pieces out?"

"I see where you're going, Dad. But I also know that you and your buddies think the world revolves around the Emerald Isle. Thanks for helping out," I said as the announcer gave us the final score, Giants 3, Padres 1.

When we got to the parking lot and were about to part company, Dad gave me a curious look that I had never seen before. He then gave Kelly a little hug (another first) and said, "You're welcome to come over for a visit anytime."

As we walked toward my car Kelly said, "Your mom is one of the nicest people I've ever met. You're a lucky guy."

I replied, "You're not kidding." Holding my thumb and forefinger an inch apart I added, "I came this close to a month of *Fried Green Tomatoes* and *The Bridges of Madison County*."

"You got that right," she replied.

When we found the Acura, I noticed that the black rubber weather strip alongside the driver's side window was pushed in toward the bottom. It looked like somebody tried using a coat hanger to pop the door lock. "Kelly, would you do me a favor and run over to the vendor by the entrance and pick up a miniature Padres bat for my nephew?" I asked as I handed her a $20 bill.

"Sure," she replied as she snatched the bill out of my hand. Without asking questions she walked toward the entrance. I don't know much about car bombs except that they're usually located either under the driver's seat, the dashboard, or the hood. As she walked away I carefully ran my hand under the passenger seat and found nothing. I walked around to my side and repeated the procedure until my fingers touched a hard, plastic object. I withdrew my hand as carefully as possible and reached into the console for my flashlight. With both of my knees on the parking lot pavement, I turned on the flashlight and placed it on the floor so that it would illuminate the space under my seat. As I leaned forward to rest my head on the floor, a bead of sweat ran down the side of my face. When my eyes adjusted to the light I let out a loud sigh as I recognized the object to be my nephew's Darth Vader action figure. While I was down there, I looked under the dash and noticed nothing unusual.

After getting to my feet, and brushing off my knees, I popped the hood and began my final inspection. I noticed a red wire running under the air filter and bent down lower to have a closer look. When I reached the lowest point in my bend, I was sure I had detonated a bomb. My body flinched in one huge spasm and I banged my head hard on the hood as I bolted upright. In a dazed state I heard Kelly say, "I'm so sorry, Jason. I had no idea you'd react like that."

When my eyes refocused I saw Kelly holding a miniature blue baseball bat and realized she had spanked me on the butt. "I think you had better drive home," I said as I cradled my head and eased myself into the passenger seat.

Chapter 7

ON Thursday morning we slept in until 9:30 AM and Kelly was extra attentive, perceiving that our relationship had gone to the next level with the meeting of my parents. She made crab omelets and asked a lot of questions about what my mom was like at various stages of my development.

I found a parking spot two blocks from my office and checked my watch just before walking through the door. It was 11:33 AM. As I entered Duffy Investigations, the first thing I saw was a file cabinet lying sideways on the carpet. I pulled my gun and stepped into the reception area. My heart sank. Lying on the floor was Jeannine with a gag in her mouth and her hands and feet tied together. Her skirt was hiked up around her waist and my first thought was that she had been raped.

When she heard the door open, she let out a muffled scream. She had her back to me and probably thought the perpetrators had returned. When she realized it was me, she started to cry. I removed the gag, untied her and held her as she hyperventilated and went into a panic attack. I found her prescription for Xanex in her purse and gave her a double dose. After about five minutes she was calm enough to talk. In the meantime I called the police.

"I look awful! I know I look awful!" she exclaimed between gasps.

"Tell me what happened," I said.

"Two men in black ski masks came in right after 9:00. They pointed guns at me and asked who else was here," she gasped. "I think I said, 'nobody' but I'm not sure. Then they tied me up, put a gag in my mouth and searched the office. They took both of our computers."

"Did they hurt you or do anything to you?" I asked as I prepared myself for the worst.

"Yes! It was horrible!" she screamed and again started to cry.

In as calm a voice as I could muster, I said, "If you'll tell me what they did I can help you when the police get here."

After stammering a couple of times she said, "The big one grabbed me by the arm and smudged my blouse. I tried to struggle, but the little one pulled my hair by my French braid and said if I didn't shut up he was going to tie the braid around my neck and hang me from the ceiling fan." Her hands began to shake.

"Then what happened?" I asked.

"They tied me up and threw me on the carpet," she stammered.

"Did they do anything else to hurt you?" I asked. She nodded and her chin quivered uncontrollably. "What?" I asked.

"They broke my nail!" she blurted out as she held up her middle finger, flipping me off. I sat with her and waited for the police. I guess her skirt hiked up as she struggled to get free.

A squad car arrived about ten minutes after I called, and the officers made sure we didn't touch anything until the place could be dusted for prints. We learned from Jeannine that the perps wore gloves, so the cops let me walk around to see if anything else was missing besides the computers. About a half-hour later Walter Shamansky made his entrance. He spoke with the patrolmen, then made his way into my inner office where he found me looking at a group of files thrown across the floor. He said, "You really ought to consider hiring a cleaning service. The slovenly look doesn't cut it in La Jolla."

"This was the work of the Russians. I'm sure," I said.

"How do you know?" he asked.

"They took everything relating to the case, including all of Cory's photographs. Nothing else appears to be missing," I said. "Any chance of getting a search warrant for Cerise's office?" I asked.

"I think the chances are pretty slim that they'd bring everything back to the office. If we get a warrant now and come up with nothing, it will be three times as tough to get another one on this case," he said.

"So what are you going to do?" I asked feeling my adrenaline pumping. "My receptionist was assaulted at gunpoint, my office was robbed and we have a very good idea of who did it."

"While you were in here I asked your gal if the perps had accents," he said.

"And?" I asked.

"Red-blooded Americans, both of them," he said.

"What about the parade of hired guns Cory photographed going into Cerise Records on Monday? It could have been a couple of those guys," I said.

"It's possible, but I don't think so. From everything I've learned so far, Koflanovich is a careful man. I can't picture him running an open casting call for a robbery," he said.

I had to admit that Shamansky made a lot of sense. As I calmed down my brain started functioning again and I said, "When I was at the Ukrainian Citizen's Club most of the guys under 40 had no accent. I think they were the Chofsky clan from Tecate."

"That listens," Shamansky said. "Is this the branch of the family that's been in the US for almost 100 years?"

"One and the same. In fact, I recently learned that John Koflanovich changed his name when he entered the United States. It was Ivan Chofsky," I said.

"All in the family," he said. "I like it even better. But now the hard part is getting cooperation from Tecate PD. If we're reluctant to get a warrant on Koflanovich, they'll never approve one for a local company that employs recently discharged service men."

I said, "I know exactly how I'm going to pay you back that favor." I then proceeded to give him the details of my plans for the weekend.

After the police left I told Jeannine I was hiring a bodyguard for her and the office. "Not a stranger," she said. I made a few suggestions, but none met with her approval. Finally she said, "Delbert Henson."

Fingernails scraped down a chalkboard in my mind. I could taste terrycloth in my teeth. Delbert Henson was in my therapy group with Jeannine for about a year. He suffers from delusions of grandeur. Every week Delbert would tell us a story where he ended up the hero. His self-lauding style and air of superiority made most of his fellow group members gag. They would tell him he was full of shit and get angry with him for making absolutely no effort to change. Jeannine never said a word about him in group or in individual therapy sessions. I always assumed she didn't like him because he was about 100 pounds overweight, wore dirty T-shirts, and even dirtier sneakers to every session. He was the exact opposite of Jeannine.

"I think we need someone who is licensed to carry a gun. Somebody who understands police techniques and could actually defend you if these guys ever decide to come back," I said in a boss-like tone.

Jeannine replied, "If you hire Delbert to protect me, I'll clean up the office and keep coming to work. If not, I'm going to need a very long vacation. He still goes to the Center. He's seeing Jake."

"You're not dating him are you?" I asked.

"I haven't talked with him since we were in group together. But I know that if he's here with me I'll feel safe, like I do when you're here," she said.

Hearing Jeannine equate me with Delbert Henson made my muscles flinch. Maybe it was the Xanex talking. She had just been through a terrible shock. But, knowing Jeannine as I do, there would be no changing her mind now that she's taken a stand. It was either Delbert and Jeannine or no Jeannine. I owed her after what she had just been through. "I'll talk to Jake, but I'm not sure he'll allow it," I said hoping I had found an acceptable out. Jeannine had always been good about obeying authority figures.

"If he says no I can always go on disability," she said.

Ouch. A Workers Comp claim for a business with one full-time employee would skyrocket my rates. I'd also have to pay for a temp while she was out. But, more importantly, Jeannine knew everything that was in the missing computers. Also, I felt an obligation as her former therapist to keep a close eye on her mental health after going through today's ordeal. "If Delbert is willing and Jake doesn't have me committed for suggesting the arrangement, I'll ask him to start in the morning, on one condition."

"What?" she asked with a pout.

"When I'm in the office Delbert patrols outside," I said.

"That would be OK," she said.

I spent the rest of the day helping Jeannine put the office back together. I decided to bring in my home computer. On it I kept a brief summary of each day's events since the start of the case. I also called my sister and arranged to borrow one she kept in her garage.

It had been one week since I was hired and time to find out if I was going to continue the investigation. I called Chelsea and gave her a summary of the week's events, including the break-in, the robbery and the shooting. When I finished I asked, "Do you think I've shown enough progress to remain on the case?"

"Am I still the prime suspect?" she asked.

"You are," I replied, "but SDPD is now very aware of the suspicious and criminal activities of Cerise Records."

"I'll retain you for another week, Mr. Duffy, but patience is not one of my virtues. I expect to be off of the suspect list by this time next week if you want to continue the investigation," she said and hung up.

Chapter 8

ON Friday morning I picked up Jeannine and drove her to the office where we hooked up my sister's spare computer. Once again, Jeannine was working her magic on the Internet and by 10:00 AM I was scamming labor temp services. After a mere 23 strikeouts I hit pay dirt just after 1:00 PM. San Diego Tech-Temps acknowledged their relationship with Yuliya after I ranted about quality issues with their new electronic technicians.

I wanted to drive over immediately and sign up as a temp. But I had to stick around and conduct a job interview with a man who could leap tall buildings in a single bound. No, it was not a bird; not a plane; it was DELBERTMAN. Jeannine buzzed me to say Delbert Henson had arrived. A few seconds later Beauty and the Beast came through my doorway. Delbert sure knows how to put on the dog for a job interview. I think he was wearing the same dirty T-shirt and sneakers he had worn the last time I saw him three years ago. "Hello Delbert," I said as I shook his beefy hand. "How are you doing these days?"

"Spectacular, Mr. Duffy," he said. "Did you miss me?"

"Miss you," I said, "why, according to Jeannine we can't get along without you." Delbert displayed a set of nicotine-stained choppers and nodded his approval. "I have a damsel in distress situation that calls for someone with your unique abilities."

"Ooh," he said as he rubbed his mitts together and raised his caterpillar eyebrows.

I continued, "Somebody broke in here yesterday and tied up

Jeannine. She's afraid to be alone and wants someone to protect her when I'm not around. It's a temporary job until the bad guys are in the pokey. It pays eight bucks an hour, plus all the coffee you can drink."

"It sounds like there could be some real danger," he said.

"Jeannine didn't put up a fight and they didn't hurt her," I said.

"I'm not sure," he said. "I have a lot of important things I do during the day."

I replied, "I'll get you a security guard uniform and any time I'm around you can go on patrol around the building."

"Deal!" he exclaimed, then jumped out of his seat and shook my hand. "When do I start, boss?"

"9:00 AM Monday morning," I said. I told Jeannine to find a local uniform store and arrange for Delbert to be outfitted appropriately this afternoon. She could accompany him since I would be leaving for the day and I wanted to make sure Delbert didn't ask for a red cape to be custom fit onto his uniform shirt. I ended our meeting with a couple of personal hygiene tips and made a mental note to send him on time-consuming errands whenever client meetings were scheduled.

Getting signed up at the temp service was a breeze. I completed the paperwork, had three work shirts and laminated credentials in less than an hour. They assigned me to a shipyard first thing Monday morning, but I had other plans.

Chapter 9

ON Saturday morning at 8:00 AM I entered Yuliya behind a group of four people wearing Tech-Temp shirts. One of then, a young Latino woman, asked if I was new. "First day on the job," I replied, and got directions to the Men's Room. I wandered around a bit, getting a feel for the layout of the plant. It was a two-story structure, encompassing about 20,000 square feet. Along the wall bordering the street were eight offices, four downstairs, and four upstairs. Only one of the offices was lighted. I assumed this belonged to the weekend boss. The Men's Room was directly across from the offices, about forty feet away. All of the offices had large picture windows looking out over the main floor. One of the windows had a nice set of drapes. This was my target. My problem was that I could be seen from the main floor if I tried picking the lock to get into the office.

When I was in my first year of college at UCSD, I cruised through my General Education subjects until I got to College Algebra. There, I hit a wall. By midterms I knew I needed help. Since I was earning decent money with my band, I hired a tutor, Carl Jaffe, who had a rather nerdy appearance and personality. One day I asked him what he did for fun and he invited me to his dorm room. I was sure it was going to be a favorite computer game, but instead, Carl put on an astounding magic show. For the grand finale he had me put him in handcuffs, then wrap a chain around him and secure it with a big Yale lock. I then walked out of the dorm room to the end of the hall and back, as instructed. When I returned, Carl was lying on his bed with his uncuffed hands behind his head and said, "What took you so long?"

He swore the locks were real and I begged him to teach me how to pick a lock. Carl told me he would do so if, and only if, I passed Algebra with a B or better. It was a huge struggle, but I got my B. Carl taught me everything he knew and I've owned a set of burglary tools ever since. Today I would see if my countless hours of practice paid off. But I still had to figure out a way to do it without being seen.

I looked around the restroom and saw a freestanding cabinet. Inside were cleaning and bathroom supplies. I grabbed a bottle of Windex and a rag, then walked out of the restroom and up the stairs like I owned the place. No one said a word. I went directly to the draped office and looked back toward the assembly floor. A couple of women were looking my way and one of them pointed at me. I pulled out my Windex and began squirting the picture window. I worked my way across the pane, periodically glancing at the floor. The women were apparently satisfied that I was on the cleaning crew and went back to work. It took about 30 seconds for me to unlock the door.

Inside were two rooms. The outer reception area held a desk with two chairs to the right, and a large leather couch against the left wall. In the middle of the room was an oak door leading to the inner office. Fortunately, the drapes were drawn, so I didn't need to worry about being seen. I relocked the door and went into Peter Chofsky's office. I was very pleasantly surprised to find that the computer was still on and I didn't need to call my computer geek friends to help me get past a security system.

Since I didn't see my stolen computer lying around, I did the next best thing and brought up the *My Documents* files. There I found a folder named Duffy. The first file I selected was named Pix. Inside were images of the pictures Cory took outside Cerise's building. This was hard evidence that the Russians had done the robbery. As I neared the end of the picture files, I found one of Kelly and I walking out of her condo building the evening we met my parents at the Padres game. There was also a picture of the four of us at the game, and a shot of Jeannine outside of her apartment house. This was getting scary. I can handle them coming after me, but my anger boiled over at the thought of them stalking my loved ones. I flashed on an image of Kelly minus half a pinky and felt like ransacking the office. When I got my emotions under control, I emailed the file to my Yahoo account.

Next, I opened a file called Bio and, sure enough, there was the kind of background information about me that I would supply a client as a private detective. I'm sure all of this stuff is somewhere in cyber space, but it sure looked like they hired a PI to check me out. I emailed the whole folder to myself and moved on to a folder named Cerise. This was huge, holding maybe 75 files. I started clicking through but found that most of the text was in Russian. I recognized one of the Tass news accounts of the kidnapping. I emailed the folder.

There was nothing labeled Doberman's Stub, but I found a folder named Tucker. Inside was a bio, much like my own, along with a copy of all four of the contract proposals. In another file was every newspaper account of Terry's murder. There was a separate file on Chelsea, complete with bio and pictures. I started to click through when I heard keys in the office door. I clicked off the computer screen, then moved with speed and stealth behind the inner office door, which was ajar. Through the door jam I could see the empty couch on the far wall. I looked around and saw a hockey stick with CCCC written on the side, mounted on the wall a few feet away. I heard a male and female in the front room. Quietly, I slipped the hockey stick out of its mounting brackets and inched my way back to the door jam. When I peeked through I saw the weekend boss unhooking the bra of an attractive young Latino woman. Her face was rather plain, but strippers would kill for that body. As they got settled onto the couch I turned away, fearing I would be unable to defend myself if I was discovered with a boner bigger than the hockey stick I was clutching.

About five minutes later I heard the Latino woman yelp and shortly thereafter heard the boss say, "I need a smoke." He took a pack of Marlboros out of his shirt that had been lying on the carpet, then pulled a green lighter out of his pants pocket. He flicked three times and got nothing but sparks. "Shit!" he exclaimed, "You got a light?"

"Sure," she said sarcastically, "I always keep one in my thong for this kind of occasion."

"Shut-up," he said and walked toward me. I straightened up as best I could and held the stick in front of me. The door was at about a 45 degree angle. I wasn't sure if it completely covered me. He must have walked around the left side of the desk, otherwise I would have seen him round the near corner. Luckily, the room was pretty dark because of the closed drapes.

I heard the weekend boss opening drawers in the desk. First he said, "God damn it." Then he said, "What the fuck?" Next thing I saw was a large naked man pulling the door away from me with his left hand as he took a full-strength, swing at my head with his right. I instinctively ducked and spun away from the wall all in one motion. When I did this, with no intention whatsoever, I inadvertently brought the hockey stick up hard into the weekend boss' package. He made a guttural scream, grabbed his crotch, and dropped to his knees, then toppled over sideways.

As I exited through the outer office, Miss Augusto was stepping into her thong. When she saw me look, she stopped what she was doing and gave me a smile. Once I was out of the upstairs office I walked quickly across the walkway and down the stairs. As I did this the sound of the weekend boss screaming, "Stop him!" echoed throughout the plant. When I reached the bottom of the stairs, three of the male workers were waiting for me, one holding a huge pipe wrench.

In these situations my motto has always been: why fight when you can bullshit your way out? I jerked my thumb toward the upstairs office and using my most indignant voice inflections exclaimed, "That Russian fuck has been screwing my wife! He was on one of your coworkers when I punched him out! Why don't you guys go rescue her and finish the job?"

The fact that the four of us were wearing Tech-Temps shirts worked in my favor. "I hate that asshole!" yelled a large guy with an anchor tattoo on his arm. "Let's go guys!" he exclaimed as he bounded up the stairs two at a time. The other two followed and I walked out the door, then broke into a sprint for my car. But there was no chase. I expect my fellow Tech-Temps turned a white Russian into a black & blue Russian.

I had about six hours to kill before meeting my friends at Jake's restaurant, then adjourn to The Belly Up for a Steve Poltz concert. I needed some more advice and determined that a night out with a couple of my friends could help considerably.

I returned to my office and read everything written in English in the folders I had emailed to myself. The pictures were slow to load, so after looking at just a few, I decided to check them out after the weekend.

When I arrived at Jake's, Justin Emerson was sipping a Heineken and schmoozing with a cute brunette bartender. Justin, now in his mid-thirties, was managing a huge club in the Kearny Mesa section of San Diego when my band first started playing the local circuit. "Hey Justin, you're looking great," I said.

"Wish I could say the same," he replied, then stood up and gave me a bear hug. "Just kidding. Actually, now that you're not burning the candle at both ends anymore you look a lot healthier. You didn't go and get married or anything like that did you?"

"Still single, but I don't know about the healthy part," I said as I lifted myself onto the stool next to him.

"Please don't tell me you asked us here to say you have some terrible disease," he said.

"No," I said, "nothing like that. It's just that I'm working on Terry Tucker's murder and there are a lot of dangerous dudes involved." I remember Justin mentioning Terry in a casual conversation a few years ago. I was hoping they kept in touch.

"Terry had more than his fair share of enemies, but what a talent," he said.

"Did you hear from him at all in the months before his death?" I asked.

"As a matter of fact, he called me about three weeks before the tragedy," he replied. "We talked for about 15 minutes about the interests, concerns and passions of the late teen, early twenties age group. I hear Calvin's joining us for dinner tonight, he'll be able to tell you a lot more about that stuff than me."

Justin was about to ask a follow-up question when Calvin walked in and we exchanged formalities. Justin let the hostess know our party was ready to be seated and we were off to our table almost immediately.

Since we were seated within earshot of twenty strangers I kept the conversation away from the investigation. There would be time to talk with Calvin later.

I had almost forgotten how much fun these guys could be. Since we all had music in common, that was the main topic for the evening. We arrived at the Belly Up in time to get one of the last vacant tables. A few minutes after our drinks had arrived, Calvin excused himself to go for a smoke. I followed him outside. "When did you take up this nasty habit?" Calvin asked as he lit up.

"I didn't," I replied. "I want to ask you a couple of questions that might help with a case I'm working." I then told him about Doberman's contract situation and asked, "What's your take on how they would have fared on the open market if Terry was still alive and they were able to dissolve their contract with Cerise?"

Calvin replied, "The file sharing problem is still huge, but the demographic profile of Doberman's Stub is through the roof. Their first CD was very good and performed beyond expectations with their target audience of males in their 20's. But, the second CD performed very differently. They expanded their demographics tremendously. They held strong with their core audience while they also developed a surprising appeal among women, ages 15 to 35. Sales of the second CD were almost double those of the first CD."

"That's really strange," I said. "I looked at some numbers last week and I could see that the second CD outsold the first, but I don't recall it being by a big margin."

Calvin said, "That's because all those hot new fans ran out and bought the first CD after they fell in love with the second one. You'd be surprised how often that happens."

"So they were on a major roll?" I asked.

"Big time," he said. "When you cross demographics all of a sudden you can quadruple the number of radio stations playing your stuff. This creates residual income from airplay, increases downloads, boosts CD sales, and drives up demand and the asking price for concerts."

"What brings in the most money?" I asked.

"Concerts" Calvin said. "Over 80% of the top 50 acts last year saw at least two-thirds of their income derived from concerts, and merchandising at concert venues. Doberman's Stub was on the verge of being a headliner on the stadium circuit. They were looking at $25 to $50 million in tour income in the next year."

"Now I'm totally lost," I said showing my exasperation. "If the big bucks are in touring, why are they in the studio instead of riding the money train?"

"It's a little complicated," Calvin said, "but I assure you there is no active performer who could come close to Terry Tucker in his understanding of what it takes to become a star and stay on top. He was like a chess master in his ability to think eight moves ahead at all times. When their first CD, *Biscuit*, was released, they established themselves as an up and coming metal band. They were the warm-up act for midrange bands attracting the same audience. When their second CD, *Don't Bury Your Bone Alone*, came out they didn't have the leverage yet to be a headliner at major venues. But, it was important that they toured right after the release to plug the album to the fans they had recently established."

"To keep the momentum going?" I asked.

"Exactly," he said. "I'm sure Terry was hoping the second CD would take off, but there are never any guarantees. Doberman made the right choice of being warm-up at stadium concerts featuring mainstream artists that would pack the house. This would ensure that they hit their performance goals with Cerise Records and, at the same time, give them a chance to expand their demographics."

"But this meant less money," I said.

"In the short term," Calvin agreed. "But long term, it was a great strategy. The increase in downloads and CD sales for both CDs went way up, and they positioned themselves for a feature tour."

"Let's get back to my original question. Why go back to the studio for a third CD when they could have gotten booked on the stadium circuit now?" I asked.

"Stardom is usually like a big monster. If you don't feed the monster it will go someplace else to get fed," he said. "This is especially true when you get into the teenage audience. They buy the most downloads and they are by far the most demanding when it comes to new material. Remember when I said they got big with women 15 to 35?"

"Yeah," I replied.

"The 15 to 25 year olds bought 80% of the music. The Beatles got huge because of their talent, but they sustained that incredibly intense level of popularity by being prolific songwriters who knew how to evolve and set trends," he said.

I switched gears a bit. "What are the chances Doberman's Stub can survive without Terry Tucker?" I asked.

"The general feeling in the industry is that the Doberman got castrated, but I think they still have a chance," he said. "I'm sure you know that Terry split songwriting credits with Nigel and that each wrote his own songs; no collaborations."

"It was sort of a *separate but equal* arrangement from what I could see," I said.

"Right. Terry's songs got the most airplay. They were metal anthems. Technically, they're terrific," he said. "But I always got the feeling that Terry was shooting for the Top 10 with every one of his songs."

I asked, "How about Nigel's compositions?"

"Frankly, I relate better to Nigel's stuff, especially his lyrics," Calvin said. "His songs are more emo, so I'm sure he's scoring big with the women."

"Are we still talking demographics?" I asked.

"As a concert promoter, my thing is demographics. I need to know who's hot and who's going to be hot six months from now. One of the nightmares of my profession is when a band breaks up just before the show I've been paying to advertise for a month," he said. "I need to know those kinds of things about bands I'm considering, and Doberman's Stub was at the top of my list when Terry died."

"So, what about Nigel?" I asked again.

"Nigel Choate fancies himself a ladies man," he said. "In order for Doberman's Stub to succeed without Terry a few important things need to happen. First, they need a big name to replace Terry as lead singer; maybe add a rhythm guitarist if their singer doesn't play. Second, they need to fire their current management and hire someone with a proven track record of taking a band to the top. Third, they need to shit or get off the pot on their drummer situation."

"Ian's drinking?" I asked.

"Drinking, coke, ecstasy, acid, you name it. They have to give him the rehab or unemployment ultimatum as soon as the CD wraps," he said.

"Do you think Terry was on Ian to clean up?" I asked.

Calvin replied, "Terry wouldn't tolerate anything that messed with his sound. I saw them onstage in San Francisco a couple of months before Terry died. Ian was definitely high and out of synch with everybody else. At one point Terry stood on the drum riser with his back to the audience and, from backstage, I could see he was screaming. If looks could kill Ian would have preceded Terry to the Pearly Gates."

"What's your take on Jack Pascal?" I asked.

"I like Jack a lot. Every successful band needs a steadying influence and Jack is their guy. He'll never show up on anybody's list for best metal bassist, but he is solid as a rock. I met him a couple of times at backstage parties and he strikes me as one of those rare musicians who will be the same guy no matter how popular or unpopular the band. He's in it for the music, not the lifestyle" he said.

"How would a guy like that respond to Ian messing with the sound?" I asked.

He replied, "My guess is he would look for Terry to fix it, like a kid turning to a parent to deal with a sibling problem."

"Do you think, if Terry hadn't died, that Ian would soon be fired?" I asked.

He replied, "I was amazed he took Ian into the studio for the third CD. Something else besides Terry's desire to succeed and Ian's lifestyle was playing a role in that decision. Maybe it was the contract negotiation, maybe not. But my guess is that it was more a question of when and not if Terry would give Ian the ax."

I could have asked Calvin twenty more questions, but the sound of Steve Poltz came drifting our way, so we rejoined Justin. "Did you go back to Jake's for dessert?" he asked.

"Has it been that long?" I replied. The show was excellent. A couple of Steve's old band mates from The Rugburns showed up to help out on the final set.

I woke up around 11:00 AM on Sunday morning. There was a message on my answering machine from Nigel asking me to call him when I got in. I called right away and the phone was answered by a sexy voice that was definitely not the lovely who flashed me earlier in the week. "Jason, thanks for getting back to me," said Nigel.

"What can I do for you Nigel?" I asked.

"Actually, there are two matters I'd like to discuss with you, but I'm a little indisposed at the moment. It's urgent that I talk with you soon. Do you think I might come round in the morning?" he asked.

"I'm going to be in my office at 9:00 AM. Can you make it at 10:00?" I asked.

"That will be fine," he replied. I gave him directions and hoped I would remember to send Delbert Henson out for donuts at 9:50.

Chapter 10

MONDAY morning I picked Jeannine up at 8:45 and found Delbert standing guard at the front door. He had forgotten to shave, but did manage to get the front of his shirttail tucked in. When he saw us he shoved something into his pants pocket, which appeared to already be quite full. Jeannine said hello and when he replied it became apparent that his pocket was full of Oreo cookies. I would have to come up with a way, other than a donut shop run, of keeping Delbert away from the office since he would already be stuffed full of confection and pocket lint.

I downloaded the folder from Yuliya onto Jeannine's computer and told her to review all of the pictures carefully for anything unusual. I told Delbert I thought somebody might try to mess with my car, and walked him to a stakeout position where he could watch it without being spotted by Nigel or anyone else who might call the cops on a suspicious ogre.

Just after 10:00 Jeannine showed Nigel into my office.

"Nigel, what's on your mind," I said.

"Like I said on the phone, I have two separate matters to discuss with you," he said. "First, I want to hire you to do background checks on prospective replacements for Terry. It's important that we choose carefully. The last thing we need is to announce a new frontman only to find out he has a heroin habit or that he's a convicted pedophile."

"Speaking of replacements, did Ian know he was about to get the boot?" I asked.

"There was a fair amount of open hostility between Terry and Ian. Terry threatened to make Ian bugger-off at least once a week," he said.

"How did Ian feel about that?" I inquired.

"Ian loves being a rock star. When we formed the band he was the only one of us who was an unknown. He was broke, hungry and had tremendous talent. Nobody knew he'd go nuts once he started earning those big checks," he said.

"Do you think Ian would kill Terry to keep the good times rolling?" I asked.

"My God! I certainly hope not. You think you know somebody, but I guess you never really do," he said with a lot of emotion. "I vouched for Ian. I thought you suspected the record company."

"I do. How soon do you need the reports?" I asked.

"We're actively seeking right now. Ideally, I was hoping you could jump on them as soon as possible," he said.

"I won't be able to give them my full attention until I finish up working for Chelsea. Is that going to be a problem for you?" I asked.

"It actually ties in with the second thing I'm here to talk with you about," he said. "We're going to be finishing the last song on the CD by Wednesday. After we laid down the tracks on each of our first two CD's, Terry got us a low profile gig at a local club. We played the new material in front of live audiences to see what they liked and what should be tweaked before we wrapped the session."

"What would you like me to do?" I asked.

"Jack told me you played the local club scene before you became a detective. Do you know any club owners who could set this up without causing a mob scene?" Nigel asked.

"I know just the guy to handle it. His club would be perfect," I said.

"Is this a place where your old band used to play?" he inquired.

"It was my favorite place to play," I said.

"What if we advertised the show as a reunion of your old group? Is your old lead singer still in the area?" he asked.

"I was our lead singer," I said cautiously.

"Excellent!" he exclaimed. "Can you sing in Terry's range?" he asked.

"You guys were just getting started the year I hung it up. But my shower version of *Clepto Lover* rocks the house," I said with a smile.

"Perfect! If I get you the sheet music and demo's of our new songs, could you put it together for next weekend?" he asked.

"Let me make sure I've got this right. After a three year layoff from playing professionally, you want me to set up a gig in less than one week; learn the rhythm guitar and lead vocals on a CD full of songs I've never heard before; deal with a hundred old friends calling about the reunion show; and solve Terry's murder all at the same time. Oh, and do a couple of bio investigations on the side. Is that about it?" I asked.

"It's not all that," Nigel said. "There's only 12 songs on the CD and you already know one of them. If you don't have time to learn the songs we can dub Terry in over the PA. Do your best Milli Vanilli impression and Doberman's Stub fans everywhere will be eternally grateful."

"What about all those old loyal fans who will be crushed when they find out Tsunami Rush isn't in the house?" I asked with tongue firmly implanted in cheek.

"Good point," Nigel said seriously. "We only want to do one set. Could you get your old band to cover the other sets?"

"We do a little garage jamming once every month or two. I don't think we could possibly be ready that soon," I said.

"It's like riding a bike, lad," he said.

"When I was seven I fell off my bike and broke my arm," I said.

"No worries, I heard you play in the studio. You'll do great," he said.

"I have so much going on right now, Nigel. I don't think it would be possible," I said.

"Too bad. It's going to be a huge plug for whatever club owner we drop in on," he said.

"Why does it have to be this weekend?" I asked.

"We have a lot of issues with Cerise Records and with our own management now that Terry's gone. We all want to wrap the CD and get the hell out of that damned studio as soon as possible. If Cerise Records was involved in Terry's death you shouldn't expect us to hang out any longer than is absolutely necessary. Right?" he asked.

"Let me see what I can put together," I said. "I'll call you tomorrow morning."

"Thanks Jason, I have every confidence in you. In fact, if you can pull this off I'll use your rhythm track on the CD and give you a credit. Your name will be on a couple million CD's. I need you on this one," he said as he exited.

My next project was to track down GI Jo-Jo's girlfriend. I figured with a name like Delitah she had to be either a hooker or an exotic dancer. I decided an exotic dancer would be easier to find. I called a guy I knew at UCSD, Tony Bascinelli, who was a connoisseur of San Diego erotica. I had no trouble locating him through the insurance company calendar he sends to me every year. "Tony, its Jason Duffy. How the hell are you?" I asked.

"I knew you'd eventually come to realize the value of a whole life policy, Jason. You're the third guy from UCSD who's called me this year. Let's set up a time to get together with the Mrs.," he said.

"There is no Mrs. Duffy. I'm trying to find an exotic dancer who doubles as a metal groupie," I said.

"I have just the girl for you. She digs your kind of music and she'll go ape-shit when she finds out you were the lead singer in Tsunami Rush. They'll be pealing you off her ceiling mirror," he said in a locker room tone.

"I'm looking for a particular girl. Her name is Delitah," I said.

"What do you want with her?" he asked.

"I just need to ask a few questions about her boyfriend. No hassles, no cops, just a few questions," I said.

"She's working first shift at Bottoms Up. She ought to be getting started about now," he said.

"Thanks for the info Tony. I'll call when I'm ready for that policy," I said. With the Russians chasing me it might not be a bad idea.

I had to pay a $10 cover charge for the privilege of hanging with a swell bunch of guys. As I walked in I spotted a large bulletin board with pictures of the day's featured dancers. Delitah had a big yellow star made of construction paper outlining her image. Her name was written on one of the star points.

Delitah had recently finished her set when I arrived. I took a seat at one of the back tables, knowing that she'd work her way from the stage toward the door. She appeared to be wearing a fake fur jacket over a G-string and encouraged patrons to tuck dead presidents into the waistband. When she arrived at my table she asked, "Did you like my show?"

I replied, "Unfortunately, I just missed it, but I did come here to see you. My name's Jason Duffy and I need to talk with you about Terry Tucker."

"Are you a cop?" she asked.

"No. I'm a private investigator, hired to find out who killed Terry," I said.

"Then I don't have to talk to you," she said.

"I thought you were a big fan of Terry's," I said.

"I was. But now he's dead and there's no chance of hooking up with him anymore," she replied.

"Wouldn't you like to see whoever killed him get caught?" I asked.

"I didn't have anything to do with it and I don't know who did," she said.

"Nobody thinks you had anything to do with it," I said. "Did you notice anything unusual going on in the last few weeks before Terry died?"

Delitah sat down at my cocktail table and leaned forward, "Everybody was pretty uptight about recording the new CD. Terry was born a perfectionist. The other guys in the band just don't understand that when you're a genius you do what it takes to achieve your vision."

"Did you see much of the band in the last few weeks?" I asked.

"I rode on the bus for the last mini-tour through the West Coast just before they went into the studio. But, once they started recording, some asshole Russian Nazi wouldn't let me in to see the sessions," she said.

"The big blond guy?" I asked.

"Yeah, that's him," she replied.

"Do you think it's possible he had anything to do with Terry's murder?" I inquired.

"I wouldn't be surprised. He hated Terry," she said.

"How do you know he hated him if he didn't let you inside?" I asked.

"First of all, I have a very good friend who works for the band," she said.

"Would that be GI Jo-Jo?" I asked.

"Yeah. Jo-Jo told me Terry thought he was a useless piece of shit and was always giving him a hard time," she said. "Plus, I saw him do something to Terry's car once."

"What did you see?" I asked.

"I was supposed to meet Jo-Jo in front of the recording studio at around six o'clock about a week before Terry died. The band was running late and I was just sitting in my car waiting. Then I saw that big asshole walk out of the studio and head straight for Terry's Ferrari. Then he whipped it out and pissed all over the hood of that beautiful car," she said.

"Did you say anything to him?" I asked.

"Hell no. I didn't want him waving that thing at me," she said. "Besides, he probably would have run me out of the lot and I wouldn't have been able to hook up with Jo-Jo."

"I'm not real clear on something," I said. "Were you dating Terry or were you dating Jo-Jo?"

"Well, Jo-Jo is my friend, sometimes a really close friend. But he knew from the start that I'm cosmically linked to Terry," she said.

"Did Terry know about this cosmic linkage?" I asked with a straight face.

"I tried telling him about it a couple of times, but Terry had a lot on his mind," she said.

"What about his wife, Chelsea?" I asked.

"That bitch!" she cried. "She was never right for Terry. It was just a matter of time before he realized it."

"What did she do that made you dislike her?" I asked.

"She doesn't have to do anything to piss me off. Just hearing her name is enough to fuck me up just like that!" she exclaimed, snapping her fingers.

"Is it just because Chelsea saw him first?" I asked.

"That bitch has such an attitude, like she's better than everybody else. Let's see if she'd have that same attitude if she had to schlep drinks in this joint or put out for some skuzzy club owner," she said.

I didn't think Delitah was going to volunteer anything else of value, but I decided to play a hunch and see where it went. "I heard Terry and Jo-Jo got into a fight over you. What was that all about?" I asked.

"That's bullshit! They had a little fight, but it wasn't over me," she said.

"What happened?" I asked.

Delitah replied, "I'm not gonna tell you. You'll just tell the cops. I know how it works. You give them something and they pay you back."

"Delitah, I won't say anything. If I get the reputation of telling stories to the cops I'd be out of business just like that," I said snapping my fingers like Delitah had done.

"You don't know what it's like playing with a band and being on the road," she said.

I asked, "Did you ever hear of the local band Tsunami Rush?"

"No," she replied.

"That was my band until three years ago. I helped out on the new Doberman's Stub CD last week, playing rhythm guitar on one of the songs. You can ask Jo-Jo. He was there," I said.

"If I tell you this and you tell the cops, I'll deny it and say you made it up," she said.

"I swear I won't tell the cops," I said, raising my right hand.

"OK. After a show in San Francisco, Terry got in Jo-Jo's face and accused him of supplying Ian with drugs. Jo-Jo doesn't sell drugs. Ian looked pretty high that night and Terry was looking to point the finger at somebody. He already went off on Ian and had some extra energy so he got really nasty with Jo-Jo," she said.

"Were any punches thrown?" I asked.

"Terry was pointing his finger at Jo-Jo; then he poked Jo-Jo in the chest. When he did that, Jo-Jo shoved him away with one arm. Terry responded by pushing Jo-Jo's shoulders with both hands, pretty hard," she said.

"What did Jo-Jo do?" I asked.

"He punched Terry in the stomach really hard and Terry dropped to his knees. That was the end of the fight," she said.

I asked, "Did Terry threaten to fire Jo-Jo? I can't imagine he'd just let it go."

"They made up almost instantly. Jo-Jo helped Terry to his feet. They talked for a minute or two and it was over," she said.

"What did they talk about?" I asked.

"Terry was bent over and Jo-Jo squatted down near his face, so I couldn't hear what they were saying," she said.

"Did Jo-Jo ever talk about it?" I inquired.

"Not a word," she replied.

"Thanks Delitah," I said as I was getting up to leave.

"I got a question for you before you leave," she said.

"What's that?" I asked.

"It's been pretty slow around here today. How 'bout a lap dance?" she asked.

I grabbed my back and said, "I would, but it would give me a bad case of the girlfriend guilts. But I am willing to make a significant contribution to your G-string fund." I then pulled a $20 out of my wallet and wrapped it around the side of her waistband. She gave me a big smile and bounced off toward the bar. I was left to try and figure out how to get reimbursed on my expense report without doing a lot of explaining to Chelsea.

At 3:30 PM I pulled into the parking lot of Bernie's club and tried knocking on the door. It wasn't open yet, but I was hoping to catch Bernie before the happy hour crowd rolled in. When knocking and pounding didn't get a result, I called him from my cell phone. When he answered I said, "Bernie, its Jason. Some maniac is pounding on your door."

"I thought it was just another yuppie with a daiquiri jones," he replied. "What can I do for you today, Jason?"

"It's more like something I can do to pay you back for your many good deeds. Let me in and I'll explain," I said.

Five minutes later I was in Bernie's office. He offered me a drink, but I declined. "This is going to sound pretty wild, but I think it would be terrific publicity for the club," I said excitedly.

"Spit it out," he replied. "I can see you're dying to tell me."

"Nigel Choate asked if I knew of a San Diego club where Doberman's Stub could perform its new CD to a live audience. Of course I immediately thought of taking care of my old buddy, Bernie," I said.

"If we announced that Doberman's Stub was going to play here the place would be so packed that the Fire Marshals would shut us down. If we turned them away at the door the fans would block the streets and probably riot because they couldn't get in," Bernie said as he stroked his chin.

"Nigel knows these things. That's why he asked that we bill it as a reunion show for Tsunami Rush. He figures it would draw just enough people to get a good audience reaction, but not so many that it would cause the problems you mentioned," I said.

"Would they play the whole night?" he asked.

"No. Just a twelve song set. He wants us to give the crowd what they came to see for the other sets," I replied.

Bernie asked, "Have they found a replacement for Terry already?"

"Not yet. Nigel asked me to do background investigations on prospective candidates once they start the search process. He also asked me to fill in for Terry," I said.

"Wow! Talk about a rock & roll fantasy come true! That could be one hot night for you. I didn't think you and the boys were still playing together anymore," he noted.

"Derek has an aunt with a big piece of property out in Alpine. Once every month or two we get together on a Sunday afternoon and jam. We could manage the other sets," I said. "My big worry is learning twelve new songs in time."

"When does he want to do this?" Bernie asked.

"Saturday night," I replied. "I know it's short notice, but they're all frazzled by the murder and are looking to wrap the CD as soon as possible. They did club tests on their first two CD's and feel it's important to stay with the winning formula."

"Oye! You know I've already got a band booked for Saturday night. How can I just cancel them on this short a notice?" he asked.

"Tell them you'll make it up to them by giving them three more bookings and putting in a good word for them with other club owners," I suggested.

"Those guys are really hungry. I'm sure we can work it out. What was your idea on how I could maximize publicity if I'm not supposed to tell anybody Doberman's Stub will be playing?" he asked.

"I suggest you get in touch with one of the Sunday Union-Trib music reviewers and tell him you'll give him an exclusive if he'll come out on Saturday night, no questions asked. Let him know you're billing it as a local band, but that a major group will be debuting new material," I said. "Now I have a question for you."

"What's that?" Bernie asked.

"How am I going to learn 12 new songs in the next few days?" I asked.

Bernie mulled my question for a minute then raised his eyebrows and smiled. "Get me a sharp copy of the sheet music. I'll scan it into a computer program and run it through the karaoke monitor suspended from the ceiling above the stage. Get one of your old band mates to follow along on a floor monitor and hit page down when you reach the bottom of the screen," he said.

"Bernie, you're the bomb!" I exclaimed.

I would have hung out with Bernie and worked out the details, but I needed to get back to the office by 6:00 PM to take Jeannine home. As I walked into my business at 5:55 PM I heard Jeannine scream, "Stop!"

I raced into the reception area to find Delbert sitting on Cory and pinning his arms to the carpet.

"What the hell is going on!" I shouted.

Delbert replied, "He was cursing at Jeannine and he won't apologize."

"Delbert, get off of Cory right now," I said authoritatively as I grabbed Delbert by the upper left arm and lifted. Delbert outweighed Cory by at least 130 pounds. "I don't want to see anything like this ever again."

"He's still not sorry," Delbert said as he struggled to his feet.

I said to Delbert," Cory is a client at the Mental Health Center, just like you and Jeannine. He has Tourette's Syndrome. That's what makes him curse. He can't control it." As I took a closer look at Cory, I saw twenty to thirty large black flecks on his face. I picked a pointy one out of his eyebrow that was about the size of a fingernail. "Are these Oreo cookies?" I asked Delbert.

"Uh, huh," Delbert replied sheepishly as he nodded his head.

Holding the pointy cookie bit in Delbert's face I said, "You could put somebody's eye out with this."

Delbert looked at Cory and said, "Sorry."

I sent Delbert home for the day and brought Cory into my office. "Are you up for a tail job?" I asked.

Cory smiled and nodded. "I want you to follow Ian Davis, Doberman's drummer, starting tonight. He'll probably go to the bars. Don't follow him inside, but I want pictures of who he goes in with, who he comes out with, license plate of the vehicles he travels in and a log of the time, date and location of all of this movements. Can you handle it?" I asked.

His profanity-laced reply told me he was enthusiastically in favor of the idea. I confided in him that I didn't like having Delbert around, but that Jeannine insisted and it was a short-term arrangement.

Though the casual observer would never know it by his words, Cory expressed thanks that I shared this information. "Now, go get cleaned up, then head over to The Tillerman's in Mission Beach. That's where Ian usually starts his carousing," I said.

By the time we returned to the reception area Delbert had departed and Jeannine was on her hands and knees inspecting the carpet nap for stray bits of Oreo cookie that may have been missed by the vacuum cleaner. Cory grabbed his camera and headed for the door without making eye contact with Jeannine.

"Did Nigel Choate drop something off for me today?" I asked.

She replied, "He had a very pretty young woman drop it off. She seemed disappointed that you were out." Jeannine retrieved a large manila envelope from her desk drawer and handed it to me.

As I walked her home we talked about Delbert and his temporary status. She was OK with the idea that his tenure with Duffy Investigations would end with the conclusion of the case.

I spent the remainder of the evening listening to the demo CD while playing along with my guitar. I also called my ex-band mates and got an enthusiastic agreement to do the weekend gig. After explaining my time crunch they agreed to practice without me a couple of times before Saturday.

Chapter 11

GLENDA MacPhearson is a buddy of mine from UCSD. We took Cognitive Psychology, Critical Thinking and a horrible Statistics class together. She helped me with Stats and I helped her with Psych. She was and still is on active duty status with one of the few Army installations in Southern California.

I gave her a call from my office first thing Tuesday morning and asked for a favor. I explained what I was looking for and she agreed to access the service record of Joseph (a.k.a. GI Jo-Jo) Martin. Glenda located his service jacket in LA. "It shouldn't take more than a day or two," she said.

At 10:30 AM I arrived at the San Diego County Russian Language Newspaper in the city of Vista. Uri Armanov is the proprietor, editor, publisher and chief writer of this biweekly publication. Uri's wife, Ursula, is in charge of circulation and advertising sales. Five years ago Uri paid to have his nephew, Alexi, relocate from Moscow to work as the paper's delivery truck driver. Everything worked out great for the first six months until a meth-head on a three day binge changed lanes on the 805 freeway without looking, and pushed Alexi into the cement median at 70 miles per hour. Physically, he suffered a few cuts and bruises, but mentally, he was a mess. Alexi couldn't bring himself to get back behind the wheel. After six weeks of therapy, using a technique called Systematic Desensitization, I had him driving again. Uri was effusive in his praise and told me several times to call on him if I ever needed his help.

"Jason, what a pleasant surprise seeing you again," Uri said.

"It's good to see you too, Uri. How is Alexi doing?" I asked.

"Wonderful. He's like a son to me," he said. "You said on the phone that you needed my help. What can I do for you, my friend?" he asked.

"I have two favors to ask. First, I brought along several newspaper articles written in Russian, and a hand-held recorder. If you could translate the articles into the recorder, then mail them to me in this packing box, it could be a big help to the case I'm working on," I said.

Uri agreed. "You said there were two favors. What's the other one?" he asked.

"I need some information," I replied. "It looks like one of my suspects may be affiliated with the Russian Mafia. Can you tell me if they have a presence here in San Diego?"

"The Russian Mafia is everywhere," he said while glancing from side to side. "If they are involved you need to stop working on your case. Much too dangerous."

"What are they up to in Southern California?" I asked.

"They try to suck the life out of the Russian community, just like in Russia. Here they are mainly involved in drugs, prostitution and gambling. Their victims are usually fellow Russians," he said.

"Why is that?" I asked.

"Because Russians understand how ruthless they are and won't talk about them to the police for fear of their lives and the lives of their families," he responded.

"If they generally leave Americans alone, why should I worry about them?" I asked.

Uri replied, "Since they know they don't scare Americans, the Mafia believes their only alternative is to kill them when there is a problem."

"Who are the leaders here in town?" I asked.

"Jason, if you start asking questions about any of the local leaders you will be involved for life. Probably a very short life," he said. "I won't give you any names today, because that would be like giving you a death sentence. If you come up with a name I will confirm or deny his involvement, if I know."

"Are you familiar with the Chofsky family from Tecate?" I asked.

"Of course. The Chofsky family has been in California since before the Russian Revolution. Their company, Yuliya, has hired many a Russian immigrant. The Russian community thinks highly of the them," he said.

"The articles I gave you are about Ivan Chofsky, who lived in the Ukraine until last year. His daughter was kidnapped by the Russian Mafia. I'm trying to find out if he cut a deal with them to get her back," I said.

"Why do you want to know about Ivan?" he asked.

"He now lives in San Diego and owns a business. My client's husband worked for him and was murdered. The widow thinks Chofsky's people were involved," I said.

Uri said, "I will be very disappointed if the Chofsky's are doing business with the Russian Mafia. They have made significant contributions to organizations that help Russian immigrants. I have referred some good people to Yuliya for employment. But, if they are now working with the Russian Mafia, I need to know. I would never refer anyone to a Mafia-run company."

"I'll let you know as soon as I find out," I said. "In the meantime, if you could get that translation to me as soon as possible you'll be helping me to find the truth," I said.

"It will be done today," he said and we shook hands.

As I was driving back from Vista my cell phone rang. "Jason Duffy," I said.

"It's Jeannine," she said sobbing into the phone. "Cory's hurt!"

"Don't tell me Delbert's on top of him again," I said.

"He's at University Hospital. It happened last night. A social worker called. I'm getting scared," she cried as her voice quivered.

"Have Delbert stay with you in the office. No patrols or smoke breaks till I get back," I said.

"OK. Are you going to the hospital now?" she asked.

"I'm on my way," I said.

After spending the night in the Emergency Room, Cory was taken to a Med/Surg floor to be monitored. When I reached the floor I asked to speak with his doctor.

Cory was in a four-bed room and had two roommates. He was sleeping, or unconscious, or in a coma; I couldn't tell. That thought haunted me over the next 45 minutes as I waited for the doctor to arrive. His face was badly bruised and his elbow was tucked into his body at an odd angle. At one point I tried calling his name softly to see if I could rouse him from his sleep, but one of his roommates told me he has been out since he was brought in three hours earlier.

Finally, his doctor arrived and told me that he suffered a concussion and three broken ribs. He also said Cory was up all night and will probably sleep for six to ten more hours. The hospital would keep him around for observation for another day or two.

After the doctor left the room I sat in Cory's visitor's chair and considered the possibility of asking Shamansky for a guard. But, I concluded that if whoever did this to him wanted to kill him, they would have finished the job last night. First Jeannine, now Cory; this case was getting very high risk.

When I returned to the office Shamansky called. "What's shakin' Kojak?" I asked.

"Don't give me that buddy, buddy stuff. You were supposed to call me yesterday to tell me what you found out in Tecate," he snarled.

"Sorry about that. I've been buried lately. I found out that the Yuliya gang definitely robbed my office. Unfortunately, none of the evidence I came up with would be considered admissible," I said.

"Don't tell me you crossed the line to get it," he said.

"I'm trying not to. I found scanned copies of the stolen photos along with several other computer files that tell me the Yuliya family was following Terry, and has been following me. They had pictures of me, my girlfriend, and even my parents," I said with an agitation in my voice.

Shamansky replied, "I can see how that could piss you off, but I'm still leaning toward your boss."

"What! You can't be serious. We know they're a bunch of thugs that will do whatever it takes to protect their interests. They were stalking the victim right up to his death, and it took place on their turf. What more do you want?" I asked.

"I agree. These guys are definitely willing to break the law to get what they want. But I can't get past the fact that Terry was the brains, creative force, lead singer and business leader of the band. I've talked with an industry expert who says the consensus is that the band will fold without him. It doesn't take a genius to figure out that a car won't run without an engine," he said.

"Any new developments on Chelsea?" I asked.

"As a matter of fact, I found out Terry went to Chelsea's dad, Peter Spivey, of Spivey Construction, and talked him into getting some of his real estate investors together to explore the possibility of starting an independent record label to promote the new CD. Peter spent about twenty grand of his own money in legal fees to figure out a way to make it happen. Peter and Terry made a joint presentation to a group of potential financial backers, and got into a huge argument. Terry told Peter and his investment partners to get fucked and walked out on them. When Peter tried collecting the twenty grand Terry told him it was the cost of being an asshole. Chelsea tried to intervene on behalf of her father during dinner at a local restaurant, and Terry made a scene and walked out. As he was headed for the door several witnesses heard Chelsea say, 'You know what they do to a Doberman that bites the hand that feeds him.' Personally, I consider that a death threat. I'll find out if the DA concurs later this week," he said.

"It was a domestic squabble. These things get said everyday. If you started indicting every wife who told her husband 'he'd get his,' if he kept being such an asshole, you'd have half of the female population in front of the grand jury," I said.

"To threaten is one thing, but when the husband turns up dead the next week, and the widow inherits five mil, you've got a very legit suspect. Throw in that she bought him the headphones, and her dad keeps blasting caps, and you have the makings of a solid case," he said.

"My associate, Cory Pafford, got assaulted last night while he was on a stakeout. He's in the hospital," I said.

"Jesus, those guys have it in for you. I can get a case number assigned and send somebody to the hospital to take his statement. But, at this point I'm going to treat them like two separate cases," he said. "I have a meeting in a couple of minutes, I'll talk to you soon," he said and hung up.

While I was on the phone with Shamansky, Chelsea Tucker called and left a message asking me to drive over to her house as soon as possible. Jeannine agreed to lock up and have Delbert walk her home.

Chelsea lives in a beautiful, two-story tutor house with a view of the Pacific in Cardiff-by-the-Sea. For the second time in a week, I was disappointed to ring the doorbell of a mansion and have the expected butler conspicuously absent. Chelsea was dressed in designer casual and was holding a martini. "Can I get you a drink?" she offered as she ushered me into a sitting room.

"No thanks, I still have lots of work to do," I replied.

"I'm sure you're wondering why I asked you out here on such short notice," she said and I nodded. "Last time we talked you told me to contact you if I remembered anything that Terry said in his last few weeks that was out of the ordinary. This afternoon I had lunch with my father, then came home and took a little nap. About fifteen minutes after I fell asleep I woke up abruptly with a vivid memory that felt very significant."

"What was it?" I asked.

"About a month before Terry died, he got up early, took a shower and left for the day. I went into the bathroom shortly after he left and he had scrawled some lyrics on the steamed bathroom mirror. I didn't think anything of it at the time, but now I realize the words weren't related to any of his songs," she said.

"What did it say on the mirror, Chelsea?" I asked.

"It said:
Back in the days when I was 9,
A friend was a friend,
Now I need mine."

She said, "I have no idea what he meant, but I have a strong feeling that it had something to do with what was going on in his life at the time. As I start putting things into perspective, it's clear that Terry was under a lot of pressure and not acting like himself."

"In what ways?" I asked.

"He was always a workaholic. So, at first it was hard to recognize his actions as being related to stress. But, now that I've been analyzing that last month, it's clear that he was more argumentative with me and my family. He was very demanding with the band, but toward the end, his relationship with each of the members began to deteriorate. I chalked it all up to the contract situation, but now it seems like it was more that that," she said.

"How much did the other band members know about the contract negotiations?" I inquired.

She replied, "I'm sure Terry told them as little as possible. Those guys are musicians, not businessmen. They were glad to have Terry keeping an eye on the bottom line."

"As I understand it, Terry did a lot more than keep an eye on the bottom line. I met Kirby Kaufmann and Elden Dumanis. The word *puppets* comes to mind," I said.

"You're right. Terry hired those guys because he knew he could control them," Chelsea said.

"Who do you think Terry was talking about in the song lyric? Has he maintained a relationship with anyone from elementary school?" I asked.

"I've been wracking my brain trying to figure that out. He never talked about high school or elementary school," she replied.

I then brought her up to speed with what I had learned about Cerise Records and Yuliya, Inc. I also explained why she was still the prime suspect in the case.

"Terry always knew how to push my buttons. I should never have yelled at him in that restaurant. But he embarrassed my father and was showing a callous disregard for my feelings," she said. "Now that I hear what kind of monsters he was negotiating with, I understand why he wasn't acting like himself. My dad was pissed, but he also remarked about how uncharacteristic it was for Terry to behave like he did in front of his business associates."

On the way home I swung by University Hospital to see if Cory was awake. When I arrived, his bed was empty. "Do you know what happened to the guy who was in this bed," I asked one of his roommates.

"Sure do," said a toothless man in his mid-eighties.

"Well?" I asked.

"He was mad as a hornet. Woke up cussing a blue streak and never stopped until he got his clothes back and checked himself out," he said.

"Didn't the nurses try to stop him?" I asked.

"Sure did. But I think they got disgusted with his foul language," he said.

By the time I got to Cory's apartment it was dark. There were no lights on and no response to my knocks. I called from my cell phone and left a message for him to call me as soon as he got home. I had a very bad feeling as I walked back to my car.

Chapter 12

SHORTLY after I arrived at the office on Wednesday morning Glenda MacPhearson called. "You need to see this guy's record right away, but I can't fax it and people are in and out of my office all the time, so you can't drop by."

"I understand," I said. "Tell me when and where and I'll be there."

"I think I should come to your office. I can't risk being seen around the base with this service record. Are you going to be around this morning?" she asked.

"Absolutely. You're the best, Glenda," I said.

"You owe me for this one, buddy," she said.

Glenda arrived just before 11:00 AM in uniform. "Do I shake hands or salute?" I asked.

"How about a hug?" she replied and we embraced.

"You look great," I said. "Before we get to Jo-Jo, tell me what's new in your life."

"I'm up for captain and the colonel on the base is giving me his full endorsement," she said with a smile.

"That's great. Any lucky young man looking to promote you to Mrs.?" I asked.

"As a matter of fact, I've been seeing the same gentleman for the past two years," she announced.

"I hope you brought a picture," I said. Glenda produced a shot of them both in uniform standing in front of an Army tank. "He looks like Will Smith. Is he a Tank Commander?"

"No, we just thought it would make a good picture. He's a Lieutenant in the infantry," she replied. "How about you? Is there a future Mrs. Duffy in the offing?"

"I introduced my girlfriend to my parents last week. That's a first since high school prom night," I said.

"It sounds serious for you," she noted. "OK, enough with playing catch-up. We can do that when you reciprocate for this favor. I have to get back to the base soon." She pulled out a thick brown file folder with yellow post-it's sticking out. "I can't hand this file to you or allow you to make any copies, but, I've decided to review it today and I've been known to read out loud."

"I understand," I said. "I've been known to take notes when other people are talking."

"You should have tried that when we were at UCSD," she said and I smiled. "Anyway, Joseph Martin rose to the rank of Sergeant over an eight year career with the Army. He enlisted at the age of 18 and received an honorable discharge at age 26." Glenda flipped to one of the post-it pages. "He received extensive training in demolitions for both military operations and in support of the Army Corps of Engineers."

I asked, "Do you mean as in blasting caps for excavation?"

"Blasting caps, dynamite, nitroglycerine; everything the Corps might use to move a mountain," she said.

"I thought he was a communications guy," I said.

"He was during his first tour. Martin had 'A' and 'C' Schools in Electronics and Communications when he enlisted. But when he re-upped, he transitioned to Ordnance."

"Anything significant after he made the move?" I asked.

"Oh yeah," she said as she flipped to another page marker. "He was on mine sweep detail in Iraq when a very unpopular captain got blown up handling a mine Martin was supposed to have defused. There was an investigation and it was deemed accidental. But I got the impression that the person who wrote the report didn't agree with the finding."

"Wow!" I exclaimed. "What did they do with him after the investigation?"

"He returned to the states where he worked on a dam-building project with the Corp of Engineers until he was discharged," she said.

"Did they use blasting caps?" I asked.

"It doesn't say in the report, but what do you think?" she replied.

"I think I just found somebody with motive and opportunity. You've been a tremendous help, Glenda. When this thing is over we'll do a double date someplace special, my treat," I said.

"Last time you told me that we ended up at a Ku Klux Klan rally," she said sarcastically.

"It was a heavy metal concert. I didn't know the band was so popular with the skinheads," I said defensively.

"I think it's safe to say I was the only African-American girl at the show," she said.

"Glenda, you'd stand out in a crowd at a beauty pageant," I said.

"And you'd stand out as a bullshitter at a used car sales convention," she retorted.

It was Wednesday, date night, and I wasn't even close to being ready for the reunion concert. I called Kelly and said, "You seemed so pleased that I shared my parents with you on our last date that I thought I'd invite you over to my place tonight and play guitar for you."

"Why do I get the feeling I'm being multi-tasked again?" she asked.

"Because you have the instincts of a palm reader," I replied. "As part of the investigation I have to play guitar and sing at a club Saturday night. I'm nowhere near ready and I thought I could rely on your brutal honesty to give me some feedback."

"I know this is a big case for you. If you need the time, just ask. I don't want to feel like I'm an item on your *To Do* list," she said.

"Actually, I've really missed you and I'm looking forward to telling you about it over dinner. Then if you could put up with my practice session I'll make it up to you later," I said.

"Jason, it sounds like fun. Why don't I pick up some Chinese and meet you at your place at seven?" she asked.

"Sounds like a plan, I'll see you then," I said and hung up.

I tried reaching Cory several times throughout the morning, but there was no answer. I took a ride over to his apartment and saw letters sticking out of his mailbox. After trying the doorbell several times I gave up. As I was leaving I saw one of his neighbors and asked if she had seen him. She gave me a very sour expression and said she had not. It was 1:30 PM, so I went to lunch at a local eatery, then returned later and got the same results. Since Cory lived only a few minutes away from Jack Pascal, I decided to take a chance that their recording session had ended on schedule.

I rang Jack's doorbell and after about a minute Jack appeared. "Jason, this is a surprise," he said. From his bloodshot eyes and distinctive aroma I could tell he had just smoked some pot.

"I hope I'm not intruding, but I was in the neighborhood and I have a few more questions," I said.

"No problem at all. I just smoked a bong, would you like one?" he asked.

"No thanks. I have all of these songs I have to learn by Saturday night," I replied.

"Oh yeah. The pot might loosen you up, but it's not going to help your memory. Come on in and have a seat," he said.

"I was hoping we could talk about GI Jo-Jo," I said.

"Sure, what would you like to know?" he asked.

"How did he get along with Terry?" I inquired.

"About as well as everybody else. By now you know Terry was the band taskmaster. But, somebody has to be the driving force or nothing gets done. GI Jo-Jo probably understood that better than any of us, being that he is ex-military and used to taking orders," Jack said.

"How about his relationship with Delitah? Did that cause any friction or fights?" I asked.

"Terry wasn't really interested in her. He never said it, but I always felt Terry thought of her as rock band window dressing; all part of the image. I seriously doubt he ever did anything with her," he said.

"Tell me about the morning Terry died. When you walked into the studio who was there?" I asked.

"Ian and GI Jo-Jo were working on resetting glass panels in front of the drum set. Vlad the Impaler and Mike the mic man were in the control booth," he said.

"Mike the mic man?" I asked.

"He's the sound engineer," Jack replied.

"Did you see either of them leave the studio while you were waiting for Terry and Nigel?" I asked.

"No. Ian was explaining to Jo-Jo how his changes were going to alter the sound of his drums as they reset the glass. It was only about five or ten minutes from the time I got there to when Nigel arrived. Terry came in just a few minutes later," he said.

"What happened next?" I asked.

"Terry hit the ceiling when he saw what Ian and GI Jo-Jo were doing. They shouldn't have been making those changes while we were in the middle of recording a song," he said.

"How come you didn't say anything when you saw them," I inquired.

"I was doing my mantra. Terry and Ian just had this big scene at Denny's and I was trying to get my head back to a place where I could relate to my bass. I wasn't really paying attention to them until Terry yelled," he said.

"Did GI Jo-Jo help Terry with his equipment?" I asked.

"Now that I think about it, yeah. He told Jo-Jo to get his shit out of the car, then lit into Ian for being such a moron," Jack said.

"Did Terry go off on GI Jo-Jo for helping Ian with the panels?" I asked.

"He started to," Jack replied, "but when Jo-Jo told him he marked the panel settings before moving them, that's when Terry sent him to the car."

"How long was Jo-Jo in the parking lot?" I asked.

"I don't know. I was back into my mantra, trying to ignore the shit storm happening ten feet away," he said.

"Its amazing that you guys were able to come together and finish that song with all of the problems that morning," I commented.

"We would have finished it earlier without all of the dramatics," he said. "Hey, do you want to crack out the Les Paul again and practice a bit for Saturday night? I hear you're doing vocals too."

"One last question," I said. "Don't most band members lay down their tracks individually in a recording studio?"

Jack replied, "Terry liked to <u>feel</u>, not just hear, the bass and drums. He also liked the synergy. Occasionally, he'd make one of us do an overdub, but usually it was a group effort. Thank God for Mike the mic man. Most engineers couldn't handle it."

I spent the next hour working on three songs. Afterwards I swung back by Cory's place, but still no sign of him.

I returned to the office at 4:45 PM, and twenty minutes later Cory walked in looking like he just went 12 rounds with Apollo Creed. He had a black eye the size of a pork chop and his elbow was tucked into his ribs, like it was at the hospital. "Where were you? I've been worried sick!" I exclaimed.

In a vernacular that was even more profanity-laced than usual, Cory conveyed that he left the hospital because he was angry and wanted to get even with the sons of bitches that laid him out. He was sure it was the Cerise Records people, specifically Vlad Torhan and Boris Melsin. He said they cleared it with their boss on a cell phone before beating him within an inch of his life.

"Where did you go?" I asked.

After he left the hospital, Cory went home and got his laptop and disks with several pictures of the Cerise crew. He then checked into a motel and began sending emails to various media trying to generate interest in a story on the Russian Mafia in San Diego. The only one that bit was *California Confidential*, a cable TV tabloid journalism show. Cory sold them the story and pictures for $2500.

"Why didn't you come to me before you did this?" I asked.

He said it was because he knew that I'd talk him out of it. He felt that by getting the story out in the open the Russian Mafia would crawl back under a rock and stop being a threat to me and Jeannine.

"Did they say when they'll be running the story?" I asked. Cory didn't know, but he was pretty sure it would be aired this week.

As I walked Jeannine home I explained to her what Cory had done and I thoroughly inspected her deadbolt and window locks when we arrived at her apartment. She seemed a bit anxious about the prospects of our Russian adversaries getting really pissed off and readily agreed to the precautionary suggestions I made about not answering the door, screening her calls and not leaving the apartment on her own.

When I returned to the office I called Kelly and arranged to meet her a couple of blocks from my place, so that the cars would not be a telltale sign that we were in. I met her at the rendezvous spot just before 7:00 PM and we walked to my house with the Chinese food she had picked up.

Dinner was a little tense as I explained about the bomb Cory had dropped a couple of hours earlier. At 7:30 PM we tuned in to *California Confidential*. The plan was that if the Russian Mafia story ran we would continue with our original idea for the evening, except we would do it by the light of a single candle and without plugging in the electric guitar. As it turned out they didn't run the story and Kelly really enjoyed hearing me perform for her. I was definitely amped-up for the performance, knowing that I could be on the Russian Mafia's most wanted list any day. Kelly's adrenaline was also pumping since, by default, she was thrust into this high-risk situation. That night, our lovemaking was wilder than ever. I was wrong when I thought a night at home with the little woman was going to mean getting a good night's sleep.

Chapter 13

WHEN I arrived at the office on Thursday morning I reviewed the items Jeannine highlighted from the Russian newspaper articles Uri had translated. She listened to the tapes he had provided and noted items she thought could pertain to the case. The resolution of the kidnapping was very conspicuous by its absence. Tass had gone to great lengths to describe in detail the circumstances of the abduction, bio's on the family, the suspicion of Mafia involvement and practically a day-by-day report on developments leading up to the rescue. It seemed incomprehensible that the largest news service in Russia would follow a case that closely and never mention the outcome. I interpreted this as an inference that Ivan Chofsky had cut a deal with the kidnappers. If the police had engineered the recovery, it's hard to imagine that they wouldn't celebrate their success in the paper and be hailed as heroes. But I realized that we were dealing with a very different culture.

Uri's translation gave me the name of the Odessa police lieutenant who was the primary on the case. I called Uri and said, "Thank you for the translation of the newspaper articles, they were very enlightening."

"Your welcome, my friend," he replied.

"I'm afraid I have one more favor to ask of you," I stated.

"Ask away, I am still in your debt," he said.

"The translation mentions the name of a policeman in Odessa, a Lieutenant Victor Sanchenko. It would be extremely helpful to me if you had any contacts in Odessa who could arrange a conversation with the lieutenant," I said.

There was silence on the other end of the phone for about twenty seconds, then Uri said, "I have an acquaintance named Igor Shmalko who has family in Odessa. I'm not sure if they have any influence with the police. I don't know if Igor would be willing to try to make the arrangement. And, I am skeptical that the lieutenant would be willing to tell an American what would not be allowed to be printed in the national press. For you, my friend, I will try, but don't expect too much."

"Thank you. Now I want to tell you about something you'll probably hear about in the next few days," I said. Over the next ten minutes I told him about what would be coming out on *California Confidential*. We agreed that few people took the show seriously, but that it would definitely cause a stir in the Russian community, and that it was quite possible the Mafia might seek out those responsible for the story. "Under these circumstances, if you feel that bringing in Mr. Shmalko could endanger him or his family, then I don't expect you to do it."

"Igor is not an old friend and certainly not a confidant, but I know exactly how he feels about the Mafia. He would perceive helping you as a way of striking back at the Mafia. That would be the only way he would consent to providing assistance. But, even if he refuses to get involved, he would respect what we are doing and wish us well in our endeavors," Uri said.

Nigel called just before noon. "Jason, how are the songs coming?" he asked.

"They're coming," I replied. "Another month and I'll definitely be ready."

"That's why I'm calling. I was thinking it would really help if we were able to practice our set at your friend's club on Saturday afternoon. Do you think you can make it happen?" he asked.

"Actually, I think it's a great idea. What I'd like to do today is meet with GI Jo-Jo at the club to decide who's bringing what equipment, and put together a plan for equipment changes before and after your set. Since Tsunami Rush is no longer a working band we don't own a PA system anymore," I said.

"We have a club size PA and, if you like, you can use our amps, mics, lights and everything," he said.

"I'm pretty sure Michael Marinangeli, our lead guitarist, will want to use his own stuff, but I think the rest of us would appreciate the upgrade. I'll check with the guys before meeting with GI Jo-Jo," I said.

Nigel said, "I'll ring up GI Jo-Jo and tell him to give you his full cooperation."

"Great. Can you ask him to call me right away?" I asked.

"Done," he said. "Also, I'm starting to talk with some new management candidates next week. When I get it down to the last two or three possibilities I'd like bios. If you're finished working for Chelsea by then can you help us out?" he asked.

"Sure. When I finish up, I'm all yours," I replied.

GI Jo-Jo called twenty minutes later. "Jason Duffy," I said.

"It's Jo-Jo Martin from Doberman's Stub. Nigel Choate asked me to call," he said.

I replied, "We met at the recording studio when I filled in on rhythm guitar," I said.

"I remember," he said. "You're the one with all the questions."

"That's me," I said.

"I don't mind getting together to figure out the set up for Saturday night, but I'm not answering any more of your questions," he said.

"Believe it or not, rhythm guitar isn't how I make my living," I said.

"Then I won't bother to tell you not to quit your day job," he said, laughing at his own joke.

"I'm a private investigator working on Terry's murder. I'm going to need to ask you more questions if I'm going to solve the case," I said.

"I told you I'm not answering any more questions and I don't want you bothering Delitah anymore either," Jo-Jo said.

"Don't you want Terry's murderer caught?" I asked.

"That's a job for the police. I talked to them and we're done. I don't need to discuss anything with you except technical questions about our gig," he said sternly.

"Nigel's asked me to do some work for the band. He's anxious for me to solve the case so I can get started. When I spoke with him a half-hour ago he told me he was going to ask you to give me your full cooperation. Do I need to call him back and tell him that's not happening?" I asked.

There was silence for about a minute. "This is bullshit!" he exclaimed. "You're telling me you're going to call my boss and tell on me if I don't play ball with you?"

"I'll tell you what's bullshit," I retorted. "The boss who gave you your job got murdered, but instead of you helping to find out who did it, you're doing what you can to impede the investigation."

"Fuck you!" he exclaimed.

"Then here's how it's going to go. If you don't agree to meet me and answer all of my questions honestly, I call Nigel and tell him I can't work with you. I'll tell him your behavior has led me to believe you're a suspect in the murder and that I feel the band should immediately put as much distance between you and them as possible. What's it going to be?" I asked.

Again GI Jo-Jo went silent. I knew it was a risk letting him know he was a suspect, but since I was already looking over my shoulder for the Russians, what's one more asshole who hates my guts. "I didn't kill Terry," he said quietly.

"Then step up to the plate and help find his murderer," I said. Again more silence. After thirty seconds I added, "You can always collect unemployment."

"I'm into Doberman's sound and I don't want to lose the gig, so I'll talk to you. But when this thing is over I'm gonna kick your ass," he threatened.

"When this thing is over I'm going to be advising Nigel on personnel changes. Do you think that's a good idea?" I asked.

"Fuck you. Where do you want to meet?" he asked.

"Dali Lama Yo Mama at 5:00 PM this afternoon," I said and hung up.

After my conversation I was too hyper to review Terry's bills and phone charges. I took a walk and thought about how to proceed. By the time I had calmed down I found myself in front of Schlotsky's Deli, so I stopped in for a turkey club sandwich. When I returned to the office I was surprised to see Kyle Kramer, Derek Schmidt and Michael Marinangeli, a.k.a. Tsunami Rush, in my reception room. "We've come to kidnap you," Kyle said.

It was obvious from Jeannine's hundred-watt grin that the boys introduced themselves. "We all took a couple of vacation days. If we spend some time in Alpine we actually might not embarrass ourselves on Saturday night," Derek said.

"A couple of nights in Alpine sounds great, but I can't leave until tonight," I said.

"Just reschedule," Kyle said enthusiastically. "We did it."

I replied, "I have a meeting at Bernie's at 5:00 PM today to work out what equipment we're using. Also, how the changes for the Doberman set will go down. And, I've been asked by Nigel Choate to get Bernie to agree to let them practice with me on Saturday afternoon. They don't want me to embarrass them either."

"Fine, we'll come with you just to make sure you don't bail on us," Michael said. He's been upset with me ever since Tsunami Rush broke up. It was his idea to form the band originally and he is the only one of us still working as a musician. He's been through two groups over the past three years and is in the process of getting a third one off of the ground.

Over the next half-hour I explained about my encounters with the Russians as well as what they did to Cory and Jeannine. I told them that as much as I needed practice in Alpine, I also needed a safe place to keep Kelly once the *California Confidential* story broke.

Derek called his aunt and got the OK for Kelly and Jeannine to accompany the band for a couple of spend-the-nights. When he got off of the phone he turned to Michael Marinangeli and exclaimed, "We're going to the mattresses, Pizon!"

"Do you guys think you could give me a couple of hours to get a few things done before going to Bernie's?" I asked.

"We have a better idea," Derek said, and the three of them walked out of my office. Five minutes later they returned with two acoustic guitars, a practice drum pad and an acoustic bass. We used to practice with this equipment on nights when we stayed in LA motels to avoid hassles with the police.

Before we started I called Kelly and got her to agree to the Alpine overnight. At first she seemed reluctant because she was getting her classroom ready for the new school year. It was then that I told her about the pictures in Yuliya's computer. That did the trick. "I want to come back with you tomorrow and work on my classroom," she said.

"I'll make you a deal. If the *California Confidential* story doesn't break tonight, I'll bring you back tomorrow. If it does, then you stay with the guys and Jeannine in Alpine, OK?" I asked. She agreed. I guess she saw enough chaotic violence when she lived with her family, and welcomed a safe haven.

At 5:05 PM the Tsunami gang descended on the Dali Lama Yo Mama. GI Jo-Jo had not yet arrived. I spotted Jasmine and waved her over to our table. "Do you recognize these derelicts?" I asked her, nodding my head toward my crew.

"Are you kidding? I heard this is the headline act at what's gonna be the hottest club in town this Saturday night," she said with a cheerleader's enthusiasm.

"Word isn't leaking out, is it?" I asked.

"Bernie swore us to secrecy. But the employees have been strongly urging their friends to see this legendary club band come out of retirement for one last gig at their favorite venue," she said.

"Do you mean it?" Kyle asked with wide eyes.

"Oh yeah," she replied. "We've been laying the bullshit on extra thick to make sure our best friends don't miss those Dobie dudes."

"Dobie dudes?" Michael asked with a face that looked like he just bit into a pickle.

"But we were one of the best club bands in San Diego," I said defensively.

"And I'm up for cocktail waitress of the year," she said sarcastically. "You boys are sweet. Come sit in my section," she said and led us to a table closer to the bar. "I'll tell Bernie you're here?"

Five minutes later Bernie was standing at our table. "What a pleasant surprise. I wasn't expecting to see you guys until Saturday. Kyle, congratulations," he said and extended his hand for a shake. "I heard you got married and have a baby girl."

Kyle beamed and looked at his fellow band mates; very impressed that Bernie had kept up. "Thanks Bernie," he said with a smile, "I'll bring a picture on Saturday."

"A picture. You better bring your better half on Saturday," he said, then turned to Derek. "Mr. Schmidt, did I hear you invented a new software product?"

"Just one of the team members to make it happen," Derek said.

"He's being modest," Kyle chimed in. "It was his idea and he was in charge of the team."

"Very impressive," Bernie said. "Promise me you'll come by the club sometime when it's less hectic and tell me all about it."

"I'll be glad to, Bernie. I didn't realize you started opening for happy hour. I'll stop by soon," Derek said.

"Wonderful," Bernie said then turned to Michael. "Now if only I could think of something nice to say about this guy." Bernie stroked his chin and looked at all of us. "Did you guys know that Michael has been in two bands since Tsunami Rush, but he's never called his old friend Bernie to book a gig at the Dali Lama?"

Michael replied, "C'mon Bernie, you know I was never a band manager. I just make the music; I don't make the deals."

"Are you working now?" he asked.

"I'm just starting a new band," he said. "I'll be glad to have the manager send you a demo when we're ready to perform."

"I'm glad you stayed in the business, Michael. You have a lot of talent. How could San Diego do without its angel of the sea?" he asked.

"Angel of the sea?" asked Kyle.

"That's what Marinangeli means in Italian," replied Derek.

We were all enjoying Bernie's company when GI Jo-Jo walked in the door. I hadn't yet cleared the Saturday afternoon practice session. "Bernie, Doberman's sound guy just got here. Can I introduce you?" I asked.

"Sure, I'll ask Jasmine to bring him over to the table," he said.

"How about if we take a walk over and meet him at the bar? I'll stop by your office before we leave and explain," I said. While we made our way through the cocktail tables Bernie gave me the go ahead for the Saturday practice session. As we approached, GI Jo-Jo was taking his first sip of a full glass of beer. He spotted us when we were about ten feet away. "Hi Jo-Jo, this is Bernie Liebowitz, the club owner. Bernie, Jo-Jo Martin, the sound man for Doberman's Stub." They shook hands, but Jo-Jo made no effort to shake mine.

"Nice to meet you, young man," Bernie said "My condolences on Terry's passing. He used to play here with Caliber 9 a few years ago."

"Thanks, man," GI Jo-Jo said. "Can we check out access and electrical?"

Over the next ten minutes Bernie took us through the backstage tour and how he wanted the cabling to run from the stage to the soundboard. Then, Bernie excused himself and I walked with Jo-Jo to the bar, which was now almost full. We ordered beers, and took them to a table away from the crowd.

"Let's get this over with so I can get the fuck out of here," GI Jo-Jo said.

"Fine," I replied. "Let's start with the day Terry died. I was told you carried his stuff in from the Ferrari while he chewed out Ian for moving the partitions. Is that correct?"

"I do almost all of the carrying, so what," he said flatly.

"So that means you were the last person to be alone with his headphones before they exploded," I said.

"I didn't do anything to the headphones. In fact, I didn't even see the headphones. They were probably in one of the bags," he said.

"I understand you were an ordnance technician in Iraq. Did the police ask you about your qualifications to build the device that killed Terry?" I asked.

"Why don't you ask them?" he asked.

"I'm asking you," I said.

"A twelve year old could have built it," he said. "Maybe that's why the cops didn't bother to ask."

"What are you going to tell them when they ask about the allegation that you fragged your boss in Iraq?" I asked.

"Who the fuck told you about that?" GI Jo-Jo asked with alarm.

"If I know about it, you can bet the cops know, too," I said.

"Then why aren't they coming after me?" he asked.

"Terry wasn't exactly Mr. Congeniality. You're just one of several suspects. But, eventually they'll get around to you. Why don't you tell me what happened so I can stop thinking it was you?" I said.

"Why should I tell you anything?" he said

"I thought we went over this on the phone. Do you need to hear it again?" I asked.

GI Jo-Jo said, "I was an ordnance tech in Iraq. My unit cleared land mines and unexploded ordnance. My C.O. was a prick and a chicken-shit. When there was dangerous duty he had no problem putting a new guy on it, even if he got blown up. But he would never go near anything dangerous himself. One day he assigned a very tricky procedure to a fresh recruit. The kid said the job was done, then went to the latrine to throw up. A bunch of us techs were standing about 40 yards away from the ordnance when this dickless captain came up to me and asked if the job was done. I told him the kid said it was. He told me to go check it out. I asked him if he left his balls in the states. We went at it a few more minutes, then he decided to show everybody he was a man. Instead, he showed everybody what an incompetent jerk he was. I never touched the ordnance. Once the brass got their facts straight I was cleared."

"Then why did you get run out of the Middle East?" I asked.

"Because dead captains have friends with pull. I made the mistake of going on record about what a shithead this guy was and his buddies decided to teach me a lesson," he said.

"That's it for now, Jo-Jo. If I need anything else I'll ask Nigel to get in touch," I said.

"I'll hold my breath," he said, then stood up and left of the club.

I walked back to Bernie's office, knocked twice, then entered. "Any luck with the homemade karaoke set-up?" I asked.

"Check this out," Bernie said as he stood up and walked from his desk to a worktable on the far wall. "Are you definitely going to perform the songs in the order that you gave to me?" he asked.

"Yeah. I told Nigel what we were doing and he said the order they appear on the CD works fine," I said.

Bernie handed me a small remote control. "Just have your assistant hit 'On' to get the first screen of the first song on the monitor. Then he just has to hit 'Page Down' when you're ready for the next screen. I saw you looking at the monitor when I was giving Jo-Jo the tour. What do you think?"

"I think you saved my butt again, Bernie," I said. "Hey, I've got a couple of old friends coming on Saturday that you'll be glad to see."

"Who's that?" he asked.

"Calvin Dawson and Justin Emerson," I said.

"If I ever decide to retire, Justin will be the first person I'll call," he said.

"I know he thinks of you as a role model. How long has it been?" I asked.

"Too long," he said. "I did see Calvin a few months ago. He was in town for a show and stopped by the club afterwards. I could talk to him non-stop for a week. He knows more inside information about this business than anyone I've ever met."

"I'll bet we get a few old regulars out to see their favorite band, too," I said.

"I was thinking about that yesterday. Most rock & roll fans connect with bands they enjoyed during a significant time in their lives. I'm betting you'll bring out some people who haven't been to a club all year. But they'll see the ad in the paper and say, 'hey honey, guess who's back at the old Dali Lama?' It's going to be a fun night," Bernie said.

After briefly explaining my behavior around Jo-Jo I said, "Bernie, I gotta go. You have my cell phone number. Call me if you need anything," and departed.

When I re-entered the club I saw Kelly sitting at a table by herself. I walked up behind her, disguised my voice and said, "Hey blondie, ya lookin' for a good time?"

Without a glance she replied, "Hey sailor, I thought you'd never ask." She then stood up and gave me a hug. "Do you really think it's necessary to get out of town tonight?"

"Better to be safe than sorry," I said. Then threw in, "An ounce of prevention is worth a pound of cure."

"We've been going to too many ballgames. You're starting to talk in cliché-speak," she said with a nervous laugh.

"Let me introduce you to the band," I said. I led her to the Tsunami table where intros were given and it was decided to hit the road right away. Jeannine had arrived by cab while I was meeting with Bernie and was seated with the boys. We managed to maintain a two-vehicle caravan across Interstate 8. At her request, Jeannine rode with the band in Derek's SUV. We reached the last exit for El Cajon by 7:15 PM and decided to look for a place to eat and watch *California Confidential*.

At 7:25 PM we bribed a bartender at T.G.I. Friday's to change the channel and got a drink order in before the show opened:

"Tonight on California Confidential ... Could California be in for another recall election? ... Is one of California's top pro baseball players ready to come out of the closet ... And our top story – Was Doberman's Stub front-man, Terry Tucker, killed by a Southern California branch of the Russian Mafia? You'll find out after these messages."

We managed to get our food orders in during the first two stories. I wasn't sure I would want to eat after the report.

"The music industry and rock fans of Doberman's Stub were

devastated three weeks ago when singer/guitarist Terry Tucker was brutally murdered during a recording session. While the police remain baffled, California Confidential has come to learn that the band's record company, Cerise Records, is owned by a man who has strong ties to the Russian Mafia. Here we see photos of the owner, John Koflanovich. But California Confidential has learned that John Koflanovich is really Ivan Chofsky of the Ukraine. You can change your name, Mr. Koflanovich, but you can't hide from California Confidential."

"Less than two weeks ago the agency of San Diego detective Jason Duffy, began taking a close look at Cerise's operations. Since then Duffy's office has been invaded by armed thugs on two occasions. The last time, Duffy's administrative assistant, Jeannine Joshlin, was bound and gagged while the Russians stole company computers and photos related to the case. A few days later, former National Geographic photographer, Cory Pafford, who captured these photos, was assaulted and hospitalized by men Pafford recognized as employees of Cerise Records. He has identified those men as Vladimir Torhan and Boris Melsin. Torhan was a former Ukrainian amateur boxing champion."

"It is believed that Cerise Records is funded by the owners of California sweatshop Yuliya, Inc., that has made its money on the backs of immigrants of questionable green card status, for many years. It is run by Peter Chofsky, and has been in California since the early 1900's. But, they shifted their way of doing business when the Soviet Union broke up and the Mafia gained a stronghold."

"But, what about California? Are we going to sit back while this world renowned, ruthless bunch of cutthroats infests our *beloved state? Not if California Confidential has anything to say about it. We salute Jason Duffy and his efforts to do what Interpol has not been able to achieve. Keep up the good work, Jason. California Confidential has got your back."*

"Oh my God," Kelly said slowly.

"What's the big deal?" asked Kyle. "This will probably be a huge boon to your business. We should be celebrating."

"It's a little hard to cash those big checks from the cemetery," said Michael. "Take it from a full-blooded Italian, the Mafia hates publicity. Nobody wants to be the point-man in a Mafia probe even if the FBI has your back,"

I said, "My big problem is that I'm not sure Cerise Records is affiliated with the Mafia. When Chofsky's daughter was kidnapped there was no evidence that he had any ties with them. I think it's just as possible that Chofsky is running from the Mafia as it is that he cut a deal with them to save his daughter."

Jeannine asked, "Then why would they use all those strong-arm tactics with you?"

"I don't know. Maybe that's what they think they need to do to survive. If he's running from the Russian Mafia there will be no mistaking where he's hiding after tonight's broadcast," I said.

Derek said, "I can't believe that anybody in his right mind would actually watch that crap. I saw a teaser for it last week and they were interviewing people who said they were abducted by aliens on Mission Bay. I don't know how they stay on the air."

Jeannine said, "Our new security guard once saved a child from being abducted by aliens. But I don't think it was on Mission Bay."

"Sounds more like Ocean Beach to me," said Kyle.

We finished our meal in relative silence. Traffic had thinned considerably, so the trip to Alpine was mercifully quick. We arrived at the country home of Derek's Aunt Esther at about 9:00 PM. Esther has always been very cool about supporting the band. She is also a bit on the old fashioned side, so I was curious about how she would establish the rules for the girls' sleepover. True to her image as a cool septuagenarian, Esther announced she was spending the night with her friend and would be back at 7:00 AM to cook breakfast. She also bought us a case of beer.

After a couple of beers we were ready to rock. Over the next half-hour we were absolutely terrible. I couldn't stop thinking about the Russians and how I had put everybody I cared about in jeopardy. Derek was trying to flirt with Jeannine, and Michael was pissed that we were about to destroy his reputation. As we argued, Kelly walked out of the four-car attached garage where we practiced and into the house. Five minutes later she returned to an even louder argument wearing a skimpy pair of baby-doll pajamas. Everyone went silent.

"Jason," she said in a sweet voice, "will you sing a song for me like you did last night?"

I was immediately snapped out of my argumentative funk. Before I could decide how to respond, Michael launched into a sexy old Bush tune called "Glycerine." I locked eyes with Kelly and gave a performance that came straight from the heart. It was amazing how the evening turned around. All of the emotions that were keeping us from being functional got channeled into an exciting, passionate interpretation of our favorite cover songs. If we could come anywhere near this vibe on Saturday night we would be just fine and we all knew it.

We called it a night at 1:00 AM. Kelly and I took Aunt Esther's bed. I soon found that while I was getting a tremendous energy release playing with the band, Kelly was getting turned on to the extreme. There would be no insomnia bringing me back to the Russian dilemma tonight. By the time she finished with me I was as spent as a sailor's paycheck on a wartime liberty.

Chapter 14

I AWOKE in a panic when I heard Michael open the bedroom door and yell, "Aunt Esther's here!" I jumped out of bed naked and spun around to Kelly's side of the bed only to see that she wasn't there and her side of the bed was made. Michael was laughing with an abandon I hadn't heard since Tsunami Rush broke up. "Would you like me to shut this?" he asked.

I picked up a lavender pillow and chucked it at the doorway as Michael ducked to avoid being hit. I took a shower and Derek lent me the extra clothes he packed when planning the office kidnapping. As I got to the kitchen Esther and the girls were putting the finishing touches on a hearty breakfast. The mood was refreshingly light. There was a confidence in the dining room that sent me off to battle traffic and the day's upcoming travails with a sense of hope, instead of dread.

I was in my office no more than five minutes when Walter Shamansky blew in like a level-five hurricane. "What the hell is the matter with you?" he screamed. "I can't believe you blindsided me in the press."

"It wasn't my idea. I can explain," I said.

"This stunt of yours isn't going to keep your client out of jail. If anything, it makes me believe you're trying to blow smoke up my ass," he said.

"I know you're pissed and I don't blame you. But I had nothing to do with giving that schlock show the story," I said.

"Then how the hell did they get it," he said angrily.

"My cameraman, Cory, got worked over by two of Cerise's goons. They put him in the hospital with broken ribs and a concussion. When he regained consciousness he checked himself out and went into hiding. By the time he resurfaced he had given them the story. He thought he was protecting us and had no idea how badly this was going to mess things up," I said.

"You've got to take responsibility for your people," he said.

"You've got to stop closing your eyes to the fact that these guys are running amok and you've done nothing to even slow them down," I said getting hot. "So far I've had a gunman break in on a Saturday afternoon, my secretary was assaulted at gunpoint, my place was robbed, I was shot at and my assistant was beaten senseless. And what have you done about it? Have you brought Koflanovich in for questioning? Have you searched Cerise for guns or stolen property? I don't like that Cory went to the press, but I can certainly understand it, considering that the police have done absolutely nothing to stop them."

"Can I expect to hear your little speech on tonight's *California Confidential*?" he asked.

"If you actually watch that crappy show, I just lost a lot of respect for you," I replied.

"You're right. That show isn't taken seriously by anyone with half a brain. But, the legitimate press is going to want to talk with you now to get your take. This is where you can set things right, or totally fuck things up. What are you going to do?" he asked.

"I don't know. These thugs from Cerise need to be stopped, even if they weren't the ones who killed Terry," I said.

"Sounds like you're finally realizing Chelsea is dirty. What made you come around," he asked.

"I don't think Chelsea had anything to do with it, but I do have another suspect who's looking like a strong possibility," I said.

"Cripes almighty, who's your suspect today?" he asked.

"I know this *California Confidential* thing is going to cost you a lot of time, so I'm gonna give you what I've got. Doberman's Stub has a combination roadie and sound man named Joseph Martin, a.k.a. GI Jo-Jo. He was an ordnance technician in the Army and was accused of blowing up his commanding officer in Iraq. He's dating a stripper/groupie that thought she was in love with Terry, and he was seen punching Terry not long before the murder."

"Are you sure about these things?" he asked.

"Yes," I replied, "and, he was the last person to be alone with the headphones." I spent the next ten minutes giving Shamansky the details, except for how I came by his service record. I also told him GI Jo-Jo's explanation and the fact that he has been very uncooperative.

"You done good, Duffy. See if you can keep this info under your hat when you talk to the press," he said.

"Now I have a question for you. Last time we talked you were going to be presenting your evidence on Chelsea to the DA. What did he say?" I asked.

"He likes her. Have you talked with her father? Terry made him look like shit in front of his business cronies and Chelsea was livid. I'm gonna take a close look at Joseph Martin, but I still have a gut feeling Chelsea got fed up. My boss is ready to ask for an indictment," he said. "Keep me posted if you come up with anything new."

After he left I called Glenda MacPhearson and discretely asked if she could check on the disposition of Jo-Jo's case. I also asked if she and her main man would like to attend the club concert of the twenty-first century. "We'll come, but only because I really don't like talking on the phone," she said and hung up.

The legitimate press was all over the *California Confidential* story. I responded by locking the door and call screening. I let all of them go to voice-mail until 10:30 AM when a caller with a Texas accent said, "My name is Billy Tyler. I'm a partner in Cerise Records. I'm the guy that got Doberman's Stub signed to the Cerise Record deal."

I picked up the receiver. "This is Jason Duffy."

"Mr. Duffy, I would very much appreciate the chance to meet with you and talk about what's been going on between you and Cerise Records," he said.

I replied, "I'd like some answers myself, but so far everyone I've met from Cerise Records has carried a gun. So you'll have to excuse me if I'm reluctant to schedule a get-together."

"You name the time and place and I'll be there. We can meet on the steps of police headquarters if you like," he said.

"Will you be alone?" I asked.

"Yes. You can dictate the terms of the meeting," he said.

I had him give me his cell phone number and told him to be on foot at an intersection two blocks from Larabee's at 12:30 PM. I then called Beaver's Mom and used my Kojak connection to get a 12:45 PM reservation for two. I arrived early and took a cruise through the neighborhood to make sure Billy hadn't arranged for his partners to stake out the area. At 12:25 PM a tall guy in a white cowboy hat appeared with cell phone in hand. I watched him for five minutes to see if he would glance at any foot soldiers in hiding. At exactly 12:30 PM I called and instructed him to walk one block in the opposite direction of the restaurant. Again, there was no sign of an ambush. So, I called back and told him to meet me at Larabee's. Enough with the cloak and dagger, I was getting hungry.

Beaver's Mom got me seated before he arrived. As he entered the dining room I could see he was in his mid-fifties and appeared to be quite fit. When he arrived at my table I stood up, but did not offer to shake hands. "Thanks for agreeing to see me," he said looking out the window at the multi-terraced alfresco dining area. "Quite a spread they have here."

"Let's get down to business, Tyler. Your partner has robbed me, shot at me and assaulted two of my staff members. I'm in no mood for small talk," I said.

"First, I'd like to assure you that I had absolutely nothing to do with any of that. In fact, I never heard of you until a California buddy of mine got me out of bed last night after seeing that horrible show," he said.

"How can you be partners with the Russian Mafia and not have a clue?" I asked.

At this point, our conversation was interrupted by a waitress I hadn't seen before, who took our lunch orders.

"I know you're not going to believe this, but John Koflanovich is not with the Russian Mafia. In fact, he lives his life in fear of them," he said. "He moved to the United States to get away from them after they kidnapped his daughter."

"I suppose he didn't cut a deal with them to get her back," I said.

"Actually, he led them into a trap set by the police. Unfortunately, they were smarter than the police anticipated and a dozen police officers were killed, along with eighteen Mafioso's. The cops managed to rescue the girl, but at a terrible price. The Russian mob swore revenge, and John closed up shop and immigrated to the US where he has family," Tyler said.

"If this is true, why does he have so many thugs with guns working for him?" I asked.

"John Koflanovich is sure the mob will eventually find him and his family. He believes the only way he can stop them is to fight fire with fire. He grew up with the paranoia that comes with living in a commie state. After what happened to his daughter, he's suspicious of everyone," he said.

"But I'm American. How could he think I'm with the Russian Mafia?" I inquired.

"I asked him the same question myself this morning. He was convinced you were with the American Mafia and you were helping your Russian comrades," Tyler said.

"How the hell did he get that idea?" I inquired.

"He said it had to do with you sneaking into his back offices and knocking out his bodyguard. Is this true?" he asked.

"I knocked out his bodyguard after he stuck a gun in my face," I said. "How did you get hooked up with this guy in the first place?" I asked.

"I own a semiconductor business outside of Fort Worth. One of my customers is Yuliya, Inc. Are you familiar with them?" he asked.

"As a matter of fact, I found some of my stolen property in their possession in Tecate," I replied.

"That's disturbing," he said. "I've known Peter Chofsky for over ten years. Anyway, I had dinner with Peter a while back and

I happened to mention that I made a nice little profit investing in some musical acts out of Nashville. About six months later he came to me with a proposal to launch Cerise Records with his cousin, John, as the president. He showed me John's resume and, frankly, it's quite impressive."

"I don't suppose he had any music industry experience on the resume?" I asked.

"That was a concern. But, Peter invested double what I put in and sweetened the deal for me by substantially increasing his orders for semiconductor wafers. It looked like a no lose situation, until now," he said.

"Is he coming after me?" I asked.

"No. In fact, he's finally convinced you aren't with the American Mafia, because you never would have gone to the press if you were. He has much bigger problems to deal with now. He's sure it's inevitable that the Russian mob will come after him and his family very soon. I just came from his place. If the Alamo had half the firepower he has, Santa Ana would have high-tailed it back across the Rio Grande so fast you'd think he was shot out of a canon," he said.

"Why the meeting? What do you want from me?" I asked.

"To be perfectly honest, I was hoping that once you learned that Koflanovich isn't associated with the Russian Mafia you'd help with damage control," he said.

I replied, "After what he did to me and my staff, do you really expect me to help him?"

"Jason, he came after you because he was convinced you were a threat to his family. After what he went through, having his only child's finger mailed to him, you can surly understand why he might err on the side of caution," Tyler said.

"So you think he was justified in what he did?" I asked.

"Of course not. But I'm also willing to consider that John grew up in a culture that preached suspicion and taught paranoia. I've been an avid anticommunist all my life. My friends were shocked when I started doing business with Yuliya, but I did so when I learned that the Chofsky's refused to return to Russia after the communist revolution. Peter Chofsky hates communism with a passion no American could ever understand. He assured me that his cousin felt the same way and I made damn sure that was the case before I agreed to the partnership," he said.

As we finished lunch our server brought coffee and our bill. "Are you going to maintain your business relationship with these people now that you know they ordered the robbery and assault?" I asked.

"No. It will take a little time, because to pull out immediately would mean laying off a lot of good people in Texas, but you can be damn sure that within the year I'll cut ties completely," he said. "In the meantime, it seems to me that if Cerise Records gets shut down, all of its assets, including the new Doberman's Stub CD, will be put in an escrow account until the legal system finishes litigating court cases and appeals."

"In other words you're saying that if Cerise Records goes down, so does Doberman's Stub," I said. Tyler paid our bill and we walked back down to the street in silence.

When I returned to my office I saw a TV camera crew and several reporters gathered outside of my building. I called Heather Gaines, a CPA who runs an accounting business in the suite next door to mine. "I need a favor," I said.

"Just name it," Heather said brightly. "I've gotten more free publicity today than ten years worth of Kiwanis Club, Toastmasters and Rotary meetings combined."

"Any chance you could drive down the block, then come back five minutes later and tell the reporters you just saw me at Schlotsky's Deli and that I won't be coming back to the office today?" I asked.

"Can I tell them anything else that might get me a little more face time?" she asked.

"Tell them I got a new lead that could change everything, but that it will take me out of town for a couple of days," I said.

Fifteen minutes later I was checking voice-mail in my office, a mere thirty messages. Uri asked that I call back as soon as possible. I reached him at his office and was told he could arrange a conference call with the Odessa police lieutenant at 7:00 AM Sunday morning on my office phone line. Uri's acquaintance will serve as interpreter.

I spent the rest of the afternoon tying up loose ends, including a conversation with Chelsea about *California Confidential*. Considering her level of aggravation I opted not to tell her about the gig Saturday night.

I spent the 90 minutes it took to drive to Alpine listening to the Doberman's Stub demo. When I arrived, the band was playing an old Blondie tune called, "Heart of Glass," with Jeannine singing lead vocals and doing quite well for an amateur. She was wearing one of Aunt Esther's vintage dresses, a string of pearls and the kind of hat one might wear to a speak-easy during Prohibition.

We managed to pick up the vibe that started last night, until it was time for *California Confidential*. Kyle said, "Last time we watched that stupid show we played like shit afterwards. Can't we just DVR it and watch it on Sunday?"

What Kyle said made sense, until I reminded myself that the gig was secondary to solving the case. "I can't ignore something that could have a direct bearing on my case. You guys can keep playing if you like."

Michael replied, "And miss the circus. Are you kidding? I want popcorn, beer and a front row seat."

We adjourned to the living room and caught the headlines, where they gave a tease for a follow-up to the Terry Tucker murder story. Aunt Esther served slices of homemade pizza while we suffered through three stories of no interest to any of us. The update was looking equally uninformative as they showed a clip of Shamansky saying 'no comment.'

> *"Finally, this just in. Police apprehended Mikhail Dracovich outside the home of Jason Duffy, the Private Investigator who discovered the link between the Russian Mafia and Cerise Records. Dracovich was spotted by a neighbor climbing a tree across from Duffy's home while carrying a high-powered*

sniper's rifle. Jason could not be reached for comment, but we heard from one of California Confidential's snoops, Heather Gaines of Gaines Accounting, which is located next door to Duffy Investigations. "Jason told me he was following an important new lead in the case and would be out of town for a couple of days."

"California Confidential field reporter Jennifer Wilde here. Did he say what that new lead might be?"

"He told me the new development could change everything," Heather said.
"Did he say when the case might be broken?" Jennifer asked.

"No. But I'm guessing it will be long before tax season. And by the way, Jennifer, if any California Confidential viewer tells me they saw me on your show, I'll pay their electronic income tax filing fee when I prepare their tax return."

When the camera returned to Jennifer Wilde she was frantically waiving her hand in front of her throat, giving the "cut" sign.

"Thanks Heather, it's so kind of you to think of our viewers while your neighbor is in so much peril."

I couldn't wait for the 10 O'clock News. I called Shamansky at his office and reached a coworker. "Call back on Monday, he isn't here."

"This is Jason Duffy. I think he'll want to talk with me tonight," I said.

"You got that right. Hold on and I'll patch you through," he said.

"Duffy, I heard Forest Lawn Cemetery is having a going out of existence sale. You might want to give them a call," Shamansky said.

"You're a riot Shamansky. Were you in on the bust?" I asked.

"No, but I did get a sit down with the gunman about a half-hour ago. I think you need to send a thank you card to the Neighborhood Watch Program," he said.

"I'm in no mood for a comedy routine. Were you able to find out if the sniper was from Cerise or the real Russian Mafia," I asked.

"What do you mean, 'the real Mafia?' Are you telling me you don't think they're mobbed-up anymore?" he asked.

"I met with an American silent partner this afternoon. He strikes me as credible and he's sure Koflanovich lives his life in fear of the Russian mob. He said Koflanovich came after me because he was convinced I was with the American Mafia and I was helping the Russians. Apparently, he knows better now," I said.

"Well, you have the real Russian Mafia coming after you now," he said.

I decided it might not be the best time to tell him about my gig at the Dali Lama. "Does Dracovich have a sheet?"

"It looks like he's been an enforcer for the mob for at least five years. In that time he's had six arrests but no convictions. Eight eye witnesses recanted their stories and two turned up missing - permanently," he said.

"So what am I supposed to do to keep out of harm's way?" I asked.

"From what I understand it's already been taken care of," he replied and paused to catch my response.

"What do you mean? What's taken care of?" I asked.

"Rumor has it that the Russian Mafia met the Irish Mafia about two hours after Dracovich got pulled out of your neighbor's tree," he said.

"My father?" I asked incredulous.

Shamansky replied, "As I understand it, about twenty sworn and retired personnel made a show of force at a known Russian Mafia bar. It was communicated in no uncertain terms that you are the son of an SDPD cop, and if any harm comes to you that every known or suspected Russian Mafioso will be hounded until they are all either in jail or deported, that is, if they survive the arrest. In the meantime, they'll be the most highly publicized group of criminals in the history of California."

"Do you think it will work?" I asked.

"The reason they came after you in the first place, according to Dracovich, is because they felt you were responsible for the publicity. They thrive in the shadows. With the Smiling Sons of St. Patrick threatening to turn into a proctology squad, the Ruskies are sure to back off. You're not worth it to them. You should keep your head down for a few days until word gets out that the contract has been pulled, but I'm sure the show of force will do the trick," he said.

"What's a proctology squad?" I asked.

Shamansky replied, "That's a group of cops that will get so far up your ass you won't need a rectal exam for the rest of your life."

"Thanks, Shamansky. I'll keep in touch," I said and hung up.

When I returned to the living room everyone was in a very somber mood. I gave them the highlights of my conversation with Shamansky. When I got to the part about the Smiling Son's of St. Patrick, Kelly beamed. When I finished she jumped to her feet, threw her arms around me and exclaimed, "Everything's going to be alright!"

The band quietly mulled the events of the last half-hour, but Kelly got it immediately. "Do you guys think we should still do the gig?" Derek asked.

"It's up to you," I said.

"I want to play," Michael stated without question.

"My life has been way too safe lately," Kyle said.

Jeannine asked, "Do you think there's a chance the men with the ski masks could show up at the club?"

Kelly couldn't keep still anymore. "You can't let an opportunity like this pass you by. You're getting a chance to do something you love at your favorite place to play in front of a group of people who probably loved you and miss you. Forget Doberman's Stub, I can't wait to hear you guys in front of a live audience. If it's anything like what I heard last night, Doberman's Stub won't want to follow you. What do you think Jeannine?"

"Kelly's right. It would be a shame if you cancelled," she said.

"Derek?" I asked.

"Isn't the drummer supposed to be the wild and crazy one? I can't be responsible for ruining that reputation by doing something sensible and sane," he said. "I'm in."

"OK, we're all agreed," Michael said. "Now let's go practice for a couple of hours so we can live up the our fans expectations."

Over the next three hours we finalized our play list and sets. About two hours into the session, Jeannine walked into our practice room wearing a surprisingly low cut nightgown she had borrowed from Aunt Esther. I'm not sure if she was trying to replicate the momentum Kelly generated last night when she inspired us with her baby dolls, but it had a very different effect on the boys. For starters, Jeannine had been fidgety since the *California Confidential* bombshell was dropped. Obsessive Compulsive Disorder can get magnified when you mix in a large dose of anxiety. Tonight Jeannine became obsessed with the nightgown's tight fitting elastic sash that ran under the bust line. Unconscious of the attention she was getting from the band, Jeannine adjusted and readjusted her breasts above the elastic sash at least twenty times.

Michael managed to continue to play without missing a beat, though he had a smile frozen across his face. Kyle and Derek kept playing too fast and too loud. The session was getting counterproductive. Just as I was about to pull the plug and call it a night, Jeannine's left breast managed to escape the confines of the flimsy bodice. Derek hit one of his symbols so hard the stand fell over and the side of the symbol landed squarely on Kyle's toe. "Aaaaayyyyyeeee," he screamed.

I said, "I think we're as ready as we can possibly be in one week. I don't want us to peak too early, so let's call it a night."

"I peaked," said Kyle. "Did you peak, Derek?"

He replied, "I peaked, but I don't think I'm quite ready to get up from behind my drums yet."

While the boys were carrying on, Jeannine quietly turned to Kelly and said, "That was a close one. My boob popped out right after the symbol fell on Kyle's toe. If they weren't so distracted I think they would have seen me."

"You might want to change into what you wore last night. Esther's nightgown is pretty but it looks a little uncomfortable," Kelly said.

"Good idea," she said.

Chapter 15

THE first thing Kelly asked me when I woke up was, "Did you call your parents and tell them you're alright?"

"No 'good morning'? No 'did you have a nice sleep?'" I asked.

"I'll bet your mother didn't have a nice sleep. Here's your cell phone. Why don't you give her a call now," she stated.

"You're right. Can I use the bathroom and get a glass of orange juice first?" I asked.

"No," she replied. "Do it now before they go out for the morning."

I tried. Twelve rings later I hung up. "They must have already gone out. What time is it anyway?"

"It's just after nine. Why didn't you leave a voice-mail message?" she asked.

"Because I have the only parents in America who don't have voice-mail or an answering machine," I replied.

"I guess we know what they'll be getting for Christmas," she said.

"I already tried. It went back to the store the next day," I said.

"I'm going back downstairs to see if Esther needs help with breakfast," she said and disappeared.

Luckily I stored Glenda MacPhearson's home number in my cell phone. "Glenda, it's Jason. Top 'o the mornin' to ya."

"Don't go givin' me none of that Irish bullshit. It's Saturday morning and if you're calling, you want something," she said.

"You didn't hear about my brush with death yesterday?" I asked.

"What happened? Did some cheating husband try to stuff your Nikon where the sun don't shine?" she asked with a laugh.

"You mean you haven't watched *California Confidential* the last two nights?" I asked.

"Why? Were you abducted by aliens?" she asked.

"You know what I'm working on. Thursday's show notified the world that I'm after the Russian Mafia, and Friday they showed a Russian hit man being pulled out of a tree across the street from my house," I said.

"No shit!" she exclaimed. "What do the Russians have to do with Joseph Martin?" she asked.

"I'm in Alpine and about to head into the city. I was hoping I could stop by your place on the way in to find out what you've learned. Would that be OK?" I asked.

"You're not being followed, are you?" she asked.

"Actually, I'm being followed by my girlfriend. Is it alright if I bring her along?" I asked.

"Sure," she said. "But we're going to be talking about stuff I can't be quoted on. I'd hate to see this come back on me."

"I understand. You can just nod at her if you want me to ask her to wait in the car. I'm sure she'll be OK with that," I said.

"I need to get out of here by 11:30," she said.

"We'll be on our way in a few minutes," I said and hung up. When we arrived at her house in Julian, I introduced her to Kelly and she called her fiancée, Tyrone, in from the backyard where he was mowing the lawn. She introduced us and told him he could go back out and finish the lawn, then take a quick shower because they were leaving by 11:30.

"Are you still playing at the Dali Lama tonight?" she asked.

"Provided I'm not sleeping with the fishes," I replied.

"Good. Then Kelly can catch me up on all this tabloid TV stuff while you're on the stage. Let's get down to the information you wanted, I really am on a tight schedule," Glenda said.

"Fine with me. I told Kelly that some of this stuff is very sensitive.

If you'd like her to go into another room, or the car, or rake the lawn for Tyrone, I'm sure she'd be fine with that," I said and got elbowed in the ribs.

"There's an eleven o'clock news show about to come on. Maybe Kelly can check it out and make sure your office hasn't been firebombed," she said.

"I'll be glad to," Kelly said. Glenda brought her into the living room, turned on the TV and asked if she wanted coffee, which she didn't.

When Glenda returned to the kitchen she was carrying a file folder with a piece of paper taped over the file name. "The deceased, Captain Carson, had friends in high places calling for Martin's head after the explosion. No matter how you look at it, he definitely could have prevented this guy's death."

"Is there more than one source?" I asked.

"I'm not going to tell you where I got this information, but I will tell you I drew this from four separate sources. One reads like a vendetta written by the dead officer's buddy. But the others sound objective and correct," she said.

"From what you read, Glenda, what do you think happened in Iraq?" I asked.

"Martin and Carson didn't get along at all. Martin thought Carson was cowardly and would delegate anything remotely dangerous to his subordinates, including freshly trained recruits. On the morning of the incident, Sergeant Martin told his coworkers that Carson was required to sign off on a new recruit's first assignment disarming ordnance. He was quoted by two sources as telling them the recruit would probably forget about a grounding wire and that when Carson made the same mistake and tried moving it, be sure to stand clear."

"Did they suspect that Martin tampered with the ordnance?" I asked.

"The captain's friend suggested that, but there was no evidence to back it up," she said. "When Carson arrived for the inspection he told Martin to do it for him and, in front of the whole squad, Martin asked if he was incompetent or just plain chicken shit. They argued for a few minutes, then Carson went off to do the inspection while Martin got everybody out of harms way. Two minutes later the ordnance detonated and Carson was killed instantly."

"What was the finding of the inquiry board?" I asked.

"They found that Martin couldn't be held directly accountable for Carson's death, but that it was definitely a preventable loss and that Martin was no longer welcome in the command. They sent him to the US to work with the Corps of Engineers while they were deciding what to do with him. Then they gave him an honorable discharge," Glenda said.

"But he orchestrated and coordinated everything that led to Carson's death. He didn't just idly step back and watch, he pushed the guy into a situation that got him killed," I said angrily.

"The brass felt that no matter what Martin did, Carson ultimately died of his own incompetence. He shouldn't have passed the buck so often that he lost his skills. The general feeling was that the Army got rid of two bad seeds and good riddance," she said.

"Can I use any of this to make a case for Martin's character and capabilities?" I asked.

"Not through me you can't," she said pointedly. "If it got out that I gave you this information, not only wouldn't I make captain, I wouldn't make honorable discharge."

"What do you think I can do with it?" I asked.

"If you have a cop friend, see if you can get him to get a court order," she replied. "A friendly judge might grant it, based on the fact that he was an ordnance tech."

"Thanks Glenda. Are you two going to make it tonight?" I asked as we walked to the living room.

"I think so," she said to me. Then to Kelly she asked, "Any breaking news to report?"

"Just a huge lawn and garden sale at Home Depot," she said.

"Tyrone! Are you ready?" Glenda yelled up the stairs. Then to us she said, "That's where we're going. We're taking a landscaping class at noon, then burning the plastic to take advantage of the sale afterwards."

"Thanks Glenda, we'll see you tonight," I said as we made our way out the door.

At Kelly's request we pointed the Acura towards my parent's house. "We can stop by to say I'm OK, then hit Little Italy for lunch so I can carb up for tonight," I said.

"Just make sure you don't carb out over your belt," she said. We continued to listen exclusively to the Doberman's Stub demo CD. She kept the conversation to a minimum so I could absorb as much as possible before tonight's performance.

When we arrived at my parent's house, my mother met us as we walked through the door, threw her arms around me and exclaimed, "Thank God you're alright! Why didn't you call? I've been worried sick!"

"I did call, but there was no answer. If you two had kept the answering machine I gave you…" I said.

"Don't start," she said, then jogged toward the backyard and yelled, "Jim, Jim, Jason's here with Kelly."

A minute later Dad walked into the living room and said, "That's quite a fix you've gotten yourself into, son."

I replied, "I'm sure you had a few bad guys come after you in your day."

"A few bad guys, yes. A whole crime wave, no," he said.

"I heard you threatened to pit the Russian Mafia against the Irish Mafia," I said with a smile.

"None of my friends like that name. Who told you that?" he asked.

"Your old buddy Shamansky gave me the highlights. Thanks Dad. It sounds like you made quite an impression," I said.

"You aren't out of the woods yet. In fact, you shouldn't even be out and about for a few days," he said.

"We've been up in Alpine the last couple of nights," I said.

"Good. Continue to lay low," he said.

Kelly chimed in, "Does that mean we shouldn't go to Little Italy for lunch?"

"You'll have lunch with us," Mom ordered. "I'll get it started right now."

"Can I help?" Kelly asked.

"Come with me dear," Mom replied and took her by the hand. "I can't imagine what you've been through," she added as they walked into the kitchen.

"That's quite a catch you got there son," Dad said as he smiled and nodded his approval of Kelly.

"If you knew where to find the local Russian Mafia Don the SDPD must have somebody monitoring their activities," I stated.

"We do, and I'm damned glad I never got stuck with that assignment," he said. "It's like working Chinatown. They keep pretty much to their own community and that community keeps Omerta better than the Italians. Nobody talks. No snitches, no outraged citizens, no jilted lovers looking to get even. The victims are too scared to serve as witnesses, and as a result, charges never stick. We keep an eye on them, but it's strictly minimal monitoring."

"Do you think your visit had the desired effect?" I asked.

"The last thing they want is to have their way of life disrupted. They put a contract out on you because you picked up the rock they live under. But once they came to understand that killing you would be a lot more trouble than it's worth, they backed off," he said.

"Then why did you tell me to continue to lay low?" I asked.

"It's an old ways, new ways issue. The young guys all carry cell phones and are hooked up to the Internet. Ten minutes after the contract was lifted those guys knew about it. On the other hand, you have the old school guys who get the word on the contract and immediately go underground to put their plans into action. You might have a gunman staking out your house, or office, or Kelly's place, who will stay in his car from one day to the next. Give one of these guys a gallon of vodka, a box of beef jerky and a pee jug and he might be good for a week," Dad said.

Kelly walked into the living room and announced, "Lunch is on the kitchen table. Come and get it." Dad looked at Kelly then back at me and gave me a big smile and a thumbs-up gesture. It's hard to believe this guy once worked undercover.

Lunch was fun and light. Kelly had the good sense not to mention the gig tonight, and Mom had the good sense not to mention my childhood. Dad seemed to be making a conscious effort to be on his best behavior. When we finished, Kelly volunteered to help Mom with the dishes. Dad said he had something for me and led me back into the living room. He told me to have a seat on the couch, then went into a closet and came out with what appeared to be a picture album that he handed to me.

Just as I thought we were about to go down memory lane, I opened the floral-covered binder and saw four mug shots complete with name and last known address. "I threw it together this morning. These are suspected Russian Mafioso's living in San Diego County who are forty years and older. I suggest you let Kelly drive, and you study these faces. Are you planning on going by your place?" he asked.

"Yeah. I need to get some clothes and a few other things," I said.

"Then swap cars with me and put on a pair of sun glasses. When you get to your house, drive by at least four times before you park. Look for people sitting in cars, enclosed vans, vehicles with tinted windows and vehicles with puddles under them," he said.

"Why the puddles?" I asked.

"It's hot outside. Somebody on a stakeout will run the air conditioner every half-hour or so. When they shut it down, it will make a puddle," he said.

We swapped keys and I agreed to return for lunch on Wednesday to swap back. Dad said, "Kelly, do you think you'd feel comfortable driving a Buick Rivera?"

"Sure," she replied, "What's wrong?"

"Nothing, Jason just needs to do a little homework on the bad guys now that he's back in the city," Dad said.

"Is there anything you need to show me about driving it?" Kelly asked.

"As a matter of fact, why don't you come with me?" Kelly and Dad went to the garage while I said goodbye to Mom. A half-hour later I had Kelly do a thorough drive-through of my block before parking. I live in a three-bedroom house in a quiet neighborhood, perched on a hill jutting out over a canyon. There is only one road in and out of this little development comprised of eight square blocks. At the entrance is a convenience store that is heavily patronized by SDPD. We got into my house without incident. The only puddle I noticed was at the base of the carrotwood tree in front of my house, and undoubtedly created by my neighbor's schnauzer, Sigfried.

I had the gut feeling that everything was OK as I opened the front door. But, since Dad put the fear of God into Kelly, I thought it would be best to put on a TV detective demonstration for her benefit. "Stay here," I said as I drew my gun. While using a two-handed grip, I executed a series of spin moves, deep knee bends and rolls that I must admit, I had practiced a few dozen times during my first year as a PI. In my practice scenarios I always imagined that my attractive female client would be very sexually aroused after seeing me in action. "All clear," I called to Kelly.

As she walked into the living room she looked me square in the eye and asked, "Who's your choreographer, Mike Hammer?"

"Would you have preferred I call out 'Anybody home,' and leave it at that?" I asked with my disappointment apparent.

"I'm sorry, Jason. That was spectacular," she said enthusiastically, and I brightened. "I just hope you had the safety on."

"Next time you're in a damsel in distress situation I'm referring you to Delbert Henson," I said, and she laughed.

Over the next half-hour we packed clothes for a couple of days, put my guitar and accessories in Dad's car and had just enough time for that brief moment of passion Kelly knew I was seeking. Afterwards she said, "Sex and rock & roll. Whoever sang, 'Two Out of Three Ain't Bad,' sure knew what he was talking about."

I replied, "It was Meatloaf and if you sit next to either Ian Davis or Jack Pascal this afternoon you'll probably catch a contact high that will take you to three out of three."

"If that roadie you and Glenda talked about is there, I'm pretty sure you're the only one I'll be sitting near," she said.

"They call him GI Jo-Jo and his girlfriend, Delitah, will probably drop by if the strip club she works at gives her the day off," I said.

"Are you suggesting I do the *girl talk* thing with her?" Kelly asked.

"I don't want you getting into any dangerous situations. But if GI Jo-Jo is working the mixing board while we're practicing, and Delitah's sitting by herself, I don't see any harm in a little friendly chat," I said.

"What do you want me to find out?" she asked.

"GI Jo-Jo had been pretty uncooperative, so I had to tell him more than I'd like to. My big concern is that he'll disappear. I think if he made that decision he'd try to get Delitah to go with him. If you could get her talking about the future of the band now that Terry's gone she might open up about their plans," I said.

"I'll see what I can do," Kelly said doubtfully.

"All you need is a good opening line. Why don't you tell her you're dating the new singer and start complaining about musicians? See if you can get the conversation to come around to her current boyfriend," I said.

"Complain about you? I could do that. How long is this practice session supposed to last?" she said with a mirthful grin.

As arranged, at 2:15 PM I called Bernie from the stage door entrance of the Dali Lama, and two minutes later we were in. After exchanging pleasantries Bernie asked, "Who's going to operate the karaoke machine?"

"I think Derek can handle it," I said.

"I have a million things to do before the show. Will he be here soon? I'm anxious to show him how to work the software," Bernie said.

"I'm not expecting him until 7:00 PM. Is that going to be a problem?" I asked.

"I guess not, as long as he knows the songs he should be OK," Bernie said.

"He hasn't heard the songs yet," I said.

"Then he's going to have a problem. Most karaoke songs are on CDG's which will automatically pause for instrumentals and changes in tempo. This home-made version that I put together is nowhere near that sophisticated. You really need somebody who knows the songs," he said.

"I know the songs," Kelly volunteered. "That's all we've listened to in the car. I've heard each of the songs at least eight times."

"Yeah, but you're not a musician," I said.

"I'm a multi-subject elementary school teacher. Who do you think serves as the music teacher?" she asked.

"You're hired!" Bernie interjected. Before I could say a thing we heard a pounding at the stage door and knew that GI Jo-Jo had arrived on schedule. Bernie let him in. He was trailed by another roadie and Delitah, who wore a sleeveless, Harley-Davidson jeans-jacket over an emerald green, sequined, sleeveless mini-dress. When we made eye contact she gave me a discrete finger wave.

"Ouch!" I quietly exclaimed as I felt my butt being pinched. Kelly doesn't miss a thing. I wouldn't want to be the class clown in her second grade classroom.

Fortunately, Bernie set up the karaoke equipment at a backstage table, rather than at the PA station where Kelly would have been forced to sit with GI Jo-Jo. She and Bernie spent fifteen minutes together while I helped GI Jo-Jo and his toady get set up.

About halfway through this process Jack arrived with a bass case in each hand. He made his way over to me and said, "Thanks for making this happen. The more things we can do that seem normal the less lost we'll feel without Terry."

"We'll see how grateful you are after I try singing and playing those new songs," I said.

"I heard you at my house a few days ago and I have every confidence you'll do a fine job," he said with a soothing reassurance. I wondered if he was stoned or just permanently mellow.

A few minutes later Nigel rolled in with the dark-haired beauty who flashed me on my first visit to the Choate mansion. He was decidedly tense as he walked up to Jack and asked, "Has anyone seen Ian today?"

From the back of an amplifier we heard Jo-Jo yell, "I got him." He then stood up, walked to the front of the stage, jumped down to the floor where we were standing and said, "He's sleeping in the back of the equipment truck outside. Ian was a little more restrained than usual last night. He'll be fine. I'll get him up whenever you need him."

"Excellent! Why don't you get him now. Pour a large coffee into him and let me know when he's functional," Nigel said. He then turned to me and asked, "Any chance the bar will have coffee yet?"

"I'll check with Bernie," I said and started toward the office. Kelly intercepted me and volunteered to handle it. Five minutes later I saw she and Delitah behind the bar measuring scoops into a filter. When she noticed me watching her with a smile on my face her expression soured and she flipped me the bird. Delitah looked interested, so I returned the gesture, letting her know she was number one in my heart.

I spent the next five minutes getting my guitar tuned to Nigel's. As we were finishing, GI Jo-Jo walked in with his arm around Ian for support. If this is better than usual I didn't give Doberman's Stub much of a chance for survival. Jo-Jo put Ian on a barstool and Delitah handed him a cup of black coffee, which he held to Ian's lips. From across the room we could hear Ian yell, "Rum! It doesn't have any bloody rum!"

After he calmed down I saw Kelly shake hands with GI Jo-Jo. A couple of minutes later Jo-Jo helped Ian to the men's room. When Ian emerged he looked decidedly more animated. Unassisted, he made his way to the bar, picked up his coffee cup and walked to the stage where he sat on his drummer's stool. He then picked up his sticks, pounded twice on his drums and screamed, "Let's rock & roll!"

I could see why Terry assumed GI Jo-Jo was scoring drugs for Ian. There's nothing he could swallow or snort that would work that fast. My best guess is that he shot up crystal meth. I turned to Nigel, who was standing next to me on stage and said, "That Starbucks is amazing stuff."

Nigel ignored me and called out the name of the first song. Ian banged his sticks together four times and we were off. Kelly did a fantastic job of keeping pace with the karaoke machine. I had two or three minor errors, but, in general, the session went well.

When we finished, Nigel walked over to me and said, "Brilliant! You've far exceeded our wildest expectations."

Jack added, "We knew you could play, but singing is clearly your strong suit."

"Your voice is different from Terry's, but we weren't looking for a tribute band imitation. I don't think the public would accept that. Your interpretation of the vocals rang true for me," Nigel said.

Ian jumped from his riser and said, "I thought you'd be the bloody shanks, but you can play with me any day." Sweat was profusely rolling down his face.

I worked out a few logistics with Nigel then said goodbye to the band. Delitah exited with GI Jo-Jo, so I walked over to Kelly, who was getting the karaoke equipment reset for the performance. "Great job on the monitor. You have a natural feel for music," I said.

"Screw you, asshole," she said. "You're always telling me what you think I want to hear."

"Excuse me," I said with an incredulous tone.

Kelly looked up from the equipment, then glanced around the area. "Oh, has Delitah gone?" she asked.

"What's it to you, bimbo?" I asked.

"You're the one who asked me to act angry with you. And, do you know what? It worked," she said.

"How about if I take you to dinner and you tell me all about it?" I asked.

"You're on," she said

We found a nice little Chinese place about ten blocks from the club. We were the only Caucasians in the restaurant, which was fine with me after studying Dad's mug-shot book earlier in the day.

Once we placed our orders I asked, "What were you able to learn from Delitah?"

Kelly replied, "What a piece of work. She thinks she's channeling Terry, who, by the way, is also pissed off at you for trying to fill his shoes."

"Do you think she was on anything?" I asked.

"I got the feeling she is always like that," she said.

"Did you get her to talk about their plans?" I asked.

"She's not sure if she's going to stay with GI Jo-Jo. She said he's dull and sometimes just plain mean. She enjoys being around the band because she likes their music, but she's not sure if she's going to like it as much now that Terry's gone," Kelly said. "I asked if Delitah was going on tour with the band, and she said it would depend on who they found to replace Terry and what kind of vibe he gave her. I got the impression she'd stay on if there was a chance she could hook up with his replacement, but won't be with GI Jo-Jo much longer."

"Did she give any indication if Jo-Jo is planning on taking off?" I asked.

"No. She didn't seem to care either way. From our conversation it was hard to believe they're a couple," she said.

"Did she say anything else I might want to know?" I asked.

"She said you have a nice butt," Kelly said and laughed.

When we returned to the Dali Lama, Michael Marinangeli was wheeling his amp through the stage door on a red dolly. We exchanged greetings and I could tell he was very excited about doing this gig. As the last of the working musicians, he had more to gain if the Union-Tribune's reviewer mentioned him in his article. "How did the afternoon practice session go?" he asked.

"Not too bad for a first run-through," I said.

"What did you think, Kelly?" he asked.

"I think Terry would approve," she retorted and left it at that.

Michael said, "I didn't mention it before, but I've gotten to be a big Doberman's Stub fan since our band broke up. The last band I was in played at least three of their songs every gig."

"What did you think about their cross-over to more mainstream stuff on the second CD?" I asked.

"At first I thought it was just OK, but after I saw how much the women liked it, I learned seven of the songs from that CD. When you played us the demo at Aunt Esther's I got really excited. It sucks what happened to Terry. I know we've had our differences after the band broke up, but, if there's anything I can do to help, just let me know," he said, then slapped me on the shoulder and walked away.

Kelly said, "I'm starting to really like him. At first I thought he had an attitude problem, but after the last couple of days in Alpine, and now this, I'm thinking there's more to Michael than he likes to show."

"He used to be one of my best friends. Tsunami Rush was his idea. We all went to different high schools at the same time. Michael recruited us from area bands to form a local super-group. The band was his baby," I said.

"What happened? Why did you break up?" she asked.

"In spite of our efforts, I came to realize that none of us can write. We were a very popular cover band but, all we would ever be is a cover band," I said. "After nine years of covering other people's songs I felt it was time to move on. I was dissatisfied with my job as a mental health counselor, and I was bummed that we couldn't develop original material. When I told the band I was leaving, Derek told us he was just about to do the same thing."

From behind us we heard, "It's the undercover rock & roller." I turned to see Derek wearing a sleek, black, long-sleeve T-shirt with a metallic blue wave cresting across his chest. As he walked toward us he said, "How many of the old crowd do you think will show up tonight?"

"I have no idea," I replied.

Kyle snuck up behind us and used Derek's sticks to play a drum solo on his shoulders. "Ooowww!," Derek cried, "I hate when you do that."

"It's for good luck. Every time I did that to you we had a good show," Kyle said with a smile.

"Good luck for who? Every time you did it I got sore shoulders," responded Derek.

"It's starting to sound so familiar," I added. It was almost 8:00 PM, time for the club to open. The first set would start at 8:30 PM and last one hour. After a twenty-minute break, Doberman's Stub will play till 11:15 PM. Then, after another break, Tsunami Rush will play two more hours. It was time to go backstage and get dressed for the show.

As we were about to clear the stage area, Jasmine dropped by to say Bernie wanted to see us at his table. I introduced Jasmine to Kelly and we all walked to Bernie's table. Jasmine led us through a large cluster of cocktail tables to a two-foot riser that held a table for twenty. This was the best view of the bandstand in the house.

"What's up Bernie?" I asked when we had all assembled in front of his table.

He replied, "I have four guests coming. This table seats twenty. If you'd like your guests to join me, I'll be glad to play host."

"Thanks Bernie. We'd love to join you," I said.

"Why don't you sit next to me while the boys get dressed. Have you met Calvin and Justin?" he asked Kelly.

"Not yet," she said.

"Well you're in for a treat. Those guys could tell you stories about Jason all night," he said and winked at me.

"Maybe this isn't such a good idea," I said with a smile.

"Don't worry about a thing," Bernie said. "Has your rabbi ever let you down?"

I replied, "Never. Take good care of her, Bernie.

At 8:25 Kyle peaked out at the crowd and saw that most of the bar and almost half of the tables were full. This was an excellent sign considering the hour. Either that or we were starting to attract a geriatric audience.

At precisely 8:30 Bernie took the stage and said, "After a three year absence from the San Diego club scene, the Dali Lama Yo Mama is thrilled to bring you the reunion of," then in a loud, enthusiastic voice, "Tsunami Rush!"

We jogged onstage, and launched into a power metal set that immediately brought about twenty people to the dance floor. Calvin and Justin arrived shortly after we started and I saw Jasmine lead them to Bernie's table. By 9:00 all of the tables were occupied and the dance floor was rocking.

About fifteen minutes before the end of our first set I noticed Nigel standing in the wings checking us out. He watched for the remainder of the set and appeared to be getting into our music. When we finished I announced, "Thanks for coming out tonight. I see a lot of familiar faces and we're having a great time playing for you again." This got a rousing applause. "We're going to take a break. Be sure to stick around for the next set. We have some very special friends joining us that are going to blow you away."

As we exited Nigel said to me, "They love you guys. That was quite a performance for a group that hasn't played in three years."

Michael, Kyle and Derek headed for Bernie's table after being introduced to Nigel. "Ask Kelly to knock on the dressing room door in fifteen minutes," I said to Michael, then I slapped his hand.

"Was it good for you?" he asked.

"Better than foreplay," I replied and he laughed.

In the dressing room I tuned my guitar to Nigel's while Jack did some kind of Zen mantra. Ian looked like GI Jo-Jo had already gotten him tweaked. Both of his feet were tapping a mile a minute and he was licking his lips continually. "How are you doing with the new songs?" Nigel asked.

"Between the afternoon session and Bernie's karaoke monitor, I should be fine," I said. "It looks like we've got a decent size crowd."

"Perfect," Nigel replied. "Thanks again for setting it up. I'd like you to look at me in between songs. If I spread my hand in front of my strings like this," he said and performed the gesture, "I want you to give me a few seconds. I'll have a note pad on my amp and I'll jot a few notes if I see something we may want to change."

"Just give me a little head bob when you're ready to go," I said.

Ian chimed in, "I could go for a little head bob after the show." This seemed to rouse Jack from the Land of Om. Before he could speak there was a knock at the door. It was Kelly letting me know she was heading to the computer, and the monitor would have the first song ready to go.

Then Bernie knocked on the door and asked if the band was ready to be introduced. Three minutes later we were standing in the wings as Bernie walked to center stage and said, "May I have your attention." He waited about a minute for the crowd to settle down, then he said, "At the Dali Lama we get a chance to see a lot of bands on their way up, and sometimes we see a few on their way down. But it's a very rare pleasure when we get to see a band as it's hitting its peak of success. But, tonight we have a very special treat. You are going to be the first live audience to see and hear the new CD of such a band. Tsunami's Rush's Jason Duffy is going to be helping them out since they recently lost a band member. Please help me welcome Doberman's Stub!"

The crowd went crazy. When I walked out onto the stage I had a flashback of old footage of the Beatles being drowned out by screaming fans. But, instead of launching into a song that would ride the tide of their intensity, Nigel gave me the spread fingers and we all waited until they settled down. Then Nigel stepped up to his microphone and said, "Thank you for that warm reception. As Bernie said, we tragically lost our lead singer and guitarist, Terry Tucker, just a few weeks ago. We're trying to decide if we should press on without him and look for a replacement, or just call it the end of an era."

"No!" shouted the crowd. "Doberman rocks!"

"When Terry died we were just finishing a CD. It was our habit to play the new CD for a live club audience before releasing it, so that's why we're here tonight. We'd like to dedicate this performance to Terry Tucker," he said and gave the head bob. We opened with a cut that was expected to be one of the lead tracks and make an appearance on Billboard's charts.

The crowd cheered wildly as we finished our first song. Shortly after they quieted down for the second song, I heard a commotion toward the main entrance. I glanced over and saw Vlad Torhan lifting a cell phone-clutching fan off of his feet. I'm sure Vlad thought he was protecting Cerise from some kind of copyright infringement. The fan was probably just letting a friend hear that Doberman's Stub was performing at the local club.

Between glances at the karaoke monitor I saw Bernie's bouncer come up behind Torhan and get him in a bear hug. Vlad threw an elbow and broke free long enough to knock the bouncer unconscious with one mighty uppercut to the chin. The fan managed to crawl away. Since the band was still playing there was no shortage of cell phones in the air. He grabbed a tall, thin, surfer dude and crushed his cell phone while it was still in the dude's hand. We finished our song and waited for the cops to arrive, expecting a long delay.

Instead, I saw Jasmine, carrying a tray full of drinks, walk right up to Torhan. As she was squeezing past him she pulled a Taser out from under her serving tray and zapped him on the arm. Vlad the Impaler turned into a spazz briefly before collapsing to the floor. Jasmine held her Taser in the air and received a tremendous ovation.

I moved back to the microphone and said, "This next one's for our favorite server, Jasmine." This got another ovation. I then added, "Don't forget to tip her generously – or else." The abundance of cell phone wielding fans resulted in a steady stream of people pouring through the door. I looked at Bernie and saw a nervous smile on his face as Justin left the table and stationed his 250 pounds of rippling muscles at the front door.

We were into our fifth song when the cops arrived and led Torhan out in handcuffs. At that point the Dali Lama was probably just above the Fire Marshall limit, but it looked like the police were satisfied that Justin had things under control. I'm sure he used his wit and charm to ease any of their concerns.

On three occasions Nigel gave me the spread fingers and made notes. Once it took him about two minutes, which seems like an eternity when almost everyone in the crowd was giving their undivided attention. At the end of the set Nigel asked the audience, "What do you think? Should Doberman's Stub try to carry on without Terry Tucker?"

The audience response would have broken a decibel meter. Nigel then added, "I'd like to give a special thanks to Tsunami Rush's Jason Duffy for filling in on vocals and rhythm guitar. If you enjoyed Jason, stick around. Tsunami Rush will be back after a little break. Goodnight San Diego."

The crowd went crazy and did not let up. The chant of "More, more, more!!!" grew louder and louder. In the dressing room Jack said, "We better give them one more or they might come in here after us."

Nigel suggested a fan favorite from the second CD, I knew the words but didn't know the guitar part. "Why don't I show you how to play it."

I replied, "I have a better idea. Our lead guitarist knows that whole CD. Let's call him to the stage and let him do it."

"Brilliant!" exclaimed Nigel, "let's go."

When we walked back onstage the crowd erupted. After about 30 seconds I held up my hand and they quieted down. "Will Michael Marinangeli come to the stage?" I looked at Michael, who was still seated at Bernie's table. He put his hand on his chest and gave me a *Who me?* look. I nodded and he made his way to the stage. I pointed for him to talk to Nigel while I explained to the crowd that we only knew one more song and needed the help of another Tsunami Rush band member to do that. Hopefully this prepped them for the fact that it would be the only encore.

GI Jo-Jo moved Michael's amp back into place and two minutes later we were delighting the crowd with the only known Doberman tune of the evening. When we finished Nigel confirmed what I had told the crowd earlier and they seemed to accept that it was the end of the Doberman set.

I made my way to Bernie's table, which was no easy task at a reunion show, and sat next to Kelly. Calvin left his seat next to Bernie and sat down next to me. "You rocked, brother," he said. "Nigel might be asking for a bio on you after that performance."

"Stop yanking my chain. What do you think of the new material?" I asked.

"I think it's going to be even bigger than the second CD. They sounded surprisingly tight, especially since they were playing with you for the first time," Calvin said.

"What about Ian?" I asked. "Between reading the monitor and watching the Russian get stunned, I didn't get much of a chance to focus in on his performance."

"He seemed OK. Personally, I think he looked a little rough around the edges, but professionally he was on his game tonight," he said.

"Any word on possible replacements for Terry?" I asked.

"I heard a couple of rumors, but it certainly seems Nigel is very actively pursuing two of the top managers in the business. I'm liking

Doberman's chances of surviving a whole lot more today than when we talked last weekend," he said.

Jasmine walked over to our table and I gave her a wave. She asked, "Hey rock star can I get you a drink?" She then put her hand on Kelly's arm, smiled at her and said, "Don't let him get a big head."

"I don't need a drink, but I can use little information," I said.

"He's serious about this detective gig," she said to Kelly; then to me she added, "What can I do for you?"

"Have you had any customers with Russian accents tonight?" I asked.

"As a matter of fact, I have a table of four drinking triple Stoly's," she said. "They have a different pronunciation for Stolichnaya. One of them insisted I learn the correct way to say it. He was serious," she said.

"Where are they?" I asked, and Jasmine pointed them out. "Thanks Jasmine, you've been a big help."

I then nudged Calvin, who was listening to Bernie talk to a group of three friends. Calvin had brought his camera along to record my moment in the spotlight. "Calvin, can you take a few pictures for me?"

"I've got plenty of you already, but sure, why not?" he said.

"Not of me. There are four men sitting right over there," I said and pointed once I was sure they weren't looking in my direction. "Can you get some close-ups from here?"

"I can do better than that. I'll just walk over and tell them I'm with Rolling Stone doing a piece on the California club scene," he said and started to stand up.

I put my hand on his shoulder and pushed him back down, "I think these guys are in the Russian Mafia. If you walk over there and take their picture they may shoot you on the spot," I said.

Calvin looked at his camera and said, "I hear this model has a really good close-up lens. I'll bet we can get some great shots from right here."

Calvin looked a little tipsy, so I asked, "Mind if I give it a try?"

"Be my guest," he replied and slid the camera in front of me. As

I adjusted the lens for a close-up I recognized one of the men from Dad's mug book.

I turned to Kelly and said, "I don't want to alarm you but one of the Russian Mafia guys from Dad's book is at a table with three friends. I'd like you to keep everybody together after the show and we'll do a designated driver caravan out of here."

"Where are they?" she asked.

I pointed them out and told her to be discreet. We didn't want them seeing anyone point at them and we didn't want one of our more inebriated group members getting brave. I had every confidence Kelly could handle the assignment. She said, "Don't worry. With all of my experience handling drunks and seven-year-olds I'll have no trouble with this group."

The final Tsunami set rocked the house. The crowd was still very excited, I was pumped and Michael was floating about three feet above the stage. As expected, the crowd peaked during the Doberman set. We managed to maintain a near full house, although Justin was able to return to Bernie's table about half way through the set. By that point the Union-Tribune reporter, who had been sitting next to Bernie, had departed and Calvin took his place. I would love to have a recording of that conversation.

I had a hard time keeping my eyes off of the Russian's table. At first glance they appeared drunk, but minding their own business. The more I watched the more it seemed they had their eyes on a couple three tables to their left. The man looked familiar, but I couldn't place him. I tried to recall as many of Cory's photos as possible, but I came up empty. Just before our last song it hit me. He was a front door guard at Ivana Chofsky's birthday party. He was probably one of the guys who took a shot at me.

The Russian Mafiosos are probably following anybody and everybody who leaves Cerise Records in hopes that it leads them to Ivan Chofsky. If that's the case then I may not be in imminent danger, but since both of these groups sent gunmen after me recently, I wasn't intending to take any chances.

When we finished our last set I thanked the crowd and called the band together, "We have Cerise Records and the Russian Mafia in the house. Let's stay together and get out of here as quickly as possible."

I had hoped to have a candid conversation with GI Jo-Jo as he packed up the equipment, but, under the circumstances, opted to just let him know to leave our stuff on the stage for pick-up tomorrow.

We said goodbye to Bernie and arranged to swing by in the late afternoon tomorrow. We left a few minutes before closing. The door guard and his date were still at their table, and the Mafia members stayed put as we made our exit.

Chapter 16

I GAVE Kelly a kiss goodbye at 6:15 AM and headed for my office. I met briefly with Uri's contact, Igor Shmalko, and by 7:10 we were on a conference call with Odessa Police Lieutenant Victor Sanchenko. Igor had a brief exchange with the lieutenant, then said to me, "Go ahead with your questions."

"I'm a detective in San Diego, California. Recently, a man was murdered who was under contract to Ivan Chofsky. I began investigating Chofsky and, since then, have been shot at, had subordinates tied up and beaten, and my office was burglarized by his cousin's men. It appears that he's connected to the Russian Mafia. Do you think this is possible?"

Igor translated his response, "No. Ivan Chofsky could never join the Mafia?"

"Why not?" I asked.

"Chofsky has a contract on his head. I know from informants that the contract is still in force," he said.

"Chofsky now owns a record company. The murdered man was a star performer who was about to leave Chofsky's company for another. So far, Chofsky has refused to cooperate with the police and is using strong-arm tactics. Why would he do this?" I asked.

"Chofsky doesn't trust the police anymore. But, he will never trust the Mafia. I tell you that with absolute certainty," he said.

"I read the Tass articles leading up to the recovery of Ivana, but there were no accounts of how she was returned. Can you fill me in?" I asked.

Lt. Sanchenko paused, "As one detective to another I will tell you if Mr. Shmalko agrees to keep this information completely confidential." Igor agreed. "Chofsky cooperated with me and consented to arrange an exchange of the money for his daughter. We set up an ambush, using 25 officers. It turned into a massacre. Twelve police officers were killed and another six were wounded. Eighteen Mafia men were killed and twelve were wounded. It is not the kind of news that gets reported."

"Why not?" I asked.

"There are still people who feel we were better off under the USSR. Bad news like this makes it look like we aren't able to maintain order," he said.

"How did the Mafia know you were waiting for them?" I asked.

"They had an informant at police headquarters," he said.

"Is it possible that Chofsky might have been working with both sides to give his daughter the best chance for survival?" I asked.

"None at all. I made it very clear to him that they had no choice but to kill his daughter. As long as she was alive she could testify against her captors. When they mailed her finger to him he knew we were right," Sanchenko said.

"Then why would he now resort to Mafia tactics himself?" I asked.

"I assume he fears the Mafia will catch up to him. He probably surrounds himself with tough men who will stand up to them. We Russians are suspicious by nature. Anyone born after the Russian Revolution into the USSR lived with the prospect of a neighbor or even an occasional family member turning him in for minor crimes against the state. I would not be at all surprised if Ivan suspects you of being part of the Mafia," he said.

"Last week a television station reported that they thought Ivan was connected with the Russian Mafia. They showed his picture and told everyone he owns Cerise Records. Do you think the Mafia will be coming after him soon?" I asked.

"If they mentioned the Russian Mafia and showed his picture, I'm sure assassins are on their way if they aren't already there," he said.

"Last night I photographed four men who I think are Russian Mafia. One is definitely living in San Diego, but I'm not sure about the others. Can I email you their pictures to see if you can identify any of them," I asked. Sanchenko agreed and gave me his email address. I attached the clearest of the pictures.

"Lt. Sanchenko, while we wait for the picture to reach you, can you tell me anything about how organized the Russian Mafia is in the United States?" I asked.

"The Russian Mafia is located throughout the world. Wherever there is money to be made you will find them. The United States has been a major target since your economy is so affluent," he said.

"Do they have their own local Mafia dons?" I asked. Igor had a problem interpreting dons, but they finally figured it out.

"Each cell has considerable autonomy, but each is beholding to Mother Russia. If a cell fails to pay its share to the home country, men like the ones you described from last night, pay a visit and collect in blood," he said with an ominous tone. As I was formulating my next question he said, "Your email just arrived."

"Do you recognize any of the men?" I asked.

He replied, "The man in the middle, with the striped shirt, is Boris Schmelnikov. He is a professional killer based here in the Ukraine. The man on his left is Dimitri Nazaroff. He finds people who don't want to be found."

"Thank you very much for your time," I said.

"You can thank me by putting a bullet in Schmelnikov and Nazaroff," he replied and hung up. I thanked Igor and impressed on him the need for confidentiality.

Chapter 17

MONDAY morning I went straight for the Entertainment section of the paper and was pleased to see the review of the Doberman's Stub show made front page and included a color photo. Of course, it was shot from Nigel's side of the stage, but I was clearly visible in the background.

In general, the reviews were favorable. I was described as "a journeyman local musician who did a commendable job subbing for the inimitable Terry Tucker." The reviewer ended his article by describing the show as being "like seeing a terrific warm-up band. It leaves you anxiously awaiting the headline act, which will come with the release of the new CD and Terry Tucker giving his farewell performance."

I picked Jeannine up at 8:45 AM and immediately became suspicious. She was smiling more than a lotto winner, and I suspected hanky panky. "I hope you behaved yourself after the show," I said.

"I think maybe I've been behaving myself for way too long," she said. "I had a great time since we went to Alpine."

"Derek has a new girlfriend every month. I don't want you getting hurt," I said with a sincere expression.

"I know. You and Kelly have been terrific. But it's not Derek," she said.

"Kyle! That son of a bitch. He's married, you know!" I chided.

"It's Michael. He was very sweet and quiet and shy and protective and I really like him," she said with a blush.

"Michael? Really? I've known Michael for twelve years and I've never met one of his girlfriends. I thought he was gay for years," I said and suddenly wished I hadn't revealed that to Jeannine.

"I guess the right girl never came along," she said with a confused expression.

"I think you may be right," I said. We had reached the office but I wanted to stay in the car and give her some advice on love and sex and heartbreak. But it didn't happen because we were distracted by the cookie-stuffed face of Officer Delbert peering into the passenger window as he leaned his arms atop the roof of Dad's car. He gave us a smile and confirmed my suspicion when he revealed his Oreo speckled teeth. "Let's talk some more later," was all I could muster.

I was tied up with calls from friends and voice-mail all morning. Most were concerning the *California Confidential* exposure, although a few were from early risers who read the paper. Two of the calls were noteworthy. The first was from *California Confidential* informing me that John Koflanovich, or one of his representatives, will be making a statement on the show this evening, refuting his connection to the Russian Mafia. They left a call back number in case I was interested in making a statement of my own.

The second one said, "Mr. Duffy, this is John Koflanovich. My business partner informs me that he met with you last week and recommends that we talk." He then left his phone number and said he would be available at that number until 1:30 PM.

I dialed the number and reached a receptionist, then a female administrative assistant before being connected to Koflanovich. Not exactly the direct connection I was expecting. "Mr. Duffy, thank you for returning my call," he said with a heavy accent.

"You are a difficult man to reach, Mr. Koflanovich. I think we could have avoided several problems if we talked a couple of weeks ago," I said.

"It sounds to me like we both were operating on incorrect assumptions," he said.

"I would still like to get together to discuss Terry Tucker's death," I said.

Koflanovich replied, "That can be arranged as long as you are willing to meet at a location I have deemed to be secure, and you come alone."

"I can understand your need for security. I hope you can understand my need for security as well," I said.

"Why would you need security? No one is chasing after you anymore," he said with some agitation in his voice.

"Well, let's see. First, I had a gun shoved in my face when I visited your office. Then one of your men broke into my office. Your relatives from Tecate entered my office at gunpoint, tied up my secretary and robbed me. Your men shot at me at the Ukrainian Citizen's Club. And, your men put an unarmed associate of mine in the hospital while he was keeping an eye on Ian Davis. So, you'll have to excuse me if I'm a little reluctant to meet in some remote location without any witnesses," I said with a fair measure of attitude.

"Ancient history, Mr. Duffy. Let us initiate Glasnost in our relationship," he said in a magnanimous manner.

"How would you feel about meeting with Detective Shamansky present? I know he has been trying to connect with you. I'd feel a lot less concerned about foul play if he went along," I said.

"That would be acceptable as long as we confine the talk to Terry Tucker and the Russian Mafia. I don't want to get into a debate about our ancient history," he said.

"I'll tell you what. I can avoid that subject if you can help my computers find their way home," I said.

"That sounds like a reasonable request. How about if we meet at 10:00 AM tomorrow at my home? You are welcome to have additional police outside if that would make you feel more comfortable," he said.

"That will be fine. What's your address?" I asked.

"First I would like to ask you a question. One of my close associates will be making a statement on *California Confidential* this evening. They are sending a camera crew to our offices. He will be telling the public that I am in no way affiliated with the Russian Mafia. His statement alone will do little to sway public opinion. But if you were present and could say how you feel about what that show stated in your name last week, it could set the record straight. Are you willing to make a statement tonight?" he asked.

I was definitely not in the mood to do this guy any favors in lieu of all he had done to me. However, I liked even less the idea that *California Confidential* had been making statements in my name without ever confirming a single bit of information. "I'll do it on one condition," I said.

"What is that?" he asked.

"I don't want to go inside your offices. Last time I was there I had a gun shoved in my face," I said.

"What if they held the interview in front of our building? You certainly don't expect us to try anything out in public with the cameras rolling, do you?" he asked.

"That would be acceptable," I said reluctantly. He then gave me his address in Del Mar and hung up.

I reached Shamansky at his desk and asked, "How would you like to meet the elusive John Koflanovich tomorrow morning?"

"Why, do you have an appointment with his hit squad," he asked.

"Mr. Koflanovich wants to make friends," I said.

"Why do you suppose he did that? Is he afraid you'll be joining Doberman's Stub on a permanent basis?" he asked.

"I thought you had more important things to do than sitting around reading the Entertainment section," I said.

"I tried the obituaries first, but you weren't there," he said with his usual sarcastic charm.

"Koflanovich wants me to go on *California Confidential* tonight and tell the world what a swell guy he is," I said.

"Knowing how much you avoid the limelight, I'm sure you turned him down," he stated.

"I'm tired of those assholes acting like they're my mouthpiece. It's time to call a spade a spade," I said heatedly.

"I can't wait to tune in," he said.

"Why tune in when you can see it live. They're shooting it in front of Cerise's building at 7:45 PM this evening. Care to join me?" I asked.

"In other words, you still don't trust them and you'd like back-up," he said.

"I'm just keeping up my end of our deal to share information," I said.

"You're a piece of work, Duffy. Sure, why not?" he said. "The way trouble follows you around like an old mental health client, it will probably just save me a trip later on."

Cory stopped by around noon to say he was sorry his disclosure to *California Confidential* nearly got me killed. I told him that after all he had been through he deserved a second chance. But, if he ever goes to the press or anyone else behind my back again, we're through. Somewhere in a tapestry of profanity, Cory conveyed that he understood.

I decided to have him tail Nigel for a while. I couldn't help but wonder why Nigel was being so generous. First, he asked me to sit in on a recording session, then offered work doing bios, then the gig at Bernie's. Each of these things served to make me like Nigel and, at the same time, distracted me from working the case.

Cory had gone back to the hospital and had his ribs wrapped. He said that the assignment would take his mind off of the pain and he was glad he still had a job.

When I returned from lunch Jeannine said, "Chelsea Tucker called while you were out and seemed upset that she couldn't reach you. She'll be out for the rest of the day, but asked for an appointment tomorrow. You're seeing her at 1:00 PM. Is that OK?" she asked.

"That'll be fine," I replied.

I then called *California Confidential* and told them I would make a statement this evening. They seemed genuinely pleased.

At 4:30 PM Shamansky called. "So, are you going to make me guard you on an empty stomach, or what?"

"I don't see the boss until tomorrow, so the petty cash fund is teetering on empty. But, if you can settle for Mickey Dee's instead of Larabee's, I think I can handle it," I said.

Shamansky replied, "There's a Subway three blocks east of Cerise. If we have to go cheap, let's at least make an effort to keep the calories down."

"Will 6:30 PM work for you?" I asked.

"Fine," he replied and hung up.

I spent the next hour getting my expense report together for Chelsea. I held off on doing totals so that I could include Shamansky's freebie on the report. I also picked up Kelly and drove her home.

By 6:40 PM I was noshing a six-inch turkey club while Shamansky was stuffing a twelve-inch meatball torpedo. I concluded that he kept his weight down by only eating when complimentary meals could be arranged.

"You disappointed me today Duffy," he said. "After reading that Entertainment section article I thought you'd be reversing your career change."

"I couldn't do that, Shamansky," I said.

"Why not? You're rockin' with the big boys now," he said.

"But then nobody would be left to chase after Terry's real killer," I said with a broad smile.

"The DA thinks I'm doing a hell of a job," he offered.

"Too bad the *profile* method of police work doesn't allow for investigating more than one suspect," I said.

"In this case, I don't think we need to go beyond your boss. But, once we lock her up maybe you can offer your services to OJ. He's still looking for the real killer, isn't he?" Shamansky asked.

"If you're so sure Chelsea did it, what are you doing here tonight and meeting with Koflanovich tomorrow?" I asked.

"Because I was told on Friday that I'm the lucky stiff that catches the clean-up work on your break-in and other crimes against Duffy Investigations personnel," he said with a look of consternation.

"But you're a Homicide Detective," I said. "If the department is treating them as separate crimes, wouldn't they go to another department?"

"You would think so, wouldn't you," he stated. "But in this era of fiscal austerity, if a detective catches a case and there are cross-over crimes during the course of the investigation, he's stuck cleaning up the mess."

"What about GI Jo-Jo? Did you conclude that having a demolitions expert who just had a fight with the victim is completely irrelevant?" I asked incredulously. This got us stares from two soccer moms who just sat down at an adjacent table.

Shamansky gave them a charming smile, flashed his badge and said, "Police business, ladies. We're having a working dinner. Could I ask you to please move to another table? This is confidential."

I would have told him where to get off, but the soccer moms were happy to accommodate Shamansky's request. Once they were out of earshot he turned to me and said, "I'm looking into it, but I'm getting the impression Terry and GI Jo-Jo were actually friends, or as close to friends as guys like that get."

"What the hell are you talking about?" I asked heatedly.

"Terry wasn't going to get rid of Martin. I don't believe that was ever an issue. Terry had a lot of respect for him as a soundman. As a perfectionist, Terry would never get rid of another detail-oriented craftsman," he said.

"What about Martin procuring drugs for Davis? What about his groupie girlfriend? What about the fight? And how can you dismiss the fact that he engineered the death of a former boss?" I said getting loud again.

"Let's walk over to Cerise Records," he said and stood up. As soon as we got outside he said, "The thing you gotta know about a guy like Terry Tucker is that he put his personal success and the success of the band ahead of everything else. If Terry yelled at Martin over a drug issue I think he was probably pissed that Martin misread the purity level of whatever he was giving Davis to keep him going."

"Where the hell did you get that?" I asked.

"Hear me out," he said. "The groupie girlfriend was another functional convenience for Tucker. He got to maintain the bad boy image while the press was around, then schlep her off on Martin as soon as the photo op was over. All of the band members confirmed that theory. I see the fight as two perfectionists having a tiff. Tucker pulls rank on him all of the time in front of the band and he lets Martin flex his muscles in front of his girlfriend to throw him a bone. You wanted to know what was said when Terry was bent over after getting punched? It was probably something like. 'Do you think that will get you some hot action tonight?' No big deal."

"What about fragging his commanding officer? Was that a big deal?" I asked as we approached Cerise.

Shamansky stopped, turned to me and said, "You said it yourself. The C.O. had influential friends pulling strings against a redneck, loner Sergeant and what happened? He got off with a transfer to the States and an Honorable Discharge."

I was about to tear into Shamansky's convoluted logic when a heavy hand clamped down on my shoulder from behind, and I heard a deep Russian accent say, "There better not be any bootleg CD's made last Saturday night."

I turned around to see Vlad "The Impaler" Torhan looming above. "Vladimir, out of jail already? Last time I saw you, you were being dragged out of the Dali Lama in handcuffs by San Diego's finest."

"San Diego's finest? What a joke. They are called pigs because they are all fat and lazy. If not for stun gun I would have introduced them all to emergency medical services," he said with a sadistic laugh.

I replied, "Where are my manners? Vladimir Torhan, Cerise Records executive, this is police detective Walter Shamansky."

Torhan made a face like he just stepped in a dog pile. "You appear less portly than your comrades," Torhan said in a lame attempt to backpedal.

"I get the impression we're going to be seeing a lot of each other," Shamansky said with a raised eyebrow.

Before they could continue, a pushy blond woman with a ponytail and a clipboard grabbed Torhan by the arm and said, "You need to go over to the make-up trailer now." She then turned to me and said, "Who are you?"

Shamansky said, "You don't recognize the one and only Jason Duffy? How did you ever get a job as a secretary with no eye for detail?"

"I'm an Associate Producer," she said indignantly to Shamansky.

"National Inquirer eat your heart out," he replied and walked away.

"I'm Emma Baldridge," she said and stuck out her hand. "I'm sorry I didn't recognize you at first. That Torhan person makes me nervous."

"Don't worry, he has that effect on everybody," I said as I shook her hand.

She said in a fast-paced cadence, "I understand you want to go on after Mr. Torhan has concluded his statement. Can I ask what we can expect to hear?"

"We've had a couple of new developments since the initial story broke, so I thought I'd bring you up to speed and comment on whatever Torhan has to say," I said while trying not to match her staccato speech pattern.

"Excellent, excellent, should make for interesting TV," she said. I wondered how excellent it will be when I tell their viewers what a slipshod operation they're running.

She did her best to try to persuade me to visit the make-up trailer, but I knew I'd never hear the end of it from Shamansky or his cronies on future cases. I'd rather be the pasty PI than the pansy PI in the eyes of SDPD.

At 7:30 PM the sun was down but the camera lamps lit up the front of Cerise's building like high noon. Five minutes later I saw Jennifer Wilde, the field reporter who did the remote from my house, standing in front of the building doing a sound check. A few minutes later she gave some instructions to The Impaler, then stood in place, waiting for her cue.

Emma tapped me on the shoulder and said, "We'll go to the studio after Torhan finishes, then to commercial. You will be on when the studio sends it back to us." She handed me an ear monitor. "Put this in your ear and you can hear what Mr. Torhan has to say. Jennifer will nod when you can make your statement."

"OK," I replied.

"Here we go," she said and walked away from me. She pointed at Jennifer and I heard:

"This is Jennifer Wilde reporting from in front of Cerise Records. Standing next to me is Vladimir Torhan, the Executive Producer of Doberman's Stub's latest CD, which is not yet titled. Mr. Torhan, it is alleged that Cerise Records is a front for the Russian Mafia. How do you respond?"

"It is ridiculous! John Koflanovich, the owner of Cerise Records, is a lawful, contributing member of the community. The Mafia is a plague on all of mankind. If Mr. Koflanovich..."

As Torhan was making his statement on live TV, two gunmen jumped out from behind a bush carrying AK-47 machine guns and sprayed him with bullets. Torhan was killed immediately. Jennifer Wilde was hit in the left shoulder and right thigh. The impact knocked her over backwards.

Shamansky drew his revolver and got off four shots from behind the communications van. The gunmen reloaded and sprayed the van. I pulled my gun and got off a few rounds as the gunmen jumped into the back of a black pickup truck and sped off. Shamansky shattered the rear window of the pickup with a long shot, but the vehicle continued out of sight. Since we had walked to the Cerise Building from Subway, we had no way of pursuing them and both knew they had gotten away.

After I had spent my rounds I noticed that the cameraman had filmed my firing sequence. I turned to the camera and said:

"Send the paramedics right away. Suspects are fleeing in a late model, black Ford F-150 pickup truck with a shattered rear window, heading west on Broadway. One of the suspects is believed to be Boris Schmelnikov of Odessa, Ukraine. He is approximately six feet tall, 190 pounds, with white hair combed back and a mostly black mustache. He has a tattoo of a

submarine on his left bicep. He is armed and very dangerous. If you see him please contact the police immediately."

As I finished my statement Emma Baldridge walked up to me, looked in the camera and said:

"For those of you who don't recognize him, this is Jason Duffy. Mr. Duffy, you were going to make a statement after Mr. Torhan had finished. Would you like to make that statement now?"

I gave Emma an incredulous look and said:
"I think we both need to see if there's anything we can do for Jennifer Wilde."

I walked back toward the victims, where Shamansky was kneeling to the side of Jennifer. Apparently, I was still in frame while Emma was engaged in a dialogue with the studio. "Is there anything I can do?" I asked Shamansky.

"Yeah," he replied, "try keeping a lower profile."

I took off my shirt and folded it into a triangle. I then unbuttoned the top of Jennifer's blouse and pressed the shirt into the bleeding wound. I held it in place for about twelve minutes, then the paramedics took over. Shamansky, who had been using his hand to press on the outside of the other entry point, followed my lead and pressed his shirt directly to her thigh wound.

While we were waiting for the paramedics I told Shamansky about Boris Schmelnikov and my conversation with Lt. Sanchenko. "I need to call that in right now," he said.

"Don't worry," I replied. "The camera was on me after the shooting, so I gave the description of the pickup and Schmelnikov on the air."

"You what!" he screamed.

"It was better than letting those guys just get away," I said.

"Bullshit!" he exclaimed. "You'll have every cowboy on the West Coast out shooting up every black F-150 they see."

"Oh, come on. We see police actions from helicopters everyday on the news." I said. "The police chase has overtaken sports as

California's favorite pastime." Shamansky grumbled, but he knew I was right.

We stayed at the scene for about an hour and talked with the assigned officers. As we were about to return to Subway for our vehicles, Emma Baldridge approached. "That was very heroic of you, Jason. We've had hundreds of viewers call in and praise you for administering first aid until the paramedics arrived," she said.

"I hope you got some kudos for Detective Shamansky, too," I said.

"Actually several viewers call in to complain about the man who had his hand up poor Jennifer's skirt," she said to me, then turned to Shamansky and said, "I'm sure you meant well."

Shamansky walked in silence. As we neared Subway I asked, "Are you still up for meeting Koflanovich if he doesn't cancel?"

"Provided I'm not buried in paperwork or getting my ass chewed off for letting a hit go down under my nose," he said.

"Will this be another of the collateral messes you'll be assigned?" I inquired.

"Who knows? I could be a crossing guard at SeaWorld by this time tomorrow," he moaned.

I said, "I'll call Koflanovich in the morning and let you know if he's still agreeable to a meeting."

I arrived at Kelly's condo at 10:00 PM. She was extremely excited. "I saw the whole thing on television. I recorded it for you. That poor reporter. Is she going to be alright?"

"Slow down," I replied. "You sound like you just won a chugging contest with Juan Valdez."

"Sorry," she said. "Is she still alive?"

"She was alive when the paramedics transported her. I don't know any more," I replied.

"I thought I was going to faint when I heard the gunshots and saw them go down. I knew you were standing right there. I didn't know if they shot you, too," she said as a tear streamed down her cheek. "I felt so helpless. Then, there you were firing your gun on camera.

It was like watching an episode of Law & Order. I was shaking for about a half-hour," she said with a quivering voice.

"I'm sorry you had to go through that," I said sympathetically. "Do you mind if I watch the video, or would it be too upsetting?"

"It's ready to go. Just hit play," she said. Unfortunately, the footage didn't capture the gunmen on tape. The cameraman stayed with the victims falling to the ground and held frame until he adjusted to focus on me firing my revolver. It was strange seeing myself talking directly to the camera.

When I refused to humor Emma Baldridge with a statement, Kelly commented, "Good for you, Jason. That bitch just wanted to milk the situation for ratings."

I was a little embarrassed when the cameraman let Emma go out of focus while she was still talking, in order to get a close-up of me taking off my shirt and compressing Jennifer's shoulder wound. I was waiting for Kelly to comment as the camera stayed on my shirtless torso a little too long. But before she could say anything I got a sinking feeling as the camera captured Shamansky reaching under Jennifer's skirt to compress her inner thigh wound. When the camera was on me the audience saw the whole sequence of events as I took off my shirt, folded it, and compressed the wound. The viewers understood what I was doing and could relate. Unfortunately, the camera skipped all of the preliminaries and just focused on Shamansky as he was reaching under Jennifer's skirt. What I'm sure was the cuff of Shamansky's white shirt dangling out of his hand, appeared on camera to be Jennifer's panties hanging down near the top of her knees. I suddenly understood the negative feedback he got from Emma Baldridge and, more importantly, I understood the weeks of hazing he would get from his fellow officers back at the station house. I suddenly wished I hadn't invited him along for the meeting with Koflanovich tomorrow. If he seemed sullen on the walk back to Subway, he would be unbearable after a morning at Metro.

"What's he doing to that poor girl?" Kelly asked with a disgusted tone.

Chapter 18

IT was the Tuesday morning before the Labor Day weekend. Kelly woke up with a case of the friskies for yesterday's hero, then treated me to a delicious breakfast. Jeannine was awed by my role in last night's *California Confidential*, and even Delbert Henson insisted on opening and closing my door for me when I arrived at work. I had the feeling I better enjoy the red carpet treatment while it lasted. Soon I'd be meeting Shamansky, coming from a squad room full of ballbusters, and John Koflanovich, who had just lost a key executive/bodyguard and must be feeling particularly vulnerable.

"We got a delivery this morning," said Delbert.

"Was it UPS this early in the morning?" asked Jeannine.

"No, it was a guy in a taxi with a big, heavy box," replied Delbert.

"Where is the box now?" I asked.

"I set it down in front of the entrance to our office," he said.

"Is anything wrong?" asked Jeannine me.

"I think I know what it is, but, just to be on the safe side, why don't you two stay here until I tell you it's OK," I said.

As expected, the box contained my stolen computers. I opened the outer shell and did a cursory inspection. Everything appeared to be in order. I was more concerned with bugs than bombs, considering Koflanovich's propensity for paranoia and sudden need for my endorsement.

I leaned over the balcony and called, "It's alright to come up now." I then called Koflanovich to confirm our appointment. His executive assistant, Svetlana Illich, told me he was making funeral arrangements at the moment but he is definitely expecting us as scheduled.

I then called Shamansky. As much as he enjoys busting my stones, I decided to play it straight and spare him the comic comments that were popping into my head. "Koflanovich is a go. Why don't we meet in front of his compound at 10:00?"

"Good, I'll see you there," he said and hung up before I could reply.

I asked Jeannine to transfer all of the new info we had entered onto the loaners and get both systems operational. I told Delbert I wanted the office door locked when I wasn't in and he was to stay on the balcony and watch the street. I showed him pictures of the Russians who were at the Dali Lama last Saturday and told him to have Jeannine call 911 if any of them showed up.

At 9:55 AM I reached the Koflanovich compound. This was quite a secluded little fortress, including five, two-story houses on a cul-de-sac. Two occupy corner lots and are undoubtedly inhabited by the security staff. I could see guards looking out of the upstairs and downstairs windows of both corner buildings. A wrought iron gate spanned the street between the corner houses and the next set of houses leading to the mansion at the end of the cul-de-sac. A twenty-foot, white, turreted wall separated the corner houses from the interior houses and anchored the wrought iron gate. Behind the walls, supporting the gate, were two thick steel interlocking walls that ran on tracks. They could be moved by remote control, and once in place, were strengthened by rebar rods that slid into holes in the street. The twenty-foot exterior wall extended all the way around the perimeter of the three interior properties, which had a steep canyon, dropping approximately sixty feet on the other side of the perimeter wall. A sentry was posted in each of the five turrets, which were connected by a walkway that resembled a medieval castle.

As I drove up to the wrought iron gate, two bodyguards

approached from either side of my vehicle. Each had a black cloth draped over his right arm. I assumed they were carrying automatic weapons. I rolled down my window and said, "My name is Jason Duffy. I have a ten o'clock appointment with John Koflanovich."

"Do you have any identification?" asked the bodyguard at the drivers-side window as the other bodyguard inspected the back seat and floor.

"I handed over my private investigator's license and said, "Detective Shamansky of SDPD will be here any minute. You had better stow the heavy firepower if you want to avoid a hassle."

"Thanks for the tip," he said and handed my ID back to me. "Do you want to wait for him?"

"Yes," I said. The bodyguard motioned for his comrade and handed him his big black bundle. The silent Soviet schlepped the two bundles into the corner house on my right, then returned and crossed his arms with his right hand reaching under his jacket. He no sooner struck up this pose when Shamansky pulled in alongside me, and got the ID routine from bodyguard number one.

Inside the compound six more bodyguards made their presence known. We were shown into a large tiled reception area. At the top of a wide, curved stairway stood Ivana, who caught my eye and waved. I returned the wave and Shamansky asked, "Friend of yours?"

"We danced briefly once, but have never been formally introduced," I responded.

"You're full of surprises, Duffy," he commented as we were led to the rear of the house and into a huge office. Seated behind an immense teak desk sat John Koflanovich in a black business suit.

Koflanovich stood as we approached, gestured to the chairs across from the desk and said, "Welcome, gentlemen. Come in, have a seat." He made no attempt to shake hands.

I said, "First of all, we'd like to express our condolences. Was Mr. Torhan with you very long?"

"It was a tragedy. Vladimir started working for me a year before I immigrated to the United States. He was a hard worker and a trusted comrade," he said.

Shamansky asked, "Do you know who killed him?"

"I don't think there is any question in any of our minds who is behind this," Koflanovich replied. "Specifically who pulled the trigger? Mr. Duffy gave us a name on the television show, which tells me you know more than I do on that subject."

I jumped in, "Should we call you Mr. Koflanovich or Mr. Chofsky?"

"You Americans have an expression that I think applies in this situation. Now that the cat is out of the bag, I suppose Chofsky would be fine," he said.

"The first thing I was hoping we could do today is eliminate you as a suspect in the death of Terry Tucker," I said. "The only way I know to do that is to talk openly and honestly about Cerise Record's contract negotiations with Doberman's Stub, past, present and future. Is that acceptable?"

Chofsky replied, "Of course."

I continued, "I had a music industry expert review the initial contract. He concluded that, although it was apparent you possess solid business skills, it appeared you didn't have any experience with the music industry or the nature of how music industry contract law has been interpreted in the courts at the time the original contract was drawn up."

"That is a fair characterization," Chofsky replied.

"In Terry Tucker you had one of the most business savvy musicians in the industry. Is it also fair to say that Terry took advantage of your lack of music industry experience to fashion a way out of the contract that would have cost you your most valuable asset?" I asked.

"I understand how you might think this would be a motive for killing him. But, you must understand, I also believed, and continue to believe, that Terry was the most talented member of the band, and without him it is highly likely the band will lose its popularity and eventually fail," he said.

"It looks like a lose-lose situation for Cerise Records," I said.

Chofsky replied, "When it comes to the American court system, there is no such thing as a sure thing. I was prepared to tie Terry up in the courts with a never-ending series of motions and hearings. I have assurances from my legal team that they could delay the release of the third CD for at least three years, and possibly as many as five if Terry tried cutting us out altogether."

"Would you be willing to allow your attorneys to disclose to the police exactly where everything stood in this process at the time of Terry's death?" asked Shamansky.

"If that is what it would take to convince you I had nothing to do with Terry's death, I will give my consent. However, I would need assurances that this information would not appear on the six o'clock news," he said, then turned to me and added, "or *California Confidential*."

"You have my word," said Shamansky. "Our interest here, and I think I speak for Jason as well, is that we spend our time as productively as possible. If we can eliminate you as a suspect we can better focus our efforts on the killer."

Chofsky wrote on a small notepad. "This is the name of the legal team handling that aspect of the contract work. I will call them later today and give permission for them to speak freely with you."

"Thank you," Shamansky said as he took the note.

I asked, "What's the status of your contract negotiation with Nigel Choate and the rest of the band at this point?"

Chofsky seemed to become a little uncomfortable. After a brief pause he said, "I get the feeling Mr. Choate is working hard to figure out his options and how best to proceed. I believe he is interviewing new management and legal counsel. Have you met the current management team?"

"Yes," I replied. "It appears Terry hired people he knew he could control."

"Exactly," he said with enthusiasm. "After meeting them, can you understand why I was not more rigorous about investigating the clauses they added?"

"I'm sure you felt you were dealing with a couple of idiots, and you were. What you didn't know was Terry's prowess in this realm," I stated.

"How would you describe your relationship with Terry after you realized he pulled a fast one on you?" asked Shamansky.

"I was angry, but not with him; with myself," he said. "I accept that Americans try to get as much as possible for themselves. I consider myself a good businessman and, as such, will not make the same mistake twice. I would never do anything that could cause me to lose my freedom."

I replied, "I promised I wouldn't bring up the difficulties I've had recently with your employees. But, suffice it to say I have a hard time believing that last statement of yours in light of my experiences."

"Mr. Duffy, I appreciate that you are a man of your word. I put my family ahead of all other priorities. I know that you are aware of what happened to my daughter in Odessa," he said. "Shortly before you came on the scene I dealt with another private investigator who told me that the American Mafia frequently assists the Russian Mafia with American affairs. He also said there were many private investigators in America who worked with the Mafia. The day you duped my receptionist and snuck into the back offices I was very suspicious of you. As soon as I learned you were a private investigator I was certain you were helping the Russian Mafia through the American Mafia. Can you understand how I came to this conclusion?"

"Who was the investigator that told you this?" Shamansky asked.

"Axel Vandevere," he replied. "I hired him to conduct surveillance on Mr. Tucker after he announced he was in a position to dictate contract terms. Mr. Vandevere prepared a dossier and maintained an activities sheet detailing Mr. Tucker's movements and meetings."

"Was Mr. Vandevere following Terry the day he died?" I asked.

"His invoice indicates that he was," he replied.

"The file Vandevere put together could be very helpful. Will you give it to us?" I asked.

Chofsky replied, "Of course. However, it is not here at the house. I'll have a courier bring it around; preferably to your office, Mr. Duffy."

"Since he already knows the way?" I asked and Chofsky smiled.

"OK, enough with the inside stuff," said Shamansky, "let's get down to what happened last night. Why did Schmelnikov blast Torhan on live television?"

"As Mr. Duffy is aware, the Russian Mafia does not like publicity. It was no secret what Mr. Torhan was going to talk about. The television stations ran promotions for the story all day. I just can't figure out how they knew it would be in front of our building," he said.

"They didn't," I replied. "They probably just staked out the *California Confidential* remote broadcast van and followed it to your building. They got lucky when they realized the shoot would take place outside in an unguarded area."

"Why did you send Torhan instead of speaking for yourself?" asked Shamansky.

"I honestly thought Vladimir would be safe," he said choking back emotion. "He was an amateur boxing champion in the Ukraine and one match away from representing his country in the Olympics. They usually don't take on individuals who have the love of the public behind them. Such moves result in demands for the police or military to enforce the laws more rigorously."

"I suppose they felt that in the United States anything goes," I offered.

"I fear that may be true," he said to me, then he turned and asked Shamansky, "Is anything being done to catch these men?"

"Absolutely. Thanks to Jason, here, we know the identity of one of the gunmen as well as another member of his organization that entered the US in the past week. Every cop in San Diego saw a picture of these men at roll call this morning and the news stations are running the photos as well. It will be very tough for them to walk around in public without getting spotted."

We could have continued asking him questions for another hour, but Father Mencavich, an Orthodox Catholic priest, arrived to discuss the details of the funeral mass. A pair of bodyguards escorted us to our vehicles. Shamansky's black Crown Victoria led the way. As we neared the end of the first block I saw a man sitting in a blue Mustang. It was Dimitri Nazaroff, the scout. His vehicle was pointed in the opposite direction and I didn't have time to stop and block him in. So I continued on as if I didn't see him and tailed Shamansky until he made a right turn. I then pulled up alongside him and pointed to a convenience store parking lot. We both pulled into parallel parking spots, then I jumped out of Dad's car and into the Crown Vic. "There's a Russian Mafia scout parked a block away from Chofsky's," I said tensely.

"Blue Mustang, sunglasses, early thirties?" he asked.

"That's the one," I said.

Shamansky got on his radio and called in for backup. "Get in back," he ordered.

"Why?" I asked as I crawled over the seat.

"I'm gonna pull up alongside of him," he said as he rolled down both passenger-side windows, "with my badge in one hand and my gun in the other."

Two seconds after we made a left turn back onto the street where Nazaroff was parked, the blue Mustang shot out of its parking space like a drag racer at the Bonneville Salt Flats. Shamansky hit the siren and stuck a portable red, flashing light onto the roof while accelerating to maximum speed. Once this little exercise in dexterity was accomplished he got back on the radio and called in our situation. Fortunately, since Del Mar is a very affluent coastal town, the number of homes and street traffic is decidedly less than most sections of San Diego. After about ten blocks we had managed to run six stop signs and a red light without seriously endangering the public. But these types of chases frequently end badly. All it would take is one young mother pushing a baby carriage and we both knew it.

Suddenly a Sheriff's Department green & white swung out in front of the Mustang from a side street. Instead of turning left, into a head-on course, the green & white turned right and moved in a serpentine fashion, making it impossible for the Mustang to pass. Nazaroff was going too fast to turn onto the street the deputy sheriff had come from and was forced to brake hard. Two blocks up the street another green & white appeared and turned toward the action. He sped to the nearest cross street and swung his vehicle into a roadblock position on the left side of the street. The first green

& white understood what he was doing and blocked to the right. It was decision time for the Russian. He could either try to ram the police vehicles and continue the chase or give it up. At that critical moment, two more green & whites turned onto our street and were closing fast on the roadblock. Even if Nazaroff could break through, he would run head-on into the backup units. He chose to slam on his breaks and extend his arms straight up through his sunroof.

Shamansky yanked him out of his seat and across the hood of the Mustang where he was cuffed. The officer in the first vehicle tried reading him his rights, but it became immediately apparent that he didn't speak a word of English. The interrogation process would be painful.

With all of the unexpected excitement of the morning, I barely made it back to the office in time to meet with Chelsea Tucker. She was sitting in the waiting area when I arrived at 12:58 PM. "I didn't think you were going to make it," she said looking at her watch.

We adjourned to my office where she took a seat. I said, "I just came from Koflanovichs' house and, as the saying goes, I have some good news and some bad news."

"Me too," she said flatly.

"Would you like to go first?" I asked.

"No. Since I'm paying for this I might as well hear what you have to say," she said without humor.

"Koflanovich has been playing fast and loose with the laws of the land, especially the way he came after me and my staff. But, I'm convinced he wasn't behind Terry's death," I said.

"What makes you think that?" she asked.

"I get the impression he felt he was playing a chess match with Terry and was feeling like he was onto a winning strategy on how he could retain Doberman's Stub at the time of Terry's murder," I said.

She retorted, "Did you bother to read the contract? He was over a barrel and he knew it!"

"Terry outfoxed him on the contract, there's no question about that. But Koflanovich had a team of lawyers work out a strategy where the third CD would be kept from release for three to five years if Terry pulled the trigger on the out clause. I didn't know Terry personally, but I get the impression his ambition would never have allowed him to sit on the new CD for that length of time. It's too good, and the band was on too much of a roll," I said.

"So what's the good news?" she asked.

"Did you see *California Confidential* last night?" I asked.

"Unfortunately, it's gotten to be a *can't miss* show for me," she said with scorn.

"We caught one of the Russians involved in the shooting a couple of hours ago," I said hoping this progress would get her off of the negative vibe she was emitting.

She summarized, "So, the extent of the good news is that we no longer have a suspect but that you helped the police with another case. That's just great. And you did it all before band practice. I'm truly impressed. You probably haven't even figured out the connection to Terry's childhood friend."

"What are you talking about?" I asked.

"I'm talking about you trying to take Terry's place!" she yelled. "I'm talking about you playing a gig with the band instead of solving the murder! I knew it was a mistake to hire a flaky musician to do investigation work! Well I've seen all I intend to see!"

"What are you saying, Chelsea?" I asked, expecting that I knew the answer.

"I'm saying: The good news is I hope you had fun pretending to be Terry and the bad news is, you're fired!" Chelsea then stood up and stormed out of the office.

Chapter 19

OVER the next couple of days I weighed my options and sulked a great deal. When I returned Dad's vehicle I brought Kelly along as a buffer to avoid talking about the case. Dad tried to draw me into a discussion over lunch a couple of times, but Kelly, sensing my reticence to talk, did a fine job of putting the spotlight on him.

Mom could tell something was wrong. When I directed Kelly to stay with Dad while I helped Mom clear the lunch dishes, she cornered me in the kitchen and asked, "What's wrong?"

"What makes you think something's wrong?" I replied.

"I'm your mother I know these things. The only time you ever volunteer to help with the dishes is when you want to get away from your father. I don't need to be a detective to figure that out," she said.

"Can we just drop it? I don't feel like talking," I said and returned to the living room. I made up a lame excuse to leave and we were in the Acura and out on the road in just a few minutes.

"Are you going to go to work for Nigel now that you have the time?" Kelly asked.

"Probably," I replied. "I still feel funny accepting employment from a guy I haven't eliminated as a suspect in a murder investigation."

Kelly asked, "Wouldn't it give you a chance to stay involved in the case?"

"Yes and no," I said. "I'd remain in contact with the band and could pick up on some things I otherwise wouldn't know about. But, my attention would be on prospective band members and management personnel and not on the murder investigation."

"Let's see if I've got this straight. Nigel wants you to check out people he's thinking of employing – right?" she asked.

"That's correct," I stated.

"Then why shouldn't he expect you to do the same thing and check him out thoroughly, as well as the rest of the band and staff, before you decide to go to work for them?" she asked.

"Good point," I said as I gave her a look that told her I had found my way.

"Does this mean you're officially finished feeling sorry for yourself?" she asked.

After dropping Kelly off at her condo I swung by the office. Jeannine greeted me and said, "Delbert brought in a package from the same guy who dropped off our computers. It's on your desk."

The Terry Tucker dossier was thick and disorganized. I could see that Chofsky did a few things to try to bring order to the file, but it was apparent that Vandevere was a slob.

Chapter 20

FRIDAY morning I met with Cory, who had nothing new or unusual to report on Nigel. He had dinner with two men in business suits, drank lightly and returned home after the meeting. I instructed Cory to stay with him for the time being.

I spent the rest of the morning pouring over Nigel's financial records. From what I could ascertain, Nigel has lived beyond his means for the past five years. His spending spree began when he inherited a large property in Northern Ireland from his Aunt, Winona Choate. Nigel leases the property to a private Drug and Alcohol rehab group that is comparable to the Betty Ford Clinic in the US. In spite of the fact that he receives a large monthly rent check, he refinanced the property twice and took out a second mortgage two months ago.

The report gave me the impression Nigel would try to avoid a protracted court battle over the third CD. His best option would be to hire a top negotiator and get the CD to market ASAP. On the one hand, it seemed that killing Terry would throw his future earning potential into serious jeopardy. On the other hand, Terry was much more financially secure and could afford to go to war with Chofsky.

As I was about to leave for lunch, I got a call. "Mr. Duffy, this is Attorney David Stein. I represent Chelsea Tucker. Chelsea was arrested this morning and she asked me to meet with you. Would it be possible to get together later this afternoon?"

"Let me check my calendar," I replied. After about 30 seconds I said, "I have an opening at 3:00 PM. Can you make it to my office in

La Jolla at that time?" Stein paused a few seconds, then asked for the address.

As soon as I got off of the line I called Shamansky, but reached only his voice-mail. At 2:15 he returned my call. "I guess you got the news, Duffy. I hope her bill is paid," he said with a laugh.

"Last time we talked the DA wasn't ready to move forward with an arrest. What changed?" I asked.

"Remember the fight Terry and Chelsea had in the restaurant shortly before the murder?" he asked.

"Yeah, it was about how Terry screwed Chelsea's father and made him look bad in front of his money people," I replied.

"That's what we thought, too. But, I went through all of the credit card receipts from the restaurant and found a couple that had the adjacent table. According to the wife, while they were bickering, Chelsea threatened to take him to the cleaners in a divorce and Terry told Chelsea he built a loophole into their prenuptial agreement," Shamansky said.

"Did you check it out?" I asked.

"Of course," he replied. "I have a copy of the agreement on my desk. The DA's office took it to two of the top family court judges in San Diego and they both agree that Terry could have divorced Chelsea without surrendering any future earnings, including the CD he was working on at the time of his death. If Terry lived and either of them filed for divorce, Chelsea would have been cut out of royalties from the third CD and, out of future sales from the first two CD's."

"I didn't think that was possible under California law," I said.

"I didn't either," he said, "but the DA says it's so and that was enough to get an indictment when linked to the fact that she bought the headphones and had opportunity to rig them with the explosives."

"How is the interrogation of Nazaroff going?" I asked.

"I've had cadavers that are more cooperative. I'm getting called into a meeting. I'll talk with you more tomorrow," Shamansky said and hung up.

At 3:00 David Stein arrived and was shown into my office by

Jeannine. "Thanks for taking the time to see me today," he said and shook my hand.

"My pleasure," I said and motioned to the chair across the desk.

"I would like to start by expressing an apology from Chelsea. She said she fired you a couple of days ago and sincerely regrets doing so," he said. He then reached into his briefcase and produced a document, signed by Chelsea, requesting my return to the case and full disclosure to her attorney. As I returned the document to him, Stein handed me a check for $25,000. "This is a retainer for your services"

"Mr. Stein, I didn't appreciate being fired, but I can understand why she did it. I'll be glad to help with the defense," I said.

"What can you tell me about the case against Chelsea?" he asked. I spent the next half-hour giving him the details that appeared pertinent, as well as the *California Confidential* situation. Stein agreed I could meet with Chelsea. "I already put you on her visitor list. Since we are heading into a long holiday weekend, the bail hearing won't happen until Tuesday afternoon."

"Is she going to make bail?" I asked.

"Almost certainly, but we can't control the court calendar. So, she'll be a guest at our women's detention facility until the hearing," he said.

"How is she holding up?" I asked.

"Not well," he replied. "She grew up in an affluent home and never saw the inside of a jail cell until today. She's scared to death," he said.

"I have a lot of experience with juveniles of the same background in similar situations. I'll do what I can to help her get through it," I said. We shook hands and Stein departed.

Chapter 21

I ARRIVED at the San Diego County Women's Detention facility in Santee at 11:00 AM Saturday morning. We had to use the telephones on either side of a glass divider. She was wearing an orange jumpsuit and her hair was a mess. "I have to get out of here," she said with arched eyebrows and pleading eyes.

"Your lawyer is the only one who can arrange that. I understand your bail hearing is set for Tuesday," I said.

"I don't think I'll make it in here until Tuesday. One woman threatened to kill me," she said as a tear rolled down her face.

"Did you hear why the DA's office moved forward with the arrest?" I inquired.

"I don't know anything and can't even think straight now," she said and sobbed loudly. She was attracting the attention of another inmate who looked like a professional wrestler.

"You've got to keep it together if you want to survive in jail," I said. "If you show fear the others will pick on you all of the time."

"I can't help it," she cried. "What else can I do?"

"Were you ever in a school play?" I asked and Chelsea nodded. "Good. Pretend you're in a play now and your role is the psycho chick that nobody wants to mess with."

For the first time in our meeting she smiled. "I couldn't do that. I don't know how," she said.

"Oh, come on. Anybody can do it. Just avoid talking to people whenever you can. If somebody threatens you, try making an animal noise back at them or say that voices are telling you to do bad things,"

I said. "Inmates tend to avoid wackos because they're afraid of the unknown, and nobody knows what a wacko might do."

"How do you know these things?" she asked.

"I used to work in a mental health facility. Lots of my former clients spent time in jail at one time or another. Trust me, it'll work. Just remember to act normal when the guards and administrators are around," I said.

"OK. So why did the DA arrest me?" she asked in a more composed manner.

"The police found a witness from the restaurant where you had your fight shortly before Terry's death. The witness said you threatened to take Terry to the cleaners in a divorce and he told you about a clause in your prenuptial agreement that would have cut you off from his income if either of you filed for divorce," I said.

"Damn!" she exclaimed. "I can see how that would look really bad. He and my dad were battling over a TV commercial. They were both putting me in the middle of their fight and I couldn't take it anymore. I wasn't going to divorce Terry, but I said that to let him know how pissed I was feeling."

"How did you react to his information about the pre-nup?" I asked.

"It was a surprise and it wasn't a surprise. Rock stars have tremendous strains placed on their relationships. Terry knew this and he knew I would never be hurting for money, with or without him. When he wrote the pre-nup he was just preparing for when I would say what I said that night. But, you've got to believe me, I had nothing to do with his murder!"

"I believe you, Chelsea. I've believed in you from the beginning," I said.

"Then find out who did this and get me out of here. I want to believe in you too, Jason," she said as a jail matron told us we had five more minutes.

"One last thing," I said. "I have a theory on what Terry was talking about in his poem he scrawled on the bathroom mirror."

Chelsea's eyes grew wide, as if a mystic revelation was forthcoming, "What is it?" she asked.

I replied, "When he said, 'Back in the time when I was nine,' he wasn't referring to being age 9 he was talking about his former band, Caliber 9. I think somebody from the band was helping him. Do you know who that might be?"

"David Cooper," she said. "Terry always said, if the chips were down and he needed somebody's help, David would always be there for him. It's got to be David, the bass player."

I started to say goodbye as the matron took Chelsea by the arm and led her out the door. When she passed by the lady wrestler, Chelsea made her eyes look very wild and she bared her teeth. The wrestler moved her arm off of the chair armrest and pulled it in to her side in a more protective posture. At that point I had no doubt Chelsea would survive until Tuesday.

I got to the office at 2:15 PM and spent the next three hours pouring over Axel Vandevere's dossier on Terry's activities in the month prior to his death. I found three items that I felt were significant or at least surprising. First, I learned that Terry and Chelsea's father were into something else besides exploring the prospects of a private label record company. This must have been the TV commercial Chelsea mentioned this morning. They met with ad agency writers and producers. Vandevere managed to talk with one of the writers and found that Terry was in the process of selling a Doberman's Stub song to be used in a custom home commercial. I had to wonder if Terry's fight with Peter Spivey might have been connected to this deal.

The second item surprisingly contradicted something Chelsea had told me. It seems Terry met with Gavin Tomko, the lead guitarist from Caliber 9, not David Cooper, the bassist. I looked both of them up in Terry's address book and left voice-mail messages explaining that I was working on Terry's murder and needed their help.

I thought I had a pretty good handle on what made Terry tick until I came across the third item. I had him pegged as a self-absorbed workaholic who spent his spare time planning his next project, song or business move. Vandevere managed to learn that Terry used Gavin Tomko's ID to volunteer anonymously at a center for troubled teens in downtown San Diego. Vandevere posed as a concerned parent who questioned Terry's commitment. The center director had nothing but high praise for Terry and revealed that he had been volunteering for the past five years.

It was date night and since I had been dominating our choice of activities since taking on the murder case, I told Kelly I would take her wherever she wanted to go. "Take me back to Bernie's club," she said. "I was jealous watching all of those other couples dancing last weekend. I want you to wear me out."

"Are you sure you want me to expend all of your energy on the dance floor?" I asked.

"I may save a little something for later if you behave yourself," she said. "There is one other thing that concerns me."

"What's that?" I asked.

"I liked your friend Glenda and her fiancée. I was disappointed that they didn't make it to your show. Do you think they may want to join us?" she asked.

I reached Glenda and learned they ducked out on the show because of the fact that GI Jo-Jo would be there and Glenda felt the need to keep her distance from him. She was glad I called back and we arranged to meet for dinner at 7:30 PM and dancing at the Dali Lama to follow.

Dinner conversation was light and fun. Glenda recounted a few stories from UCSD that brought back fond memories, even though I knew Kelly would bust my chops over a few details.

When we got to the Dali Lama I didn't even have the chance to say hello to Bernie before Kelly had me out on the dance floor, where we stayed for the entire first set. By the time we made our way back to the table I had resolved to get to the gym at least three times a week regardless of the status of the case.

Undoubtedly on a tip from Jasmine, Bernie appeared at our table at the break and attributed the full house to the wonderful publicity he received from last week's show. "In fact," he said, "we've been packed every night this week." He quickly excused himself and made his way back to the office.

When the next set started Kelly said, "I'm sure glad I wore my dancing shoes tonight."

Glenda caught my expression and said, "I have a couple of things I need to tell Jason about his case." Then, looking at her fiancée asked, "Would you be a dear and take Kelly for a spin while we talk shop?" Tyrone agreed and we were suddenly in an unscheduled meeting.

"Do you really have something for me or did you just happen to notice that I look like I'm ready to keel over?" I asked.

"I was about to return the file yesterday when I decided to take one last look at an adjunct deposition section I hadn't reviewed. I found something you may want to follow-up on," she said.

"What is it?" I asked.

"It was a deposition from the captain who ran Martin's unit before the fragged captain took over. In the deposition, Captain Anson Phillips stated that he was certain that Martin acted on behalf of all of the soldiers in the unit in response to gross dereliction of duty on the part of the deceased. Captain Phillips retired two years prior to the incident. A year later he got his son, Daniel, assigned to the unit. According to Captain Phillips, his son was killed disarming ordnance he wasn't properly trained to handle. The soldiers who served under Phillips took it very hard. Phillips felt Martin's actions were the only solution after formal complaints failed to correct the situation and two other recruits were severely injured as a result of the C.O.'s laziness and incompetence," she said.

"Wow," I said, "I guess there really are two sides to every story. Thanks, Glenda. You probably saved me three days of work."

"Three days of work and one dance," she said as Kelly and Tyrone returned from the dance floor. "Break time is over."

"Why don't we all dance?" asked Tyrone.

"That's a great idea," I said and smiled at Glenda.

Chapter 22

SUNDAY morning I was feeling a little uneasy. I had high hopes that GI Jo-Jo would help get Chelsea out of the number one suspect slot. But, it was starting to look like he wasn't the scumbag I had originally thought. I was feeling closer to being back to square one than to finding the killer. With my boss recently locked up as the prime suspect, I was getting frustrated. Kelly sensed my mood and asked if I would take her to The Eggman for brunch.

We reached the restaurant just before the post-church crush and only had to wait five minutes for a table. "I can see the case is on your mind today," Kelly said. "Would you like to talk about it?"

I spent the next half-hour giving her a synopsis of the events leading up to today. It was the first time I had laid out a case for her. As I finished I was wondering if it was a mistake to burden her with my problems.

That feeling lasted only a few seconds as Kelly shocked me with a tremendously insightful observation. She asked, "If Chofsky is so willing to play hardball with you, do you think he might have talked with the other band members about Terry wanting to get rid of one of them?"

I asked, "Do you mean to stir things up?"

"Exactly. There's nothing like a little peer pressure," she stated.

"It makes sense," I said. "He was losing in the negotiations with Terry. Vandevere probably told him Terry was in a position to afford a long court battle. Why not see if the others were as willing to live on a tight budget for three years, especially if one of them was about to get the ax?"

"Did that help?" she asked.

"Absolutely! You'd make a fine detective Miss Kennedy," I said as I reached across the table and gave her hand a squeeze.

As a fair and equal partner in this relationship, I asked Kelly if she was excited about school starting on Tuesday. She spent the entire ride back to her condo telling me about it as I pondered my next move on the case.

After dropping Kelly off, I called each of the band members. I got voice mail for Nigel and Ian, but Jack was in and agreed to see me this afternoon.

Forty minutes later Jack was welcoming me into his modest abode. He had either contracted pinkeye or had just gotten stoned. I hoped it wouldn't adversely affect his memory of a possible conversation with Ivan Chofsky. When we reached the entrance to the living room Jack said, "I know you want to talk, but I'd rather jam a little first, OK?"

"That would be awesome," I said and Jack beamed. We progressed from blues to rock to power rock to metal in about 45 minutes. When the metal jam had ended I unhooked the guitar strap before Jack could launch into the next improvisation. "Let's take a break," I said.

We moved into Jack's well-appointed living room. "OK, I guess I'm ready for you to put on the Sherlock hat. Should I shine the reading light in my eyes or something?" he asked with a toothy grin.

"Let's just kick back and talk," I said. "We touched on how Terry was negotiating with Cerise on a new contract the last time I was here."

"Yes. Like I said, Terry took care of all of that stuff. I didn't even ask him about it. I had complete faith in his ability to get us the best deal," he said soberly.

"I remember you telling me you didn't discuss it with Terry, but did John Koflanovich ever talk with you about it?" I asked.

Jack looked at me, then at a beautiful clear crystal lamp sitting on a teak end table. The body of the lamp was see-through and I could see the wall behind Jack through the lamp. Jack leaned toward the lamp, touched it simultaneously with his index and pinky fingers and the lamp swung open to reveal a glass stash box that matched the color of the wall. Jack withdrew two marijuana cigarettes. He put one in his mouth and extended the other toward me, "Care to join me?" he asked.

"Not today," I said and waited while he lit up.

After a couple of tokes he looked at me and I wondered if I was going to have to repeat the question when he said, "Mr. Koflanovich called me about a month before Terry was killed."

I waited out a 30 seconds pause to see if Jack would continue without prompting, but he was not going to make it easy. "What did he say?"

Jack said, "He explained that he was in the process of negotiating a new contract with Terry and he wanted to get my input."

"What did you tell him?" I asked.

"That I was comfortable letting Terry handle the band's business," he responded.

"What did he say next?" I asked.

"He said that Terry was trying to get out of his contract with Cerise Records and that it looked like we were headed for a long court battle," Jack replied.

"How did you respond to that?" I asked.

Jack took a long toke on his joint and held it in his lungs for so long I was afraid he was going to pass out. He then said, "Mr. Koflanovich said that it would mean the CD we just finished wouldn't get released for three years or more, and that he'd get a court order that would keep us from performing any of the unreleased songs."

I could see that Jack was starting to feel the effects of the pot. I tried to mirror his enthusiasm and appear sympathetic. "That sucks!" I exclaimed. "Doesn't he know how good those songs are?"

"I know! He's a businessman. He didn't care," Jack replied.

"What else did he say?" I asked.

"He said that without the new songs we wouldn't be able to

do a big money headline tour and that I had better have a savings account if I wanted to play Terry's game," he said with disgust.

"That's totally bogus," I commented, "What did you say to that?"

"I told him that people without soul shouldn't be in the record business and do you know what that shit said?" he asked.

"What?" I asked.

"That if Terry had soul he wouldn't be squeezing him for every nickel and get the songs out to the fans where they'd be appreciated," he said, then gave a little cough.

"What did you say to him?" I asked.

"I told him I didn't get involved in business negotiations because I have no intention of getting into the back-stabbing shit he was trying to pull," he said with a hint of pride.

"Good for you. Did he say anything else?" I asked.

Jack stood up suddenly and said, "I'm gonna grab a beer, do you want one?"

"Sure," I said and followed him into the kitchen, which was as organized and tasteful as the living room. I tried prompting Jack again by asking, "So, what did he say," but Jack was focused in on the beers and ignored me.

"I love these beer steins," he said, holding out two pewter steins with orange inlays and inscriptions in Gaelic. "Nigel gave them to me for my birthday." He did a slow pour down the side of the stein, then let the last couple of ounces splash to give it a head. He presented the stein to me and repeated the ceremony for his own benefit.

I took a long sip and sat on a tall stool, hoping we would be staying in the kitchen for a while. I was beginning to experience a contact high from Jack's weed. "C'mon," I said. "The suspense is killing me. What did Koflanovich say?"

Jack sat in an oak chair at a matching kitchen table and said, "He made something up to try to get me pissed off at Terry, but it didn't work."

I said, "Elden, your lawyer, gave me four different versions of contracts Terry proposed to Koflanovich. Each of them had a clause that would allow the band to fire one of its members. Is that what he told you about?"

Jack's jaw dropped and I could tell this news was a surprise. "Bullshit!" he exclaimed. "Koflanovich made that up!"

"Jack, I got the copies from your lawyer, not from Koflanovich. I know Terry had some problems with Ian on your last tour. Do you think the clause was put in there for Ian or was something else going on?" I asked.

"This blows me away," he replied. "We busted our asses for Terry. I know we had our problems, but the music was getting better and better. You know that. Terry was always about the music. I know he had to handle all of the other bullshit. But Terry liked to talk about where we were going when we complained about how hard he was driving us. I can't imagine him breaking up the synergy we had."

"I don't know. Maybe it was part of Terry's negotiating strategy. Did you ask him about it?" I inquired.

"No," he said and stared at the floor.

"Did you talk with any of the band about this?" I inquired.

"Nigel was always my go-between. I asked him and he said he thought it was Koflanovich trying to turn us against Terry. I really don't want to think about this anymore," he said and walked out of the kitchen. By the time I got to the living room his stereo was playing Cream's "Sunshine of Your Love." "I always like to listen to Clapton when I'm feeling down. If you want to hang out, feel free. But, I don't want to talk about that stuff anymore," he said and fired up another joint.

"I'm sorry I upset you, Jack. I had better take off. Thanks for the beer and especially for the jam. It's always a thrill to play with you. Call me if you think of anything that can help us all get back to normal," I said and walked out the front door.

I jumped into the Acura and roared off to Nigel's abode. I was very fortunate that the California Highway Patrol wasn't doing one of its famous holiday crackdowns on speeders or my insurance rates would have surely doubled. I skidded to a halt under Nigel's huge driveway awning, jumped out of the car and rang his doorbell. The lead guitar riff that followed was not keeping up with the energy I was feeling. The thirty-second riff ended and no one had answered. I rang again and, as the second riff was ending, the girl who had flashed me on my last visit, appeared at the door wearing a flimsy pink mini-negligee, carrying a giant blue martini glass and appearing completely inebriated. "Hello," she said in a throaty, sexy voice.

"I need to talk to Nigel," I said rapidly.

"Did you like my boobies?" she asked, then struck up a pose and took a sip of her martini.

"They're lovely," I said, "but I need to talk to Nigel right now. Will you tell him I'm here?" I asked.

"No can do," she replied. "That shit took off for the holiday weekend and didn't even talk to me before he left. I got a tattoo for him last weekend and this weekend he's off with God knows who and left me here alone," she added with a little slur.

"Did he leave a note or a voice-mail to say where he was going?" I asked.

"I got a tattoo of his stupid guitar on my heinie and it still hurts," she said as she slid her palm under the negligee to give it a rub.

I touched her shoulder to get her attention and said, "Did Nigel leave a message on where he was going?"

"He left me a stupid voice-mail that he was interviewing people for the band out of town this weekend and he'll be back on Tuesday or Wednesday. He didn't ask if I wanted to go. He didn't even think about me being stuck here all by myself for the long weekend with nothing to do but rub my heinie. It's not fair!" she cried and gave a big pout.

"I'm sorry he ruined your weekend. If he calls will you tell him I'm trying to get in touch and ask him to call?" I asked.

"Don't you want to stay a while and keep me company?" she asked using her sexy voice again. For a moment I considered the possibility of a brief interview to see if this gorgeous girl in her early twenties could provide any insight into Nigel's business, but quickly concluded that it would only lead to big trouble and latent Catholic guilt. It just wasn't worth it.

"Sorry, I'm working today. Please remember to give my message to Nigel," I said with a hopeful smile.

She replied, "I will if you'll give him a message for me."

"OK, what is it?" I asked.

Nigel's girlfriend turned around, flipped her negligee up in the back and mooned me. She was right. Nigel's golden guitar still had a pink hue. She held her pose until I drove away.

It was 4:15 PM and I decided a pop-in on Ian would be fruitless. I called Cory and reached him at home. He reported that Ian concluded his Saturday night at about 8:30 AM, and would probably roll into The Tillerman's sometime between 5:00 PM and 7:00 PM depending on whether or not he was hungry.

I drove to Mission Beach and pulled up a barstool in front of the Doberman's Stub poster. I was fortunate that the bartender I met on my previous visit was not on duty, so my status as a PI was unknown. Over the next hour I made a list of questions I had for Ian and Nigel. At 6:00 PM, Bert, the bartender I met on my first visit, took over and immediately recognized me. "Nosing around asking questions about Ian again, are you?"

"Why, did somebody complain?" I asked.

"Yeah, somebody complained. He doesn't like tattletale TV. So why don't you bugger off," he said with a pugnacious attitude.

"One of my employees got assaulted outside of this bar by a couple of Russians. Unless you'd like me to link The Tillerman to the Russian Mafia next time I'm on the show I suggest you change your attitude," I said.

"Like I've got to worry that my customers will believe you and stop coming," he said with a laugh.

"You missed the point, Einstein. I'm telling you to lay in a couple of cases of vodka because you'll be attracting a whole new ethnic group to your bar – Russian thugs and people who want to fight them," I said.

We were in the middle of a stare-down when Ian walked in the back door, saw me and shouted, "There's my mate. How the hell are ya, Jason?"

"I'm doing fine Ian, and yourself?" I inquired.

"Fit as a fiddle," he said to me, then turned to the bartender and said, "Double Bushie me lad."

When his drink arrived, Bert glared at me, then said to Ian, "He's talkin' about bringing the Russian's here and causin' trouble."

I expected Ian to drain his drink and immediately order another as he had done the last time we met here, but instead he said, "Are you kidding? This guy's a Dobie! We just played a gig together at a club last weekend." Then, with a more serious tone he added, "So, I don't want you telling any stories, Bert."

Bert looked him in the eyes and said, "We're cool."

We then made our way through a dozen occupied tables of well-wishers, to a relatively remote corner where a track light illuminated a huge color photo of Rod Stewart in his early thirties, wearing a soccer uniform, standing with a teammate. From the inscription I surmised the teammate is the current owner of The Tillerman, one Tommy Stark. Ian pointed at the photo and said, "That man's been like a father to me."

I couldn't resist an opportunity to break the solemn tone. "Do you mean you're really Hot Rod Junior?" I asked with mock excitement.

Ian could tell I was kidding and said, "You're a pisser, Duffy. Another Irishman messing with me head. I'm talking about Tommy Stark. He owns The Tillerman and I'd hate to see anything happen to this place."

"Bert greeted me by telling me to get out. When somebody hits, I hit back," I said. "Don't worry, I was just trying to shut him up until you got here. So, can you spare me a few minutes?"

"Anything for an honorary Dobie. What's on your mind?" he asked.

"I met with John Koflanovich yesterday and talked about the contract he was trying to work out with Terry. I know he contacted each of you. Jack was very helpful in filling me in on their conversation, I was hoping you could do the same. Did he tell you that you could end up in a three-year court battle and wouldn't make much money till it gets resolved?" I asked.

"Yeah. That was about the gist of it," he said as he looked at the poster.

"I know Terry was in a position to financially withstand that kind of battle. Were you?" I asked.

"Of course not. But it was just a negotiating thing. Terry was bluffing to get us the best deal. It was just business bullshit. I didn't put much stock into what Koflanovich had to say," he said with slightly more eye contact.

"I saw the four contracts that Terry proposed. Each of them had a clause enabling the band to fire one member. Who do you think he had in mind?" I asked.

Up to that point Ian had been merely sipping his drink. After I asked the question, Ian downed what remained in one large swallow and said, "I need a refill. Can I get you one?"

"Will you answer my question before you go?" I asked.

"Let's stop pretending," he said increasing his volume. "You know it was me he wanted to oust."

"That's just it, Ian. Everybody else thinks it was you, but I don't. Right now it's just a hunch, but, if you'll answer a few more questions I think I can convince the police that it wasn't you," I said.

"The police think it was me?" he asked with astonishment. "I thought they just arrested Chelsea."

"They did, but that was before they learned somebody was about to get the sack. That's what the cops call motive. Chelsea's dad is rich enough to hire a dream team of lawyers and they know it. Personally, I'm sure she didn't do it and it's just a matter of time until she's cleared," I said.

"So they think I'm guilty just because I knew I might get fired?" he asked with agitation in his voice.

"They also think you moved the glass partitions to help shield yourself from the blast, since the new configuration would have given you more protection," I said, presenting my discarded theory as fact.

"It had to do with echo! I didn't know there was going to be an explosion!" he boomed, and several of his compatriots stared at our table.

"I'm working with the primary investigator and I think I can convince him that you weren't involved, but I need you to answer a few questions honestly if I'm going to be successful," I said.

"What do you want to know?" he asked while staring into his empty glass.

"I don't think Terry would have accepted you into the band three years ago if your substance abuse problem had been apparent. If this is true I need to know when you started hitting it hard and why," I said.

"Can I get a refill first?" he pleaded.

"No. Tell me now," I said, not wanting to give him time to come up with a bullshit story.

"I always liked the drink, but I didn't get carried away in the beginning," he said. "You're right, Terry never would have allowed me in the band."

"When did it pick up?" I asked.

"As I got famous I started dabbling in a few drugs, then I would drink myself to sleep," he said. "I guess it snowballed."

"That doesn't fit very well with my theory," I said. "I think fame brought more parties, but your first CD brought the fame. I don't see Terry carrying you if the heavy abuse surfaced early on. I'd guess it didn't get to be a problem until the last six months."

"You think something happened and you want to know what," he stated. I raised my eyebrows and leaned forward. Ian continued, "OK. After the last CD there was a lot more infighting and I responded by running away rather than getting confrontational. I didn't want to take sides. Once I became a total fuck-up nobody gave a shite what I thought. Is that what you wanted to know?"

"What was the infighting about?" I asked.

"The second CD attracted a different kind of fan. Terry wanted to stay true to our metal roots, but Nigel wanted to transition into more romantic songs. Terry didn't like the idea of losing power. It definitely changed the way they started acting toward each other and I didn't want to be caught in the middle," he said.

"I understand and I believe you, Ian," I said with empathy. "Did you ask Terry about the contract?"

"No. I knew he was pissed at me and I didn't want a donnybrook," he said.

"So, what did you do?" I asked.

"I called Nigel. He's been like an older brother to me. I knew Nigel couldn't afford to get cut off for three years and he had some influence with Terry," he said.

"What did Nigel say?" I asked.

"He told me that my behavior would be the only thing that would make Terry want to take time off. He said that I needed to stop fucking everything up. I knew he was right, but I wasn't expecting Nigel to whack me while I was down like that," Ian said.

"Do you think it's possible Nigel was involved in Terry's death?" I asked.

"No! That's ridiculous!" he exclaimed. "He'd never do anything like that," he added with less enthusiasm.

"It sounds like you're not telling me something," I commented.

"It's just a feeling. It's probably nothing," he said.

"Tell me," I said.

"I can't. I'd feel like I'd be ratting out a best friend," he said.

"The only way this is going to work out for you and the band is if we get to the truth. Nothing's going to be right for you until that happens." I said.

"I don't want you telling Nigel you got this from me, OK?" he asked and I nodded. "Nigel has some lads from back home that most would consider hooligans. I've been wondering if maybe Nigel told those Teddy Boys that he was having troubles with Terry, and one of them took it upon himself to help Nigel out."

Do you know any of their names?" I asked.

"No. I ran into them once at a club and Nigel made a point to not introduce me and took his leave as quickly as he could get them out of there," he said.

"Is Nigel with them this weekend?" I asked.

"Nigel doesn't keep me up on his itinerary," he said.

"Let me check it out," I said. "In the meantime, see if you can stop acting like you're trying to drown your guilt. I'll see what I can do with the local bobbies."

"You're a prince, Duffy," he said as he walked me to the bar.

"Another Bushie?" asked Bert.

"No Bert. Give me a glass of Watney's," he said and gave me a smile and a nod as he downshifted to beer.

As I started home I got an idea that could have a huge downside, but seemed worth the risk. I changed course for Rancho Santa Fe to drop in on the owner of the pink and gold guitar tattoo. When I reached the estate the sky had just gotten dark. I waited through four thirty-second guitar riffs before Nigel's girlfriend finally flicked on the entrance chandelier and opened the door. "Change your mind Mr. Whats-yer-name?" she asked.

"It's Jason and I couldn't get that beautiful tattoo out of my mind. What's your name?" I asked.

"I'zz Victoria," she said with a slur.

"You aren't entertaining anyone else are you Victoria?" I inquired.

"Nope," she replied. "I'm in this big house all by my lonesome. C'mon in." As she led the way to the living room she didn't stagger, but was decidedly careful in her movements, as if she was making a conscious effort to appear sober. "Would you like to ravish me on the davenport or would the settee be more to your liking?" she asked.

"Actually, I have a girlfriend and a great deal of Irish Catholic guilt. It will take a couple of stiff drinks before I could get past that," I said with a smile.

"You better not tell Nigel you're Irish Catholic if you know what's good for you?" she said with one eye half closed.

"Why not?" I asked.

"Because he and his asshole buddies don't like Irish Catholics," she said.

"But he has an estate in Ireland," I said.

"Protestant Ireland. Why don't you make the drinks," she said as she pointed at the bar.

I mixed enough to fill one large martini glass. I then took two glasses and filled them half way. I topped mine off with water and

Victoria's with vodka, then returned to the sofa where she was reclining on large pillows. "Have a drink with me," I said. Victoria took a large swallow and made a face.

"You sure make a stiff drink," she commented.

"The stiffer the drink the quicker I get rid of the guilt," I said.

Victoria held up her glass and said, "Then let's drink to a quick stiffy," she said and laughed hysterically at her joke. "Tell me about your girlfriend."

"That will only make the guilt last longer. Let's talk about something else, like Nigel's asshole buddies. Is he with them this weekend?" I asked.

"I don't want to talk about them. They suck," she said and took another long draw on her drink while I poured the rest of mine in a large vase holding a fichus tree.

"Ready for another one?" I asked.

"Schlow down stud," she slurred. "I want you to last all night."

"I know," I said. "I'm just anxious to get in the mood."

"Knock yourself out," she said.

I stood up, retrieved her glass and walked to the bar. Victoria didn't seem any closer to passing out than she had when I arrived. This time I made hers one-third martini and two-thirds straight vodka. "Let's have a toast," I said as I handed her the large V-shaped glass on a thick stem.

"What are we doin' for?" she asked as she started to drift.

"Let's drink to your gorgeous blue eyes," I said.

"I'll drink to that," she said and took a big gulp. Her eyes widened and she said, "That woke me up," as she shook her head from side to side.

Desperate times call for desperate measures. "Mind if I put on some music?" I asked.

"Think somebody's getting in the mood," she said.

There it was, just as I suspected. No self-respecting British rocker could possible own a CD collection without Pink Floyd's *Dark Side of the Moon*. It's a tremendous rock classic, but has always had the power to put me to sleep when I was tired but just couldn't nod off. "How ironic," Victoria said as the music started to play.

"What's that?" I asked.

She replied, "First I mooned you, now you're playing *Dark Side of the Moon* for me."

"I'll drink to that," I said and clinked her glass. She took a sip and stared at an aquarium built into the wall. We sat quietly listening to the CD for about five minutes, then I heard the sound of liquid pouring onto the rug. I poured my drink into the fichus vase, removed the glass from Victoria's hand, then set out in search of Nigel's office.

I found it on the first floor next to a guest bedroom. Unfortunately, I didn't luck out like in Tecate. Nigel had a password-protected computer and 15 minutes of my best guesses did nothing to unlock it. I spent the next half-hour going through a January-December accordion file filled with monthly bills. I took out a small spiral pad and noted the phone numbers of calls to Ireland from his phone bill. I also wrote down Nigel's travel itinerary. I was about to leave when a picture on the wall caught my eye. It was of a large group of twenty-something men wearing orange sashes walking along a road with spiral barbed wire separating the sash wearers from an angry mob. British soldiers in red jackets were posted at ten-foot intervals. Upon closer inspection I spotted Nigel flipping off one of the mob members. A small brass plate affixed to the picture frame said, "Help Charles Darwin – Kill a Catholic."

I was enthralled. I spent another half-hour looking at trophies, nick-knacks and other memorabilia relating to Northern Ireland and, of course, rock & roll. I made my way from picture to picture all the way around Nigel's spacious office. When I reached the doorway, there was Victoria with an angry scowl on her face. "What the hell do you think you're doing?" she asked.

"I'm just checking out Nigel's pictures. I love the one over there with Nigel and Jimmy Page," I said with a smile.

"Then why is Nigel's bill folder sitting on the desk?" she asked with remarkable clarity.

"I was hoping it was an autograph file, but, you're right, it was just bills," I said. "How did you sober up so fast?"

Victoria opened her hand to reveal some spent capsules and said, "amyl nitrate." She continued to stare at me with intense suspicion. "I think you had better leave."

"OK," I said and walked out of the office.

"I'm going to have to tell Nigel about this," she stated.

"That should be interesting. Let's see; you tell him you seduced the guy who played in his band last weekend, then you got drunk, passed out and caught him looking at his pictures in the study. What do you think he'll say?" I asked.

Victoria replied, "I'm not gonna tell him any of that. I'll tell him you bullshitted your way in here and when I wasn't looking you snuck into his office and snooped around."

"And then Nigel confronts me and I ask him if the pink hue has faded off of the electric guitar on your heinie," I said as I reached the door.

When I opened the door Victoria wiped her face with her hands and said, "Please tell me we didn't get it on."

"Victoria, we didn't get it on. I was too grossed out when you peed in the fichus tree vase," I said as I walked to the Acura, then sped off with my trusty spiral notebook in my back pocket.

Chapter 23

I CALLED Dad at 8:00 AM and told him about what I had seen in Nigel's office. "He's an Orangeman," Dad said.

"University of Syracuse?" I asked skeptically.

"No. We're talking about the Order of Orange. It's been around since the 16 or 1700's. O'Malley talks about them," he said.

"Any chance I could talk to O'Malley later today?" I asked.

"No problem. I'm meeting him at Casey's around 5:00 this afternoon. Would you like to join us?" he asked.

I hesitated a moment, wondering if this would make me an honorary member of the Irish Mafia. But I definitely needed to find out as much as I could before Nigel returned. I had better things to do than spend the entire day in front of my computer, so I agreed.

My next call was to Ivan Chofsky's cell phone. His assistant, Svetlana Illich, answered, "What is it, Mr. Duffy?"

"I need to meet with your boss today," I said.

"Not possible," she said.

"Why not," I inquired.

"He is at funeral, then meal with family," she said. "Call back tomorrow," she added and hung up. I called back immediately. "What?" she answered.

"Where is the funeral?" I asked.

"St. Nicholas," she replied. "Mass at 9:00 AM, burial at cemetery behind church at 10:00 AM."

"Where is St. Nicholas?" I asked.

"North of Escondido," she replied and hung up again.

I didn't have time to attend the mass. I jumped into a dark suit and headed for the North County. I arrived at 9:50 AM and found two police vehicles with four uniformed officers guarding the gated entrance.

At the front of the barricade I recognized Chofsky's bodyguard who I had tipped about Shamansky's arrival. He had a word with the officers and I was admitted. He pointed out a path winding around the modest stone church that didn't have the usual Spanish architecture found in most churches in California. Behind the church was a six acre cemetery, bordered by a wooded area on two sides and a canyon to the west. About a hundred yards away was a group of about twenty mourners. As I approached the group I recognized Father Mencavich from my visit to Chofsky's home. When I reached the mourners I looked at Ivan Chofsky and something was wrong. I only met the man once, but he appeared different. Maybe it was the light. I took another couple of steps toward him and two bodyguards grabbed me by my upper arms and directed me away from the flock. One of them was the man who led me and Shamansky to Chofsky's home office. He asked, "What are you doing here?"

"I came to pay my respects," I said and flexed my muscles once they let go of my arms.

"Mr. Koflanovich cannot talk with you today," he said. "You must go at once."

"I was there when Torhan died. What's wrong with me attending his funeral?" I asked. Before he could answer a shot rang out from the tree line and Chofsky flipped onto his back as if his legs had been suddenly kicked out from under him. Several mourners screamed, Father Mencavich ducked behind a headstone and I could hear the engine of a dirt-bike roar off in the distance. I ran to Chofsky and realized immediately that a body-double had been shot in the face, just above the jaw. I think the sniper may have realized it too because the force of the blast had detached a snap-on toupee from the look-alike's bald pate.

I made my way to my car with the rest of the fleeing mourners as the police were unsuccessful in controlling the stampede. I had more important things to do than recount my involvement in the case with the Sheriff's Department for the remainder of the day. I drove straight to Del Mar and called Chofsky's phone a few blocks from the compound.

"What is it?" answered the charmless Svetlana.

"It's Jason Duffy. I just came from the funeral where your boss's look-alike was murdered," I said accusingly.

"I don't know what you are talking about," she said.

"Put Ivan on the phone or I'll call the police and tell them he arranged for the murder of some poor actor so that the Russian Mafia would think he was dead," I said.

"Hold line," she replied and three minutes of silence followed as I pulled up to the gate in front of the compound.

Another Russian "waiter" approached my car with a black towel over his hand. "Who are you!" he demanded.

"Jason Duffy," I said. "I'm on the phone with Svetlana Illich. She's going to tell you to let me in soon."

The guard rested the barrel of his gun on my half-open window and said, "I hope you are correct, sir."

Svetlana came back on the line and said, "I will meet you at gate," and hung up. I wish she would stop doing that.

Five minutes later Svetty had me comfortably ensconced across the desk from Ivan Chofsky, who was wearing a black suit and tie. "I understand you witnessed the shooting at the cemetery," he said with little emotion.

I didn't want the conversation to start off on an adversarial note, so I simply said, "The poor guy never had a chance."

"Did the police or anyone get a look at the shooter?" he asked.

"He was in a wooded area and escaped on a dirt bike seconds after your look-alike went down. Nobody saw anything," I said.

"Tragic," he commented and we paused for a few seconds of silence.

"I need to ask you a few questions about your conversations with the surviving band members regarding your negotiations with Terry," I said.

"My negotiations were with Terry. Nobody else participated in them before Terry died," he said.

"Are you telling me that you didn't call each of the band members and tell them they were going to be without money for three years if Terry started a court battle?" I asked with the tone of a prosecuting attorney.

"It sounds like you already know the answer to your question," he said.

"I spoke with the band members about these conversations, but I get the impression one of them was not entirely truthful with me, so I would like to get your version of each of these chats, alright?" I asked.

"I am continuing to negotiate with the band and don't think it would be appropriate to discuss negotiating strategy in the middle of the process," Chofsky replied.

"I need an answer to these questions. We can either do it here and I will use discretion, or I can ask Detective Shamansky to have this conversation with you at police headquarters," I said.

"What makes you think he's going to do what you tell him?" he asked.

"Because I'll tell him you set up some poor schlep to get killed so that you could try to fool the Russian Mafia into thinking you're dead. It could easily get you deported back to Russia," I said and waited for Chofsky to reply.

He pondered what I had told him and said, "Alright; I'll trust your discretion."

"Who did you call first?" I asked.

"I called Mr. Davis," he said.

"This will go a lot faster if you just tell me what you told each of them instead of me playing twenty questions with you for the next three hours," I said.

"I told Mr. Davis that Mr. Tucker was putting me in a position where I had no alternative but to tie the band up in court. I let him know that my attorneys estimated the length of time to conclude that type of case, after appeals, to be approximately three years, and that during that time the new CD could not be released and the band could not play any of the songs in concert. I also pointed out that without the support of a new CD it would be unlikely that a concert promoter would advance Doberman's Stub to stadium tour headliner, and may steer clear altogether if they got the impression they could be drawn into the lawsuit. This is essentially what I told each of them," Chofsky said.

"What else?" I asked.

Chofsky stared at me for about ten seconds before continuing. "I pointed out that Mr. Tucker had the financial resources to withstand a long legal siege, but I thought it only fair that I make the other members of the band aware of the repercussions of a protracted court battle."

"How did Ian respond when you gave him this news?" I asked.

"He used a substantial amount of foul language to express his displeasure at this revelation," Chofsky said. "Once he calmed down he said that he trusted that Mr. Tucker would act in the band's best interest, and he would abide by the consensus opinion."

"Is that when you told him about the clause Terry put in the contract proposals enabling him to fire one of the members?" I inquired.

"That is correct," he said. "Mr. Davis became very upset and verbally abusive. I couldn't tell if it was directed at me or at Mr. Tucker. He concluded his tirade by hanging up before I could respond."

I asked, "What was Nigel's response to this bomb?"

"Actually, I contacted Mr. Pascal next. I believe Mr. Davis called Mr. Choate while I was discussing the matter with Mr. Pascal. By the time I reached Mr. Choate he was aware of the details of my conversation with Mr. Davis. I was not able to reach Mr. Choate immediately after my conversation with Mr. Pascal, and it is my opinion that he discussed the matter with Mr. Tucker prior to my call," he said.

"Considering that Nigel is the co-writer and, by default, second in command, why didn't you confront him first instead of giving him the most time to prepare a response?" I asked.

Chofsky looked out his window for a moment and mulled his response. "As the Japanese say, I wanted him to save face."

"It sounds like you were laying the groundwork for a coup," I noted.

"Mr. Tucker wielded power like a dictator. I merely attempted to introduce a little democracy," he said.

"But in the end the dictator was overthrown," I stated.

"You certainly don't suspect one of the band members," Chofsky said with more enthusiasm than at any point in our conversation.

"Why not?" I asked. "You planted the seeds for a revolution. Why are you surprised that one of these guys might have planted the bomb? If a band member was sure he was about to get tossed out of the band and cut off from his income stream, who else would have a better motive?"

"Mr. Tucker was not a likeable man. I understand he recently embarrassed some other business partners and had a major falling out with his wife, who I need not point out, was just arrested and jailed for the murder," Chofsky said with a raised eyebrow as he tapped a pen point on a legal pad.

I could tell Chofsky felt he had gained the upper hand in our conversation and was anxious for it to end. I needed to run a bluff to keep the ball rolling. "Chelsea has been withholding some information that is embarrassing in nature, but will give her an alibi for the murder. I expect the charges to be dismissed within the week."

"What is this alibi?" he asked.

"I swore to Chelsea and her lawyers that I wouldn't reveal it under any circumstance, allowing them to break the news when it would result in the charges being dismissed," I said.

"I'm being open and honest with you," he said.

"I'm not facing deportation for getting someone killed, not to mention the crimes you orchestrated against me and my staff. We're nowhere near even in this relationship. What did Nigel say when you called him?" I asked.

"Mr. Choate tried to assure me that no final decisions had been made regarding litigation and that we needed each other and both would suffer greatly from a stalemate," he said.

"What else did you tell him?" I asked as if I knew, even though I was fishing.

Chofsky once again gazed out his window, mulling a decision on what would be prudent to disclose. "I tried to bolster his confidence." I flipped my palms skyward in an effort to prompt him to elaborate. "I told him that our A&R consultants attribute the band's sudden surge in popularity to the Nigel Choate compositions."

"Was this news to Nigel, or did you get the impression he already knew this?" I asked.

"This was a revelation to Mr. Choate, I am certain," he said.

"How do you know?" I asked.

"Up to that point he had held a stern, adversarial tone. When I offered this fact his manner changed and the way he said, 'really,' gave me the impression he was genuinely surprised," Chofsky said.

"Did he ask you to elaborate?" I asked.

"No. But he did offer to avail himself to the negotiating process if I reached an impasse with Mr. Tucker," he said.

"Did you take him up on his offer?" I asked.

"I kept him apprised of new developments, and I'm glad I did considering he had to step into Mr. Tucker's role," he said.

"As I understand it, he's in the process of hiring an established manager who will assume that role," I stated.

"He is seeking new management," Chofsky said, side-stepping part of my question.

"Have you reached an agreement on the release of the new CD?" I asked.

"We reached an agreement on two major points," he said. "First, I conceded that the escape clause was a mistake on my part and substantially diminished my position. Second, Mr. Choate conceded that Mr. Tucker was a tremendous talent and his absence will substantially diminish the band's current and future value as of this date. So, we agreed to release the new CD under the terms of the old contract."

"What about future CD's?" I asked.

"We agreed that Doberman's Stub would remain with Cerise Records, and they would receive a raise within a rather wide range, depending upon the reputation and quality of Mr. Tucker's replacement and the performance of the new CD. The exact amount is to be negotiated by the new manager, who will be selected by the band. It is a win, win situation for all parties," Chofsky said with his first smile of the day.

"Except for Mr. Tucker, of course," I said.

"Of course," he replied.

"I assume if you paid an investigator to follow Terry when he was alive, you are also paying an investigator to keep an eye on Nigel. Is that correct," I asked.

"Mr. Vandevere has been monitoring Mr. Choate's activities," he replied.

"May I see his file?" I asked.

"Mr. Vandevere has the file," he responded.

"Will you call and instruct him to meet with me tomorrow, giving full disclosure?" I asked.

"I will. Now if you will excuse me I need to make some calls to Mr. Torhan's family."

"Thank you for your time and candor," I said, and hoped Chofsky's constricted sphincter speech patterns hadn't rubbed off on me. Miss Illich escorted me to the gate.

At 5:00 PM I walked into Casey's Bar and spotted Dad with three of his fellow Friendly Sons of St. Patrick. I recognized O'Malley from the occasional backyard barbecue, but had never seen the other two. "Have a seat, son," Dad said as I approached. "You remember Lieutenant O'Malley."

I extended my hand to O'Malley and said, "Thanks for agreeing to meet with me."

"Glad to be of service," he replied.

"Son, these are Detectives Seamus Fallon and Brendan Gillhouly. Guys, this is my son, Jason," Dad said with the smile of a proud father.

After the handshakes Fallon said, "We know you're here to discuss a case so we'll take our leave. It was a pleasure meeting you." Gillhouly agreed and they walked to the far end of the bar where a small group was watching an East Coast baseball game on television.

"So Jason," asked O'Malley, "how can I help you?"

I spent the next five minutes describing what I had seen in Nigel's office. When I told him about the inscription on the picture frame, Dad chimed in, "Those bigoted bastards."

O'Malley asked, "Any idea what town they were in?"

"I think I saw a Portadown sign. Does that sound familiar?" I asked.

"That's where the Orangemen cause the most trouble every year," O'Malley said.

"Give Jason a little background," Dad said to O'Malley.

"The Orangemen are members of the Order of Orange. They formed as a terrorist organization back in the 1700's. Every year they hold parades all over Northern Ireland to celebrate a massacre led by William of Orange at the Battle of Boyne," he said.

"Are you telling me that the government allows a terrorist organization to exist and hold parades?" I asked.

O'Malley replied, "The Orangemen try to put their own spin control on history by saying they formed as a counter-terrorism group, and that today they are just a fraternal organization. But, you ask any Catholic living in Northern Ireland about the Orangemen and every single one will have a story about how Orangemen terrorist activities have affected at least one of their family members or ancestors. The Brits have been using them to do their dirty deeds for a couple of centuries. But this is the first time I've heard of them killing a Catholic on American soil."

"The victim wasn't a Catholic. I don't think it was any kind of political statement. The motive was money," I said.

Dad interjected, "But the method had Northern Ireland written all over it."

"Tell me about the bomb," O'Malley said.

"It was concealed inside an expensive set of headphones. The ear pads were packed with BBs, and each contained a blasting cap. It was detonated when the victim turned on his audio recorder," I said.

Dad said, "It sounds like the perp might have been nearby or had a friend or family member potentially in the blast zone."

"I agree," said O'Malley.

"Why?" I asked.

O'Malley said, "Blasting caps and shrapnel have been commonplace bomb ingredients for a hundred years. But, most of the time it involves a blasting cap inside a jar of nails or screws. Lots of bang for the buck and it leaves nasty looking corpses. The bomb you described could only have pushed the BBs into the vic. Maybe a couple of small pieces of plastic get blown away from the headphones, but probably not enough to seriously hurt anybody else."

O'Malley said, "Blasting caps are everywhere and not difficult to come by. They cause a small explosion that triggers a more potent explosion when positioned next to something like TNT. A blasting cap explosion is definitely powerful enough to push shrapnel into a human being. I'd call the device you described a cheap clean bomb."

With business out of the way, Dad invited the other cops to join us and insisted on bringing up the fact that I am dating a Kennedy. I suffered through about fifteen minutes of cop probes before I was able to change the subject. "Do any of you know a PI named Axel Vandevere?" I asked.

Fallon replied, "I met him on a case a couple of years ago. What do you want to know?"

"He did some work for a guy I don't trust. I'm wondering what your take is on him," I said.

Fallon took a swallow of beer and said, "I asked around about him when I was on the case. I heard he used to work for Interpol until he drank himself out of a job. My experience told me it was probably an accurate assessment. The guy is smart and picks up on little details one day, then drinks on the job the next. If you're lucky enough to catch him when he isn't either drunk or hung over you'll probably be impressed."

On the way home I called Axel Vandevere and arranged to meet him at his office tomorrow morning. I could tell by the tone of his voice that he was not happy about having to share information with another private investigator.

Chapter 24

AT 9:00 AM I arrived at the office of Axel Vandevere Investigations in a crumbling strip mall on the outskirts of an industrial park in National City. Vandevere sat at his desk smoking a cigarette. He wore a gray hat with a black band that looked like it was popular during the thirties. "You must be Duffy," he said.

"That's right, Jason Duffy. Thanks for seeing me," I said and looked at the torn plastic chair on the other side of his desk.

"Have a seat," he said as he waved at the chair with his hand.

"Koflanovich gave me the file on Terry Tucker and promised your full cooperation on what Nigel Choate has been up to," I said.

"Personally, I think a PI should do his own homework," he said, then took a huge drag on his cigarette.

"We're all entitled to our opinions, but your boss says he wants you to answer my questions, so I suggest you cooperate," I said leaning forward.

"Vandevere blew a plume of smoke toward me and replied, "Why don't you tell me what you know, and I'll let you know if you're going in the right direction."

I replied, "Did your boss tell you that I'm working with SDPD on this and he faces deportation if I don't get full cooperation?"

Vandevere said, "And you think I'm such good pals with Koflanovich that I'll do whatever you say?"

I replied, "I think Koflanovich is the richest client you've seen in quite a few years and your income will go right back in the toilet the minute he gets deported."

"I like a man who keeps an eye on the bottom line," he said with a nicotine-stained smile. "OK, I don't want to sit here with you all day. Get on with your questions," he said.

"How long have you been following Nigel Choate?" I asked.

"Since Tucker's funeral," he replied.

"If you want this to go quickly, tell me the most significant things you've observed," I said. "What about his friends from Ireland?"

"Those guys are nuts. Their MO is to go to an Irish bar and start fights. Sometimes they dress in green and act like they're buddy-buddy with the locals, then suggest another Irish bar and beat the snot out of their new friend or friends once they get them outside. Other times they'd walk into near empty bars wearing orange sashes and pick fights," he said.

"Did Nigel get recognized?" I asked.

"No. He always wore a wig and a fake beard," he said.

"Any other mischief besides the beatings?" I asked.

"O'Toole's Bar in Clairemont keeps a two-tier party bus in their parking lot for parades and ballgames. I saw those hooligans blow it up a couple of weekends ago," he said.

"Did you see what they used to blow it up?" I asked hoping it involved a blasting cap.

He replied, "A fuse. They just took off the gas cap, shoved a fuse in, lit it, then drove to a spot across a canyon from the lot, where they watched it explode and burn. They laughed and carried on so loudly while it was going up in flames that the bar patrons heard them over the roar of the fire and tried racing around the canyon to get them. But, by the time they got there all they found was an empty parking lot with the words 'Orangemen Rule' spray painted in orange on the pavement."

"Do you know their names?" I asked.

Vandevere stood up and walked to a stack of file folders. He removed one sheet and handed it to me. The names Warren Bates, Devin Billingsly and Theodore Pine were typed neatly under the heading: Choate Associates of Interest. "Any chance you ran a rap sheet on these guys?" I asked.

"You may find this hard to believe, but the cops don't run errands for me," he said sarcastically.

"Let's talk about the day Terry Tucker was killed. Were you at Denny's that morning?" I asked.

"I was," he said.

"Tell me what you saw after Terry left," I said.

"He left Denny's alone and went to the recording studio," he said.

"What about his stop at 7/Eleven?" I asked.

"Is this a trick question?" he asked.

"You didn't follow him, did you?" I asked.

"I may have had an errand to run. I don't have a staff like some PI's," he said with a squint of the eyes.

He probably made a liquor store run and I didn't see a point in trying to get him to admit it. "Were all of the band members at the studio when you arrived?"

"Yes. Terry was walking in the door when I got there. He left his trunk open. About five minutes later Joseph Martin came out and made two trips carrying Terry's belongings into the studio," he said.

"Did Martin grab and carry or did he take some time at Terry's trunk?" I asked.

"Grab and carry. No chance he could have swapped headphones at that time. He was empty-handed when he approached and he was moving at a pretty good clip. No dallying whatsoever," he said.

"Were you in the lot when the explosion happened?" I asked.

"Actually, I was in the adjacent lot, but I was watching the building when it happened. The band must have just taken a break because I saw the drummer go to the trunk of his car to take a snort of hooch. Choate walked out right afterwards, then BOOM!" he said with sudden emphasis.

"What did they do?" I asked.

He replied, "Davis hit the pavement behind his car like he was afraid there would be a second explosion. Choate immediately ran back into the building."

"One more question. Do you know where the hooligans stay when they're in town?" I asked.

"Occasionally they stay with Choate, but most of the time they stay with a friend at a dump in Southeast San Diego," he said and gave me the address.

"Do you have a name for the friend?" I asked.

"Desmond Thompson," he replied.

I thanked him for his time and let him know I would be back in touch.

On my way to the courthouse I gave Dad a call and asked if he could check out the names Vandevere had given me. He said he'd be happy to help bring down the Orangemen.

I arrived outside the courtroom at 1:15 PM, just as a bailiff was posting the order in which the cases would be heard. Chelsea was listed third, which told me I had at least forty-five minutes before bail would be set. Shamansky arrived at 1:25 PM, just moments before the grand entrance of Reginald Rutherford, a legend among California criminal attorneys. Chelsea's father was at his side. Chelsea's attorney, David Stein, had apparently been demoted to the second string once the superstar was brought on board and walked three steps behind Rutherford.

"Chelsea's up third," I said to Shamansky, "can I talk to you in the juror's lounge?"

Shamansky nodded and we walked out of earshot. "What's on your mind, Duffy?" he asked.

I spent the next ten minutes giving him a synopsis of why I suspected Nigel. When I finished he said, "You have a new suspect every time I see you."

"Chelsea's already rich," I said. "Nigel's fortunes go in the dumper if Terry goes to war with Cerise. Chofsky was doing all he could to fuel the fires of dissent. And, Nigel hangs with a violent gang of hooligans."

"I already have my suspect right where I want her," he said and folded his arms.

I said, "So let's see. Right now you have a suspect with a sparkling record being defended by a lawyer who's never lost a case. On the other hand, there's Nigel, who's running out of money, has motive, opportunity and a posse that likes to blow things up. Why not hedge your bets?"

"Let's see which way the judge goes," he said and walked back toward the courtroom.

When the judge called the case, Reginald Rutherford entered a plea of not guilty. He said, "Judge Stafford, this is a classic case of what is wrong with police profiling. The only reason this poor woman spent the past four days in jail is because SDPD chose to cut corners. Mrs. Tucker has never been arrested. She had no financial motive. Her father is very wealthy and she will never want for money. The prosecution has built a case on the fact that she inherits life insurance and had an argument with her husband shortly before his death." He then spread his arms, looked at the gallery and added, "Will all of you married people who have never had an argument with your spouse please raise your hand?"

There was much laughter and no show of hands. The judge banged his gavel. "Quiet!" he said.

Rutherford added, "I move to dismiss the charges."

The judge replied, "I put a little more faith in the police and district attorney's office than you, Mr. Rutherford. Motion denied. However, I expect to see a more compelling case when we go to trial"

Rutherford then asked that Chelsea be released on her own recognizance.

"In lieu of Mrs. Tucker's record and ties to the community, I am setting bail at $10,000," Judge Stafford said.

The prosecutor, Jeffrey Del Rio jumped to his feet, "Judge, this woman is a millionaire. She could easily jump bail and live comfortably anywhere in the world."

"My ruling stands, Mr. Del Rio. You will be notified of the court date. I'm sure I will be hearing motions in the interim. Good day gentlemen, Mrs. Tucker."

Shamansky looked like he had been punched in the gut. I'm glad I gave him the alternative before the hearing. I don't think he would have talked to me afterwards. I planned on having a chat with Chelsea after the hearing, but Rutherford escorted her past the press and was intent on controlling every second while she was in the proximity of the courthouse.

My cell phone rang as I was getting into my car. "Jason Duffy," I said.

"This is David Cooper returning your call," he said. After a mere three messages Terry's old band mate was finally responding.

"Thanks for getting back to me. Chelsea hired me to find out who killed Terry and I understand you were helping him in the weeks before his death. I was hoping you'd talk with me about what you were working on," I said.

"The only reason I'm talking to you is because of Chelsea being arrested. I'm not going to talk about what I did for Terry on the phone. If you want to meet me near my house I'll fill you in," he said.

"No problem. Where do you live?" I asked

"Morrow Bay," he replied

"That's 300 miles from here!" I exclaimed. "Can't we just talk now?"

"I have a good reason for not wanting to talk on the phone. What I have to say could help Chelsea. If you want to hear it you'll have to cruise up the coast. What's it going to be?" David asked.

"How long will it take me to get there?" I asked.

"If you leave now you'll beat rush hour and should get here in five to six hours. I'm going to have dinner at Carla's Country Kitchen at 7:00 PM. It's a block east of Morrow Rock, you can't miss it. Be in the parking lot around 7:45. Come alone and don't come in the restaurant. Wait for me to come out. I'll be wearing a black MTV sweatshirt. After dinner I'll take a walk on the beach. Catch up to me after you're sure you're not being followed. Then we'll talk," he said.

"Should we set up a password or a secret handshake?" I asked, more than a little annoyed at the hoops he was making me jump through.

"Do you want to do this or not?" he asked.

"I'll be there," I replied and hung up.

I spotted Morrow Rock at 7:25 PM from about ten miles away. It sits just barely off of the shoreline and is over 700 feet tall. I did a report on it in junior high. It's actually an extinct volcano, although it looks more like a giant boulder. I rolled into the parking lot of Carla's Country Kitchen at 7:40 and was looking for a nearby gas station to use the restroom when Cooper appeared in the doorway. He was about my age, had long dirty blond hair and a beard.

I gave him a head start, then followed. I took off the dress shoes and socks I wore to court and jogged on the beach until I caught up with him. "OK, I'm here. Why the cloak and dagger?" I asked.

"Hand me your cell phone," he said.

I did so and he had it apart in three seconds. He inspected the insides for about a minute, then returned it to me and said, "Leave it off." He then took something out of his pocket that was just a bit larger than an ink pen and passed it over my body.

"You're not in the CIA are you?" I asked.

"I'm in the computer security business," he said.

"In other words you're a hacker," I said.

"I've had a few government agencies keeping close tabs on me. I'm sure my phone is bugged and we're probably being watched. But their technology isn't developed to the point where they can pick us up over the sound of the waves crashing on the beach. The rock gives them fits too," he said and smiled.

"What were you doing for Terry?" I asked.

"Research," he said. "At first he had me checking out John Koflanovich, a.k.a. Ivan Chofsky."

"Was he using Chofsky's past as leverage in the contract negotiations?" I asked.

"Terry wasn't like that. Most people he worked with saw him as a Type A personality with a maniacal drive to succeed. What people don't know is that he really was a good person. He did all kinds of charity work and didn't take advantage of other people's problems. He had me checking out Chofsky because he had the same suspicions you blabbed to that horrible television show," he said.

"I didn't blab to anyone. One of my employees gave them that story after two of Chofsky's thugs put him in the hospital. The day Vlad Torhan was shot I was going on the air to tell the public how *California Confidential* has screwed up the story," I said.

"No shit?" he asked with amusement.

"What other research did you do?" I asked.

"Terry was very good at analyzing industry data. He was sure that Doberman's Stub was about to explode. I discreetly floated a rumor that they would be going free agent in search of a new record company. I then intercepted emails between executives to get a feel for what the market would bear," he said.

"That's not what you brought me up here to tell me," I said.

"No. It concerns the final research project he gave to me. Care to guess who he wanted me to check out?" he asked.

"Nigel and the boys from Portadown?" I asked.

"I'm impressed," he said.

I asked, "What did you find out?"

"Let me ask you a question first. Do you think Nigel is responsible for Terry's death?" David asked.

I replied, "Without a doubt. The only mitigating circumstance I can imagine is if one of his hooligan buddies heard Nigel carping about the contract negotiations and took it upon himself to make Nigel the star."

"Is that what you think happened?" asked David.

"No. I think Nigel was the ringleader and even morons know enough not to kill the goose that lays the golden eggs without permission," I said. "So, tell me about the research you did on Nigel."

"At first it was just Terry's gut telling him Nigel's friends were going to be a problem. After seeing their pictures all over Nigel's house, he ran into them at a club one night, a few weeks before he died, and got a very bad vibe. I tapped into an international network and found that all three of them have criminal records. One in particular, Devin Billingsly, has a history of sadistic charges. He started out strapping home made mini-bombs to the household pets of Irish Catholics, then worked his way up to farm animals. He was arrested on three occasions for detonating bombs that resulted in human death, but he was never convicted. Once, the prosecution had a witness, but she suddenly disappeared a week before trial and Billingsly walked. I have no doubt he did the handiwork on the headphones," he said.

"What else can you tell me about the hooligans?" I asked.

"All of them are Irish citizens. Warren Bates had a work visa and came out to San Diego to help with his uncle's landscaping business for a year," he said.

"Do you remember the name of the uncle's business?" I asked.

"It's called Emerald Landscaping. The uncle's name is Paul McDougal. I checked him out, thinking bad blood may run in the family, but he came up clean. In fact, I got into his emails and found one to Warren's mother explaining that he was pulling the plug on the employment arrangement because of character issues and other major concerns. He kept it pretty general, not wanting to hurt his sister with details, but I got the impression that McDougal is a straight shooter and wanted nothing to do with Bates," he said.

"Did you find out if it's the kind of landscaping outfit that mows lawns or the kind that comes in after construction projects?" I asked.

"They do major construction contracts and, get this, during the time Warren was there they worked almost exclusively on a huge multi-tract project in Sorrento Mesa. While Emerald was landscaping one tract, the general contractor was excavating adjacent tracts," David said.

"Sounds like a great place to pick up blasting caps," I said.

"Exactly," said David.

"Any info on Theodore Pine?" I asked.

"Unfortunately, Teddy Boy is very low tech. I don't know much beyond his nickname, which is synonymous with ass-kicker in Great Britain," he said.

"Does Nigel pay bills or do banking over the Internet?" I asked.

"He'll make an occasional purchase, but he's careful and I've checked him out in ways you couldn't imagine," he said.

"I have a theory that Nigel recommended the headphones to either Chelsea or Terry. I'll ask her about it tomorrow. I'd like to get you the name of the manufacturer. Is there a way to do that safely without driving back up here?" I asked.

"Use the email drop-box I set up for Terry," he said and shook my hand, pressing a note that contained the email address. If you don't want the feds on your tail I suggest you take a circuitous route back to your car."

"One last question," I said. "Was Gavin Tomko helping Terry, too?"

"Gavin would let Terry use his ID so that he could go out in public without getting overwhelmed by fans. He doesn't know anything about this. You can talk to him if you like, but it will be a waste of time," David said, then broke into a jog. I climbed up the first beach access I could find, and walked a few neighborhoods before retrieving my car.

Chapter 25

AT 9:00 AM Wednesday I called Chelsea from my office. As expected, I reached voice-mail and left a message. I spent the next hour deciding how I was going to proceed with Nigel. There didn't seem to be any advantage to maintaining a friendly relationship since I was sure that if Victoria didn't tell him about my visit that Ian would. I sent David Cooper the email we talked about and hoped his hacking skills could give me a clearer picture of how the murder went down.

I hadn't given up on the possibility that the original headphones Chelsea had given to Terry were somewhere other than a landfill or the bottom of the Pacific Ocean. I felt it was important, once Nigel knew he was a suspect, that someone keep a close eye on him at all times in case he decides to move Terry's headphones to a safer place. This would mean long stakeouts and, considering Cory's broken ribs and his desire to do something to make up for the *California Confidential* fiasco, I felt it best not to bring him in on this one. I called Dad and asked him to lunch.

"Didn't you tell me Wednesday night is date night for you and Kelly?" he asked.

"It is, but there are a lot of things happening quickly. I may have to postpone with her this week," I said.

"Don't do that, son. She'll feel like she's always playing second fiddle to your career. Cops have just about the highest divorce rates of any profession and PI's experience many of the same strains. Like it or not, you got a lot of publicity from that television show and should be busy with cases for years to come," he said. "I'm no expert on relationships but I'll bet Kelly's busting to tell you about her new class now that school just started. Let her tell you all about it on the ride over here and at dinner. Afterwards she can help your mother in the kitchen and we'll talk. What do you say?" he asked.

Dad was helping me and I appreciated it. For so many years we instinctively said no to each other. "OK. How about if we come over at 7:30?" I asked.

"Your mother will be thrilled. We'll see you then, son," he said and hung up.

Less than a minute later the phone rang and I thought Mom nixed the idea because of a prior commitment. I answered the phone before Jeannine could pick up by asking, "Is there a problem?"

"Is this Jason?" Chelsea Tucker asked.

"Chelsea, I'm sorry. I thought you were someone else. I'll bet it felt great sleeping in you own bed last night," I said.

"You have no idea," she said with a nervous laugh. "I don't think I would be alive today if it wasn't for your advice about acting psycho at the jail."

"I wish I could give you a couple of days to get your head together after that ordeal, but I really need to meet with you today," I said.

"I understand. Tell me when and where and I'll be there," she said, no longer exuding the supreme confidence she demonstrated in the past.

"Why don't I stop by your place. You may want to avoid the public for a while if possible," I said.

"It's almost eleven. If you want to come over now I'll make lunch," she said with a slight quiver in her voice.

"That would be terrific. I'll leave here in ten minutes," I said.

"I've been craving a chicken club sandwich for two days. Will that be OK?" she asked.

"Great. Should I stop for anything?" I asked.

"I'm out of Diet Coke, would you mind?" she asked.

"No problem. I'll see you soon," I said and hung up.

I then called Kelly's cell phone and left a message asking if she would like to have dinner with my parents.

Just as I was about to leave the office, an email came in from David Cooper, which said, "Devin Billingsly purchased three sets of Delatorre headphones from a distributor in Ireland."

About six blocks from Chelsea's house I pulled into a 7/Eleven to pick up a six-pack of Diet Coke. I'm usually a fanatic about locking my car door. I learned the hard way when I was eighteen years old and had my guitar stolen while I was at a friend's house for no more than twenty minutes. Since then I've locked my door except when I stop at a gas station or a convenience store, because they usually have huge windows facing their parking lots. I took three steps toward the 7/Eleven and froze in my tracks. It suddenly hit me that Terry stopped at a 7/Eleven after he left Denny's the day he was killed. Nigel went to the restroom as they were leaving, giving Terry the impression he was alone when he stopped for his iced tea, but Nigel could very well have followed him and swapped the headphones while Terry was getting his Super Big Gulp.

When I arrived at Chelsea's house she was every bit as friendly and energized as she was on the phone. "Why don't we eat first, then talk," she suggested.

"That's fine with me," I said and followed her to the dining room. I have seen many people shortly after being released from jail, including several first-time offenders from affluent homes. They are almost always either depressed or angry. Never have I seen anyone have such a positive metamorphosis as Chelsea Tucker. We ate and exchanged small talk. Then Chelsea cleared the table, refreshed our soft drinks, and sat down across from me. "Are you ready to talk?" I asked.

"I think so," she replied and took a deep breath.

"I'm 99% certain I know who killed Terry. It's somebody you know and the normal response is that you're going to want to lash out at him, then you're going to want to tell the world it wasn't you who did it. But, if you do that he'll have time to get rid of evidence and our chances of catching him and punishing him will be hurt. So be honest with yourself and tell me if you're going to be able to keep it a secret," I said.

"I want to know, Jason," she said while maintaining eye contact.

"Promise me you'll let me and the police handle it and not do anything to get retribution," I stated.

"I promise. After what I just went through I can guarantee you that I have no intention of ever getting a parking ticket."

I said, "Before I tell you I have a couple of questions. First, tell me why you decided to purchase the brand and model of headphones you gave to Terry."

"He was complaining that he had a problem with outside noise when he listened to his audio notes between songs. I was in the process of trying to find a pair that touted extraneous noise reduction when Terry came home one day and said he heard that Delatorre Electronics put out a line that would do a great job," she said.

"Did he say who gave him the recommendation?" I asked

"Nigel told him they were a little heavy but would take out 90% of the background noise he'd get in the studio," she said.

"Did he recommend a particular model?" I asked.

"No. He just told Terry that the more expensive ones would do the best job," she said.

"How many expensive ones were there to choose from?" I asked.

"There were quite a few, but only three of them claimed to radically reduce outside noise," she said.

I spent the next fifteen minutes telling her what led me to the conclusion that Nigel had killed her husband. "If all goes well we should nail him within the week," I said.

"Can I tell my attorneys?" she asked.

"No. They all have their own agendas. Not that I could ever imagine Reginald Rutherford taking advantage of an opportunity to grab a front-page headline," I said sarcastically.

"I see your point. Too bad Daddy has to pay him all that money to work on my defense," she said.

"Nigel isn't in custody yet and you're not off the hook either. Let him do his thing; it could work to our advantage with the DA's office," I said.

"How so?" she asked.

"After going out on a limb and arresting you they normally wouldn't want to give up on you as the prime suspect. But the prospects of Reginald Rutherford making them look like fools could help open their eyes to Nigel; especially if we aren't able to produce the headphones you gave to Terry or get a confession out of one of Nigel's hooligan friends," I said.

"Thanks for agreeing to come back to work for me. I was such a brat. I got so wrapped up in myself I couldn't see that you were doing everything you could to help me," she said emotionally.

"You've been through a lot in a short period of time. I'm really glad you hired me back because I just wasn't able to let it go during my brief period of unemployment," I said. Chelsea gave me a hug, walked me to the door and said goodbye.

When I got back to the office I had two messages. The first was from Walter Shamansky and the other was from Nigel. I called Shamansky first. When he came on the line I said, "This is the Rutherford legal team returning your call."

"How is your Nigel theory coming?" he asked.

"It's getting stronger by the hour. I just came from Chelsea's house and guess who recommended the brand of headphones?" I asked.

"He didn't happen to put it in an email or a note, by chance, did he?" Shamansky asked.

"No, but I did learn some interesting facts about his hooligan buddies," I said.

"Such as?" he asked. I told him what David Cooper had told me without revealing my source. "Let me buy you dinner tonight. I'm in a manpower bind and was hoping we could come up with a plan of attack."

"I already have dinner plans, but let me see if I can cut you in. I'll call you back in ten," I said and hung up.

I called my parent's home and mom answered. "Could you handle another guest for dinner?" I asked.

"Anybody I know?" she asked.

"Detective Walter Shamansky," I replied.

"I think you better get a green light from your father first," she said.

"Good idea. Is he around?" I asked.

"Hold on," she replied.

Two minutes later I put in my request and Dad said, "We're not exactly on the best of terms."

I said, "I was going to ask you to help me by staking out the perp. Shamansky just called to say he agrees with me but is in a tight spot because of arresting Chelsea. He wants to get it right and needs our assistance."

"OK, he's invited to dinner, but tell him not to expect any pigs-in-a-blanket," he said.

"Promise me we won't hear the word Pollack or any other ethnic slur," I said, and there was a long pause. "Kelly's very sensitive about that stuff. I don't think she'd want to come back to your house if you embarrass Shamansky."

"You're worse than your mother. Alright, I'll treat him like he's related to the Pope," he said.

I called Shamansky back and told him what I had in mind. He was shocked by the invitation, but appreciated the help.

I decided to avoid Nigel altogether and had Jeannine call and tell him I was going to be tied up with a group of Russians for the rest of the day, but would like to meet with him tomorrow. He agreed to meet me at his home at 10:00 AM.

As we drove to my parents' house I told Kelly that Shamansky was joining us, but we would hold the shop-talk until after dinner. "In the meantime, I'd like to hear about your new class." She spent the rest of the drive telling me all about it. Sometimes people just need to vent. Fortunately, there wasn't a pop quiz at the end of our trip since my focus frequently drifted to my meeting with Dad and Shamansky.

We arrived fifteen minutes before Shamansky. Dad and Walter were cordial to one another, like the leaders of two warring countries at a peace summit. I could tell both hoped something positive could be accomplished, but both were basically distrustful of the other.

The dinner conversation centered on Kelly. For me, it was like a chick flick double feature. This time Mom kept jumping in and relating the conversation to when I attended school, so I was forced to pay closer attention. Shamansky chimed in periodically. I had a feeling he would be attentive to Kelly considering his penchant for attractive young women. He also addressed me with a new respect that I could tell came more from the fact that I was dating a looker than out of deference to my parents.

When dinner was over Dad suggested that the men grab a beer and adjourn to the backyard. When we got out there, Dad said, "Let's get down to business. I understand you need some help with the case."

I gave a ten-minute summary, highlighting new developments and facts that emerged since our last conversation. When I finished the summary I said, "I have a meeting set up with Nigel tomorrow at 10:00 AM. I'm trying to decide whether to confront him with the facts or give him a false sense of security while I continue to build the case."

"What would be the advantages of a confrontation?" Shamansky asked.

"Nigel thinks he's gotten away with it. He's proceeding with his plans to replace Terry and hire a top notch agent. I think he's under a lot of pressure as the businessman of the band. If he finds out we're on to him he could very well make a mistake."

"Like what?" asked Shamansky.

"I think it's possible that the headphones Chelsea bought for Terry could still be around. If not, the other two purchased by Billingsly could help build the case if they're recovered. Nigel or his girlfriend might try to dump them if they're at his house. Or, he could call the friend in Southeast San Diego to make sure they're gone," I said.

"What would be the advantage of keeping Nigel in the dark a little longer?" Dad asked.

"I'm almost certain the hooligans are back in Ireland. Nigel just got back from there today. Unless they returned with him we won't be able to bring them in," I said.

Shamansky said, "We'd have a much better chance of breaking this open if we could get Nigel's posse back in the country and put the four of them in separate interrogation rooms."

"So how do we get them back here?" asked Dad.

"Give me a minute, I'm getting an idea," I said.

"How about if I get us another round of beers while you figure it out," Dad said.

"Great idea, Jim," said Shamansky. "Can I give you a hand?"

"Sure," Dad said with a quizzical look on his face. I don't know what they talked about in the five minutes they were gone and, frankly, I didn't care.

"So let's have it," said Dad when they returned. "What's your idea?"

"Shamansky, I suggest you and I pay another visit to Chofsky. You read him the riot act for getting that actor killed at the cemetery and threaten to have him deported. I'll suggest that if he can help us catch the killer you'll call it even. We make Chofsky tell Nigel he doesn't want the band worrying about their safety, especially after Terry and Torhan's deaths, as well as the shooting at the cemetery. He tells Nigel that he'd be glad to assign one of his security men to each of the band members. Or, as the new leader of the band, he could bring in his own men. He goes on to tell Nigel that he prefers men from his own country and, if Nigel would feel more comfortable with Brits, he'd pay them a salary of $40K per year and sponsor them for a work visa. So that it doesn't seem too staged, he tells him the bodyguards would be expected to perform security duties at his compound once things calm down and the band isn't touring. But, he wants them in place within the week and he wants to meet them as soon as possible. One bodyguard for each band member," I said.

Dad and Shamansky were silent for about a minute, then Shamansky said, "I love it."

"Good plan, son," Dad added. "Where do I come in?"

"I'd like to get a look inside the house in Southeast San Diego. I need you to stake it out, establish a pattern of comings and goings and be my look-out while I check it for headphones and blasting caps. If we know they're in there, you can get a search warrant once the boys are back in town and at the house," I said.

Shamansky said, "Me and your dad had a hard time hearing that last part, but I like what we've heard so far."

We went back inside and spent another hour drinking beer and talking with the women. I wondered if Dad realized he was enjoying the company of a non-Irishman.

Chapter 26

I MET Dad at 5:00 AM a half-block from Desmond Thompson's house in Souteast San Diego. I wanted to get a look at the layout to figure out how and when I would do my locksmith thing. Dad was surprised to learn I acquired that skill at UCSD. When he questioned my ability to do it under pressure I told him about my experience in Tecate, and he was genuinely amused when I told him about inadvertently cracking the boss in the package with a hockey stick.

At 5:45 AM a guy in his mid-twenties emerged from the house and got into a gray, late-nineties Toyota pick-up and pulled away. I gave it a few minutes before getting out of the car, then I walked around the block and was pleasantly surprised to learn an alley ran behind the property. It was bordered by an old six foot redwood fence, but had a chainlink gate that gave me an excellent view of the rear of the house and a detached garage that sat within the perimeter fencing.

After I left Dad, I drove to the Denny's where Terry Tucker ate his last meal. I told the hostess, "I'm very particular about the service I receive. Would you be sure to seat me in Cassie's section?"

"You'll probably have to wait longer," she replied.

"I don't mind," I said, then walked outside and fed quarters to a newspaper dispenser.

Twenty-five minutes later I was seated in Cassie's section and reviewed the menu while waiting for her. "I remember you," she said as she appeared at my table. "I saw you at the Dali Lama a couple of weeks ago and I told my boyfriend, 'He sat at my station and asked a bunch of questions about Doberman's Stub and now he's playing with their band,' it was pretty cool," she said.

"And here I am again," I said.

"What can I get you today?" she asked.

"How about a Grand Slam with orange juice," I said. "And I have one more question."

"What do you want to know?" she asked.

"Last time I was here you said that Nigel, the English guy, went to the bathroom while Terry, the guy who was killed, left the restaurant," I said.

"Yeah. That's what happened," she said.

"Do you remember if Nigel was in the bathroom long or just in and out?" I asked.

"In and out. I remember saying to myself, 'Jeez, I thought the British always washed their hands.' I even mentioned it to my boyfriend when we saw him at the Dali Lama," Cassie said.

"How long would you say it was from the time Terry left and when Nigel left?" I asked.

"Just a few seconds. Terry paid the bill while pee-pee hands was making the pit stop," she said.

"Pick-up Cassie," I heard from behind.

"I'll be back," she said and deftly snagged three plates from the counter and delivered them to a family of six, then returned for three more. She took care of a few more people and returned with my breakfast.

"Did you happen to notice either of them out in the parking lot?" I asked.

"I sure did. Both of them had really hot cars. The British guy left us some rubber as he pulled out of the lot," she said.

"So it looked like he was in a big hurry?" I asked.

"Oh yeah. It looked like he was trying to catch up to his buddy," she said, then responded to a request for more coffee.

It took five minutes to get from Denny's to the 7/Eleven. As I pulled into the parking lot I saw what I was hoping to see. The reason I almost never lock my car door at convenience stores is because they usually have huge plate glass windows looking out at the parking lot, so the shoppers can keep an eye on their cars and the police can watch out for robbers. But, some stores get carried away with putting big promotional posters in their windows to drum up business, and this is definitely one of those stores. There was enough space in between posters where someone could see in or out of the store if they focused their attention at one of the narrow slots. But there was not enough space for a person getting an iced tea to notice someone in the parking lot out of his peripheral vision. Nigel could have easily made the switch without being seen.

I walked over to the fountain drinks area and checked out the sight lines to the parking lot. Unless Terry was parked in one of two particular slots, there was no chance he could have spotted Nigel in the lot.

At 10:15 AM I found myself listening to Nigel's doorbell and hoping, for once, that a real butler would answer the door. Instead I got Victoria with a mean expression. "Are you gonna tell him?" she asked.

"Did you?" I asked and she shook her head. "Then mum's the word," I said and followed her to Nigel's office where he was seated behind his desk.

"Jason, how was your long weekend?" Nigel asked.

"It was fine. I heard you got out of town," I replied.

"I flew across the pond and checked in with the relatives. "Any new developments?" he asked.

I replied, "I hate to say it because I know he's trying to work a deal with you, but Koflanovich is still looking pretty bad. While you were gone I talked to Jack and Ian again and they told me about how he tried getting you guys to pressure Terry to settle for less than you're worth."

"He is on a bit of a power trip," he said. "But, I'm not so sure it wasn't that big blond gonstermonker that did in poor Terry."

"You mean Vlad Torhan, the guy who got shot?" I asked.

"If you ask me, the Russian Mafia knew he was behind it and punched his ticket because he was out of control," Nigel said.

"That's a possibility," I said, "but, if I were you, I still wouldn't do anything to piss off Koflanovich until this thing is sorted out."

"Blimey!" he responded.

"Anyway, I just wanted to find out if Koflanovich said anything to you that was different than what he told the other guys," I said.

"I think Ian got called first, then Jack. Ian called me right afterwards, so I was prepared when I got my call," he said.

"From what they told me it sounded like the usual contract posturing to try to get an edge during the negotiations; lawsuit threats and worst case scenarios," I said.

"Exactly," Nigel said.

"They also told me about the clause in the contract where Terry could fire one of the band members. Ian was pretty upset. Do you think it was just Terry's way of telling him to shape up or ship out?" I asked.

"Something like that. Terry was a perfectionist. He was mad at Ian, but I really don't think he would have thrown him out. It was probably just a scare tactic to get him into rehab," Nigel said.

"That's all I've got for you today, Nigel. I'll let you get back to work," I said as I kept my eyes off of the hooligan pictures. "I'll keep you posted if there are any new developments."

Nigel stood up when I did and stuck out his hand, "I appreciate that, Jason. Be sure to tell Chelsea we all know she didn't do it." Victoria magically appeared as I was walking toward the door. I had no doubt she had been eavesdropping on the entire conversation.

When we got to the door she gave me an insincere smile and said, "Don't hurry back," then shut the door without waiting for a reply.

I checked in with Jeannine and was told that Shamansky set up a meet with Chofsky at 1:00 PM. I skipped lunch and arrived about 15 minutes early. This meant I got to spend quality time with Mikhail and Rovi, both of whom appeared to be failing their ESL classes. We bonded when Mikhail pointed his AK-47 at my steering wheel and demanded to see my gun. The Badinov Brothers played with it like a new toy for about five minutes before returning it to me.

When Shamansky arrived we were escorted to Chofsky's office once again by poor Ivana's prison matron, Svetlana.

"Sit down gentlemen, I'm afraid I don't have much time for you today," he said.

"You're gonna have to make time unless you want to spend the next 72 hours at police headquarters," said Shamansky in a 'bad cop' voice that startled me.

"What's this about?" demanded Chofsky trying to meet force with force.

"It's about an underpaid actor laying on a slab in the morgue because you chose to use him as an expendable pawn in your war with the Russian Mafia. It's about deciding whether you should be deported. Are you getting my message?" asked Shamansky.

"It is most unfortunate that the poor man was shot. But I'm not the one who pulled the trigger," he replied.

"Then I suggest you study up on the laws regarding employers putting their employees in highly dangerous situations that result in their death. You're going to find case after case of the employers doing prison time," Shamansky pontificated.

"Have I not been completely cooperative with you?" he asked.

"He has been cooperative," I said hoping my good cop role would not be too transparent. How many cop TV shows could this guy have watched? He probably lives for the Minsk farm report on satellite.

"I don't care," railed Shamansky at me. "My job is to keep the citizens of San Diego safe from guys like this. What are you doing sticking up for him anyway? Didn't his guys shoot at you in the parking lot of the Ukrainian Citizen's Club?"

"He thought I was in the Mafia," I said.

Shamansky replied, "Another error in judgment that nearly cost another life."

"What do you want me to do?" asked Chofsky, who apparently guessed that he was over a barrel and would have been in handcuffs by now if he was actually being busted. "I have no interest in going to prison or back to Odessa. You have my full cooperation. What do you want?" he asked.

We spent the next fifteen minutes laying out what he was to say to Nigel. When we finished he asked, "Are you certain it was Mr. Choate who killed Mr. Tucker?"

I replied, "Yes, and it probably wouldn't have happened if it wasn't for you calling each of the band members and giving them the impression they'd be better off without him."

At first it looked like Chofsky was going to argue this point, but, realizing the futility, simply said, "I'll call Mr. Choate this afternoon."

"Call him now," said Shamansky. "I want to hear it."

Chofsky was able to get through to Nigel and was very credible. He laid out the whole scenario on the phone and Nigel told him he liked the idea of bringing in his fellow countrymen. Nigel told him they could be in San Diego by Saturday and Chofsky set a 3:00 PM meeting to receive them at the compound.

"Meet me at the Starbucks down the street in five minutes," I said to Shamansky as we were escorted to our vehicles. "That went rather well," I said when we had our coffee.

"Saturday doesn't give us much time if you're still planning on an unauthorized tour of the guest accommodations," Shamansky replied.

"I'll have to go in tomorrow. The owner left the house at 5:45 AM. It didn't get light out till after 6:30. I could try going in first thing if my dad says the rest of the immediate neighbors leave for work at a more reasonable hour," I said.

"What time did Jim get started this morning?" asked Shamansky.

"Five o'clock. I was planning on having Cory relieve him at 5:00 PM. He has a van where he can do stakeouts without being seen while he watches. I'll have a better idea of an exact time after I talk to Dad," I said.

I looked at my watch – it was 3:44 PM. "I had better head southeast before Dad attempts to introduce himself to Cory," I said.

Shamansky broke into a hearty laugh and said, "I could sell more tickets to that than a widows & orphans fundraiser at the stationhouse."

I laughed and added, "I can see it now. He'll have Cory handcuffed in the back of his van with a bar of Irish Spring between his teeth." Shamansky convulsed as we got into our cars and pulled away.

At 5:22 PM I hopped into the passenger seat of Dad's car, which was now parked on the opposite end of the street. "Cory's in the white van at the other end of the block. How about if we go have dinner someplace and put together a plan of attack?" I asked.

"That's Cory? I thought it might be Axel Vandevere," he said.

"Vandevere's probably sitting on Nigel," I said. "I'd introduce you to Cory, but he suffers from Tourette's Syndrome and manages to offend everyone he meets."

"Then why is he working for you?" Dad asked.

"Because he was born to do stakeouts and he's the best photographer I've ever met. He did some work for National Geographic," I said.

"I'm impressed," he said, but I detected a note of sarcasm. "There's a Black Angus between here and the freeway entrance. Why don't we meet there in fifteen minutes?" I asked.

"What's wrong with your mother's cooking?" he asked.

"Do you really think she should be listening to us plan a break-in?" I asked.

"I'll call and tell her we're bonding," he quipped, this time without masking the irritation in his voice. I guess sitting in a warm car for 12½ hours will do that to you. After checking over Dad's notes I told Cory what I wanted him to monitor. Fortunately, he brought along a night vision scope.

Black Angus was a zoo. There were about 10 people ahead of us waiting for a table. We managed to get a small cocktail table in the bar after five minutes of standing. When our waitress came by I asked if we could order dinner in the bar and she gave me the thumbs up. "What do you think Dad?" I asked and he rolled his eyes and nodded his head. After we made our dinner selections I said, "Nigel's bringing his boys to California by Saturday. That means I've got to go in tomorrow."

"One day doesn't give you much of a picture. It could be dangerous," Dad said.

"Not nearly as dangerous as doing it when we have three extra guys to keep track of," I replied.

"I've been thinking about it all day. Your best shot is first thing in the morning, right after he leaves for work. It'll be dark until 6:30. There's a neighbor that left for work at exactly 6:00. Nobody else on the block did anything more than bring in a morning paper. The rest of the workers all left between 7:00 and 8:30."

"You don't think it would be better once most of them have gone?" I asked.

"Too much activity. Mommies walking babies, seniors walking themselves and their dogs. And, I saw a couple of guys who came home for lunch. It either has to be first thing in the morning or after dark, when you run the risk that the guy will stay home," he said.

"Tomorrow morning it is. You said you've been thinking about it all day. Why don't you tell me how you'd do it," I said.

"Since you asked, I don't mind if I do," Dad said and took a slug of Harp. "First, I'd borrow two phone company jumpsuits. I saw a ground-mounted telephone box near the north entrance to the alley. I could hold an ohmmeter and hang out at the box acting like I was running tests without anyone giving me a second look. If you can borrow that white van from Cory, I can also get two SBC magnet signs for the sides to make us look official. You take a large white tarp and tent it in front of you while you work on the backdoor lock and, more importantly, when you work on the garage door lock facing the street. You need to be in and out of there in a half-hour, twenty minutes would be better."

"Can you get the jumpsuits and signs tonight?" I asked.

"Not a problem," he said as our food arrived.

Chapter 27

DRESSED in my Southwestern Bell Corporation jumpsuit, I gave the Acura keys to Cory at 5:20 AM and got an expletive-laden briefing on Cory's observations. He thought he got one good shot of the owner's face when he arrived home at around 9:30 PM and staggered up his front sidewalk.

After swapping vehicles with Cory, I drove the van around the corner to an open space next to the phone box. I then placed the magnetic signs on the van and set out a couple of Day-Glo orange cones to look official. I walked back to Dad's Riviera and waited with him until Desmond Thompson left for his landscaping job. A light rain started falling in the last few minutes before Desmond departed. "The guy works in outside construction. Do you think work will be cancelled?" I asked.

"Not if it stays like this," Dad replied. "But if it comes down harder it could be a very short day."

"Good thing Friday is almost always payday in construction. Even if it rains hard, he'll be sure to go in for his paycheck, right?" I asked.

"He'll pick it up and cash it before he comes home if he's like every other construction guy I've ever known," Dad said.

When Thompson emerged from his house at 5:47, he spread his arms out, palms up and looked at the sky. He then went back in the house and it suddenly occurred to me that he could get paid biweekly. Fortunately, he returned two minutes later wearing a Raider's baseball cap and departed in his truck.

We left the Riviera and walked to the van. With Dad huddled in close, I picked the lock on the telephone box in about twenty seconds, "That's scary," he said.

"Benefits of a state school education," I said. With the white tarp under my arm I walked down the alley, through the gate and to Thompson's back door like I owned the place. I tented the tarp against the door with me underneath and, with a small flashlight in my mouth, picked the backdoor lock almost as quickly as I sprung the lock on the phone box. I entered the kitchen and immediately noticed the faint sound of music coming from the second floor. Maybe Desmond isn't conscientious about shutting off his radio in the morning. I decided to move as quietly as possible just in case I wasn't alone.

I walked into the living room and quickly found the stereo. A set of headphones was attached, but it was too dark to see the manufacturer's name. I flicked on my penlight, found the Delatorre label and my heart started racing. I located the serial number on the bridge and determined that it was one of the three sent to Billingsly's home in Northern Ireland.

A fairly expensive stereo sat on a makeshift cinder block and wooden plank shelving unit. Stuffed into one of the cinder block holes was a second pair of Delatorre headphones. Again I checked the serial number and again it was from the same shipment sent to Billingsly.

Since there was music emanating from the second floor it was time to find out if there was another stereo or just a clock/radio set to the wrong time. I made my way up the stairs, thankful that I didn't encounter any squeakers. They led me to the back of the house. The music was coming from a bedroom facing the street. I edged past dark bedrooms on the left and right, then past a bathroom on the right. As I approached the room with the music I heard a noise that sounded like a CD hitting a hardwood floor on edge, "Shit!" came a husky female voice accompanied by the sound of bare feet on flooring.

I spun into the bathroom, stepped into the bathtub and pulled the shower curtain partially closed so I couldn't be seen from the hall. It all happened so fast, I wasn't sure if she heard me. My heart pounded as I strained to hear sounds. Suddenly, the music went off and I heard bare feet on hardwood, then the silence that would follow if she continued onto the hall carpeting. Two seconds later I held my breath when I heard bare feet slapping the bathroom tile. I reached for my gun, but realized it was on the other side of my jumpsuit. I couldn't hold my breath much longer. I balled my fists as I expected the shower curtain to be ripped back at any moment. Instead, I heard the sound of urine splashing in the toilet bowl. I let out a controlled breath hoping it would be masked by the splashing sounds. I inhaled as the sound of toilet paper rolled, then took a deeper breath when she flushed.

I heard a few more footsteps on tile, then nothing. I assumed she had walked back onto the carpeted hallway and risked a peek from behind the curtain. But, she hadn't departed. She was standing in front of a medicine cabinet mirror that, luckily, wasn't aimed my way. She looked to be in her mid-twenties, with medium length black hair and an exceptional figure. Her face was decidedly less attractive. She wore a green T-shirt that barely covered her butt. After adjusting her bangs she rinsed her fingers.

I thought I was home free until she pulled off the green tee shirt and turned toward the shower. Before the shirt had cleared her eyes I ducked back behind the shower curtain, but knew it was just seconds until I'd be discovered. Suddenly, a hand shot past my elbow and turned on the hot water, then she reached in further and turned the knob labeled cold. As water streamed down my SBC jumpsuit a set of perfectly manicured white nails grasped the shower curtain. But, before it could be pulled back, the telephone rang in another room and the nails were suddenly gone. I jumped out of the shower, grabbed a towel and ran it over me quickly. I then mopped up the puddle I had caused on the bathroom floor and ran into a darkened bedroom across the hall. I waited for another three minutes, continuing to towel off, until she emerged from the bedroom in her birthday suit.

When she stepped into the shower I went into the bedroom and found a small stereo system. Attached was another set of Delatorre headphones. As I was turning them over to check the serial number the phone rang three feet away from me. I immediately heard a squeak from the shower knob and I tossed the headphones back to where I found them and quick-stepped back to the next bedroom.

Peaking around the threshold of the guest bedroom I saw her toweling off as she talked on the phone. When she turned her back to me I quickly and quietly made my way downstairs

I then carried the tarp and the towel I had acquired to the front of the garage, once again, made a little tent and used my lock picks to gain access. There was now a light rain falling. I glanced at my watch and I had been in the house for twenty-five minutes. The inside of the garage was dark. I used my penlight to look at tools and boxes. Nothing seemed unusual or out of place. I was about to leave after less than five minutes when I spied a black trunk covered with a faded Union Jack sticker on the side. A small Yale lock secured the trunk - child's play for The Great Duffdini. In less than fifteen seconds I was looking at an impressive array of blasting caps, timers, wires and five sticks of dynamite. Using my penlight, I pushed some of the wires out of the way and saw a square black plastic tube with a red top. On closer inspection I learned that it contained BBs.

I was feeling pretty self-satisfied as I shut the trunk without exercising the stealth I used in the house. Suddenly, I heard a huge dog barking out on the sidewalk. Peaking through a narrow gap between boards I saw an angry rottweiler tethered to an elderly woman. "What is it Thor?" she called. "Who's in there? Should we call the police, Thor?"

Using my strongest voice, knowing that I needed to reach the tympanic membrane of an old woman holding a barking monster in the rain I let out a, "Rrrrrroooouuuuwww," sound that cats make when they're cornered and have to fight.

"Down boy! Leave that cat alone! What the hell is wrong with you? You nearly pulled my shoulder out of it's socket you bad boy!" I heard her berating the dog all the way down the block. At first I thought it was funny until I realized that neighbors might have heard her and may be looking out their windows to see what's going on. I gave it another five minutes before exiting the garage and walking out the back gate.

When I got back to the van it was 6:43 and Dad was pissed. "Do you know how long you were in there? I thought you got caught," he said with immense stress in his voice.

"It's all in there. I found the headphones in the house and blasting caps and BBs in the garage," I said.

We drove to a nearby IHOP where I told him the whole story. Before we went our separate ways I called Shamansky from the parking lot. As expected I got voice-mail. I said, "Southeast San Diego was better than the Mission Valley Mall. I found everything we were looking for. Ten more minutes and I would have had Jimmy Hoffa and the co-conspirators from the grassy knoll. Call me."

Dad looked at me like he used to when I'd make noise in church. Then his scowl turned to a smile and he said, "You turned out alright Jason. Keep me in the loop."

When I returned to my office I sent an email to David Cooper asking for a quick bio on Desmond Thompson. I had the feeling Desmond would be sitting in an interview room at the police department very soon and background could help us push the right buttons.

I was in the middle of entering notes to the case file when Shamansky called. I told him he was working too hard and deserved a lunch break. He agreed and said he was longing for a Larabee's shrimp salad for the last half-hour. I pointed out that it was only 10:15 and suggested we meet at 11:30.

As I was getting ready to leave for lunch an email came in from David. It read: "Message received. I'll check him out today. I was up most of last night after I came across an ad in a European music industry publication, pitching the newest Doberman's Stub CD, *Bite Me, Big Dog* (working title). The publication has been out for at least a week, but in reading the instructions for placing an ad they are very emphatic that all new-release advertising must be placed at least one month in advance. That means Cerise Records placed the ad either just before, or immediately after, Terry died. What does that tell you?"

It's possible it meant nothing. The magazine might sell blocks of ads that would allow Cerise to download their text shortly before going to press. The rule could be bendable or breakable by paying a premium price. But if it is a hard and fast rule that would mean Chofsky had prior knowledge of the murder plans.

I replied to David's email: "See if you can find an invoice to determine the date the ad was placed and paid for."

Beaver's mom gave me the red carpet treatment for the first time when I arrived at Larabee's at 11:45. I was concerned that Shamansky would be pissed that I was late, but when I walked into the dining room and saw the girl of his dreams fawning over him, I knew my tardiness would not be a problem. After we shook hands and established that I remembered our waitress, she took my drink order and disappeared.

Shamansky looked at his watch and, suddenly all business, said, "Let's have it. What have you got?"

"I found the two Delatorre headphones shipped to Devin Billingsly near the downstairs stereo. I then went upstairs and found a third pair of Delatorre's plugged into another stereo," I said with a smile.

"Very good work. Did you match up serial numbers?" he asked.

"I was able to confirm the downstairs pairs. But, when I got upstairs I had company and didn't have time to verify the serial number, but it looked exactly like the picture of the model Chelsea gave to Terry," I said.

"Tell me what happened when you got upstairs," Shamansky said and I gave him the details. "Did you get anything else?" he asked and I took him through the items found in the garage.

"Does Desmond Thompson have a sheet?" I asked.

"Not much," he replied. "He had a DUI a couple of years ago and two speeding tickets. That's it."

"I'm told we'll have no problem finding rap sheets on each of the hoodlums from Northern Ireland," I said.

"It sounds like you've tapped into a hellofa source," he said.

"I can't give any details on him, but I can tell you the bombshell he laid on me just before I came over here," I said, then proceeded to recount our emails.

Shamansky said, "I want to pop the hoodlums as soon as possible, but we need to establish probable cause for a warrant. Considering that we just arraigned Chelsea for the crime, it's going to take some imagination."

I replied, "Nobody is saying Chelsea built the bomb. You could tell the judge you think Nigel helped her and utilized his terrorist friends who visit frequently. Tell him I was at Nigel's house and overheard him say, 'We better get rid of everything at Thompson's house when you get to town.' Do you think that would fly?"

"You'd be sticking your neck out on that one, lying to a judge," he said.

"I'm not lying to a judge, I'm lying to a cop," I said with a grin.

"I can live with that," he replied.

When I returned to my office I saw Michael Marinangeli sitting on Jeannine's desk, interlocking his fingers with hers. "Hey dude," he said when he saw me.

"Hi Michael," I said. "Drop by to give Jeannine a hand?"

"Just doing my best to get a date with this lovely lady," he said, then gazed into her eyes.

"Good luck," I said and turned to go back into my office.

"Jason, hang on. I also wanted to tell you something. Have you got a minute," he asked.

"Sure," I replied and waved him into my office.

He shut the door and I was sure he was going to start asking uncomfortable questions about Jeannine. But instead he said, "Nigel Choate called me yesterday and wants me to audition for Doberman's Stub. I'm meeting them at Jack Pascal's home studio tomorrow morning. Can you believe it?" he asked with the enthusiasm of a teenager.

"Wow!" I managed to say. "What did Nigel say?" I asked.

Michael replied, "He said he liked the way I played with the band

and that he was planning on leaving right after the Doberman set, but hung around another half-hour to hear me play. It sounds like I've got a real shot," he said. "You don't seem all that happy for me."

"I'm sorry. I think it's great that you're getting recognized for your incredible talent. It's just that we still haven't caught the bad guy and the Russian Mafia is still in the picture. Just keep your eyes open and don't trust anybody, and I mean anybody, until this thing gets sorted out. OK?" I asked.

"Got it," he replied.

"One more thing. If anybody asks you about what I'm doing with the case, make sure you don't tell anything you learned from Jeannine or me. Alright?" I asked.

"OK," he said with a slight bit of irritation in his voice.

"That said, now go out there and knock 'em dead," I said with a smile. Michael gave me a fist bump and departed.

At 4:15 PM I got a call from Dad. "Guess who just arrived by cab?" he asked.

"They must have jumped on the first flight after getting the call," I responded.

"Are you sure you want Cory relieving me at 5:00?" he asked.

"I want him there to take night pictures if they try moving the trunk tonight. But, he could definitely use some help. I'll hang in there with him until they turn in for the night. If somebody leaves I'll be able to tail him," I said.

"I could do another shift," Dad said.

I said, "This thing could drag out a few more days. I need you fresh. I'll be there by 6:30."

I called Shamansky and told his voice-mail of the hooligans' arrival and my plans to stay with Cory on the stakeout. If the stars were aligned just right I suppose there was a chance that he'd get the message in time to find a judge who would issue a warrant on a Friday night, but I thought it highly unlikely.

As I was getting ready to leave I got a call from David Cooper. "Don't use my name during this conversation," he said instead of hello. "The guesswork is over. The ad was placed and paid for the day before Terry was killed. I have no doubt this guy was in on it. He had to be."

I responded, "Is it possible to find out if Nigel made any moves in the US or the UK that would indicate he knew he was coming into a large sum of money soon. Particularly any activity the day Chofsky placed the ad."

"I'll see what I can do, but I didn't have much luck with his US accounts last time I looked. Maybe he was a bit less security conscious in the UK, but I doubt it. You either are or you aren't. You'll have to find another link. I gotta run," he said and hung up abruptly.

At 6:18 I got into the passenger seat of Dad's Riviera and told him about the latest development. He said he wanted to hang out until we heard from Shamansky. He didn't have to wait long. Shamansky called just before 7:00 to say he reached his favorite judge at a wedding rehearsal party, "Nothing's going to happen tonight, but I have his assurance that if I bring the warrant to his doorstep at 7:00 AM, he'll sign it."

"That should work," I said. "How do you want to play it with Chofsky?" I asked.

"I think you should show up at the compound wearing a wire at the time Chofsky is supposed to be meeting with Nigel. I'll send a couple of black & whites to hang out at the gate while you're in there. Tell them the house was raided, the boys were picked up, the headphones and bomb kit were found and the boys gave up Nigel. Tell them about the ad and how you know they were in it together. If we're lucky one or both of them will say something we can use at trial," Shamansky said.

"My dad's here. He wants to know if he can be of further assistance," I said.

"Ask him if he wants to be an unofficial consultant at the stationhouse tomorrow while I sweat the hooligans," he said. When I did, Dad broke into a smile that didn't want to go away.

"We've got a big affirmative on that one, Kojak. Do you think he should stay here all night on the stakeout or do you want him fresh for the interrogation?" I asked.

"Tell him to get his ass in bed ASAP," Shamansky replied as I held the cell phone so Dad could hear.

"Yes sir!" Dad said enthusiastically.

Dad headed home with that same smile glued to his mug. I climbed into Cory's vehicle, explained the situation and was pleased to learn he had a sleeping bag in the back of the van. I carefully explained all of the circumstances where I wanted Cory to wake me up, then got into the sleeping bag as soon as night fell. I laid awake thinking about contingency plans for almost an hour before drifting off. At 11:00 PM Cory woke me up to say someone just went into the garage. Although the door was left ajar, we didn't have the angle to see inside, so we waited about a half-hour, then saw Devin Billingsly emerge with only a flashlight in his hands. At least he hadn't removed the trunk. Cory said he might have had something in his other hand when he entered. He took a photo through the night scope. We'll know more tomorrow when he enhances it with his software.

Just as I settled back into the sleeping bag my phone rang. "Jason Duffy," I answered.

"No names," said David Cooper, "I've got something for you that might help if you get a chance to interrogate the hoodlums."

"Let's hear it," I said.

"Warren Bates and Devin Billingsly both have a couple of years of college and passing grades. Theodore Pine, however, is dumber than a 286 with a virus. He would have flunked out of high school if he weren't an All-Conference rugby player. The other two have a few minor convictions, mainly for Orangemen related activities that got out of hand. But Pine spent three of the last five years doing time. Where the other two might get the benefit of the doubt with a jury, Pine looks like a career criminal. If you can't get him to flat out roll on his mates, you should have no trouble outsmarting him," he said.

"Thanks, dude. You're the best. Anything else?" I asked.

"I'll call if I get anything important," he said and hung up.

Chapter 28

I WOKE up at 6:30 AM to a profanity-laden argument coming from Cory and someone in the passenger seat that escalated into shouting. I pulled myself up on the van console that separated them and in my loudest whisper I yelled, "Shut up! Are you guys trying to blow our cover?" Then to the stranger in uniform, "Who the hell are you?"

"Lieutenant David Jensen, Special Weapons and Tactics," he said. "You must be Duffy. Is this asshole with you?"

Cory started to respond, but I held my hand up, looked at Cory and he stopped. I replied, "This is my photographer and he has Tourette's Syndrome. Leave it alone."

"I don't put up with that shit from anybody. I don't care what he has," Jensen said getting worked up again.

"He can no more control his swearing than a guy with Parkinson's Disease can keep himself from shaking," I said.

"I don't want to hear excuses, just get him the fuck out of here," he said.

"You're the asshole, Jensen," I said.

"I don't like you Duffy. You should think about who's gonna have your back here today," he said.

"You don't have to like me, just do your job by not telling the bad guys we're here," I said.

"Your guy is a liability in this situation and I don't want him on the scene," he said while glaring at Cory.

"Normally I'd fight you on Cory's right to be here. But, I need him to take the pictures he shot last night back to his lab and enhance those images," I said to Jensen. Then, to Cory I said, "I really need to know what was in that guy's hand when he walked into the garage. Call me as soon as you know."

Cory nodded and I exited the van behind Jensen. When we got back to the SWAT truck, filled with his men, Jensen climbed into the back, turned around to me and said, "Why don't you wait out here? You probably need a stretch after being in that van all night."

"That's fine with me," I said. "I thought the guys who are going in might like to know the floor layout and which rooms the perps are going to be in. But you probably prefer surprises."

"Is that Jason Duffy out there?" said a voice from inside the SWAT truck.

I stepped to the door opening and said, "Who's in there?"

"Dennis Kerrigan. My dad was on the force with your dad. I was at a couple of your backyard barbecues when I was a kid," he said.

"I remember you. How are you, Dennis?" I asked.

He replied, "We'll catch up later. Now get in here and tell us about that house. I'm one of the guys going in."

I looked at Jensen who said, "Whatever," and sat between two of his men.

"I then climbed into the truck and conducted as thorough a briefing as possible without disclosing how I came by this knowledge. I didn't tell and they didn't ask.

At 7:45 AM Shamansky arrived with a warrant in hand. He took charge once he got in the truck, "Did Jason brief you on the layout?" he asked.

"We got a lot more than we expected," said Jensen. I wasn't sure if this was a compliment or if he was still pissed about Cory.

Shamansky continued, "Here's how it's going down. We have to give them a chance to let us serve the warrant peacefully, but I think they're going to give us trouble. That's why you guys are here. We suspect that these men built the bomb that killed Terry Tucker, and we think it was built here. I was going to have you launch gas grenades into the upstairs windows, but I think we'll need maximum visibility in case one of these guys goes for a stick of dynamite or some other explosive."

"Do we know they have dynamite?" asked Kerrigan.

Shamansky shot a look at me and replied, "The owner of the house works for a construction outfit next to an excavation site. We know they use dynamite at the site, so there's a good chance they picked up some dynamite when they stole the blasting caps that killed Tucker. The stuff might be in the house and it might be in the garage if they have any brains. The warrant covers both structures."

Over the next fifteen minutes Shamansky laid out his plan and Jensen asked questions. At 8:07 AM Shamansky rang the front doorbell while four SWAT guys with a battering ram took up a position by the back door. A minute later he rang the bell again, holding the warrant in his left hand and his 9mm pistol behind his back in his right hand. Kerrigan and I had our backs to the exterior wall away from the front window. It was decided that I could go in because I had knowledge of the items being sought in the warrant, and time might be of the essence once we got inside to keep evidence from being destroyed.

The door opened up and I heard, "What can I do for you, mate?"

"Detective Shamansky, San Diego Police. I have a warrant," he said.

"COPS!" screamed Devin Billingsly.

Shamansky whipped his gun around his body, shoved it in Devin Billingsly's ribs and pushed him inside. I followed behind Kerrigan through a small entryway into the living room. I started to look for the headphones when I became aware of a huge ogre of a guy sitting at the head of a table in the adjoining dining room, with a cereal bowl in front of him. Suddenly, he jumped out of his seat and dove through a bay window that overlooked the side yard and garage.

I followed Kerrigan into the dining room in time to see him roll through the glass on the lawn, then bounce to his feet and dive through the garage window. Billingsly screamed, "NO!" just before a massive explosion leveled the garage and knocked us all to the floor.

A few seconds later a battering ram knocked the back door open and SWAT poured in both doors. The cops that came in the front door ran straight up the stairs and three shots were fired immediately. The SWAT response that followed sounded like the ending to the movie *Butch Cassidy and the Sundance Kid*. "Come out with your hands on your head or I'll throw in a grenade," we heard in a booming voice.

"They'll destroy the evidence," I said to Shamansky with panic in my voice.

Shamansky shook his head and Billingsly yelled, "He's bluffing!"

After 100 rounds of ammunition smashed through the master bedroom door, Desmond Thompson was no longer taking orders from Devin Billingsly. Two minutes later Desmond tromped down the stairs in baby blue boxers and was followed by the girl I encountered yesterday morning. She was wearing the same green T-shirt and with her hands on top of her head she was commanding way too much attention, while Warren Bates was still on the loose. "Did you find Bates?" I asked the guy who was bringing up and admiring the rear.

"I didn't see him," he replied without looking at me.

Jensen heard this and yelled, "Jackson, Anderson, Dickson, go up there and find that guy!"

Dickson popped a new magazine into his weapon and followed the others up the stairs. "We want him alive," shouted Shamansky. Over the next ten minutes we found the two sets of headphones in the living room and became increasingly aware of the total silence on the second floor. Finally, Jensen went up to check on his men. He came back down a couple of minutes later and told us Bates was nowhere to be seen.

"Keep a close eye on him," Shamansky said to Kerrigan as he let go of the handcuffed Billingsly. He then turned to me and said, "Come with me." We walked up the stairs and half-way down the hall when he called, "Shamansky and Duffy in the hall."

"Let's get the headphones," I said and Shamansky nodded. The door was open and Officer Jackson was staring at the closet.

"He must have gone out the back door last night," Jackson said.

"They came here by cab. Thompson has the only vehicle and it's parked outside," I said.

"Well he ain't here," said Jackson.

I looked at the stereo and immediately noticed that the headphones were no longer plugged in. I stepped quickly to the shelving unit that held them, along with speakers and numerous CD's, but no headphones. "Damn," I said and dropped to the floor for a look under the bed.

"He ain't there either," Jackson said.

I rummaged through drawers while Shamansky checked the closet, but no sign of the headphones. We looked for about ten minutes, then moved to the guestroom where we suspected Warren Bates was staying. A check of his open suitcase containing his passport and clothing confirmed that he was here. I looked out the room's gable window and saw the space where the garage had been. I also saw several cops and seriously doubted that Bates could have climbed down the side of the building and past the cops. In fact, there wasn't anything to climb on even if the cops weren't there to notice.

We tossed the room and failed to find the headphones, then continued from room to room but came up empty. When we got back downstairs I checked the serial numbers of the two sets we recovered, in case the one Chelsea had purchased was moved to the living room, but no luck. They were the same sets I had seen the previous day. After an hour and forty-five minutes of searching we gave up.

Outside, Shamansky told the crime lab guys to look for any sign of blasting caps, BBs and a BB box. While he was helping to define the areas he wanted combed thoroughly, I walked to the border of the yellow police tape across the street. There were several neighbors on the other side of the tape checking out the cops and SWAT team. I peaked inside the SWAT truck and saw Kerrigan talking to

Jensen. I decided not to interrupt and hung out by a few of the neighbors.

A little five-year-old boy holding his mother's hand kept pointing at the house and telling his mom, "I saw Santa. Santa's here. Is Santa coming to our house?"

Kerrigan and Jensen emerged from the truck and Jensen walked back toward the house. "Did you find what you were looking for?" asked Kerrigan.

"Not everything," I said and remembered that I turned my phone off before approaching the house with Shamansky. I checked my messages and got a voice-mail from Cory who conveyed that Billingsly had a pair of headphones in his hand when he walked into the garage. He had only the flashlight when he emerged a half-hour later. He must have rigged a bomb to destroy the evidence and not bothered to tell Pine.

I started to explain this to Kerrigan when the five-year-old went limp in the knees as his mother tried leading him away. "I wanna see Santa! I wanna see Santa!" he cried adamantly.

"What the hell is that all about?" Kerrigan asked.

"Want to be a hero?" I motioned for him to follow me. When we got to the fire truck hosing down the smoking embers of the garage I said to Kerrigan, "Tell the fire chief you want him to put their ladder up there so you can look down the chimney."

"Say what?" asked Kerrigan with a squint.

"Why do you think the kid thought he saw Santa?" I asked.

Kerrigan smiled and started barking orders. Ten minutes later, with a pistol in one hand and a flashlight in the other Kerrigan called, "I got him!" When they got down to the ground Kerrigan got a round of applause from the spectators, fire, and police personnel. He stuck his arm out toward me to give me credit, but I shook my head and waved him off.

I felt a hand clamp down on my shoulder. Jensen said, "Who said you never get a second chance to make a first impression? You're alright, Duffy."

"You've got a hellofa team, Jensen. You've done a great job with them," I said and meant it.

Shamansky broke up our little fence mending session to say, "Let's get you downtown and wired. Nigel should be at the compound in about an hour. No time for lunch today."

As we rode to the station house Shamansky said, "I'm sure glad we got Bates, but I'm not exactly feeling the thrill of victory,"

"I know what you mean. Just before we found Bates I got a message from Cory. He enhanced the picture he took with the night scope of Billingsly walking into the garage last night and guess what was in his hand?" I asked.

"The headphones?" he asked with a wince. I nodded. "He must have booby-trapped them."

"It worked," I replied. "He took out the number one booby in Southeast San Diego. I found out last night that Theodore Pine was our best bet for rolling over on his mates. He had an IQ lower than the tree he's named after. He also has a long criminal record and was the only one of the three with very little to do with killing Terry."

"Damn! What about the other two?" he asked.

"Some college, passing grades, no felony convictions," I said.

"Shit! They'll probably lawyer up and hope Nigel can get them out of it," he said with disgust. "By the way, where are you getting this information?"

"You don't want to know who and you don't want to know how," I said with a tone of mystery in my voice.

"Now you've peaked my interest," he said.

"Let's just say it's a guy who can get into other people's computers quicker and easier than I got into the house we just left," I said.

"Maybe he could be a resource in the future," he said.

"He's being watched by agencies I never even heard of, and I doubt he'll be reachable once this case is over. He was a friend of Terry's," I said and Shamansky let it go.

"Have you been thinking about what you're going to say to Choate and Chofsky?" asked Shamansky.

"I'm gonna tell Nigel we found the headphones, the blasting caps and the BBs. I'll also tell him that while Teddy Boy was trying to be fiercely loyal, he came down with a case of the stupids and a couple of smart cops tricked him into giving it up," I said.

"Perfect. Very believable. As far as I know, the names have not been released to the press as yet. Even if Choate watched the noon news or heard a radio report, he shouldn't make the connection," he said.

"He's conducting an audition for a new guitarist this morning, so I doubt he'll be seeing or hearing any news," I said.

"Good. I think once you tell him, you should make like it was all Chofsky's idea, and that he might be able to cut a deal if he rolls on the mastermind," he said.

I replied, "Chofsky's got a compound full of guys with automatic weapons. I was thinking of maybe a less direct approach."

"No! For a few seconds you'll have them by the short hairs - squeeze and twist. Try to get them to turn on each other," he said.

"What if they decide that getting rid of me is the best solution?" I asked.

"Then show them the wire. Tell them 50 cops have been listening to every word and the wrath of God will come down on their heads if they do anything to you. They'll lawyer up at that point, but they won't touch you," he said with more confidence than I felt.

"What if they both just deny everything and don't go for the bait?" I asked.

"Then we bring them in and hope we get somebody to roll. I think we'll still have a shot. The Irishmen aren't going to want to do time in the US where they'll be away from family, friends and the Orangemen. One of them might give us Choate if we work a prisoner exchange deal," he said.

When we arrived at Shamansky's desk in the stationhouse, Dad was across the room chatting with one of his buddies. He looked serious and as he approached us he said, "Sounds like you had some fireworks out there."

"We got some of what we were looking for, but not everything," I said to him.

Shamansky said to Dad, "Your son was a big help, Jim. He did you proud. I'll brief you in a few minutes, but first Jason needs to get wired and out to Chofsky's place."

"Do what you need to, Walt. Let me know when you're ready," Dad replied and walked back over to his friend's desk.

"Walt?" I asked Shamansky.

"It doesn't sound right coming from you," he said, then picked up the phone. "Dispatch, it's Shamansky. Are the two B&W's ready? ... Good, we'll be down in ten," he said and hung up. To me he said, "Take off your shirt."

I did so and Shamansky expertly attached the microphone and transmitter. "How will I know if you're getting the transmission?" I asked.

"The guys in the truck will have your cell phone number. If they can't hear you they'll call and tell you the instant they lose you. Just make up an excuse to go out and talk to the cops, and they'll strap on a new one. But trust me, I've used this model a hundred times. I know the range and the layout of the compound. There shouldn't be a problem," he said.

I stood up and Dad walked over carrying a bag. "Your mother packed you a lunch. I figured you wouldn't have much time."

I could tell Shamansky was dying to display his humor, but didn't want to piss Dad off, so he held his tongue.

At 1:18 PM I arrived at the compound in a black & white. After a minor hassle with Svetlana she escorted me to Chofsky's office. The doors swung open and Chofsky was standing behind his desk. The thick-paned, tinted French doors behind the desk that overlooked half of the swimming pool were open. As I walked in I could hear Ivana splashing in the pool and talking to someone I couldn't see.

"I don't have much time for you, Mr. Duffy. Besides the interviews with the men you helped bring into the country, I also have another business meeting taking place right now. So quickly, what can I do for you?" he asked impatiently.

"I need you to call Nigel in here," I said.

"He is in the meeting. This will have to wait," he said assuming I didn't have the clout that Shamansky carried.

"His friends were arrested this morning and told us Nigel swapped out the headphones Terry's wife gave him with the one containing the bomb. We need to talk right now," I said.

Chofsky picked up his telephone, dialed and said, "Bring Mr. Choate to my office." He then walked to the French doors and closed them. As he was doing so he gave a tight-lipped smile and waved at Ivana. I felt sorry for her, knowing what she had been through and what was coming. Chofsky pressed his fingertips together and had a worried look on his face. He was about to say something when Svetlana swung the doors open and Nigel walked in.

"What's going on?" asked Nigel.

I replied, "The police raided Desmond Thompson's house first thing this morning. They found the headphones Chelsea gave to Terry along with two of the three pairs that were sent to Devin Billingsly in North Ireland."

"Bollocks!" he exclaimed.

I continued, "They also found blasting caps and a box of BBs."

"That's ridiculous! Why would they do that? They know Terry was my mate. I can't imagine how this is possible," he said with as much conviction as he could muster.

"Well, actually we have some answers to those questions already," I said. "Your friends Devin and Warren weren't giving anything up. But the other guy, Teddy Boy is quite another matter. He had every intention of keeping your secret, but he lost a battle of wits with a couple of smart cops. We know about how you swapped out the headphones at 7/Eleven."

"Bollocks! I had nothing to do with it!" he exclaimed.

"Before I left to come over here, Detective Shamansky called the 7/Eleven to find out if they have a surveillance system, and guess what? They got robbed three times last year so they put cameras on the parking lot to record the faces of robbers before they put on their ski masks," I said.

"Aha! Now I know you're lying! There aren't any cam…" Nigel's voice trailed off as he realized what he was saying.

I replied, "See how easy it is to give it up? This is the kind of thing that got Teddy Boy to slip up. You knew Terry would be stopping there for his usual Super Big Gulp of iced tea. They had posters all over the windows so you didn't have to worry about being seen by him," I said.

"Do you believe this shite?" Nigel said to Chofsky, who remained silent.

I continued, "Mr. Pine has a big problem with spending the rest of his life in a California prison. As an accomplice he could get as much time as everybody else. But, since he told us Warren stole the blasting caps and Billingsly built the bomb, he really didn't have much of a role in the killing. The DA agreed to a prisoner exchange with Northern Ireland. The details still have to be worked out, but the bottom line is that Pine agreed to five years near his family, friends and fellow Orangemen versus life where he'll never see a familiar face again. Pine has been to prison before. He knows what it would be like at a facility with no friends. He took the deal."

Nigel asked, "Then why are you here instead of the cops?"

"The cops are here," said Chofsky.

Nigel looked at me and I said, "Because I don't believe this was your idea. I think Mr. Chofsky laid out Terry's plan for a protracted legal battle that would have shut down your cash flow for the next three years, and you asked him what you could do to get the deal done. I think Terry put you in a position where he wanted to punish you for your excessive spending and felt a legal battle would get him more money in the long run and get you back under his thumb in the short run. You didn't think it was fair and Chofsky suggested something that would solve all of your problems."

"You're out of line Mr. Duffy. That is preposterous," Chofsky said with his chest puffed out and his thumbs looped under his lapels.

"Then why did you place an ad for the new CD in a trade publication the day before Terry was killed?" I asked. When he couldn't come up with a response I turned to Nigel and said, "The DA always comes down hardest on the mastermind. If you tell the police that Chofsky took advantage of you while you were in a vulnerable spot, you could get a deal like Teddy Pine. Probably a few more years, but with good behavior you'll only have to do one-third of your minimum sentence. If you keep denying everything while everybody else cuts deals, you're screwed."

Chofsky boomed, "Get a lawyer and keep your mouth shut!"

Immediately after he shouted all hell broke loose. A hail of gunfire seemed to come from everywhere. I instinctively dove to the carpet, looked up through the French doors, and saw several paratroopers with automatic weapons floating quickly toward the inside of the compound. Chofsky bolted through the French doors toward the swimming pool. He got about three steps onto the decking when a bullet struck him in the forehead. I rolled onto my side as I heard the sound of Ivana getting out of the pool.

By this time Chofsky's guards were returning fire and drawing the attention of the paratroopers. I ran out the French doors and dove behind one of several large brick planter boxes that ringed the pool area. When I peeked over the edge of the box I was horrified to see who Ivana had been talking to. It was Jeannine. At first my brain had trouble processing what I was seeing. Why would Jeannine be in Chofsky's backyard? Then it hit me. She had come with Michael to his audition, and her presence must mean he was asked to join the band.

Jeannine was in a squatting position with her hands over her ears, and her eyes closed. I ran to her, bent down, pulled one of her hands away from her ear and as calmly as possible said, "Jeannine, it's Jason. Come with me."

Her eyes opened wide and focused on me, "Let's go!" I shouted over the gunfire. I laced her fingers in mine and pulled her to a standing position then started to run. She kept pace all the way through the French doors. I brought her around the desk and guided her down to the floor alongside Nigel. "Wait here!" I shouted.

I pivoted and ran back to the deck where Ivana was down on all fours calling to her father in Russian. Keeping my head down I ran to her. "He's gone, Ivana," I said.

"No!" she screamed. I put my arm around her waist and carried her on my hip back through the French doors to where Jeannine and Nigel were hunkered down behind the desk.

"Nigel, where's the rest of the band?" I asked while breathing heavily. He pointed toward the door. "Show me!" I exclaimed.

He led us out the office doors and into the hallway. I asked Ivana, "Is there a safe room in the house?"

She looked confused, "What?"

"Do you have a safe room in case you're attacked?" I asked.

As we reached the huge dining room where the band was set up she said, "The bomb shelter."

Upon entering the dining room Ian and Jack were asking what was going on while Michael ran to Jeannine, threw his arms around her and said to her, "Thank God you're alright. I was going out of my mind." She sobbed loudly into his shoulder.

"Listen up!" I screamed above the cacophony of everyone talking at once. When I had their attention I said, "Ivana is going to take us to a safe room."

"Bomb shelter," she corrected me.

"Let's go," I said and pointed Ivana's shoulders at the door. She started walking down the hall when we heard a loud crash in the front of the house. "Faster!" I exclaimed in an excited whisper. She ran and we kept pace all the way into the library. She pressed a hidden button under the lip of one of the shelves and a panel next to the bookshelves retracted, revealing a metal door with no handle and a box the size of a fire alarm unit with a green display screen. Ivana put her thumb on the illuminated scanner and the door opened instantly. As soon as we entered she thumbed another scanner and the door closed.

"The panel on the outside is closing now. We should be safe," she said.

"What's this?" asked Nigel.

We walked over to a desk that held two television monitors. Ivana opened up a laptop computer and turned it on. She then hit a couple of keys and the monitors came on. One showed the area in front of the bomb shelter and the other was an interior camera showing the front door, which was wide open.

"What the hell is going on?" asked Ian.

I replied, "It looks like the Russian Mafia sent a skydiving hit squad into the compound."

"They killed my Daddy," Ivana whimpered and started to cry.

"How many are out there?" Ian asked.

"There must be at least a hundred of them," she replied. Actually, I think it was closer to twenty, but I had no problem letting Ivana think it took a small army to kill her father.

The bomb shelter looked comfortable. It held two single beds, a stocked kitchen, bathroom, radio, TV, DVD and a short-wave radio. "Do you know how to work the short-wave radio?" I asked Ivana. She nodded and wiped tears. "See if you can reach the police."

When I said this, Nigel reached into his pocket and came out with a small pistol that he pointed at Ivana and said, "Put the radio down, Ivana."

"What are you doing Nigel?" asked Jack.

Nigel replied, "Ask Jason, he has all the bloody answers today."

Everyone looked at me and I said, "Nigel and his hooligan buddies killed Terry."

"Why?" asked Ian.

"You know why," answered Nigel. "Terry was going to sit back and let us go bankrupt while he worked out our deal with Cerise. You called me right after Koflanovich called you. You didn't like it either."

"There's a lot of things I don't like but I don't go around killing people," Ian stated.

Nigel replied, "No, you just go get fucked up and pretend that everything's fine. Well I couldn't do that. We're on the brink of being one of the biggest bands in the world. I wasn't going to sit back and see my personal life go down the crapper while Terry lived off of his rich wife. We're hot, but in this business you cool off fast if nobody hears from you for a few months, never mind a few years."

Jack said, "We could have talked to him. It was probably just a bluff to get the record company to cut us a better deal. Did you even ask him about it?"

"I talked to him, but he wouldn't listen. I think he was jealous that the ladies were into my songs and not his. He wasn't going to let it go three years, but he had no problem tying everything up for at least a year," Nigel said.

I interjected, "It wasn't just the money for you Nigel. Terry wasn't thinking about Ian when he put that clause in the new contract proposals about getting rid of a band member. He wanted to get rid of you."

"Is that true?" asked Ian.

Nigel replied, "You guys have no idea what goes on behind the scenes. We weren't really that big until our second CD. What made us huge was all the women who loved my songs, not Terry's songs, my songs. But do you think he would recognize that and treat me with the respect I deserved? Not a chance. He was going to run things his way, and if we didn't like it, too bloody bad. So I stood up to him and he told me that if I think I'm such hot shite maybe I should get my own band together. Bloody ingrate deserved what he got!" Nigel had worked himself into a lather and had a crazy look in his eyes.

"What happens now, Nigel?" asked Jack.

Nigel looked around the room. His eyes settled on the TV showing the front door. Everyone looked at the monitor to see what caught his eye. It showed four men in sky-blue jumpsuits, carrying automatic rifles. "What are they looking for? I thought you said Koflanovich was dead," said Ian.

I responded, "He faked them out with a look-alike once before. I'm sure they were told to make certain it doesn't happen again."

Nigel said, "I hate to be a party pooper but it's time for everyone except Ivana to go greet our guests."

Ian said, "You're daft if you think I'm going out there," and he lunged toward Nigel. Nigel pulled the trigger and whizzed a bullet a few inches to the right of Ian's left ear. "I'm fucking deaf," he screamed.

Nigel said, "You're gonna be fucking dead if you don't go out that door right now," as he pointed to the door.

"Why are you keeping Ivana here?" asked Jeannine.

I replied, "He doesn't want her putting her thumb on the scanner again."

"Amazingly astute for a Catholic Irishman, Mr. Duffy," said Nigel. "Now I suggest you get out there before the blue-boys show up on the library monitor."

"You're not going to get away with this, Nigel. Why kill your mates?" asked Jack

He replied, "The only people who know about this room are either dead or here with me. I plan on sticking around for maybe a week. Let all the cops and crime scene people do their thing, then waltz out of here and go someplace where I can continue to write and record. Now, if you don't leave immediately I'm going to shoot you and toss you out myself."

I took a final glance at the monitors and saw no one. The heavy door popped open and the five of us made our way across the library as the door closed behind us and the panel slid back into place. "There's a set of stairs on the other side of the kitchen," I said, "follow me." Serving as point man, I peaked into the kitchen and saw two of the paratroopers walking into an adjacent pantry room. We quickly crossed in front of the doorway while their backs were turned.

The door to the back stairs was ajar. Jack was guarding the rear of our little group. "Shut the door," I whispered to him when we were all on the stairs. Fortunately, it was a new, expensive house so we didn't have to contend with noisy stairs. When I reached the top I peaked around the corner and saw a long hallway with several open doors. "Let's go," I whispered as I ascended the last stair and moved into the hall. Jeannine was directly behind me, followed by Michael. As soon as Jeannine was completely into the hallway I saw the tip of a machine gun come whipping around the corner along with a leg in a mid-calf skirt. Before she made eye contact she started firing. I threw a cross-body block into Jeannine, knocking her into Michael and back into the stair well. Three rounds blew holes in the wall to my right. I landed on the hall carpet and yelled," Svetlana!"

She stopped firing immediately and shouted, "Ivana?"

"It's Jason Duffy," I retorted and directed our group into the hall. When Svetlana reached us I said, "Ivana is in the safe room with a killer."

"What is safe room?" she asked.

"The bomb shelter," Jeannine said.

"Do you have any more guns?" I asked.

"Come," she replied and walked to a nearby bedroom. At the foot of the bed was a large cedar chest with two large brass bands adorning what looked to me like a pirate's chest. Svetlana pushed two of the many beveled rivets holding the bands, and the chest opened quickly to reveal five AK-47's and numerous ammo clips.

"Everybody take one," I said as I snapped an ammo clip into one of the weapons.

"I don't want one," Jeannine said as she continually shook her head.

"Then make sure you stay close," I said and the continual shaking changed to continual nodding.

"Does anybody have any shooting experience?" I asked.

Jack said, "I grew up in the country. My dad taught me to shoot when I was twelve. I was pretty good."

Nobody else said anything. At my request, Svetlana gave them a quick lesson in loading and firing. When she finished I asked, "Svetlana, do you have any idea how we can get back into the safe room?"

"Bomb shelter," she scowled then immediately smiled as she held up her thumb.

"What about the TV monitors?" I asked.

Once again she simply said, "Come," and walked out of the room. We all followed her into her bedroom about two-thirds of the way down the hall away from the back stairs, but not quite to the exposed railing overlooking the front foyer. Just as we were closing ranks inside her room, shots rang out in the hallway coming from the back stairs. Jack hit the floor with a thump and I was sure he was dead until he started firing his weapon. Before any of us could do anything to help, Jack stopped firing, turned back to us and said, "It must have been the guys from the kitchen. I got 'em."

I took this as an extremely good sign. I knew since that fateful day in the alley behind the Dali Lama that I had the stones to pull the trigger. Since I first applied for my PI license I visited a shooting range for practice at least once a month. But, I still don't know if I could hit a moving target, especially a moving human target. At least I knew one of us could and, under the circumstances, that was a huge plus.

After Jack made his announcement, Svetlana sat at her desk, opened her laptop computer and began typing furiously. As she pounded the keys I noticed for the first time that for a forty-something woman, she might actually be attractive with a little effort. "Done," she said as she closed the computer and stood up.

"What's done?" I asked feeling like she had just hung up on me once again.

"Bomb shelter monitors turned off. They will not see us coming," she said as she breezed past me to assume the point position. "This way," Svetlana said as she led us to the back stairs. As we stepped over the two Mafioso's that Jack had killed, Svetlana put a hand on Jack's shoulder and said, "Good boy. You walk with me in front."

I had just been demoted and I didn't care. I took up the rear position with Jeannine directly in front of me. Ian stayed right behind Jack and was looking like the only thing he wanted to kill was a bottle of Jameson whiskey.

We cautiously made our way back to the library. When we got there I shut and locked the hallway door. As I did this, Svetlana headed straight for the panel release switch and it retracted. "Stop!" I yelled in a hushed scream. "He'll shoot Ivana if you just barge in with your gun."

For once Svetlana was listening to me and froze in her tracks. "You have better idea?" she asked. In less than a minute I laid it out and everyone except Svetlana found hiding spots away from the doorway. Jack unlocked the library door, checked outside and left it ajar. He then took up a firing position behind an L-shaped, stone and copper planter box that joined the wall between the hallway door and the first of the library bookshelves. Svetlana thumbed the scanner, then dropped to the carpet. When it popped open, she pushed it wide and called, "Ivana, it's Svetlana! Are you in there?"

"Svetlana, don't come in!" screamed Ivana.

Svetlana replied, "I've been shot. Your father is alive. He is in hallway. Please pull him into bomb shelter."

At this news both Ivana and Nigel appeared in the open doorway. In an amazing display of acting, Svetlana made eye contact with Ivana and said, "He is awake. Get him in here before they come back."

I was counting on my theory that Nigel and Chofsky had been co-conspirators in hopes Nigel would immediately recognize the value of Chofsky's money and contacts to help him out of this jam. I was also hoping Nigel didn't see the big hole in Chofsky's forehead as he exited the office. Ivana believed what she wanted to believe and instinctively ran toward the library door. Nigel lowered his gun so that it was a couple of feet from Svetlana's head when a short burst of shots rang out and Nigel's right arm exploded just below the elbow. The little square gun fell directly in front of Svetlana and she retrieved it, stood up and aimed it at Nigel's head.

"No!" I yelled and Svetlana glanced my way. Nigel had dropped to his knees and was holding his right arm with his left hand. She lowered the gun, then kicked Nigel in the face with all of her might. He flipped backwards and banged his head on the floor as he landed on his back.

"Daddy's not there!" cried Ivana. Jeannine ran into the hallway and threw her arms around her. After a brief moment, Jack herded them back into the library and locked the doors.

Svetlana stood over Nigel, "What did you do to that little girl? She demanded, then suddenly stomped on his shattered arm."

Nigel let out a scream of incredible intensity. As I charged toward Svetlana before she could finish him off I heard Ian say to Jack, "We could have used that scream on the *Biscuit* CD."

I grabbed Svetlana by the shoulders and moved her away from Nigel, "Everybody inside the bomb shelter!" I yelled. Once we were inside it was apparent that Jeannine had explained our ruse to Ivana. She sat on one of the beds and wept into her hands. "Can you operate the short-wave radio?" I asked Svetlana.

She gave me a look of disgust and replied, "What do you think?" as she sat down and started flipping switches.

Svetlana connected me with a police dispatcher, who patched me through to Shamansky. "Jason, I'm with your dad outside the compound. Are you OK?" he asked.

"I'm inside a bomb shelter. Everybody's OK except Chofsky. He was killed instantly," I said.

"You mean a safe room?" he asked.

"Yes. It's inside the library. What's going on with the paratroopers?" I asked.

He replied, "They have a helicopter inside the compound, but a SWAT guy hit the fuel line and it's on fire."

"Anybody I know?" I asked.

"It was a different team than the guys you met this morning. We lost your transmission right after the shit hit the fan. Did Nigel give it up?" he asked.

Nigel was listening to my conversation and I didn't know if Shamansky was planning on keeping the Teddy Pine story going, so I replied, "Not only that, we can now add five counts of attempted murder. By the time he gets out of prison he'll be lucky if he can get a gig playing at his old folks home."

"Arsehole," Nigel said.

"Oops, I almost forgot. Nigel got his arm shot off. I guess he'll have to settle for being somebody's prison bitch for the next 30 years," I said.

"It sounds like he's listening to us. Call me back in a half-hour. We should have everything under control by then," he said and was about to hang up when he said, "Jason, are you still there?"

"I'm here," I said.

"Your dad wants to talk to you," he said and was gone.

"Jason, are you alright?" Dad asked.

"I'm fine. I can't talk, but tell me about the interrogations," I said.

He replied, "I think they're expecting Nigel to roll in with a cadre of lawyers and everything will be alright. So they're not talking. Forensics got a positive result when they tested Billingsly's hands for gunpowder," he said.

"Anything from the other couple in the house?" I asked.

"Desmond hasn't said a word, but the girl, Marilyn Hempstead, has been cooperating," he said. "She didn't know about Terry Tucker, but she was very helpful when it came to remembering when they got the missing headphones, what they looked like and how everybody told her not to take them out of the house because they could get the guys in trouble," Dad said. We continued to talk another twenty minutes. Jack kept his gun trained on Nigel while Svetlana tied a tourniquet on his arm in a less than gentle manner.

"The grounds are clear and Shamansky is in the library. He wants you to open the door now. I'm signing off," Dad said. I told Ivana to thumb the scanner.

When the door opened Shamansky walked in with two SWAT officers, pointed at Nigel and said, "Gentlemen, there's your man." The officer on the left helped him to his feet.

Nigel said to me, "You never would have made it as a professional musician. Your vocal range is too limited and your rhythm guitar is just a knock-off of other people's style. I was just jerking you off to keep you out of the way."

"And a fine job you did on that one, Nigel," I said as I tried to ignore the sting of his biting critique.

"What about me?" asked Michael Marinangeli.

"You are the real deal. Your buddy totally screwed you. If it wasn't for Duffy you'd be playing to full stadiums and making more money than the bloody president," Nigel said as the officers led him out the door.

"Tough break Michael," I said.

"Are you kidding me?" he replied. "When we were upstairs in that hallway I prayed for the first time since I was a little kid. I asked God to keep Jeannine safe and told Him if He did I'd never ask for another thing." Michael put his arms around her and she started to cry.

Chapter 29

OVER the next three days I was in touch with Shamansky on a regular basis. The DA's office was pressing hard for the death penalty since it was clearly premeditated. Shamansky said that the death penalty threat was the DA's way of getting Nigel to roll over on his buddies. In exchange he was offered 25 years to life. With good behavior, that translates to eight and a third years before becoming eligible for parole. Nigel's attorney might have considered the death penalty talk to be just so much sword rattling had it not been for the fact that Jack and Ian changed the home page of the Doberman's Stub Official Web Site to ask fans to demand justice. It had a flattering picture of Terry and a very unflattering one of Nigel flipping off the media. The caption read, "Let's get Terry and Nigel together again in the hereafter. The text strongly urged fans to email the San Diego County DA's office to ask for the death penalty for Nigel Choate. A link was included and twelve thousand emails and text messages were received in the first 24 hours. They were forwarded to Nigel's attorney and made a strong impression.

On Thursday morning Shamansky called to say he just concluded a meeting with the DA and was told all charges against Chelsea would be officially dismissed. He asked the DA if he could give her the good news and got the OK. "Would you like to be the one to tell her she is officially off the hook?" he asked.

"I love giving good news," I replied. "Can I tell her today?"

"The sooner the better. Make sure her attorney calls the DA's office by tomorrow at the latest," he replied.

I gave her a call as soon as we got off of the phone and she asked if I would like her to make lunch for us once again. I accepted.

Two hours later I was seated at her kitchen table with a Diet Coke from the twelve-pack I brought along. When I told her the charges were dropped she let out a loud sigh and said, "In a way it feels like it's over, but I don't think it will ever really be over."

"You're never going to forget about him, but eventually most of your memories will be of the good times," I said.

As we finished lunch I said, "There's one other matter I'd like to discuss."

"What is it, Jason?" she asked.

"At Nigel's trial it will come out that Cerise Records owner, John Koflanovich, a.k.a. Ivan Chofsky, may have been in on the conspiracy to kill Terry. He was killed in the Russian Mafia raid on his home. I just wanted you to know that his sole heir is a 17 year-old girl who was kidnapped in Russia and had a finger chopped off. She has lived like a prisoner ever since, but still managed to turn out to be a terrific kid."

Chelsea said, "So if I were thinking of suing Chofsky's estate it would actually be this poor girl who would take the hit for her father."

"I just thought you should know," I said.

"Before you go I have something for you," she said as she got up from the table and left the room. When she returned she was carrying a guitar. "It's not very expensive and he never used it on stage, but Terry wrote all of his Doberman's Stub songs on this guitar."

I strummed it and said, "It's incredibly easy to fret."

"That's what Terry said. He could play that guitar all day and night without getting tired. I can give you a letter of authenticity if you like," she said.

"This is a keeper, Chelsea. I won't be selling it," I said.

"I'm really glad you feel that way," she said.

After placing the guitar in an expensive Fender case, she handed it to me then picked up a white envelope on a table by the door. "My dad wanted to thank you personally but he had to go out of town.

He said to tell you not to open it until you get back to your office." She gave me a hug and said, "Thanks for everything, Jason."

Once inside the Acura, I opened the envelope and a check for $50,000 fell out. The note said: "Thank you for believing in my little girl. The enclosed check is my way of showing my gratitude. Should the thought of sending it back cross your mind, consider that her attorneys would have cost me 10 times that amount. I'm sure I will be referring you to my friends and associates. Regards, Peter Spivey."

A lot of thoughts crossed my mind, but sending back the check was definitely not one of them. Considering their contributions I decided that Jeannine and Cory would be getting Christmas bonuses.

When I got back to the office Jeannine told me that my mother had called. After we exchanged hellos she said, "I know it's last minute, but your father and I would like you and Kelly to join us and the Kerrigans for a little dinner party here at the house Saturday night to celebrate you closing the case, and Dennis getting a citation."

"Mom, I've got a problem with this," I said.

"Do you and Kelly have other plans?" she asked.

I replied, "No, I have a problem with joining the Irish Mafia."

"I asked you not to use that term," she said.

"It doesn't matter what we call it. Ever since Dad found out I was dating a girl of Irish heritage he assumed I want to become a member of his exclusive little club," I said.

"There's nothing wrong with having friends," Mom said.

"I agree. I have lots of friends. I have Italian friends, African-American friends, Mexican friends. We're Americans, Mom, not Irishmen," I said, getting a little worked up in the process.

"I understand what you're saying, Jason, but your dad and I grew up in a different era. We were taught to trust our own people. Right or wrong when you learn these things from parents you love and trust, it stays with you," she said.

"That may be so but it doesn't make it right. You might see it as me humoring my father. But, you have to understand, I see it as perpetuating racism. I think it's high time the Duffy family sign on as 100% American," I said wishing there was a way of making my feelings known without upsetting her.

"Does this mean you're not going to join us?" she asked.

"We will if you agree to integrate the festivities. Invite Detective Shamansky and a date to the party, and we'll be glad to join you," I said.

"OK, give me his number and I'll give him a call," she said.

"Are you going to ask Dad first?" I asked.

"I'll tell him, but I'm not taking no for an answer. What you said is true and I'm ashamed I wasn't a better example for you," she said.

"I didn't mean to shame you, I just think it's time we evolve as a family," I said.

"Say no more. I'll see you and Kelly Saturday night. Cocktails at 7:00 dinner at 8:00," she said.

Chapter 30

FRIDAY morning I joined Jeannine and Delbert in the waiting room and said, "Delbert, I have your final paycheck. As I said when I hired you, the job was just for the duration of the case, which is now officially closed. With your help it was a success." I handed him an envelope. "I added an extra two weeks pay as our way of saying thank you for a job well done."

The information about the severance package didn't seem to register. Instead his eyes focused on the box I had carried into the room, wrapped in red paper with a blue ribbon and bow. "What's that?" he asked.

"This is a little something extra that I got for you," I said as I handed him the box.

Delbert removed the wrapping paper with one mighty swoop of his beefy hand, "Oh my God, what is it?" he asked even though the contents were clearly marked on the cardboard box within. Using two hands he ripped open the box and his eyes lit up when he saw that it contained 24 packages of Double-Stuff Oreo cookies. "Cool. I never saw this many Oreos in one place; not even in the grocery stores. Let's eat some," he said as he ripped one of the packages open.

"It's only 9:30 Delbert. Don't you think it's a little early for cookies?" I asked.

"Isn't this like a going-away party?" he asked.

"Of course it is," said Jeannine. "May I have a cookie?"

Delbert stuck his mitt into the package and came out with about six cookies. When I saw that his hands hadn't been washed I picked up the package and offered it to Jeannine. She carefully selected one cookie as Delbert shoved half of what was in his hand into his mouth. "OK, I'll join you," I said.

"I have a present for you, too," Jeannine said.

"Really," he replied, spraying cookie fragments as he turned his head toward her.

Jeannine reached under her desk and removed a box wrapped in paper that said, "We'll miss you," all over it. Delbert put his cookies down for a moment and removed the paper deftly. He opened the box and his jaw dropped. Not a pretty sight. With eyes full of wonder he removed a Superman long sleeve T-shirt. "This is awesome! Look at this!" he exclaimed as he pointed to the red cape on the back of the shirt that hung down with another foot of material below the front and sides. Delbert pulled it on over his uniform shirt and immediately made muscles with his arms.

"I have a great idea," I said. "Why don't you take the rest of the day off and wear the shirt over to the Center to show everybody."

"You're a really cool boss," he said, grabbed his case of Oreos and headed for the door.

"Don't forget your paycheck," I said sticking the envelope in his hand.

He tossed it into his box of cookies and said, "I won't forget it in there." In a moment he was out the door with a smile and a lot of double-stuff on his face.

At 11:30 AM I met Shamansky at Metro headquarters to look at a couple of line-ups. Two of the Russian paratroopers survived gunshot wounds and were now deemed healthy enough to be identified. The police wanted me to see if either of the survivors was involved in the shooting of Vladimir Torhan. I was hoping to see one of the guys from the Dali Lama the night I played with Doberman's Stub, but it was not to be. I did manage to identify all four of them when I was shown photos of the deceased. "Can I get a copy. I know a police lieutenant in Odessa who will sleep a lot better once he knows these guys are on their way to hell."

"You got it," Shamansky said. When we got to the copy machine he said, "Your mother invited me to dinner tomorrow night."

"I know," I replied. "They want to celebrate me and Dennis Kerrigan not screwing things up."

"I'm not going to be the token non-Irishman am I?" he asked.

"Absolutely not," I replied, "unless you bring an Irish girl as a date. But I wouldn't recommend it. I'm trying to reverse the adverse effects of social inbreeding."

"Then count me in," he said as he handed me my prints.

"Was my dad any help during the interrogations?" I asked

"Actually, he was a big help. We weren't getting anywhere with either of the hooligans. It was apparent they were going to stonewall us until Nigel showed up with the legal team. Then, toward the end of the day I was taking a last shot at Billingsly when Jim came into the interrogation room and said he was the warden from the city jail. He said he had family in Belfast who were blown up by Orangemen and he had a special cellmate for Billingsly, and wanted to take him right away, before any lawyers showed up."

"What did Billingsly say?" I asked.

"He got really nervous and asked who the cellmate would be. Your dad told him it was a Catholic from Portadown whose daughter lost an arm in an explosion during the Orangeman parade last year. He said the prisoner was 6'4" and 250 pounds of pure muscle. I guess your dad did his homework on the bombing because it was clear Billingsly knew all about it and went into a panic. From the way he reacted I'd guess Billingsly was in on the blast and was sure the Irishman was about to tear him apart. He gave a full confession in about 15 minutes. I was truly impressed," Shamansky said.

I got back to the office at about 2:30 PM and found Jeannine talking with Ivana. A burly looking bodyguard-type accompanied her and sat on the waiting room couch with a blank stare. "Ivana, this is a pleasant surprise," I said.

"I wanted to say goodbye," she said. "I'm going to be living with my uncle and his family in Dana Point. I also came to thank you, Jason."

"You thanked me at your house," I said.

"Uncle Peter had his lawyer contact Mrs. Tucker. He said he was expecting her to file suit, but she told him that you spoke with her about me and she isn't going to take me to court. I'm sure this will make it a lot easier fitting in with my new family," she said.

"What are you going to do with Cerise Records?" I asked.

She replied, "Mr. Tyler has taken over, but he's in the process of selling. He's giving the surviving members of Doberman's Stub a great deal on the third CD, then releasing them from their contract."

"That seems very generous," I observed.

"I think everybody is trying to avoid giving all of the money to the lawyers," Ivana replied.

"That certainly sounds like the best way to go for all concerned," I said.

"Are you going to miss living in a castle?" asked Jeannine.

"Not at all," she replied. "I have to get going, but I brought along a couple of going-away presents." She reached into her large purse and handed Jeannine a snow globe of the Kremlin. "Here's a nice replica of the best-known castle in all of Russia."

Jeannine held it on her fingertips and looked delighted. "This is beautiful," she said.

Ivana then handed me a CD in a special case. She had hand-painted a cover that said, *Doberman's Stub Live at the Dali Lama Yo Mama*. "The sound man, Mr. Martin, recorded the show. I thought you'd like to have a copy of it," she said.

"I love the art work. How does it sound?" I asked.

"You sound terrific, but, I was told to warn you that it can't end up on the Internet, OK?" she asked.

"It will go no further that my living room and the sound system in my car," I said. "Thank you so much for doing this."

Ivana beamed at my reaction, then gave us hugs and departed.

An hour later I got a call from Jack Pascal who asked if he and Ian could meet me at my office tomorrow at 10:00 AM. I agreed.

Chapter 31

AT precisely 10:00 on Saturday morning Ian walked into my office, followed by Jack, Michael and Jeannine. "You're up awfully early," I said to Ian.

"I'm being told it's the first day of the rest of me life," he said.

Jack added, "He's checking into the Betty Ford Center at noon."

I shook Ian's hand and said, "Good for you. It looks like perfect timing for a new beginning."

"I figure if it worked for Aerosmith, I can make it work for me," he said.

Michael added, "And, he's going to be busy breaking in a couple of new band mates soon."

"That's one of the reasons we asked to meet with you this morning," Jack said. "We think Nigel had the right idea when he talked about hiring you to investigate potential band members as well as new management. We value your opinion tremendously and have narrowed the choices for Terry's replacement to three people. We want to have the new member signed by the time Ian gets discharged. Can you help us out?"

I asked, "What about the new manager. Are you going with Nigel's choice?"

Ian said, "He has a good reputation, but he sounds like a fast-talking salesman to us. We also need a concert promoter to book the tour for the new CD."

Jack said, "We actually need your services for a while. We want profiles on the prospective band member, promoter, manager and record companies. What do you say?"

A smile crept across my face. "I think it sounds terrific. I may be able to help you with the concert promoter right away."

Michael said, "I told them you'd be recommending Calvin Dawson and they were stoked."

"Calvin's a friend of yours?" asked Jack.

"We go way back. I have the highest regard for him as a promoter and as a person," I said.

Jack replied, "I'm sure it will help Ian get through rehab knowing we'll have a top-notch promoter working on getting the tour together while he's working on getting his head together."

"Affirmative," Ian said enthusiastically.

Jeannine had been quietly sitting at her desk playing with the snow globe Ivana had given her. For a moment she came out of her own little world and asked, "Have you thought of a name for the new CD?"

Ian replied, "We're thinking of calling it, *The Metal Musings of Cain and Abel*, but we want to make sure Chelsea Tucker doesn't object. Can you check on that for us, Jason?"

"No problem. By the way, do either of you guys recognize the guitar on my wall?" I asked Ian and Jack.

"If I don't miss my guess, that's the guitar Terry used to write his songs," Jack said. "I've got some great stories about that guitar, but they'll have to wait. We can't keep Betty waiting." In a minute they were gone.

On the drive to my parent's house I asked Kelly, "Would you like to hear the hottest CD never to hit the airwaves?"

"This sounds interesting," she replied.

I popped in the CD Ivana had given me. After the first song I asked, "What do you think?"

"I think with a new singer and a better lead guitarist they could be the next Doberman's Stub," she said with a grin.

When we reached the house, the Kerrigan's had already arrived. Introductions were made, hors d' oeuvres were passed and Dad delighted in his role as bartender. Bob Kerrigan brought along the citation his son had received. Dad insisted that Dennis recount what had happened at the scene.

When he finished, Bob lifted his beer and said, "To another generation of Irishmen helping their own." Mom, Dad and Kelly immediately looked at me to see how I would react.

Before I could throw a wet blanket on the festivities the doorbell rang. "I'll get it," I said avoiding the toast issue for the moment.

I knew it would be Walter Shamansky. The question was whether Walter could talk the aspiring actress from Larabee's into accompanying him this evening. I had kept Kelly apprised of Shamansky's wishful thinking infatuation since the first time we had lunch. I could see her jockey for position to get a look as they walked in the door.

To my amazement, Shamansky had brought along Svetlana Illich. For the first time I saw her in chic, modern cloths, make-up and an attractive new hairstyle. "Surprised?" she asked me as she walked in the door, then kept walking before I could answer. Some things never change.

Shamansky was reading my expression and loving every minute of it. As he shook my hand he asked, "How's that for cultural diversity."